W9-AXW-229

Hartford

In loving memory
of
Louise Garcia

KEEPERS
OF THE RING
3

HARTFORD

Angela Elwell Hunt

PROPERTY OF
UNITED METHODIST CHURCH LIBRARY
HUNTERTOWN, IN

Tyndale House Publishers, Inc.
WHEATON, ILLINOIS

Copyright © 1996 by Angela Elwell Hunt
All rights reserved
Cover illustration copyright © 1996 by C. Michael Dudash
Back cover photo by Bill Bilsley
Map on page vii copyright © 1996 by Kirk Caldwell

Scripture quotations except the one noted below are taken from the *Holy Bible,* King James Version.

The Scripture quotation on p. 123 is taken from the *Holy Bible,* New International Version®. Copyright 1973, 1978, 1984 by International Bible Society. Used by permission of Zondervan Publishing House. All rights reserved. The "NIV" and "New International Version" trademarks are registered in the United States Patent and Trademark Office by International Bible Society. Use of either trademark requires permission of International Bible Society.

Library of Congress Cataloging-in-Publication Data

Hunt, Angela Elwell, date
  Hartford / Angela Elwell Hunt.
    p. cm. —(Keepers of the ring ; 3)
  Includes bibliographical references.
  ISBN 0-8423-2014-8 (alk. paper)
  I. Hartford (Conn.)—History—Colonial period, ca. 1600–1775—Fiction. 2. Connecticut—History—Colonial period, ca. 1600–1775—Fiction. 3. Indians of North America—Connecticut—Fiction. 4. Pequot War, 1636–1638—Fiction. I. Title. II. Series: Hunt, Angela Elwell, date Keepers of the ring ; 3.
PS3558.U46747H37 1996
813'.54—dc20   96-11716

Printed in the United States of America

01 00 99 98 97 96
7   6   5   4   3   2

TABLE OF CONTENTS

CONNECTICUT
1765

Boston

Windsor

Hartford

Wethersfield

Connecticut River

Saybrook

Mystic

Long Island Sound

AUTHOR'S NOTE

I had never heard of the Pequot Indians, much less of the brutal assault upon their fort at Mystic, until I read Captain John Mason's eyewitness account of the event. On a clear spring day in 1636, several hundred Pequot Indians, including women and children, were burned alive in their fort at Mystic.

The Pequot War, as related in this story, is absolutely historical. The sections signed "John Mason" are from the actual account he wrote a few years later. Pequot captives were sent to the West Indies to work the sugarcane, others were made slaves to the Puritans, the Mohegans, and the Narragansetts.

My soul was shaken to the core as I read the story. How, I wondered, could men and women who professed the name of God rejoice to hear their enemies "frying in the fire"? What happened to the Puritans' desire to evangelize the Indians?

The situation reminded me of the Crusades, when well-meaning knights mounted their horses and rode off to the Holy Land with the express purpose of spilling the "infidels'" blood. Time and again throughout history, the great deceiver has twisted our fervor and misdirected our energies toward hating the outsiders Christ commanded us to love.

But God has always had a people—men who will stand up for truth and right, women who are steadfast in their faith. And always, love reaches across a span of hate and pain to bring us to reconciliation and peace.

There is very little difference between one man and another,
but what little there is,
is very important.

—*Anonymous*

PROLOGUE

The tomahawk against the flesh of his palm completed him, made him whole.

From his hiding place secure in the dense forest outside the English village, Sassacus studied the hint of thinner darkness against the eastern horizon. Soon Sun Woman would begin her walk across the sky, and the English would venture forth to plant and hoe in their fields. And when the timid turtles had thrust their heads out of their village, he and his warriors would exact their revenge.

Their tomahawks cried out for blood. Five springs had passed since the Dutch and English had first come to the shores of the winding river the Indians called Quinnehtukgut. These alien intruders, armed with biting muskets and booming cannon, stripped the land and erected stuffy dwellings of timber and stone, then put up fences as though to keep the forest out. From inside one of the houses, a dog howled. Sassacus's mouth twisted with the faint beginnings of a smile. A dog's howling meant death approached. A good sign.

As patient as a spider, he again weighed his tomahawk in his hand and waited. Amid the blue-green shadows slender fingers of golden light had begun to probe through the dense foliage and brighten the ragged carpet of the forest floor. This place had been home to his father and grandfather, to ancestors since the time of the great flood. Until the arrival of the interlopers, his people, the Pequot, had lived in relative peace with their neighbors, the Mohegans and Narragansetts. When trouble occasionally flared, Pequot warriors proved their reputation and courage. From the Quinnehtukgut to the great salt lake, the Pequot tribe was the most proud, most numerous, and most successful. Today they would prove themselves again.

From all around, the land spoke to him. The sun's warmth and the insect hum of the woods joined with the drumming of his heart to call for courage. He would answer. Within the hour he would at last silence the cry of spilled Pequot blood and slake the tribe's thirst for vengeance.

The bloodletting had begun on the river. Three winters ago, Sassacus's father, Tatobem, had been killed by Dutch traders even though the tribe obeyed his abductors' orders and paid a large tribute to ransom him. When news of Tatobem's murder reached the Indian village, Sassacus silently picked up his father's pipe, signaling his intention to assume his father's place as sachem. Even the wisest and most esteemed of the elders had fallen silent and waited to hear what Sassacus would do.

He did not hesitate, but led them in a swift and merciless attack upon the Dutch trading post. When all the white traders within were dead, the warriors looted the goods and went home, their anger satisfied and their dignity restored. Sassacus had thought the fire in his own heart quenched, but some flames were easily rekindled.

Fifteen feet away a warrior suddenly crouched in the brush as if he had heard something. Nervous flutterings pierced Sassacus's chest as he listened, but after a moment the warrior turned to Sassacus, his face utterly blank. Nothing yet stirred in the field or the village beyond. But they would come forth. They always did.

Soon after the Pequot attack on the trading post, a band of western Niantics murdered an English captain who had hired them to guide him and his party down the river. After plundering the ship, the renegade Niantics sank the boat and scattered in the woods.

For some reason Sassacus could not understand, the English came to *him* and demanded retribution for the murdered captain's death. Under the watchful gaze of the armed English soldiers, Sassacus agreed to find and hand over the man's killers and allow the English to purchase land in the river valley. Eager for peace, he also agreed to pay four hundred fathoms of wampum, forty beaver skins, and thirty otter skins. In return, the English promised to send them a trader from whom they could purchase muskets, axes, and kettles.

But the promised trader, John Oldham, never made it to Sassacus's village. He was murdered off the shores of Block Island, probably, Sassacus suspected, by a roving band of eastern Niantics or Narragansetts. And like a fool who scratches his head when his foot itches, two English captains and one hundred twenty men burned an Indian village on Block Island, then sailed into Pequot Harbor and demanded that Sassacus hand over Oldham's killers, one thousand fathoms of wampum, and several Indian children as hostages to secure the peace.

The memory of that impossible request edged his teeth even now. As hard of hearing as they were hard of heart, the English would not listen to reason. After a brief skirmish, the somber-faced Englishmen left the village.

But Sassacus had learned. He knew they would return. He called a conference of the elders, who agreed with him that the time had come to act. The English would press for more and more land, and they possessed superior weapons that would allow them to take it.

Runners spread the news that a war party would be needed. Throughout the next several days warriors streamed into Sassacus's village to strike the war post. Yesterday they had danced until the entire camp worked itself into the frenzy of war.

At dusk Sassacus and one hundred seasoned warriors had set out upon the river and paddled northward. Their canoes cut through the black waters so quickly that lacy white garlands of foam decked their bows. The men traveled silently, the only sound a silken breeze whispering through the pinewood. With his inner ear Sassacus heard the sibilant whispers of the spirits of the water call to him over the soft lap of the oars: *Punish the English for this injustice. Teach them. They cannot strike our people as if we have no hearts.*

A strange, cold excitement filled his heart. Some of the elders had cautioned that the English could not die, that they were spirits. But Sassacus had the last word. "They have come to us because some of their number died on the river," he said, looking steadily at his counselors. "They can be killed. We have some of their long guns, we have our own weapons. But it will not be said that the Pequot have no heart for war."

Through the smoke of the council fire, the elders had nodded soberly. Sassacus listened to the distant memory, taking courage from the strength of will shining in the elders' eyes. Shifting silently, he straightened and stared toward the English village. Already a living warmth radiated from the risen sun, and a tingle of anticipation spread through his limbs. The white men's dog continued its mournful wail.

A dozen men and two women, all dressed in the heavy clothing of the white people, walked into the field. The men talked and jibed carelessly with one another, their arms loaded with bags of seed and hoes. The women carried baskets and kept their eyes down. Even at this early hour, they slumped in weariness.

A warrior at the edge of the woods gave the signal, and Sassacus sprinted forward, his bloodlust at a fever pitch. With the thrill of the chase in his nostrils, Sassacus raised his tomahawk and dashed toward his prey, the silence of the woods broken by the shrieking war cry of the Pequot.

Daniel

*A brother offended is harder to be won
than a strong city:
and their contentions are like the bars
of a castle.*

Proverbs 18:19

As fast as lightning on a summer night, Daniel flew over the moist forest floor, his moccasined feet barely imprinting the earth. Fifty feet away, Taregan matched Daniel's pace easily, darting like a shadow among the trees and tangled shrubs that had begun to wear the bright gold-green of spring. The buck bounded ahead of them, bolting erratically in the zigzag flight of panic, but Taregan kept pace with the animal, instinctively anticipating its movements.

The buck swerved sharply to the left and darted through a cluster of brush, and Daniel stopped, bracing himself against a tree. He could still hear the steady thump of the animal's frightened canter, the swish and crackle of branches bending or breaking in the animal's headlong flight. Then, a sudden thrashing sound and a triumphant cry.

Daniel flung his knife into the ground, disgusted. Once again, Taregan had made the kill. Though they had worked together to flush the animal and track it through the woods, Taregan's arrow had brought the animal down.

Scowling, Daniel retrieved his knife, wiped the blade clean on the soft leather of his leggings, then advanced toward the faint rustling sounds in the brush. When he reached Taregan, his brother had already opened the jugular vein and tied the animal's legs together.

"It was a clean shot," Taregan said, standing back to admire the beast. "And a good buck. We will have meat for many nights, and Mother will like the skin. Mayhap one of us will get a warm jacket from this beast."

Taregan, of course. Daniel shoved his knife into his belt and leaned down to look at the buck, unable to meet his brother's triumphant gaze. Mother always made the best jackets for Taregan, her favorite.

"Will you give me some help?" Taregan asked, struggling to lift the heavy animal. The buck was huge, probably 170 pounds, and slippery with blood.

"Squat down," Daniel ordered. When Taregan crouched before him, Daniel heaved the carcass over Taregan's back so that two legs draped over each shoulder. "You killed him, you can carry him."

Taregan didn't answer, but stood up, staggering slightly under the load. "Are you sure you don't want to help me?" Taregan called, struggling to lift his head under the deer's weight.

"Yes, I'm certain," Daniel answered, staring at the beast's lifeless eyes. The black orbs wore a faintly mocking expression. *Your brother wants your help now, but he will emerge alone from the woods with me on his back, Daniel-boy, and your mother and father will heap praise upon his head while you stand behind with nothing to say. . . .*

"It is also my kill," Daniel muttered in a burst of anger.

"What are you babbling about?" Taregan turned carefully, lazy laughter in his eyes. "You helped me track him, but the kill was mine. One arrow, straight through the heart. I don't think Father could have killed him so cleanly." Ducking beneath the deer, he lifted his head and studied the cloudy sky. "Come, we should hurry. The wind smells of rain."

"Do you think I don't know it?" Daniel did not wait for his brother, but charged ahead into the woods.

▼▲▼▲ They were four miles from home, an hour's walk, and Daniel left Taregan behind on the trail. The river raced with him along the deerpath, its silver waters flashing white in the slanting rays of the spring sun. The rain-heavy wind roiled the surface of the river into choppy waves, but Daniel kept his eyes fastened to the trail beneath his feet as his thoughts raced like a rabbit.

How unfair life was! Fifteen winters ago he and Taregan had
been born from the same womb, yet he could not imagine two
more different people in all the earth. Though outwardly they
looked as alike as two halves of an apple, inwardly they were
as different as fire and water. Mother often pointed out that he
and Taregan both possessed unique gifts, yet the things that
mattered—hunting, fishing, and tracking—came as naturally
to Taregan as if he had been born to an Indian tribe. Daniel
knew he and his brother had the same amount of Indian blood
flowing in their veins, but he had never been able to compete
with his favored twin. He dreamed of the day he would finally
prove that the elder son—a distinction he clung to though he
had come into the world scant seconds before his brother—was
not the lesser.

He was more like his father, Daniel supposed, more *English*.
Of course, he had not fully understood what being English
meant until those people came to settle in the river valley. As a
small child, Daniel had thought his father a demigod, a red-
haired man strikingly different from the surrounding Indians
and, as such, one who was respected and revered by them. Like
the Indians, Fallon Bailie knew how to survive and thrive in the
forest, but he possessed a broader knowledge than the native
tribes about the wild world beyond and the true God. Daniel's
mother, Gilda, was a rare treasure, too, for she had been born of
an English mother and an Indian father. Fully Indian in appearance but for her striking blue eyes, Gilda Bailie understood the
ways of the Indians, but she also knew how to read and she lived
according to the book of God, which she kept on a small table in
their house. With the patience of the gentle stream that trickled
by their house, she taught her boys how to read and write even
as she taught them how to skin the animals Fallon brought to her
cooking kettle.

Jogging home, Daniel submerged himself into the memory of
the day he discovered that his father was not the only Englishman in the world. Indian scouts had brought word of invaders
on the river, and Father had set out with his knife and his toma-

hawk. Daniel and Taregan were eleven years old, and they followed cautiously, obeying their father's command to stay out of sight until he signaled that all was well.

They followed the ancient deerpaths until they came to a natural bend in the river. Strange wooden islands had been tied to trees along the shore, and light-skinned men with heavily bearded faces walked to and fro on the strange wooden crafts as well as on the land beyond. They spoke a language Daniel had never heard; it was neither the tongue of his parents nor the tongue of the Algonquin tribes.

Fallon Bailie cocked his ear toward the men, then he smiled. "Dutch," he said simply, stepping boldly out of the brush. The sight of so many men, women, and even children seemed to cheer him immensely, and he approached with an upraised hand and called out a greeting. A handful of the bearded men spoke Fallon's language, and Daniel watched in amazement as his father extended his hand and introduced himself to all.

Since that day many other foreigners had sailed down the winding length of the river they called the Connecticut. True Englishmen, who looked and talked like Fallon, had joined the Dutch, and the colonists had established themselves in three towns: Windsor, Hartford, and Wethersfield. One man, Reverend Thomas Hooker, brought a group of somber-faced men and women who settled in the city known as Hartford and immediately raised a timber building they called a church.

"What is a church?" Daniel had asked one afternoon as he and Taregan followed their father home after a visit with the English.

"It is a place where men and women worship God," Father answered.

"What is worship?" Taregan asked.

Father paused and looked up to the sky as if the answer were revealed there. "It is praying and praising God. Worship takes place when we celebrate him."

"But we do that all the time," Taregan pointed out. "In our

home and in the woods. Why do these people close themselves in a building? Are they afraid?"

Father frowned as he searched his thoughts for an answer. Daniel had seen that thoughtful expression often since the foreigners had come to dwell in the land. "The English and Dutch set aside a special day for worship, and they like to praise God together," Fallon explained. "There is no home large enough to hold all of them, so they have built a special cabin like the longhouses of the Iroquois. A church is supposed to be home to the family of God."

"But we have no church house and yet we are part of the family of God," Daniel argued. "You and Mother have always said that God is our Father."

His father smiled and ran his hand through Daniel's hair. "Yes, Son, we are part of that family, for we worship the same God as these folk." He paused, searching for words. "When I was a youth in England, I visited many churches of glass and stone. I saw how man attempted to imitate the vaulted skies o'er our heads, the pillaring trees that surround and shelter us. Everything on earth points to God, but man continues to prefer the works of his own hands over creations straight from the breath of the Creator. Many of these folk from across the great salt sea believe they dare not worship or live outside their houses. They are blind to God's handiwork in the flight of a bird, nor can they hear his voice in the wind. They struggle and work to please God by their efforts, and yet the heavenly Father is long-suffering toward them. We must be patient, too."

That afternoon in the woods Taregan had nodded as if he understood completely, but Daniel suspected that the words made no more sense to his brother than they did to him.

A sudden thrashing in the bushes just ahead jarred his thoughts from the past, and Daniel looked up to see Taregan pressing forward on the trail in a steady run. He would beat Daniel home even with a buck on his back!

"Oh no, you don't," Daniel yelled, sprinting toward the house.

▼▲▼▲▼ Grinning despite his exhaustion, Taregan commanded his feet to move faster. He passed the huge oak tree that marked the entrance to their home, then slowed and staggered. Sweat dripped from his brow, and the sticky blood of the buck had soaked his bare chest and stained his breechcloth. He felt every inch a victorious hunter.

"Ho, now!" Fallon called, stepping out of the house to greet his sons. "What a fine buck! Daniel, you didn't make your brother carry that beast all the way, did you?"

"He wanted to," Daniel said, glaring for a moment at Taregan as he leaned forward to catch his breath.

Taregan let the deer slide from his back to the ground, then groaned as he stretched his cramped arms. "It was not too heavy a buck, Father. I could have carried it farther."

"Go tell your mother what you have brought," Fallon called, a mingling of pride and amusement in his eyes. He pulled his knife from its leather sheaf at his belt. "Since you have done the hard work, Daniel will help me with the skinning."

After stretching again, Taregan moved toward the house. The wide, cozy building of earth and timber looked more like an Iroquois longhouse than the grass and straw wigwams of the nearby Pequot villages, but Taregan liked the difference. Father had built the house in the style of Ocanahonan, the village where he and Mother had been born. Though Father often spoke of that village where English and Indian had lived with each other in peace, Taregan privately thought his stories as mythical as the Indian legends the elders loved to tell around the campfire. Ocanahonan, Father said, was home to nearly two hundred folk who believed in God the Father and Jesus the Son. For twenty years the town had existed on the banks of the Chowan River in a place called Virginia, but in 1607 the great Powhatan chief Opechancanough had destroyed it.

Taregan rapped softly on the door and heard the quiet murmur of his mother's voice. "Come in, my son."

She rose from her stool as he entered. "My brave hunter," she said, her smile shimmering like sunbeams on the surface of the river as she placed her hands on his shoulders. "Look at you! I see that you were successful in your hunt."

"Yes, Mother," he answered, his cheeks burning under her proud gaze. "Daniel and I tracked the deer for a few miles, then I brought it down with a single arrow. It is a fine buck; Father and Daniel are skinning it now."

"We shall have meat," Mother murmured thankfully, moving toward the door. Her soft leather skirt swayed gracefully as she looked out at her other son and her husband.

As Taregan reached for a woven cloth to clean himself, he watched his mother and thought that no woman in the world was as lovely. He felt closer to her than to his father, for the Indian blood of her ancestors flowed closer to his heart than it did Daniel's. After thirty-four summers, Gilda's face and features still shone with the bloom of youth. She was not worn with toil and worry like so many of the Indian women in the nearby villages, nor was she stiff and fearful like the English women in the river towns. She moved and spoke with the graceful air of one who is at home in many worlds. She was possessed of the wisdom of the Indians and the skills of the English. Often Taregan thought of her as a bird: intelligent, direct, and free.

"You should be helping your father and brother," she said, turning to him. A faint note of reproach underlined her words. "They will think I am spoiling you."

"Two will have no trouble doing the work of one," Taregan answered, grinning. He picked up the water bucket. "They don't need a third pair of hands. Do you need water? I can fetch that for you when I wash by the creek, so no one will say I am spoiled."

"Faith, but you are a foolish boy," she said, waving him away. But she smiled and Taregan knew she was happy with him.

▼▲▼▲▼ As the sun sank toward a livid purple cloudbank piled deep on the western horizon, Gilda bowed her head over the meal she had prepared. "Blessed are you, Lord, for pro-

PROPERTY OF UNITED METHODIST CHURCH LIBRARY HUNTERTOWN, IN

viding this meat," she prayed, squinting through one eye to
check on the piety of her sons. "Blessed are Taregan and Daniel,
for you have given them speed and endurance. Blessed is their
father, for you have given him the wisdom to teach the things
that matter most. And blessed am I, for living with three men
who make me so very happy."

"Amen," Fallon boomed from the head of the table, and
Gilda's heart warmed when he caught her eye and smiled. As
was his custom, he lifted the wooden bowl containing the
chunks of venison and gestured for the boys to pass it to their
mother.

Gilda scooped out a handful and placed it on her bark plate,
then motioned for the boys to eat their fill. With the ravenous
appetite of youths, they attacked the meat, and Gilda sighed in
relief for having hidden a bowl of the savory venison for Fallon.
He could eat his fill later. These two boys, hungry as winter
wolves, would not leave much for their father.

Fallon munched on a handful of dried corn as he watched his
boys gorge themselves. Gilda caught his eye and shrugged as if
to say, *boys will be boys*. He winked at her, understanding completely.

He had always understood her, ofttimes even better than she
understood herself. After escaping the massacre at Ocanahonan,
Gilda had been reared by the Indians; Fallon had been sentenced
to die by Opechancanough but by the grace of God had escaped
this fate. Near death from fever and exhaustion, he'd been discovered in the woods by Captain John Smith, who promptly
shipped him off to England. Years later, when Fallon had
returned to Virginia and was reunited with Gilda, the young lovers had found themselves torn between the English civilization
at Jamestown and the Indian confederacy of the Powhatan. The
Indians, led by the fierce Opechancanough, attempted an outright massacre of all English people, and the surviving settlers at
Jamestown were afterward so affrighted that no Indian within
a hundred miles of the city was safe.

Gilda and Fallon left Jamestown to find Ocanahonan, but

nothing remained of that place save a few buried relics and charred timbers. Taking Gilda north, Fallon had carefully skirted the Powhatan lands and followed the seashore until he reached the land of the Pequot.

The Pequot lived in the lands of the Quinnehtukgut River; the lands north and west were inhabited by the Mohegan and Narragansett tribes. All three tribes were of the Algonquin family, so they spoke dialects of the same language Fallon and Gilda had learned with the Powhatan. It was in this place, with these people, that, for the first time in years, Fallon and Gilda felt safe. After building a timber and mud lodge in the manner of the houses at Ocanahonan, they settled in to await the birth of their first child.

A woman from a nearby Pequot tribe assisted at the birth, laughing when a second baby followed immediately after the first. "He will not be left behind," the old woman said, catching the second child as Fallon held the firstborn. Since that initial glimpse of her sons, Gilda had known that her boys were very different. Though they shared golden skin, dark hair, and eyes the color of a summer sky, the first baby came into the world with a worried frown between his brows; the second squalled in protest that he had momentarily found himself alone in the womb.

Fallon named his elder son Daniel, "God is my judge," and Gilda called the bawling child in her arms Taregan, an Indian word for "crane."

"For it is my prayer," Gilda said, stroking the baby's damp hair in the hope that he would stop crying, "that your heart will be as pure as the crane's snow-white breast."

Her beloved crane was now stuffing his mouth like a bear, still trying to finish before his brother. "If you two are interested," Fallon said, interrupting the boys' feeding frenzy, "Tomorrow I must go to Nixkamich's village. I must speak to the sachem."

"Why?" Gilda asked, lifting the nearly empty bowl from its

place. Taregan made a last grab at a sliver of meat on the bottom of the bowl; she playfully slapped his hand.

Fallon shook his head and leaned his crossed arms upon the table. "I wish I had better news to take to the wigwam of my friend. Three nights ago Sassacus led an attack on the village at Wethersfield. They killed six men, three women, twenty cows, and a horse. The English at Fort Saybrook saw his warriors taking two captive women downriver. Sassacus struck the war post. This time the English are certain that the warriors were Pequot."

"Sassacus attacked to avenge those who died on Block Island," Gilda said, standing from her place. "Don't the English know this?"

Fallon shook his head. "The English know only that nine of their people are dead and they now have an excuse for war. Nixkamich will be drawn into the battle unless he can speak to the elders."

"Nixkamich and his people had nothing to do with Sassacus," Gilda said, eying Fallon intently. "Since they have become Christian, they take no part in these tribal rivalries—"

"But they are Pequot," Fallon said, his smile strained. "And though our friends follow our God, they will not disassociate themselves from their tribesmen. If the Pequot go to war, I fear we shall be caught in the middle."

The boys stared at their father, stunned by the seriousness in Fallon's voice. "Surely we will side with the English," Daniel said. "The Pequot haven't a chance against the English guns, and if Sassacus *did* attack Wethersfield—"

"No, if the English come we will fight with Nixkamich!" Taregan protested. "He has done nothing wrong, and his people are our people. We could not turn our backs on them, not ever—"

"Therein lies our problem," Fallon said, lifting his hand to end the debate. "We shall have to see if Nixkamich's wisdom can give us an answer to the dilemma."

"I want to go with you," Daniel said, looking up.

"I'll go, too," Taregan answered, flashing a quick look at Gilda. "Unless, Mother, you need me. . . ."

Gilda shook her head, grateful for his attentiveness, then he grinned at his father. "I'll go. I wouldn't miss it."

"At first light, then, we'll set out," Fallon said, pushing his chair away from the table. "Be ready, my sons."

After a quick breakfast of bread and dried corn, Taregan helped
his father and brother slip their canoe out of its hiding place
along the riverbank. The sight of the birchbark canoe always
filled Taregan's heart with a mingling of joy and sadness, for he
and his father had built it two summers before. Daniel had not
wanted to help, so as Fallon and Taregan worked, Daniel sat on
the riverbank and sulked. Taregan thought he understood the
reason for Daniel's moodiness.

Fallon had taught both boys to swim at an early age and to
paddle a canoe when they were old enough to grip an oar. But
one day he had taken the twins to a stretch of rapids in a fork of
the river, and Daniel had been so paralyzed by fear that he could
not row. The canoe capsized, nearly drowning Taregan.

Since that day, Daniel had shown little love for the river. But
he was not frightened this morning. He strode quickly down the
riverbank, his knife strapped to his thigh, his bow and quiver
slung across his back. Gilda waited at the riverbank with Fallon,
who wore the brightly embroidered jacket she had made him,
and she paused to give Daniel a quick embrace and whisper
something in his ear.

"Do you think we will have time to hunt?" Taregan asked,
eying the weapons.

Daniel shrugged. "Why not? While you and Father sit with
the old men around the fire, I will join the warriors in the woods.
Mayhap I will bring home a buck tonight!"

Taregan shrugged and sprang easily into the bow of the
canoe. Daniel knelt in the center, and Father took his place at the

rear and pushed the boat off into the water as Gilda waved good-
bye.

Taking up his oar, Taregan sighed in contentment. Slanted sunlight shimmered off the glowing green foliage of early spring,
and his heart lifted as it always did when he rode the river. Birds
crisscrossed the water, calling to each other in their distinctive
tongues; insects whirred from tall grasses growing at the river's
edge; wavelets made soft slapping sounds beneath the canoe. As
if by some unspoken consent, Fallon and Daniel observed the
sanctity of the river's peace as well, and the time passed in
silence.

The sun had not yet crossed a quarter of its distance across the
sky when Daniel pointed toward a clearing in the brush. Fallon's
expert paddling sent the canoe hissing up onto the sand. Taregan
sprang out of the boat, his knees stiff from kneeling, and helped
pull the canoe onshore. Carefully, Fallon stepped out, his eyes
scanning the trees beyond the clearing.

No matter how certain a man was of his friendship with the
Pequot, one did not casually venture near their villages. Taregan
knew that the eyes of half a dozen scouts had been watching during their progress upriver, and he worked silently to beach the
canoe and hide it in the underbrush.

Now they stood on the riverbank, waiting. The wind whispered as if announcing their presence, and Taregan scanned the
trees, alert for any movement or unexplained rustling. Then a
sharp hissing sound rent the air as a spear landed squarely at
Fallon's feet.

His face cracked into a lopsided smile as he pulled the spear
from the ground and examined the painted design along its
shaft. "Your aim is growing as weak as your eyes, Nixkamich,"
he called, his voice echoing over the shore. "You nearly clipped
my moccasin with your blade."

"How do you know I did not mean to hit you?" a voice
answered. A leafy screen parted, and an Indian stepped forth
from the bushes. Tall and broad, the sachem was a dignified
chief of late middle age, with a small round paunch bulging over

the leather belt of his breechcloth. His face was sharply angled, with a jutting brow, sharp eyes, and a long nose, but an expression of genuine delight lit his face.

Fallon bowed his head before the esteemed warrior. "If you meant to hit me, I would be in heaven even now," he said, smiling. "In truth, your skill grows sharper with each passing season."

"What brings Wematin to us?" the chief asked, using the name the Indians had given Fallon. Taregan smiled inwardly. If anyone was a "brother" to the Pequot, it was his father.

"I wish to open my heart," Fallon said, placing his hand upon his chest, "and allow my sons to learn from your warriors. I would smoke with you around your campfire and share my tobacco."

"Then you are welcome to my wigwam," Nixkamich answered, stepping aside so that Fallon could follow on the trail.

▼▲▼▲▼ Surrounded by a palisade of felled trees, Nixkamich's village was a small encampment of about twenty families. Many of his warriors, the sachem explained, were hunting and would return this day or the next. With stately dignity he led Fallon and his sons past the fields of planted crops to the birchbark-covered wigwam where he lived with his wife and children. There were few furnishings in the house. A group of furs and skins covered the floor of beaten earth, a few weapons and a small wooden cross hung from notches in the poles that supported the roof. The chief skirted the hearth in the center of the dwelling, then took a seat in front of his backrest. Knowing that the Indians considered it bad manners to discuss business while standing, Taregan quickly followed his father's example and sat as well.

For a long time they sat without speaking. The sachem pulled out his pipe and inhaled a long, deep breath. A trio of barking dogs ran past the open door, stirring up dust as they ran, and a horde of squealing, nearly naked children followed, prodding the dogs with pointed sticks.

Taregan marveled at the way the adults ignored the children. Though the Indians were terribly fond of their young ones, they rarely rebuked or scolded them. *It is as if they know maturity will come soon enough,* Taregan thought, his eyes scanning the circle of wigwams outside.

A movement near one of the wigwams caught his eye, and Taregan tilted his head to see past his father's shoulder. A girl stood in the sunshine, her soft buckskin dress heavily embellished by beadwork that could not disguise the ripening woman's figure beneath it. Dark hair flowed over her shoulders like a glowing tide. Her tilted eyes crinkled into a smile when his eyes met hers.

"Can that be Dena?" he whispered, elbowing Daniel and nodding in the girl's direction.

Daniel had worn a frown ever since learning that the warriors were away, but he turned at Taregan's question and studied the girl. "So, the chief's little flower has bloomed at last," he whispered, but a stern look from Fallon shushed both boys.

Taregan knew he ought to turn toward the sachem, but his eyes would not leave the girl. He gasped in surprise when she gave him a discreet little wave, then flushed as a rush of warmth flashed over him. As his face burned, he turned toward the chief, wondering if she now laughed at him.

Nixkamich passed the pipe to Fallon and rested his hands on his knees. "I am glad you have come, for I have wanted to speak to you as one man speaks to a brother," he said, nodding gravely at Fallon.

"I have wanted to speak to you, too," Fallon answered. He paused to puff on the pipe.

"Mayhap Spirit of God speaks to both our hearts," the chief said, nodding. "It speaks to me of the English who have come to live on the river."

Fallon passed the pipe back to the chief. "The message I would give you concerns them."

"I have welcomed them in peace and in the name of the God you taught us about," the chief said, his eyes darkening, "and

yet my heart does not rest easy. You know that God has given us
the beasts of the woods to feed us and to clothe ourselves and
our children. To kill animals for any other reason would offend
the great Giver of life."

"I agree," Fallon answered. "God has been gracious to us, and
we should not kill for no reason."

"But the English bring tomahawks, bells, mirrors, hatchets,
and the burning white water to trade for the skins of animals,"
Nixkamich said, tipping his head back to better see his guests.
"Our hunters are killing beasts we do not eat for skins we do not
wear. And our women clamor for needles, scissors, knives, and
other things they say they can no longer do without." The chief
paused and looked through the open door toward the other wigwams of his village. "Our fathers and grandfathers did without
these things while they hunted the deer and beaver and bear.
And always the woods were full of animals. The Giver of life
gave freely what we needed."

A frown creased the old warrior's brow. "Many days ago a
group of Englishmen came from one of the villages on the river
and offered to buy our land." Nixkamich shook his head. "As if
land could be bought! I told him that land was a gift from the
Great Spirit and could not be given away. This made the Englishmen angry. They raised their fists and said that God had given
the land to them." The chief frowned in honest confusion. "How
can this be? How can a man, who lives only a few summers,
claim that which lives forever? We can allow the English to live
in peace where they have built cities, but one day they will die,
and their houses will fall. The land can never belong to them. We
will allow them to use it now, but it must be kept for our children's children. We, too, are children of God, and this land holds
the bones of our fathers and grandfathers. This is our place. This
is what my heart says to you."

The chief paused to puff on his pipe, then passed it to Fallon,
a sign that he had finished speaking and awaited Fallon's opinion. Taregan watched for a moment as Fallon took the pipe and

smoked, his eyes on the ground before him. He knew his father searched for the right words.

Finally he spoke. "The English come from a place where land is passed from father to son and bought and sold. Though the land outlives them, still they do this."

The chief smiled. "A wigwam, a bow, a blade, can be owned because they can be picked up and carried from one place to another. But the land . . ." He opened his hands and spread them to indicate the woods beyond. "How can a man say the earth is his when he walks upon it and lives within it? The land feeds and shelters us. We can no more claim to own it than a dog can say he owns the man who brings him food. I can more easily own the air in my body and the sunlight on my skin than the land I walk upon."

The corner of Fallon's mouth rose in a conspiratorial smile. "I understand, my brother, but the English will not. They come from a place where houses are walled and each man protects his fields lest another man walk across them. I have walked in the heart of their stone cities. I have seen how they live in fear. They find safety behind walls of wood and stone. They do not want strangers within their villages."

"We have allowed them into ours," Nixkamich answered, nodding gravely. "And now I wonder if we were wise."

"The time has passed for looking behind, now we must look ahead," Fallon said, passing the pipe back to the chief. "The English are angry with the Pequot because Englishmen have died upon the river. The English think that you and the other Pequot sachems can find these murderers and surrender them to the English captains."

The chief's expression did not change, but a vein in his forehead swelled like a thick, black snake. "How can we do such a thing? A murderer would not remain in our village. We would cast him out."

"But the English say the killers are Pequot."

"If they are, they are not of our band. Is the great English king responsible for the actions of every English man?"

"The king upholds the law, and English law demands that those who kill be killed."

"The Pequot are responsible only to themselves and their gods, and my village lives by the words of the God on a cross. You, my brother, know this better than any Englishman."

Fallon took a quick breath as if he would speak, then he pressed his lips together and said nothing. Silence hung as thick as smoke in the tense atmosphere, then Fallon smiled and the mood lightened.

"You do not live under English law," Fallon said, clasping his hands. "And you have been a good friend to my wife and my boys. But the English who are coming are not like my family. They do not understand Pequot ways, and they do not wish to learn from you. They are like a great bear, slow and steady, but terribly hungry. Their claws are sharp."

"I have killed many bears," Nixkamich said, lifting his head. A gleam shone in his eye, and for the first time Taregan noticed the necklace of pierced bear claws around the chief's neck. "But only when I needed food and fur. I will not kill a bear if I have no need of killing."

"You have spoken well," Fallon answered, nodding to the chief.

▼▲▼▲▼ After the somber council between his father and the sachem, Taregan and Daniel left the men and walked through the camp in search of other entertainment. Several young Indian boys dodged between the wigwams, using sticks to bat an inflated pig's kidney. Daniel picked up a stick and joined them.

Taregan hesitated. For the first time in his life he had no desire to join the younger boys' games. Beside a small bed of newly planted corn, just beyond the wigwams, Dena waited, her hands behind her back, a shy smile upon her face.

A burning heat rose from the back of Taregan's neck and spread up to his ears as he walked slowly toward her. The smile she threw him was friendly, and yet there was something else in

it as well—a sort of admiring appraisal that took his breath
away. He and Dena had been friends forever, for he and his family had often visited Nixkamich's camp, but until today he had
thought of Dena as a pudgy child, the spoiled and pampered
daughter of the chief. But the chubby child had grown as slender
and tall as he, and the eyes that rose to meet his flashed with
understanding and challenge.

He would have stuttered had he spoken, but fate did not give
him a chance. Just as Taregan drew near the girl, Daniel
appeared between them, a bright sheen of perspiration on his
face.

"Aren't you going to play and give me a chance to beat you?"

"Not now," Taregan said, swiveling his eyes past Daniel.

"Why not?" Daniel caught the direction of Taregan's gaze and
turned. He paused, then threw his brother an understanding and
cocky grin. "So, something else has caught your eye! Come now,
brother, surely you haven't been bewitched by this child?"

"I don't want to play, so let me be," Taregan answered, giving
him a killing look. Daniel offered a stick, but Taregan pushed his
hand away.

"What's wrong?" Daniel jerked his chin upward. "Are you
afraid I'll make you look bad in front of her?"

Taregan glanced at Dena. Still smiling, she had tilted her head
to listen, but her smile seemed somehow diluted by Daniel's
arrival. Since he and Daniel looked alike, perhaps she debated
whether she would prefer the older brother. . . .

"You can't make me look bad," Taregan said, turning to
Daniel. "I'm faster and stronger than you."

"Oh ho! A challenge! Would you like to prove it?"

Their eyes locked in open warfare. "I'll prove it right now."

"What then, a footrace?"

"Is that the toughest test you can think of?"

Daniel grinned and thumped his chest. "A race to the tall oak
on the other side of the meadow, then we must climb it until one
of us pushes the other off the tree. The one who falls must wait

until the winner begins the run back, then he can try to salvage his honor."

Taregan looked again at Dena. Though she had a rudimentary understanding of English, their heated exchange had happened too quickly for her to follow. Still, her dark, watchful eyes had missed nothing. She leaned forward, aware that they argued, and interested in the outcome of the race.

"Agreed." Taregan whipped a strip of leather from his wrist and tied back his hair.

"Now, then." Daniel threw his stick to the ground and strode purposefully toward the opening in the village palisade. Taregan thrust his shoulders back and followed, the gentle heat of the sun upon his chest and Dena's eyes at his back. *Father God, give me the strength of the sun, the swiftness of a deer, the quickness of a climbing squirrel.*

The way the brothers moved carried its own excitement, and soon a tribe of other boys had gathered around them. Nearly a dozen hunkered down beside Daniel and Taregan in the open field outside the palisade, and one of the youngest boys held up his hand.

Taregan leaned forward, caught up in the thrill of competition. Though of fairer skin than the boys around him, his heart beat in the same fierce rhythm, his spirit soared as high as the eagle's. He would show them all that he had become a man, he would prove himself to Dena, and finally he would silence Daniel's mocking, challenging eyes.

"Yiii!" With a loud whoop, the little boy's arm came down, and the contestants bolted across the field. The earth seemed to thunder with the sound of the boys' determined sprinting. Taregan steadied his breathing as his feet flew over the golden green grass, pulling him out of the pack, but from out of nowhere a Pequot boy blazed past with the ease of a deer. He turned to toss Taregan a cocky smile, then stumbled and fell, rolling across the ground. Laughing, Taregan leapt over the fallen challenger, then raced on toward the tree.

The oak rose in front of him before he had time to study it, but

Taregan threw himself up, willing his feet and hands to cling to the bark so he could scamper into its branches. For a moment he hung like a dead thing, his feet clawing the gnarled oak, then his toes gripped a protuberance through the leather of his moccasins and he pulled himself upward. Within a moment he had crept onto an overhanging branch about ten feet off the ground, but Daniel and the others had also reached the tree and begun to shinny up, each in their own fashion.

Taregan ignored the others and watched his brother climb. Daniel's face was contorted beyond its usual shape, almost unrecognizable. His eyes were narrow slits of determined rage, his mouth two stiff, straight lines. Daniel dug his fingers into the oak's bark with the tenacity of a raccoon, then scrambled toward the limb where Taregan crouched, waiting.

Through howls of glee from the Indian boys, Taregan faced his brother and felt his tension rise. The sulky look Daniel habitually wore had been refined to hatred; he played this game with purpose. Taregan stood and leaned forward, taking care to plant his feet firmly on the limb beneath him.

Clutching at branches above and beside him, Daniel moved like an awkward kitten onto the branch, propelled more by anger than confidence. "Now, my brother, you will learn who is the greater warrior," he said, one fist clenched and lifted as if he planned to fight.

Taregan moved forward, sure and certain on the unsteady limb. "And the one who falls will wait until the victor is on his way back, in truth?"

"Wasn't that what I said?" Daniel retorted, his mouth tipping in a faint smile.

"That's what I heard," Taregan answered, his eyes settling upon his brother's face. Daniel took a half-step forward, and Taregan resisted the impulse to retreat. Daniel was gasping from exertion. With any luck, he'd swing, lose his balance, and fall on his own accord.

Daniel drew back his hand and struck out, but Taregan warded off the first blow. Shifting his weight upon the limb,

Daniel leaned to one side, scrambling back a step as if to lure Taregan to the relative solidity of the stouter end of the branch, then he clung to an upper limb and jumped upon the branch, sending a massive shudder along the branch under Taregan's feet.

The boys perched in the tree howled in delight and expectation as Taregan pinwheeled to keep his balance. Daniel gave an angry shout and came forward, striking wildly, forcing Taregan back farther on the length of limb. Taregan made a quick lunge toward Daniel's arm, but the older brother managed to grab Taregan's wrist. With a sudden downward jerk, Daniel threw Taregan off balance.

For an instant Taregan was certain he would fall. Like an eagle in flight, he flapped along the branch, dreading the ground beneath him, but one of his fingers caught an overhead branch that gave just enough support for him to catch and keep his balance. Fired by adrenaline and the certainty that something deeper than boyish rivalry lay behind Daniel's challenge, Taregan screamed an ancient war cry. His shout was cut off by a wrenching kick to the stomach. He gasped as his legs parted and he fell, straddling the branch. As colors exploded in his brain, he clung to the rough bark beneath his palms and struggled to catch his breath. The ground below was a swirling green blur, but above it a shadow approached. In determined desperation, Taregan lifted his arm and swung wide, hitting Daniel's leg.

The yowling of the boys swallowed Daniel's cry as he fell, hit the ground, and rolled in a mad tumble down the hill. The yips of delight evolved into a chorus of laughter, and Taregan grinned, knowing that only his brother's pride had been truly injured. Now Daniel must lie still while Taregan scampered down, then the race would go to the swiftest of foot.

But Daniel did not lie still. Rising on his hands and knees, he cast a quick look at Taregan, then sprinted toward the camp as if the hounds of hell were giving chase. "Wait!" Taregan yelled, but Daniel obviously had no intention of playing by the rules he had ordained.

Dumbfounded, then furious, Taregan slid down the tree

trunk, cutting his chest against the jagged bark. Anger fueled his pumping feet, but still he did not win the race. By the time he burst through the opening in the palisade with the pack of boys at his heels, Daniel was already bent over before Dena, panting. Upon his shining face he wore a smile of triumph.

Taregan felt himself trembling all over, and a heat rose in his chest and belly. He recognized the surging emotion for the pure rage it was, but he dared not speak to Daniel. To protest that his brother had cheated would only bring him further dishonor before Dena. Daniel would answer that Taregan lied, and he would look like a poor loser.

He turned away from Daniel and leaned against the logs of the palisade, his lungs burning within him. The other boys surrounded him, jabbering in confusion about the race, but Taregan waved them away. He lowered his head, smarting under the sting of humiliation, and a shadow crossed his on the ground. He scowled and looked up, expecting to see a grinning boyish face, but Dena stood before him, her eyes clouded with some tender emotion he could not bear to see. He had hoped to win her admiration, not her pity.

"I watched you run," she said slowly, her eyes like clear black glass. Though he tried to look away, he could feel the magnetic pull of her gaze.

"It was not a good race," he finally managed to whisper.

She stood silently, her eyes relentless in their silent questioning, and after a moment she spoke again. "You run like a deer," she said matter-of-factly. "You are as swift as you are kind."

"Kind?" He nearly choked on the word. Daniel would tease him without mercy if he overheard *this* conversation.

"Yes, kind," she answered. "Many summers ago, you came and visited my father. The other boys were calling me Little Fat Bear, and your brother joined them and laughed at me. But you did not."

She did not smile, but Taregan felt those dark eyes rake his face, searching for a reply. "I have always thought you beautiful," he said simply, lifting himself up to stand erect. He gulped in a deep breath of fresh air as a breeze ruffled the hair that had fallen around his face.

Her eyes softened, and her admiring gaze gratified him. "I will speak to my father about you," she said, tilting her head to one side. "You have grown up, Taregan Bailie, and you will need a wife. I am old enough to marry. When you are ready, if the idea pleases you, come and ask my father for me."

For a moment, the world swirled around him, and Taregan was not certain he understood what she meant. But there was no mistaking the seriousness of her voice or the gravity of those dark eyes. She spoke about her marriage, which could take place as soon as summer.

Spellbound by sensations that were new and compelling, his heart slammed into his ribs. This glorious creature had just declared her love—for *him!* Taregan felt his heart skip, and his palms grew moist as all sense skittered into the shadows of his brain. From this day forward, her name would be carved into his heart, her voice would ring in his ears, her beauty would fill his eyes.

Deliberately, she leaned forward and gave him a childish peck. That whisper-like contact, so brief and yet so personal, seared his soul and sent shafts of lightning coursing along his veins.

Standing weakly in the electric silence between them, Taregan nodded. "You have my word, Dena. I will speak to Nixkamich very soon."

She finally gave him the smile for which he had been hoping. "I will wait for you, Taregan. No man but you shall have me."

Laden with deer, raccoon, and the carcass of a bear, the hunting party returned that afternoon. The village at once became a hive of activity as the women took the animals from the hunters and began to strip the skin and quarter the meat. The hunters' wives tossed generous hunks of meat into iron kettles over the fire, then smoked other portions for eating later.

Nixkamich invited Fallon and his sons to remain overnight. "I would have the other warriors hear your words about the English," he said simply.

Daniel groaned when his father accepted the invitation. He wanted to go home, to sleep in the comfort of his own roofed house, not in a crowded wigwam amid stinking, sweaty bodies and mangy dogs. He rolled his eyes, exasperated, then caught his father frowning at him. Daniel pulled out of the circle of men and left to find his own entertainment.

A group of hunters had set to work on the bear, and Daniel crept closer, watching in fascination. The heavy fur pelt, which would be dried and stored for the coming winter, had already been stripped away. Solid chunks of bear fat sat upon leaves on the ground, and Daniel knew it would be preserved in skins and used for polishing the warriors' hair, bodies, and bows. One man had extracted the bear's intestine and placed it in the sun to dry. Once it had toughened, it would be twisted and used for bowstring.

Though the people of Nixkamich's village had heard and accepted Fallon's words about the true God and his Son, Jesus, the old superstitions had not completely died away. The hunters who worked on the animal carcasses treated their kills with reverent appreciation. "I am sorry I had to take your life, my brother," one hunter chanted as he sliced his knife through the tough sinews of the bear's claw. "But I thank God for providing you, and I wish you a speedy journey back to the place from where you came." From time immemorial, Daniel knew, the bear's great strength had earned unique reverence from the Indians. A special pit would be reserved for the bear's bones, and the dogs would not be allowed to touch them.

A pair of children had picked up the bear's claws and pretended to roar and snarl at each other. "No, no," one of the women casually rebuked the children over her shoulder. "Our brother bear has great strength and courage. You must never mock him."

If this bear had such strength and courage, Daniel thought, glancing around for some more interesting activity, *why is he now dead? Cunning matters, not strength.*

A melodic laugh caught Daniel's ear, and he glanced toward the sound. Through an opening between two wigwams he saw Taregan and Dena walking together, their heads bowed toward one another.

Jealousy hissed in Daniel's heart. Taregan's shoulders shook as if in mirth—how could he laugh after his shame and disgrace this afternoon? Daniel had finally bested Taregan in front of the sachem's pretty daughter, and yet the loser behaved as if he didn't know that his honor had been besmirched. And Dena, for all her loveliness, was no wiser. Daniel had won, through craft and cunning, and yet Dena had given him only a troubled look. She should be laughing with *him!*

He closed his eyes and clenched his teeth. Women loved Taregan—even Mother laughed more easily with him than she did with Daniel. This morning she had giggled and waved good-bye at Taregan while she drew Daniel to her and whispered "Don't struggle so, my son." What had she meant? He didn't *struggle* against Taregan. Beating him was easy when he applied his wit.

Infuriated, Daniel went to find his father. Fallon sat in a circle around the village fire with the sachem and his elders while a warrior rehearsed the details of the hunt. The mood was light;

the night punctuated with laughter. The hunters relaxed around the fire with full bellies and content hearts. Soon the coals would be banked, and the entire company would disperse into the wig-wams.

"Father," Daniel whispered, sinking onto the ground beside Fallon, "Taregan spends all his time with Dena, Nixkamich's daughter." He snorted. "He is smitten. He behaves as if he would take her to wife."

His father lifted an eyebrow. "So soon? He is but fifteen."

"That's what I thought," Daniel agreed, crossing his legs. "Tar-egan should spend his time with the warriors or the elders, or even the other boys. But instead he walks with *her*, and a silly look fills his eyes."

From across the fire, Nixkamich lifted his hand and gestured to Fallon. "What does your boy say?" the sachem asked, his eyes gleaming through the gathering dusk.

Fallon nodded in respect. "Daniel thinks my other son is fond of your daughter."

The chief smiled. "She is my eldest child, and the nearest to my heart. A union would be a good thing. We should join our clans forever and share grandchildren."

"But Father—," Daniel protested.

Fallon held up his hand, warning Daniel against further inter-ruption with a stern glance. "Why should they not be promised to one another?" he answered, resting his elbows atop his knees. "Surely God would smile on their marriage."

"In one or two summers, it shall be done," Nixkamich fin-ished. "If God wills."

"If God wills," Fallon echoed, smiling at the sachem.

Reining in his temper with difficulty, Daniel tried to smile.

▾▲▾▲▾ Fallon made sure that Daniel and Taregan were properly bedded down on grass mats in the sachem's hut, then he paused outside in the silvery moonlight for an honest talk with the chief.

"My friend," he said, his eyes scanning the darkening village for signs of movement, "I hope that you will not forget the words I have spoken here. The English are angry; they will want Pequot blood in return for those who died at Wethersfield." '

"But you say the English worship the same God we do," Nixkamich replied, pulling his blanket around his shoulders. "A Christian would not kill his brother."

"Sassacus is not a Christian," Fallon answered. "Nor are the other Pequot sachems. Yours is the only village following the true God; the others walk a path the English hate."

"Then we will tell the English that we follow the Christ," Nixkamich said, his eyes serene. "They will not harm us."

"They may not believe you," Fallon said, struggling for words. From what he knew of the Puritans, they were a strict group who had left England because they would not compromise matters of religious belief and conduct. From the gossip of Dutch traders on the river, Fallon had heard that they actively fought against religious and cultural behavior they considered ungodly. Rumors whispered that a woman in Massachusetts, Anne Hutchinson, stood on the brink of exile from that colony because she claimed God could and did speak directly to her heart.

Could the Puritans accept as fellow believers these Indians who heard the voice of God in the wind? Who lived openly and happily at peace with both the spiritual and physical worlds? The Pequots of Nixkamich's village shared all things in common, loved freely, shunned sin, and worshiped truthfully, but Fallon thought it likely that the Puritans would see Indian civilization as sinful, depraved, and barbarous. The standard by which they measured conduct and civility was altogether different from that of the Indians, but how could they insist that their standard was the right one? Fallon suspected that peace could best be kept if the two cultures remained separate.

"Promise me you will speak to the other sachems," Fallon said finally. "They must avoid the English if possible and give no cause for affront. If Sassacus's thirst for vengeance has been satisfied, urge him to leave the English in peace."

Nixkamich nodded gravely. "I will consider your words, my brother," he said. "Soon I will journey to speak with Sassacus."

▼▲▼▲▼ A narrow deer path pointed a curving finger through the trees, and Daniel skulked along the trail, studying the prints in the moist earth. His ego still smarted from Gilda's effusive praise of the buck Taregan had brought home, and he was further goaded by the fact that with scarcely any effort at all, Taregan had won the most desirable girl in the river valley. Daniel had to find his own buck, one he could bring down without help. He'd find it, shoot it, track it, and carry it home as a trophy to prove that he was every bit as skilled and adept as Taregan. Even Dena, when she heard of it, would be impressed.

He crouched in a leafy thicket off the trail and waited for the better part of an hour as the woods vibrated softly around him. The trees seemed to him a prison wall, the sun-shot leaves overhead a suffocating ceiling that threatened to smother him. A branch bobbed in the wind, raining dew upon his head, and Daniel frowned, wishing there were some other way to earn his father's approval. If only he could work in one of the English villages! He was quick with numbers and a ruthlessly efficient trader when Gilda took the family's wares to the trading post.

Mayhap some day, he mused, *I can convince Mother and Father to move to one of the English villages. Then I could have a trading post of my own, with axes and arrows and swords and iron knives—*

A rustling sound caught his attention and Daniel tensed, every nerve in him strung to perfect tune. A stately buck sauntered onto the path, a doe and fawn following. The buck blinked, surveying the area, his nostrils quivering as he flushed out the various scents of the woods. His antlers were majestic, fully five feet from point to point, and for an instant Daniel's courage failed as he imagined himself impaled upon those sharp tips. . . .

Still hiding in the brush, he grimaced and reached for his bow.

After nocking the arrow, he stood and pulled back the bow-string, praying that his aim would be true. Staring at the center of the buck's chest, he steadied his trembling arm and released the string.

The thrum of the bow spoiled the silence, the buck darted away, but not before the arrow had buried itself deep within the animal's flank. The doe and fawn fled into the woods as Daniel stood and screamed in elation, thrilled and somewhat surprised that he had managed to strike the deer. But within a moment, the leaves stopped moving, the forest lay silent. He would have nothing to show for his efforts unless he tracked and killed the buck, but an animal injured in the flank could run for miles before dropping.

Curbing his excitement, he hurried through the brush, his eyes alert for bright crimson dots of blood among the greenery. He would have his buck, and his father's approval, before the sun set.

▼▲▼▲▼ Daniel tracked the deer for over an hour and finally found the great beast at the bottom of a gully. The stag panted heavily, its sides heaving with every breath, its flank mottled with spots of blood. Standing at the top of the ridge, Daniel lifted his bow, but the buck stood at such an angle that he could not hit the heart. To shoot from this place would only wound the creature again and possibly send him into another frantic flight.

He would have to descend into the gully and slit the animal's throat. Taregan could have done it, and Father, too, by creeping silently down and throwing an arm around the beast's neck while the edge of the knife struck invisibly, like a snake.

The buck's head was hoary with old age; of certain he was a grandfather, a prince among the herd. Slowly, regally, the animal lifted his crown of antlers, his nostrils quivering as he snuffed the air. Daniel tensed. In a moment, this king of beasts would smell his fear.

Goaded by desperation, he slipped sideways down the

muddy edge of the ravine until he stood a few feet from the buck. The massive head turned toward him, the rack of antlers sharp and as wide as Daniel was long. The buck's dark eyes gazed on him with derision, daring Daniel to take a step forward. One cloven hoof pawed the ground, the head lowered slightly as the buck prepared to defend himself. For a moment woven of eternity, the buck stared until Daniel's heart raced and his fingers fluttered in fear.

Instinctively, he took a half-step back. "I did not mean to harm you, brother," he babbled, hoping that the Indians were right about animals understanding sincere human speech. "Go your way, back to your wives and children."

The buck snorted sharply; the sound cut through Daniel like a knife. Fear poured from his loins in a warm rush as he scrambled up the ridge and ran away.

He would have to go to the river and wash, or Taregan would surely know that Daniel had shamed himself. He would have to invent a story about the missing arrow, or else claim that the buck had escaped him in the brush. But then Taregan would taunt him for being a poor tracker and hunter.

Safe on the ridge, Daniel sank to the ground, the heaviness in his chest weighing him down like a millstone. Why not admit the truth? He was the eldest son and should have been the best son, but Taregan would beat him in every contest involving courage, strength, or physical skill.

As long as Daniel lived in the primitive, cursed wilderness, Taregan would defeat him every day.

▼▲▼▲▼ The delicious scent of his mother's cookfire quickened Daniel's plodding pace as he neared his home, but the sight of Englishmen in the clearing stopped him abruptly. At least half a dozen strangers stood outside the house with his father, muskets in their arms and at the ready. Daniel froze. What had happened?

He could not see Taregan or his mother, and Daniel guessed

that his father had sent them into the house as the strangers approached. Taregan probably stood at the window, mayhap even now he aimed a musket through one of the slits in the shutters. But what should *he* do? His hand gripped the handle of the knife in his belt, but the dampness of his leggings reminded him that he was no warrior. If Father needed help, he should count on the son in the house, not the one in the field.

"We are seeking the Pequots who attacked Wethersfield not many days ago," one of the men was saying, his voice echoing over the empty field. "The traders say you know every savage in this land."

"I know many Indians," Fallon answered, his voice composed and as steady as his posture, "and very few savages. The warriors you seek do not live in these parts."

"Where *do* they live?" the leader barked. Dressed in the blazing red of the English army, he was a tight little man with green eyes and a bearded face that did not look capable of any pleasant emotion.

Fallon did not answer, but squatted to idly scratch on the ground with a stick. A soldier next to the leader lifted his musket into firing position. "Answer Captain Mason when he speaks to you, sir!"

Fallon lifted his face and gazed at the man with chilling intentness for a long moment. "The Indians who attacked Wethersfield acted to defend their honor and send a message. Your people, Captain, have committed many wrongs against the Pequot. Tatobem, one of the Pequots' greatest sachems, died at white men's hands even though his people paid to ransom him, and eight months ago a Pequot village on Block Island was burned—"

The second man squinted down his rifle. "Where are the murdering devils now?"

Fallon shrugged. "I do not approve of bloodshed in the first place or the second," he said, pointing toward his scratchings on the ground. "And here, by the sea coast, is where you will find the sachem you seek." He looked up at Captain Mason. "But if I

were you, I would not make the journey. I would rest, knowing
that the Indian anger has been assuaged."

"How can we not go after them?" Mason demanded, thrusting his hands on his hip. "They killed nine people, sir, and took
two young women captive."

Fallon lifted his brows. "Were the women returned safely?"

"Yes, thank God. The Dutch rescued them for us."

"There would have been no rescue if the Pequot had not
allowed it. Be grateful that so few died, sir, and leave the Pequot
in peace. Their ways are not your ways."

"Are they yours?" Mason asked, his eyes narrowing as he
studied Fallon's face.

At that moment, Taregan opened the door of the house and
stepped out into the bright sunlight. The captain's men immediately tensed and trained their muskets on the boy in the doorway.

Daniel felt a sudden chill, and fear like the quick, hot touch of
the devil propelled him forward. *You won't point a gun at my
brother!*

"Ho, Father!" he called, smiling broadly though everything in
him wanted to scream. "God nearly smiled on me today! I saw a
buck, a huge one, with antlers as broad as an oak!"

As he had hoped they would, the Englishmen turned from
Taregan to stare at Daniel. "Mayhap God has smiled on us," Captain Mason said, rubbing his beard with a meaty hand. "You
seem a prosperous man. If you will grant us hospitality, sir, we
would stay and eat with you and your family. The day is far
spent, and we would be happier camping upon your property
than in the woods."

"This land is God's, as is everything upon it," Fallon
answered, holding out a welcoming hand to Daniel. "My wife
will cook for you, and you shall eat with us. And as you sleep
tonight, I pray God will direct your hearts away from the path of
bloodshed toward peace. You have your captives returned, the
bloody score is evened. Let it rest, gentlemen. Let it rest."

▼▲▼▲▼ "Hey, boy."

Daniel turned his head from the warmth of the evening fire toward the circle where the Englishmen had spread their cloaks to sleep. His mother and father had already disappeared inside the house, and Taregan had gone down to the stream to fetch water for the morrow. Most of the English slept, already snoring after their hearty meal of corn and venison, but the dark-haired man who had held the musket on Father lay awake by the fire, his granite eyes locked on Daniel.

The man was slim but powerfully built, with a long, narrow brown face, deeply seamed by the sun and more than forty winters. Unlike the other Englishmen, he wore his long, dark hair free about his shoulders. An intense quality of animal assurance clung to him like a mantle.

Daniel's tongue felt thick and heavy in his mouth. "What?" he finally asked.

"Tell me about the buck you almost brought in today. Mayhap we could find it again, together."

The man waited as if he expected a reply, but Daniel could not think of anything to say.

A cocky, sure smile gleamed from the center of the man's face. "I have to admit I'm more than a little surprised you couldn't bring the buck in. The traders say your father is as good a tracker as the Indian guides. They say that even though his blood's British, he's Indian in his heart."

Daniel stared at the ground, uneasy. This man could read his mind, had guessed his humiliation. . . .

"The traders also say," the man went on, an oily tone creeping into his voice, "that your mother is very beautiful. Tonight I have seen that they are right. And your brother, he takes good care of her, doesn't he? He has not left her alone since we arrived."

A vague note of accusation rang in his voice, and a flash of anger swept words from Daniel's heavy tongue. "We take care of one another. We are a family."

The man held up a defensive hand. "Whoa, boy, don't lose your temper on my account. I can see you're as angry as a beaver

with a toothache, and it wouldn't be polite of me to offend my
host, would it? Especially since *your brother* provided the deer
that fed us tonight."

Frowning, Daniel hugged his knees and watched the dying
fire. "I don't like to talk about my brother."

"Then we shall talk about you. What's your name, son?"

"Daniel Bailie."

"Nice to meet you, Daniel. I am Garvin Black." The man's
bright smile seemed to hang on nothing in the darkness. "When
I saw you tonight, I said to myself, 'Now there's a boy with
pluck.' You came rushing out of those woods with fire in your
eyes, ready to help your father. Not a bit like your brother, who
had been hiding in the house with your pretty mother. So I knew
right away which of you was the most gallant. You are, aren't
you, Daniel Bailie?"

Daniel jerked his head away, afraid he'd reveal the shame
written in his heart. *No!* he wanted to shout. *No, you're wrong —
I'm a coward. I can't kill a deer, I can't paddle in the river rapids, I
can't do anything as well as Taregan.*

But he bit his lip and said nothing.

"Ah, and you're humble, too. Humility is a good quality, Daniel Bailie, especially in a young man on the brink of his future."
The man rolled onto his back and folded his hands over his
chest. "Mayhap we should talk in the morning. Find me alone
before we pull out, and we'll talk about your plans, young Bailie.
It is a pity to let your talents go to waste out here in the woods,
don't you think?"

The fire winked out, and Daniel sat in the darkness for a long
time, thinking.

▼▲▼▲▼ The birds began their incessant calling as soon
as the gray dawn moved across the clearing, and Garvin Black
spat the taste of bitter whiskey from his mouth as he woke.
Another cursed night on the ground when he could be home in

his bed! Then he sat up, abruptly, remembering where he was. Most of the others were still asleep around the cold campfire.

He shivered and rubbed the sleeves of his doublet. A heavy April dew had covered them completely during the night. The double lace collar of his shirt was ruined, limp with the humidity of the morning mist, and muddy clay stained the heavy fabric of his breeches. The leggings over his calves were torn in several places, and under the heavy woven material his legs looked unnaturally scrawny and pale.

Groaning, Garvin adjusted his garters, brushed himself off, and stood, tossing his damp blanket over a bush. Remembering that he had seen a stream nearby, he tramped through the woods. His sleep-fogged brain begged for a bracing splash of cold water on his face.

The sound of voices made him pause when he reached the stream. The two brothers frolicked there, as alike as handsome birds of a feather. With their classically sculpted features and striking blue eyes, in a proper doublet, breeches, and hat they could easily pass for English nobility. But here in the wilds of New England, wearing nothing but leather breechcloths and painted leggings, the brothers' savage nature could not be denied. They cavorted in the water like two young bear cubs, taunting and splashing each other until he spoke and halted their revelry: "And which of you would be my friend Daniel Bailie?"

The nearest boy turned around, water shining on his wide brow. The other boy's face darkened with distrust.

"Do you remember me from last night? I don't think I look much different in daylight." He stepped out from behind the tangle of shrubbery, casually slipping his hand into the pocket of his doublet. "Daniel, my friend, will you introduce me to your brother?"

Daniel lifted a bare shoulder in an awkward shrug. "My brother is called Taregan."

"You held a musket on my father," Taregan said, a thread of anger in his voice.

"I cry you mercy, don't be holding that against me," Garvin

went on smoothly, smiling at Daniel. "Your father was not being very helpful. But after his wonderful hospitality, I'd like to repay his kindness by helping you."

His words brought a hard frown and a glint of temper to Taregan's face, but Daniel pushed his bottom lip forward in thought. *Smart boy.* "Have you spent much time in civilization, boys? Have you traveled to Hartford? Been as far as Boston? Have you been to the docks where huge ships bring treasures from the east?" He raised his hand and spread it slowly as if he could summon the riches of the world by a single gesture. "In the city you can find beautiful girls, delicious foods that melt in your mouth for sweetness, treasures unheard of in these parts and heretofore unimagined. All these could be yours, my young friends, if you would come away with me. You could leave this shack and return with me to Hartford. Captain Mason is always looking for trackers, and since both of you already speak English—"

"I can read and write, too," Daniel inserted, snapping at the bait like a starving turtle.

"But he doesn't want any part of the English army," Taregan argued, splashing closer.

Garvin suppressed a smile. "That is good. I'm not always with the army; I'm only with Captain Mason to scout out these lands. I own a merchant company; I import riches from all over the world. Colonists will soon fill this land from one edge of the horizon to the other, and I need someone to help me manage the Indians. I need a young man who knows his way in the woods and speaks the Indian tongue. I could use both of you, or either of you." His eyes flickered over Daniel's expressive face. "But I need someone who is useful in the woods—and out."

"We could not live in the city," Taregan objected, clenching his fist. "Our father would not allow it. We belong here, this is our home."

"You are old enough to chart the courses of your own lives," Garvin said, pretending to study his nails. "In England, lads your age have already been apprenticed to a trade. They behave as men, they do not splash in creeks like little boys."

Daniel flushed deeply, but Taregan did not take offense. "We care not what the English may do," he said simply. "We are not English."

"Can you not speak for yourself?" Garvin asked, turning to Daniel. The boy's face contorted in a spasm of frustration. Garvin knelt at the creek's edge, scooped up a handful of water, and wiped his face and beard. When he looked up again, neither boy had moved.

"We will be leaving soon," he said, standing. "If you ever decide to come to Hartford, ask for Garvin Black at the trading post by the dock. Someone will know how to reach me." He turned to go, then tossed a comment over his shoulder. "I could use one of you immediately. In fact, Captain Mason could use an expert guide today. He is not familiar with Pequot lands and is most insistent on reaching them as soon as possible. We have heard that the Pequot are about to join with the Narragansett and the Mohegan tribes to wipe our settlements from the land."

Taregan laughed. "That is a lie," he said, total conviction in his voice. "Uncas of the Mohegans would never cooperate with Sassacus of the Pequot. They've disliked each other ever since Sassacus became sachem. Uncas had married Tatobem's daughter, you see, and thought he should be sachem. He is jealous—"

"Mayhap our intelligence is incorrect," Garvin interrupted, shrugging. He paused and looked again at Daniel. "Do come, Daniel, when you've tired of this place. I can help you discover a world of which you have never dreamed."

"Why would we grow tired of our home?" Taregan asked, lifting his hand to the sky. The warm sun gilded his handsome features. "This land feeds, shelters, and teaches us. We are friends with the English and the Indians. We want nothing more than to live our lives here in peace—"

"You talk like one of the barbarians," Garvin said, barely managing to conceal the contempt that rose from his soul. "You think this land is rich? I can see that you are children, but I had no idea the renowned Fallon Bailie had reared a pair of fools. Don't you know that the more land a man owns, the greater he is? And this land on which you stand is not yours at all—it belongs to King Charles."

"King Charles?" Daniel's brow furrowed in deep thought.

"The king of England, for whom these lands were claimed years ago. King Charles lives across the sea in a palace of ten thousand rooms. On his shoulders he wears furs unlike any you've ever seen, and he is crowned with gold and diamonds. The food at his dinner table today would feed your family for a year! Hundreds of great seafaring ships are his to command, and thousands of men stand ready to do anything he asks. And soon those men, their wives, and their children will fill these lands, *English lands,* and those who do not join us are fated to be trodden underfoot."

Taregan thrust his head back and laughed. "What a story, Garvin Black! I almost believed you!"

But Daniel did not laugh. Troubled thoughts stirred behind his deep blue eyes.

Garvin flattened his smile. "I may have told a lie once or twice, but I am speaking the truth now," he said simply. "More and more ships will come to this land, and soon the Indians will be forced to flee. Choose your friends carefully, young lads, and mark my words. You will remember them."

Taregan waited until the Englishman had left the creek, then he playfully splashed Daniel's bare back. "Come, Daniel, let's bathe ourselves in King Charles's water!"

"Stop it! I do not want to play games."

"In truth, surely you did not believe him!" Taregan strode through the thigh-deep water until he faced his brother. Daniel's eyes were narrow, his face pinched with worry.

Taregan tried smiling, but sensed immediately that it was a bad idea and gave it up. "Forget what he said. He is only a stupid Englishman who thinks he can frighten us with threats. Nixkamich says the English are made of nothing but smoke and big talk."

"I think this man spoke truly. Father has been to England, and he has talked of their mighty cities and their king. It is true that the wooden ships come more and more frequently to the river villages; each day more Englishmen walk in this valley. And they are powerful—we have no cannon, no muskets except those we trade for in the English villages."

"Why do we need cannons and guns? You can't kill meat for the table with a cannon, and there's not an Englishman in Hartford who can shoot and track a deer as well as Father."

Taregan's words fell on deaf ears. Daniel splashed up the bank.

"Where are you going?" Taregan called after him.

"Home."

"I'll beat you back."

Taregan bolted out of the stream and ran through the brush, pacing himself to remain one step ahead of his brother's pounding footsteps. When they burst into the clearing outside their home, the Englishmen had circled around Fallon once again. This time, Taregan noticed with relief, their muskets hung casually at their sides.

"Are you sure we can't convince you to come with us?" Captain Mason asked again. "We need a guide through the woods. We hope to find this Pequot chief and reason with him—"

"Leave Sassacus in peace," Fallon answered, with a cautionary lift of his hand.

"Peace?" Mason laughed. "Where, in the name of God, are we supposed to find peace in this godforsaken wilderness? There's a savage behind every tree, a heathen camp beyond every hill—"

"Peace is not to be found in the world," Fallon answered, his eyes darting toward his sons. His gaze held Taregan's for a moment, and he smiled. "Peace enters a man's heart when he reconciles himself to God. A few of the Indians have found this peace, and they ask nothing more than to be left alone."

"And I suppose you'll be trying to tell me that the fountain of youth flows just over the next hill," Mason said, laughing. He shouldered his musket and held up his hand. "We'll be off, sir. We thank you for your hospitality, Fallon Bailie."

"Wait," Fallon called, stepping forward. He stood face-to-face with Captain Mason. "Let me be your emissary. I will speak to Sassacus and gather the answers you seek. I will come to Hartford and tell you what the Pequot sachem has said."

Mason hesitated, and Taregan realized for the first time that the man wasn't at all eager to enter a wilderness where the Indians were at home and the English virtual strangers.

"You would do this?" the captain asked, lifting a bushy brow.

"I would. And let us hope there will be no more bloodshed."

"I'll have to report to the General Court of Connecticut by the first of May. Please, sir, bring me Sassacus's reply within three days."

"You have my word."

Captain Mason nodded in approval and shouted a command to his men. The others fell into a straight line and began the march into the woods. Taregan sighed in relief as the group walked away, but a creeping uneasiness rose from the bottom of his heart when Garvin Black turned and winked at Daniel.

A court was called and met in Hartford on Monday, the First of May 1637, who seriously considering the very sad condition of the English, for those Pequots were a great people, being strongly fortified, cruel, warlike, and munitioned. The English were but a handful in comparison. But the Pequots' outrageous violence against the English, having murdered about thirty of them, their great pride and insolence, constant pursuit in their malicious courses, with their engaging other Indians in their quarrel against the English who had never offered them the least wrong, who had in all likelihood espoused all the Indians in their country in their quarrel, had not God by more than an ordinary Providence prevented. These things being duly considered, with the eminent hazard and great peril the English were in, it pleased God so to stir up the hearts of all men in general, and the court in special, that they concluded some forces should forthwith be sent out against the Pequots, their grounds being just, and necessity enforcing them to engage in an offensive and defensive war. . . .

Captain John Mason

▼▲▼▲ After learning of the court's decision, Garvin Black smiled in satisfaction. Despite Fallon Bailie's recently arrived word of assurance that Sassacus did not plan to war against the English, John Mason was as relentless as the tide: difficult to withstand and impossible to stop. The captain wanted blood on his sword, not only to defeat the Pequots, but to annihilate them so they might serve as an example to the other tribes. Mason had already spoken of enlisting Uncas of the Mohegans to ensure that tribe's cooperation. With the ninety men of the Connecticut militia and a company of Mohegan warriors, success was nearly guaranteed. They faced only the tricky problem of navigating the river without arousing attention from Pequot scouts, and about that difficulty Garvin Black had thought long and hard.

The Bailie boy, the one who smelled of discontent like a cheap scent, would serve nicely as a scout. As the advancing army passed by the Bailie homestead, Garvin could pluck the boy as easily as a ripe apple. Daniel Bailie would know how to lead the troops and mislead the Pequots; that boy alone could prove to be the edge of victory for the fledgling colony. And when the Pequot were gone, the lands cleared, and Fallon Bailie arrested for complicity with the enemy, Garvin Black would claim that prosperous homestead for himself. He smiled in grim satisfaction.

He'd take the woman, too, if she didn't prove too troublesome.

The web he'd begun to weave a few years ago was finally taking shape. He had acquired his first stake in the trading business when he intercepted the ransom the Pequots paid for their sachem, Tatobem. After hiding the booty of furs and wampum, Garvin urged the Dutch traders to kill the old man lest the Pequots descend in an attempt to free their chief. That bit of mischief had cost him many a night's sleep once he learned that the old man was father to the fierce Sassacus, but when renegade Niantics murdered the English captain John Stone on the river, Garvin pointed a finger at Sassacus and the Pequot, hoping to rid the woods of his vengeful and clever enemy. The wily savage managed to escape English retribution, but Garvin knew the terms of his arrangement with the English. With the proper words and promises in the ears of a band of renegade river Indians, Garvin had made certain that Oldham's trading ship would fall prey to pirates off Block Island. And John Gallop, the trader who had happened upon the attack and discovered the hacked-up body of John Oldham, could not tell one Indian from another. Again, the Pequot bore the blame.

The dismemberment of a leading Bay trader was offensive enough to give the edgy Puritan leaders an excuse to wage full war upon the Pequot. The English captains were quick to believe Garvin's reports, for he had years of experience in the frontier. It

was far easier to believe in murderous, cannibalistic savages
than to doubt a civilized white trader.

Smiling to himself, Garvin turned from the posted proclama-
tion of war and strode toward Captain Mason's garrison.

▼▲▼▲▼ Under the command of Captain John Mason,
the Connecticut army left Hartford on the fifteenth day of May.
Uncas brought a sizeable party of Mohegan warriors in canoes
while the Englishmen traveled in three ships: a pink, a pinnace,
and a shallop. For most of the day Garvin Black stood at the rail
of the pinnace with his hand over his mouth, smothering the
smile that threatened to creep across his face. For all their blustery bravado, the English had failed to plan for the often shallow
waters of the Connecticut River. Though none of the English
boats were particularly large, still they frequently ran aground.
The depth of the water was no problem to the Mohegans, who
either slipped their flat-bottomed canoes through the shallows or
stepped out and carried them forward, but the English stuck like
flies in molasses whenever the grassy river bottom caught hold
of the ships.

The Mohegans, impatient with delays and the helplessness of
the English, sent Uncas to declare that he and his men would
move overland through the woods and meet Captain Mason at
Fort Saybrook. Garvin watched as Mason considered their
request. The captain's face clouded with doubts and misgivings,
and Garvin knew he weighed the risk of offending the
Mohegans by denying them liberty against losing them altogether if they chose not to keep their word and join in the battle
to come.

Garvin stepped closer to his captain. "Sir," he said, clicking
his heels together smartly as he lowered his voice, "why not
send Captain Underhill with the Mohegans? If you have cause to
doubt Uncas's fidelity, mayhap Captain Underhill can hold him
tight to our purpose."

The captain's green eyes narrowed as he turned to confer with

Garvin. "If I allow the savages to go," he said, lowering his voice
to a near whisper, "how then are we to progress through these
hostile forests? We are altogether ignorant of the country, and of
the people who dwell along these shores—"

"Begging your pardon, captain," Garvin struggled to keep a
note of triumph from his voice, "but do you recall Fallon Bailie
and his sons? I am certain I can convince one of the boys or Master Bailie himself to accompany us. All three speak the savage
tongue as easily as they do English, and they know this land as
thoroughly as any Indian."

For the sake of the waiting chief, Captain Mason drew his lips
into a tight smile. "Are you sure Bailie will help us?" he whispered to Garvin. "His reception of us was less than enthusiastic."

Imitating the captain, Garvin tossed a confident smile at the
Indian. "Bailie is English, is he not? And if he will not help, of
certain one of his boys can be persuaded. I took the time to cultivate a friendship with the boy Daniel, and I'd stake my life on
my conviction that he will join our cause."

Mason abruptly thrust his hands behind his back and nodded
toward Uncas. "So be it. The Mohegans will go overland with
Captain Underhill and wait for us at Fort Saybrook. We will continue on our present course. But the shallop will go ahead with
Garvin Black to find another scout to help us navigate this river."

"Aye, sir," Garvin answered, nodding.

▼▲▼▲▼ On the third day of the river journey Garvin
Black stood in the bow of the shallop and pointed with his sword
to the small clearing that led to the Bailie homestead. "Pull right,
over there," he shouted to the oarsmen. Even before the shallop
hit bottom, he sprang from the boat and splashed through the
reeds onto shore. A lazy column of smoke rose in the distance.
Good. At least Mistress Bailie waited in the house. Mayhap
Fallon Bailie would be more disposed to give aid if his lovely
wife's voice were lifted in entreaty.

Gripping his musket, Garvin Black strode up the bank and motioned for his men to follow.

▼▲▼▲ Sitting against a backrest outside the house, Daniel stopped whittling when a flock of waterbirds suddenly took to the air. He heard the rustling in the brush before he saw the men. The company coming in his direction was sizeable, and the intruders moved with the heavy, lumbering tread of Englishmen.

His pulse quickened as he looked down the path. Could Captain Mason be returning so soon?

"Taregan!" he hissed in the direction of the house. His brother's tousled head appeared in the window. "Men are coming!"

Taregan closed the shutters and disappeared, and Daniel knew he would wait and listen from inside the house. Their mother worked in the field and might not return for some time; their father was away, hunting. Instinctively, Daniel knew his first concern should be for his mother's safety.

He stood and puffed out his chest, stretching himself to his full height.

Garvin Black and a company of a dozen men burst through the brush on the river side of the clearing, their muskets raised as if the enemy lurked behind every tree. Garvin walked with a stalking, purposeful intent, and his dark eyes scanned the doorway and window of the house as he moved closer. Finally he stopped, took in Daniel in one sweeping glance, then threw Daniel a secretive smile.

"Are you my friend Daniel or the other one?" he asked, his voice pleasant and completely at odds with the menacing expressions on the other men's faces. Garvin dropped the butt of his musket to the ground, and the other men with him seemed to relax slightly.

In a rush, Daniel released the breath he'd been holding. "I'm Daniel, Master Black. What—why are you here?"

"I am looking for your father." He glanced around the clear-

ing again, taking a pouch of tobacco from his doublet pocket as
he did so. "Is your father home?"

"My father has gone hunting," Daniel answered, finding reassurance in the man's willingness to stop and smoke.

"And your mother?"

"She is—away."

"You are alone, then?"

Daniel resisted the impulse to look toward the house. He was
certain Taregan's blue eyes were pressed to a slit in the shutters.
"I am alone. How may I help you?"

"In truth, I am glad you asked." Garvin pulled a pipe from the
pocket of his red uniform and paused to light it. "I need a favor,
son. For killing more than thirty innocent Englishmen, the General Court of Connecticut has declared war on the Pequot. Uncas
is leading a party of Mohegans; Captain Mason is leading the
Connecticut army."

A spasm of panic shot across Daniel's body like the trilling of
a bell. "W-war?" he asked, dimly aware that he stammered like a
child. "You would kill the Pequot? But my father told you that
the bloodshed had stopped, and it would be wrong to involve
Uncas, for he has never liked Sassacus. They've been fighting for
years—"

"I cry you mercy, hush," Garvin said, stepping closer. He
placed his heavy, solid hands on Daniel's shoulders, and the
calm warmth of his touch soothed Daniel's alarm. Here was an
adult, a rational man in the midst of confusion.

"I am trying to stop the bloodshed, can't you see?" Garvin
whispered, looking over his shoulder as if he feared his men
would hear. "But I need help. Uncas travels by land, Mason is on
the river in two large ships that can't make good time. I need
someone to take me to Sassacus by the fastest possible route, and
it's important that he not know I am coming. He would only
send warriors to warn us away." He paused and scanned the
perimeter of the clearing again. "I had hoped to convince your
father to join me."

"My father is away," Daniel repeated, lifting his chin. "But I can take you to Sassacus, Master Black. I know the way, and I know the signals the Pequot warriors use to identify themselves in the woods."

"Can you take me to Sassacus's village?"

"Weinshauks?" Daniel crinkled his brow. "I could, but the sachems are meeting now at Mystic. All the great sachems and their warriors are there to celebrate the spring planting dances."

"All of them? Dancing?" Interest gleamed like fire in Garvin's eye. "How marvelous, Daniel. Come, you shall lead us, but we must go at once. Gather what you need, but hurry, for we are in a race against the Mohegans."

Spurred by the delightful sense of being useful, Daniel darted toward the house. Slamming the door open, he grabbed his leather shirt and slid his knife into his belt.

"You should not go," Taregan said, lifting his head from the window where he had watched the entire encounter. "Something about this man is not right. Father does not trust him, nor does Mother."

Daniel turned on Taregan in a sudden flash of defensive spirit. "Didn't you hear him, snooping ears? He is trying to save the Pequot. You know Uncas would like nothing better than to see Sassacus and his people destroyed. Have you forgotten the love of your life? Dena is a Pequot. How do you know Uncas would not lead the English to make war even on Nixkamich's village?"

"Nixkamich and his people have harmed no one."

"That's why I've got to stop Captain Mason. I'm going, Taregan, and I don't care what you think. You're just jealous because Master Black likes me!"

"I think you're wrong." Honest fear gleamed in Taregan's eyes, and he stepped forward and grasped Daniel's arm in an iron grip. "Don't go, Daniel. What will Mother say when she comes back? What would Father tell you to do if he were here?"

"Mother will know that I have gone to do a man's work," Daniel said. With a colossal effort, he wrenched his arm free from Taregan's grasp, then pulled a handful of pemmican from the storage barrel. He stuffed the dried food into a leather pouch, then tied it to his belt. "And Father will be proud of me. Tell them not to worry. I will be back as soon as I have shown Master Black the way to Mystic."

"Do I have to fight you to keep you here?" Taregan demanded somewhat desperately. He moved to stand in front of the door, his feet spread, his arms crossed. He seemed to swell, sizing Daniel up as if he could forcibly hold him until their father returned.

Daniel was not worried; cunning could win over mere strength. "You could fight me," Daniel said, keeping his voice level. "You could sit on me and pin me down. You could knock me senseless. But you would eventually have to release me. And I am leaving here with Garvin Black. If you hold me, I will leave later and follow the English on the river. If you tie me up, I will escape. Nothing you can do will change my mind."

Surprise blossomed on Taregan's face. Daniel laughed, gripped his bow and quiver, and slipped past his brother to join Garvin Black and the Englishmen.

▼▲▼▲▼ To Daniel's complete and utter delight, the English treated him like a peer. Garvin introduced him to the others as "my friend, Master Daniel Bailie," and the men were quick to ask his opinions about tracks, trails, and the various fowl and animals they passed along the way. He was momentarily confused when the shallop was joined by the two larger ships commanded by Captain Mason, but Garvin Black merely shook his head and put a finger across his lips when Daniel threw him a questioning glance.

"Say nothing about what I have told you to Captain Mason," Garvin whispered later. "He thinks I am determined to make war against Sassacus. He does not know that we will try to win peace once we arrive."

When Daniel nodded and kept silent, Garvin Black placed a soft felt hat upon his young scout's head and declared him captain of the shallop. Propped up in the bow of the boat, pride surged through Daniel's chest as he pointed out the navigable passageways of deep water. Despite his dislike for the river, he knew it as well as he knew his mother's face, and more than once he felt Garvin Black's approving eyes upon him. Daniel smiled, thinking of how proud his father would be when he heard that his son would help rescue the Pequot.

Late Wednesday afternoon, just after the three ships arrived at Fort Saybrook, the wind died. The men camped on the open ground while they waited for the wind to rise again. Though Garvin assured Daniel that he was a crucial part of the expedition, he was not permitted to hear the heated discussions that came from inside the fort where Captain Mason and his officers plotted their strategy. But the soldiers gossiped more than Indian women, and by nightfall on Thursday, Daniel knew that the Pequots at Mystic had sixteen guns with powder and shot. The Pequots had also heard rumors of war on the wind, and they expected the enemy to come from the direction of the sea.

"If you can show us a way to get to Mystic by venturing through the Narragansett land to the east," Garvin Black said, spreading a parchment map before Daniel, "we shall prove very successful in this endeavor."

Daniel peered at the map, recognizing several landmarks and geographical formations. "Here," he said, pointing to a narrow tributary east of the Pequot fort. "Sail past Mystic into Narragansett Bay, and speak to their sachem for permission to cross his land. If you come on a mission of peace, he will allow it."

"I'm certain he will," Black said, studying the map in the torchlight. He glanced up at Daniel and gave him a fleeting smile. "Sleep well, boy, and I'll see you on the morrow. Then we shall sail as you have said."

Gilda's heart leapt to her throat when someone shook the latch on the door. "Fallon?" she called, her pulse fluttering.

"Who else?" the familiar voice answered, and her husband came in, smelling of earth and sweat and blood.

She threw herself at him in a desperate embrace. "Oh, Fallon, I'm so glad you're back. Taregan has told me such a tale, I don't know what to do!"

"What happened?" Fallon dropped his weapons on the floor, his eyes sober and dark.

She quickly told him about Garvin Black's reappearance, his story about war upon the Pequot, and Daniel's insistence that he join the English. Wide-eyed, Taregan confirmed every word.

Fallon sat before the fire, then wiped his eyes with his hands. "I had hoped we could live here forever in peace," he said simply. "But the English are too afraid."

"Afraid?" Taregan asked. "They did not look afraid. They have muskets and shot."

"War is nothing but fear cloaked in courage," Fallon answered. Exhaustion was written upon every line of his face, but his eyes crinkled as he smiled and turned to Gilda. "I'm afraid I must leave again, my dear."

"Will Daniel be safe? Fallon, what will they do with him?"

"I do not think they intend to harm him," Fallon answered, reaching behind him for a new bowstring. "They obviously need someone to guide them, so he will be safe. But I do not trust these men, especially Garvin Black. Something about him disturbs my spirit."

Fallon got stiffly to his feet, leaning hard upon Gilda's shoulder. "It will be a long journey." He looked at Taregan. "Take care of your mother while I am gone, Son."

"I will, Father."

"Must you go now?" Gilda asked, already knowing the answer.

Bending down, he kissed her lightly. "I can be miles downriver in a couple of hours while the moonlight holds," he said, resting his forehead against hers. "I hate to leave, but if I go now I'll be half-returned in a few days."

"Go, then," Gilda said, pressing her hands to his chest. "Fetch our son home as soon as you can."

She rose from her place and readied a pouch of pemmican and smoked venison while Taregan pulled a pair of new arrows from his quiver. Fallon accepted these supplies without comment, then paused at the threshold and looked back.

"Go on," Gilda said, aware that he studied her as if she were some unparalleled work of art. She gave him a crooked smile. "Go fetch our headstrong son, and then we will give him a talk about running away."

"All right," Fallon said, taking a step into the blackness. From out of the night, his voice floated on the wind to her. "I will fetch Daniel home."

▼▲▼▲▼ The English sailed past the Pequot fort on Saturday afternoon and into Narragansett Bay that evening. They remained aboard ship all day Sunday, keeping the Sabbath. The concept of Sabbath-keeping was not new to Daniel, who often heard his parents read from the Bible on the day they called "the Lord's day," but the English gathered together to recite a strangely poetic set of prayers that seemed to have little to do with the realities of living. Even so, the flowery, lyrical words flowed easily into his brain, and Daniel made a mental note to tell his father that the English had placed religion on a properly lofty pedestal.

The peace of the Sabbath was altogether put aside on Monday

morning. Captain Mason landed his ships and marched fearlessly into the camp of the Narragansetts, reporting later that the sachem urged the English to attack the Pequots. "He said he did approve of our design," the captain told the men assembled around him, "though he thought we were too weak to deal with the enemy. He said the Pequots are very great and skillful in war. Thus he did speak somewhat slighting of us."

Daniel frowned when the men laughed uproariously at the captain's remarks. The Pequot *were* fierce and warlike when pressed. If the English truly desired peace, why did they laugh at the threat of the enemy? They ought to be on their knees, praying for peace and mercy from Sassacus.

On Wednesday morning the entire company marched from the shore to a Narragansett village twenty miles distant. The Indians of this village, distrustful of the English, stationed warriors completely about their fort, not allowing the English in.

Captain Mason clenched his jaw when he saw the armed warriors. "We shall meet mercy with mercy and force with force," he said, snapping his fingers toward his men. Instantly, a circle of English soldiers surrounded the Indian warriors.

Captain Mason walked to Daniel's side and leaned down while keeping his eye on the warriors outside the fortress. "Tell them that none of them shall stir out of their fort this night upon peril of their lives. If they will not suffer any of us to come into their fort, so we will not suffer any of them to go out, lest they warn the Pequots that we are in the area."

Daniel walked forward and translated, his voice a melancholy treble in the stillness of twilight. The Indian warriors did not stir, but kept their spears and tomahawks in hand. The English did not relax either, but stood with muskets and swords at the ready.

"We are in for a long night," Garvin Black murmured, placing his hands on Daniel's shoulders. "Better get some sleep, son. The morrow will bring either the making or the breaking of us."

▼▲▼▲ Fallon paddled easily down the river and into the bay, thankful that the English were such a large company that they left a plain trail. Their ships, large and inelegant in the moonlight, floated offshore in Narragansett territory, a telling clue to the English strategy. The Pequots would not expect a landing or attack from this direction. They would be ill prepared, especially now when the sachems were gathered for the spring festivals at Mystic.

He allowed the waves to push his canoe ashore, then he jumped out, pulled it far up the beach, and overturned it. After scanning the shoreline to be certain nothing moved in the darkness, he crawled beneath his boat to sleep for a few hours. He had been traveling almost constantly since leaving Taregan and Gilda, sleeping in the boat whenever possible, and the gap between him and the English had narrowed each day. But he would need strength to confront Garvin Black.

And his son.

▼▲▼▲ The tension around the Indian fort eased considerably when the morning light revealed that neither side had ventured to harm the other in the darkness. A delegation of the Narragansett sachem's warriors came out of their fort, bragging about how much they hated the Pequot and how many they would kill if the English would give them muskets. But the English would have to fight fairly. Noncombatants—women, children, and the elderly—must be spared.

"How gallantly they make their solemn protestations," Captain Mason remarked as the latest arrivals boasted of their willingness to join the expedition. "Each warrior speaks of killing Pequot warriors as if the enemy were rabbits."

Daniel looked at Garvin Black, hoping to hear that Captain Mason had made a mistake, but Garvin's narrow face was inscrutable. He had not mentioned his desire for peace in several days, and Daniel had begun to wonder when talk of killing would fade into discussions of peace.

With a handful of Narragansett warriors, the army continued the long overland march toward the Pequot fort. For want of water and provisions, many Englishmen fell by the way. Captain Mason gave them neither pity nor help.

After marching for twelve miles, Daniel led the men to a ford of the Pawcatuck River. "This is where the Pequots usually fish," he said, gesturing toward the spot where the river narrowed and the water ran shallow. "If you truly wish to parlay for peace, this might be a good meeting place."

Captain Mason bid the company halt and refresh themselves in the water, but the determined look on his face did not soften. "We will press on," he said, staring grimly at the country ahead. He lifted a hand and pointed toward the horizon. "Aren't those fields in the distance?"

Daniel squinted toward the captain's pointing hand, then nodded. "The Pequots' cornfields, sir."

"Then we are close. We will march all night if necessary."

As Captain Mason stalked ahead, Daniel hung back and waited for Garvin Black. "What of your purpose, Master Black?" he asked, keeping his voice low. "I thought you wanted to reach the Pequots before Captain Mason. You spoke of pressing for peace—"

"Ah, boy, don't be worrying about such things," Black answered, his eyes fixed on some spot in the distance. "Whatever happens will be done according to God's will, haven't you heard the captain say so? We will follow his orders and trust him to do the right thing."

▾▴▾▴▾ After a hard march of many hours, the English slept that night under the stars and within shouting distance of the Pequot fort. Captain Mason threatened death for any soldier or Indian who so much as made a sound.

Within the Mystic fort the Indians whooped and shouted in celebration. At one point in the night Captain Mason knelt beside Daniel and pointed eagerly toward the palisade. "Can you hear the words of their song, boy?" he whispered, his voice hoarse. "Why do they dance tonight?"

Daniel closed his eyes and concentrated on the warbling chant of the tribal singer. "They rejoice," he said, opening his eyes to look at Captain Mason, "because they saw your boats sail by some days ago. They have concluded that you are afraid of them and will not come near. They insult your name and rejoice because they will not have to fight."

"They are insulting us, are they?" the captain said, a sneer hovering about his bearded mouth. "On the morrow we'll give them true cause to insult us. Sleep well, Daniel, and stay in the rear during the attack. I promised Garvin Black that I'd return you safely to him when every last Pequot is dead."

"Dead, sir?" The word stuck to his tongue. "But surely there can be a resolution to this trouble. Sassacus is a friend of my father's, and Father could win a hearing for you and your officers—"

"We are done with talking," Captain Mason answered, preparing to skitter away, crablike, in the darkness. "Sleep, Daniel, and stand clear on the morrow. Such things may happen that are not fit for young eyes."

▼▲▼▲▼ Lying on his belly on the moist earth, Fallon heard the Pequots singing and saw the rustling bushes that covered the English army and their Indian comrades. So the English meant to attack after all! Taregan had told him that Garvin Black wanted to parlay for peace, but this ambush had no look of peace about it. The English were settling in for a siege, or worse, and Daniel had thrust himself into the center of a storm about to break.

Fallon crept forward, automatically placing his hands and knees in the moist hollows of earth where the sodden leaves would make no sound. As quietly as a night shadow he moved toward the English, his senses keyed for the sight or scent or sound of his son. Let the English do their dirty work; Fallon's first concern was for Daniel.

There! Amid the rows of bodies pressed into the grass outside the fort, one form was thinner than the others and possessed of that dear shape which Fallon knew doubly well. No matter that Daniel would deserve a severe rebuke when he had been safely restored. If Fallon could only get the boy away from these English and back home, then he could teach Daniel how to read the inner hearts of men.

Pausing in the shade of a low-growing shrub, Fallon rose up on his knees and cupped his hands about his mouth. Gauging his breath carefully so the sound would reach Daniel and not beyond, he gave the cry of a whippoorwill—a familiar bird in summertime, but still far away from the Connecticut River valley in spring.

The familiar shape tensed, the head lifted. Fallon rose to his feet and bent forward. "Come on, Daniel," he whispered, his eyes glued to his son. "Tell them you want to relieve yourself and come away. Tell them anything, but come apart from them. Come now!"

The boy stood and looked about uncertainly, and Fallon caught his breath as another shape rose up to confront Daniel. Daniel must have murmured a suitable excuse, for the second man slipped back down against the grass as Daniel stepped forward.

Again, Fallon cupped his hands to his mouth and drew in a breath to give the signal. But a branch snapped behind him, and he froze as cold metal pressed against the base of his skull. "Surprised, are you, Fallon Bailie?" a cold voice hissed in the darkness. "Well, you're not the only one who learned to move in the woods without making a sound." Garvin's voice was filled with mockery. "And how interesting to encounter you here at the end of my musket, nonetheless. I suppose you've come about your boy."

"I want to take him home," Fallon said, still watching as Daniel searched the treeline, listening for the whippoorwill. "He knows nothing of war. Let me take him. He has guided you to this place; you have what you wanted."

"But such a boy would be very useful to me in the future." The metallic pressure against Fallon's neck eased, and he turned slowly. Black stood behind him, his face longer and darker in the night shadows. "Keep your voice low, Bailie. I'd hate to have anyone sound the alarm. Sure as you're alive they'd believe you and your boy were guilty of treachery. And we'd have to kill you both." His musket remained trained on Fallon's head as he went on. "I'd hate for that to happen. Your boy could be very useful indeed. I've spent some time with your son, Master Bailie, and I may know him better than you do. He is quite enamored of the English lifestyle and thinks your hand is altogether too heavy upon him. He is an English boy, anyone can see it, and yet you've done your best to keep him away from King Charles's colonists—"

"I have protected him from English avarice and greed," Fallon answered, clenching his teeth. "Just as I have protected him from Indian brutality. Evil lurks in the hearts of all kinds of men, Master Black."

Garvin lifted an eyebrow. "Spoken like a true Puritan, Bailie. Total depravity. Irresistible grace. And what think you of mercy?"

"What?" Fallon blinked, not understanding.

"There is mercy in my depraved heart," Garvin answered. "And because I am a merciful man, I will not sentence you to the traitor's death you deserve, but will hand you over to the captains at Fort Saybrook."

"I am no traitor!" Fallon hissed, sudden anger flaring in his soul.

"Indeed, you are, for you have come here to warn the Pequot, our enemy. Only my quick thinking and action has saved this company from an ambush."

"I have come only to fetch my son home! Give him to me and I'll go—"

"Who would believe such a thing?" Garvin interrupted, the barrel of his musket kissing Fallon's cheek. "No one. You look like an Indian, it is known to all that you call the Pequot brothers, and your presence here is undeniably an effort to thwart our advantage in this war. No, Fallon Bailie, you are a traitor and worthy of a bullet hole in the head. But I am far too wise to usurp God's position as judge, and so I will let the captains decide your fate. In the meantime, I will take good care of your son. And your wife, too, if that would please you."

Breathing raggedly in impotent anger, Fallon turned again toward the fort and weighed his options. He could stand and fight this devil, but Daniel was in a vulnerable position. If Fallon were injured or did any harm to this scoundrel, who could say what might happen to Daniel?

His eyes watered as he sought and found the silhouette of his son, still scanning the trees for the one who had called. Slowly, carefully, Fallon lowered his weapons to the ground and raised his hands in a gesture of surrender.

▼▲▼▲▼ The assault began shortly after daybreak. Captain Underhill led one contingent of men; Captain Mason the other, and together they stormed the two openings of the fort. Within a moment of the attack Daniel heard the cry *"Owanux! Owanux!"* and knew that the Pequot had recognized their English attackers. Secure in their fort, the Pequot had no means of escape.

Then we wheeling off fell upon the main entrance which was blocked up with bushes about breast high, over which the captain passed, intending to make good the entrance, encouraging the rest to follow. Lieutenant Seeley endeavored to enter, but being somewhat cumbered, stepped back and pulled out the bushes and so entered, and with him about sixteen men. Whereupon Captain Mason seeing no Indians, entered a wigwam, where he was beset with many Indians, waiting all opportunities to lay hands on him, but could not prevail. At length William Heydon, espying the breach in the wigwam, supposing some English might be there, entered, but in his entrance fell over a dead Indian, but speedily recovering himself, the Indians some fled, others crept under their beds. The captain, going out of the wigwam, saw many Indians in the lane or street, he making towards them, they fled and were pursued to the end of the lane where they were met by Edward Pattison, Thomas Barber, with some others; where seven of them were slain. The captain facing about, marched a slow pace up the lane he came down, perceiving himself very much out of breath, and coming to the other end near the place where he first entered, saw two soldiers standing close to the palisade with their swords pointed to the ground. The captain told them that we should never kill them after that manner, we must burn them. Immediately stepping into the wigwam where he had been before, he brought out a fire brand, and putting it to the mats with which they were covered, set the wigwams on fire. Lieutenant Thomas Bull and Nicholas Omsted, beholding, came up, and when the fire was thoroughly kindled, the Indians ran as men most dreadfully amazed.

And indeed such a dreadful terror did the Almighty let fall upon their spirits, that they would fly from us and run into the very flames, where many of them perished. And when the fort was thoroughly fired, command was given that they should fall off and surround the fort; which was readily attended by all, only one Arthur Smith being so wounded that he could not move out of the place, who was happily espied by Lieutenant Bull, and by him rescued.

The fire was kindled on the northeast side to windward; which did swiftly over run the fort, to the extreme amazement of the enemy, and great rejoicing of ourselves. Some of them climbing to the top of the palisade, others of them running into the very flames; many of them gathering to windward, lay pelting at us with their arrows, and we repaid them with our small shot: others of the stoutest issued forth, as we did guess, to the number of forty, who perished by the sword.

Thus were they now at their wits end, who not many hours before exalted themselves in their great pride, threatening and resolving the utter ruin and destruction of all the English, exulting and rejoicing with songs and dances: but God was above them, who laughed his enemies and the enemies of his people to scorn, making them as a fiery oven. And thus in little more than one hour's space was their impregnable fort with themselves utterly destroyed, to the number of six or seven hundred, as some of themselves confessed. There were only seven taken captive and about seven escaped.

Of the English, there were two slain outright, and about twenty wounded.

Captain John Mason

▼▲▼▲▼ Daniel watched in horrified amazement as the fort at Mystic went up in a fiery blaze of smoke. Screams and agonized shrieks of women and children mingled with the warbling war cries of warriors who tried valiantly to wound the torturing enemy.

"Mach it! Mach it! Enough!" cried the Narragansetts, horrified that the assault had violated the ancient Algonquin code that forbade harming women and children in battle. As the fire continued to rage, keening wails and the eerie death songs of elderly folk who could not flee the flames sent shivers down Daniel's spine. Along with the sickening scents of blood and burning flesh came the paralyzing realization that without his help the English could not have reached this place, could not have assaulted the Pequot, who were brother to his father.

A new kind of fear shook his body from toe to hair, twisting his face as guilt avalanched over him. He thought that single moment would embody the worst sights and sounds and smells he would ever experience, but then Garvin appeared from the brush carrying a colorfully embroidered leather jacket—*his father's*. In that instant, Daniel suspected that his previous horror was but a shadow of the nightmare to come.

"I'm sorry, Daniel, my boy," Black said, dropping the jacket upon Daniel's outstretched hands. "I saw a man slip out of this jacket in the woods and make his way toward the fort. When I went to investigate, I found this at the edge of the clearing. I couldn't help but recognize it. We all envied it when we saw your father wearing it. And he kept his word; he came to warn the Pequot and entered the fort before the attack began."

A rise of panic threatened to choke Daniel; his throat worked as he stammered in denial. "Father wouldn't have come here! He's at home, with Mother—"

"Look at this coat, Daniel," Garvin insisted, holding it before Daniel's terrified gaze. "Is there another like it in the world? Who else but Fallon Bailie wore a jacket like this one? He came here, I tell you, to warn his friends . . . and apparently he has paid for his loyalty with his life."

"Why did you have to burn the fort?" Daniel said, fighting back bitter tears as he lifted his eyes from the jacket in his grasp. "You knew he was inside! You said the English wanted to sue for peace. You said you'd convince Captain Mason just to talk so the Pequots wouldn't fight—"

"You want to talk to murderers?" Garvin snapped, pointing to the flaming fort. "Thirty Englishmen have been killed, Daniel! How many more will have to die before the Pequot understand that we will not sit back and do nothing? We aim to live here, by God, and no murderous heathen savages are going to stop us."

"Leave me alone!" The bitter gall of sorrow burned the back of Daniel's throat as he fell to his knees and stared at the flames beyond. As the conflagration consumed the stoutest branch of the Pequot nation, Daniel's cries mingled with the wailing from the fort and the roar of the fire.

One hundred fifty warriors from other tribes had been present at this feast, Daniel later learned, and all had perished with their fellows in the fire of English vengeance. But as the young man wept, he cursed the Pequot for winning his father's loyalty.

Taregan

Thine own friend, and thy father's friend,
forsake not;
neither go into thy brother's house in the day
of thy calamity:
for better is a neighbor that is near
than a brother far off.

Proverbs 27:10

Taregan and Gilda passed the days of Fallon's absence in a nervous blur. Taregan spent much of his time on a small rise overlooking the river, his eyes riveted to the southern horizon from which Fallon's canoe should come. Finally, after several days, he spied the small sail of an English ship.

"Mother!" he called, racing toward the house. "Someone comes!"

Gilda dropped the buckskins she had been sewing and hurried toward Taregan. "Is it your father?" she asked, twisting her mane of dark hair into a knot at the nape of her neck.

"It is an English ship," Taregan answered, giving her a careful, hopeful smile. "Mayhap Father was invited aboard with Daniel."

Gilda looked at him with something very fragile in her eyes, then squared her shoulders and followed him to the rise overlooking the river. Men in dusty English uniforms hurried over the ship's deck; the bow pointed toward the landing where Taregan stored his canoe.

"They are coming to see us," he remarked, scanning the deck for some sign of his father.

"Yes," Gilda answered, her voice sounding as if it came from far away.

A party of men leapt from the deck into the shallows, then followed the trail leading to the house. "We should meet them at home," Gilda remarked absently, turning back. "Your father would want us to meet them at the house."

Taregan and Gilda walked silently through the woods. The treetops stirred with the whisper of a warning breeze, and the sun-shot leaves arching the path trembled overhead. Mother and son moved without speaking into the clearing, then the silence was broken by the rumble of men's voices and the steady tramp of feet through the grasses. Presently the men broke through the woods and entered the clearing. Try though he might, Taregan could not see his father among them.

A group of about three dozen English soldiers filed into the empty space without speaking. An odd coldness settled upon Taregan, a fearful and darkly textured sensation like a gust of scent from a rotting corpse. The sight of Daniel standing between Captain Mason and the man called Garvin Black did little to dispel Taregan's fear. Daniel's face was cold, stony—frozen into a more bitter expression than Taregan had ever seen before.

The captain left the line of his men and marched smartly toward Gilda. Halting abruptly, he gave her a formal nod. "Mistress Bailie," Mason called, his voice ringing over the clearing as if he addressed a multitude instead of one woman and her son. "It is with deepest regret and sorrow that I tell you that your husband, Fallon Bailie, was among those killed at Mystic, the first site of battle in our war against the Pequot."

"No," Gilda murmured, her hand going to her throat. She gave the captain a dazed, crooked smile. "Surely you are mistaken, sir. My husband would not have fought in the battle, he left only to fetch Daniel home."

Mason clasped his hands in front of him. "I'm sorry, ma'am, but there is no mistake. Garvin Black saw him enter the fort before the attack, and later his jacket was found near the entrance to the Indian fort. We know he was friendly with the Indians; 'tis only logical that he intended to warn them."

"No." Gilda covered her face and began to weep, but Taregan only half-heard her. A sudden darkness rose behind his eyes as he stared at the tall, thin man who stood with a protective hand on Daniel's shoulder. Why was *that* awful man by Daniel's side in Father's place? Could Taregan's instinctive dislike of Garvin Black have been rooted in a premonition of disaster? Had the Spirit of God tried to warn him? Why, then, hadn't he been able to stop this terrible thing from happening? Father had gone to

Mystic to find Daniel, not to warn the enemy. So why hadn't Taregan fought with all his strength and will to keep Daniel home, even if it had meant seriously hurting his twin. . . .

"How did it happen?" Gilda asked, her voice shattered.

"We think he took a shorter route through the woods and came to the fort before we did," Captain Mason said, frowning. "He knew their secret trails, and gaining access to the fort would have been no challenge to him. The Pequot were eager for news of us and our party. Apparently he left his coat behind so he would better blend in among the woods."

"He would never willingly leave his coat," Gilda said, stubbornly shaking her head. "Never."

"Who knows what a man will do when his life is in danger?" Mason asked, shrugging. "The Pequot are fierce, and your husband knew that all too well. But we have soundly punished them, ma'am. The fort at Mystic is totally destroyed."

Gilda blinked slowly, and Taregan automatically slipped his arm around her slender shoulders. This had to be a mistake! Fallon Bailie was destined to live long in the land he had tamed for his family. He would grow old and gray under the mushrooming shelter of trees that had provided him with a place to call home.

Daniel stepped forward and held out the embroidered jacket like a peace offering. "Mother," he said, his voice breaking.

Gilda let out a tiny wail of mounting sorrow, and as Taregan pulled her to him she crumbled like wet parchment in his embrace.

"Your son Daniel has done a great service for us, Mistress Bailie." Captain Mason went on as though oblivious to Gilda's grief. "He led us to the enemy and guided our attack."

Taregan had heard enough. "The Pequot are not our enemy!" he snapped, pressing his mother's head to his shoulder as he glared at the captain. "I will never believe that they intended to do harm to the English."

"You are an ignorant boy, then," Captain Mason answered, fixing Taregan in his penetrating gaze. "Uncas himself gave witness to Sassacus's treachery."

"Uncas has been feuding with the Pequot for years," Taregan shot back. "And yet they managed to live in peace."

"Do you deny that our people have died along the river?"

"Though men have died, how do you know the Pequot are to blame? My father always said evil can thrive in the heart of any man, be he English or Pequot, Mohegan or Narragansett. But the sachems know the value of peace. Why should they rise up to kill one another when the diseases of the English have killed so many? Before the English and Dutch came in their wooden ships, over thirteen thousand Pequot lived in this river valley. In the last five years, the smallpox has killed all but three thousand. *Our* people have died along the river, sir, and now you have determined that you will kill the rest."

"We are soldiers; we follow the orders of the General Court," Mason answered, snapping his heels together. He bowed again to Gilda. "'Twould be impossible to identify your husband's body, Mistress Bailie, so my men pulled one from the rubble and will bury it if you show them where you want it planted. Then we must be on our way back to Hartford. If you have victuals in the house, mayhap you will be good enough to share them with the men who have labored to bring this soul home."

"There is food in the house," Daniel said, speaking for the first time, and Taregan was surprised again by the cold light gleaming in his eyes. "I will find whatever is to be had."

Two men carrying a covered stretcher entered the clearing; Captain Mason nodded a thank-you toward them. The wind ruffled the canvas over the body, and Taregan caught a glimpse of a blackened hand with charred, distorted fingers. 'Twas nothing like his father's freckled hand. How many times had his father's hand guided his around a bowstring, around a fishing hook? Confronted with cold reality, Taregan blinked back unexpected tears.

"You will never convince me that my husband is dead," Gilda said, her voice as stiff as her back. "But every human being deserves a decent burial. You may bury this man under that tree yonder." She pointed toward a tall oak that rose like a sentinel over the house. "But first you must allow me to prepare the body."

"It is not a pretty sight," Mason said, holding out a restraining hand.

"You forget, sir, to whom you speak." Gilda pulled herself from Taregan's embrace. The indomitable pride of generations of Indian leaders held her head high. Taregan noticed a flash, like light caught in water, when her angry gaze fell upon the captain. "I have seen men tortured, flayed alive, burned at the stake. I have escaped the wrath of the Powhatan and Opechancanough's massacre at Jamestown." She shook her head. "There is nothing, sir, that I have not seen, and you will not keep me from doing my Christian duty."

Relenting, Captain Mason stepped back, and Gilda took a wobbly step toward the stretcher. Taregan ducked his head to look into his mother's eyes.

"Mother? Can you do this?"

"Bring me your father's Bible and a clean cloth," she answered, staring past her son with wide, unseeing eyes. "And a blanket."

She moved toward the stretcher, and Taregan pressed his lips together, stanching the flood of emotions that wanted to pour from his heart. It didn't seem possible that his father could be dead, but he would not taste that sorrow now. His mother needed him, and Daniel was too busy taking care of his English friends to spare her any comfort.

▾▴▾▴▾ Despite the warmth of the spring sun, even Daniel's lips felt cold as he stood by the oak with his mother, brother, Captain Mason, and Garvin Black.

Gilda held Fallon's Bible in her hands, and her voice trembled as she read: "Yea, though I walk through the valley of the

shadow of death, I will fear no evil: for thou art with me; thy rod
and thy staff, they comfort me."

Rods and staves are for beating the sheep. Are you beating me, God?
Daniel's tortured mind cried as he clenched his fists. His mother
read on.

"Thou preparest a table before me in the presence of mine
enemies. . . ."

*My enemies? Taregan is my enemy now. I see nothing but blame in
his eyes. He thinks if I had not gone off with Garvin Black, our father
would not have died. But loyalty killed him, not me! If he had thought
more of me than of the Pequots, he would be yet alive.*

"Thou anointest my head with oil; my cup runneth over.
Surely goodness and mercy shall follow me all the days of my
life. . . ."

*All the days of my life Taregan and Mother will hate me. I have
taken her husband; I have killed my own father as surely as if I fired the
fort myself. He would not have tried to warn the Pequots if I had not
led the English to Mystic. I heard the whippoorwill's cry, I know he
called to me. But like a coward I waited instead of going out to look for
him. I was afraid to stumble around in the dark. So Father gave up on
me and tried to save the Pequots instead.*

"And I will dwell in the house of the Lord for ever."

Gilda closed the Bible and held it close. "Father God," she
prayed, bowing her head, "a host of warriors has entered
heaven, many of whom—" her voice trembled—"were faithful
fathers and loving husbands. Bless them for their love, holy God,
and comfort our hearts as we finish the course you have spread
before us." She grew quiet and swayed upon her feet as if she
would faint, but Taregan was quick to slip a supportive arm
about her. "I was just thinking that Nixkamich should have been
here," she whispered, her eyes riveted to the shrouded form on
the ground. "And Achak, and Chansomps, all your dearest
friends. But they, too, are waiting in heaven. You have all left us.
You are all gone, and we must wait on God to show us how we
are to survive without you."

Two of the soldiers lowered the blanket-wrapped form into

the earth. As the Englishmen began to cover the body with dirt, Taregan gripped his mother's arm and led her back to the house. Daniel waited by the graveside until the men had finished. To the side of the grave he saw a huge gnarled root showing its dark power as it pushed at the earth. His father lay under the earth, too, somewhere, his power stolen from him by misplaced loyalty . . . and a cowardly son.

While Taregan consoled their weeping mother, Daniel went through the family's barrels of provisions. The English had not enjoyed a decent meal since leaving Hartford. After eating their fill of the family's smoked meat, dried corn, and pemmican, they relaxed around a campfire in the clearing outside the house. Though Taregan glared at him through the window, Daniel remained outside in the circle of boisterous soldiers, preferring their company to the quiet mourners in the house. While the men near him joked around the fire, he thought about the events of the past few days, fastening his eyes to the leaping flames as if he could find the answers he sought in them.

"You can tell your mother, Daniel," Captain Mason called across the clearing, "that God himself worked in a most miraculous fashion to preserve us. John Dier and Thomas Stiles were both shot in the knots of their handkerchiefs, but received no hurt. Lieutenant Seeley endured a shot in the eyebrow with a flat-headed arrow, but the point turned downward harmlessly, I pulled it out myself. Lieutenant Bull had an arrow shot into a hard piece of cheese, having no other defense—"

"Which may verify," Garvin Black interrupted, leaning on one elbow near the fire, "the old saying, 'a little armor would serve if a man only knew where to place it.'"

The bumptious crowd roared with laughter, and Daniel glanced quickly toward the shuttered window, afraid that Taregan would think that he, too, was making merry. Taregan was still shocked by their father's death, but Daniel had lived with that reality for several days. The cold-blooded heartlessness of his father's murder and the brutal battle at Mystic haunted his waking hours and ushered terror into his dreams. In the whisper

of the wind he could still hear the anguished screams of the
Pequot women and children, the warbling death songs of the
warriors as they charged bravely toward the English muskets or
ran to perish with their loved ones in the flames.

Had his father had time to prepare himself for death? Had he
known the English would fire the fort? He should not have died
with the enemy Pequots, he should have remained at home!

Daniel's stomach churned at the memory of the meals he had
eaten around Pequot fires; his hands burned at the thought that
he had wrestled boys from the Pequot tribe. Garvin Black was
right—the Pequots were an uncivilized, heathen, barbarous lot!
Fallon Bailie had been foolish to ever believe they could be
redeemed. Daniel's love for his father twisted like hair caught in
a flame, and he knew he would never again recall his father's figure or voice without dredging up memories of the bitter morning when his innocence had been swept away in a flood of fire
and blood.

"It was a fearful sight to see them frying in the fire," Garvin
Black was saying as the others leaned forward, enjoying the
retelling of the battle now that the danger was safely past,
"and horrible was the stink and scent thereof. But the victory
seemed a sweet sacrifice to God, who has worked so wonder-
fully for us—"

"How dare you."

With numb astonishment Daniel realized that his mother had
entered the circle. Her quiet voice interrupted Garvin Black, and
every man in the group turned guilty eyes toward her as she
stood in the shadows of the house, her dark hair lit by the moon
behind her. With one pale hand she clutched her shawl about her
throat, and with the other she pointed directly at Garvin Black.

"How dare you gloat over the deaths of godly men. You say
my husband was in that fire; so was Nixkamich, his friend. The
sachems were at Mystic to celebrate the spring festivals." Her
voice was a high stiletto, piercing the darkness. "Nixkamich was
a Christian; he served the God you say brought this great victory."

She said nothing else, but melted away into the shadows.

When the sound of the creaking door reached him, Daniel slumped in relief. Captain Mason looked quickly to Garvin Black, who only shrugged and tossed a stick into the fire.

"Perhaps it is time we slept," the captain said, looking at the silent men in the circle. "We have a long journey tomorrow. There is yet another Pequot village north of this place. Uncas and the others will expect us there by midday." He lay back upon the earth, then tipped his hat forward so that it covered his face.

The others murmured their assent and stretched out on their cloaks. Confused and out of place, Daniel stood and looked toward the house. A single lamp burned through a half-open shutter, and he moved toward it, then stopped when he saw Taregan staring at him through the window, his eyes wide with accusation.

With a sudden flash of defensive spirit, Daniel turned his back to his brother and stooped to make his bed with the English.

▼▲▼▲▼ Gilda was not surprised when Daniel entered the house an hour after the English soldiers had gone to sleep. Even though she was certain he fought the rising tide of his own guilt, he was still her son and Taregan's brother. They were a family; they needed each other on this night of all nights.

But defiance poured hotly from Daniel's blue eyes as he glared at his brother. "What is it you would say to me?" he demanded of Taregan, clenching his fists. "He was my father, too! Do you think I do not mourn him?"

"I have nothing to say to you," Taregan answered, but his jaw clenched as he stood. "You seem to have settled matters in your own mind."

"You know nothing, Taregan; you were not on the battlefield. I was. I saw the fire and heard the screams. Arrows fell in a whistling cloud around us, and we are fortunate to have escaped with our lives."

"When did the arrows fall?" Taregan said, balefire in his eyes. "*After* the English attacked and set fire to wigwams filled with women and children? Were the warriors of Mystic wrong to defend their homes and families?"

"It all happened so fast. Uncas swore to Captain Mason that the Pequot had tried to convince the other tribes to kill every Englishman in the land. Our father was English, Taregan! We have come to the place where either the English or the Pequot must die, and God willed that the English should win. How can you doubt that we were right to punish the brutes who caused our father's death?"

"Our father was a brother to the Pequot and to the Mohegan! He wanted to warn them, to save their lives! And yet the English wantonly murdered innocent people!"

"What about the English who have been murdered on the river? They were innocent!"

"Sassacus did not know who killed those people. The English themselves have admitted they do not know from which tribe the murderers were."

"You are a coward, Taregan! Because you remained here with Mother, you blame me for taking a warrior's part—"

"You? A warrior?" Taregan's laugh was clipped by anger. "Your courage failed before a deer in the woods. How am I to believe you would fight men?"

"Be silent!" Gilda could not listen a moment more. Her sons' angry voices shredded her broken heart. Once these two had been the best of friends and companions, but since they had begun to grow into men, they had not ceased to squabble and fight. She stepped into the quivering space between them and lifted her hands, then turned to Daniel. She wanted to ask him a thousand questions about what had happened at Mystic, but this was not the time. Taking a deep breath, she forced herself to think of urgent matters at hand. "I heard Captain Mason say that tomorrow they plan to attack a village north of here." Her eyes fell upon Fallon's Bible. *God, give me strength.*

"North?" Taregan asked. "But that's—"

"Nixkamich's village." She turned to Daniel and looked fully into his eyes. "Though he and his warriors are gone, the women,

children, and elders remain in their wigwams. Would you have
them die in the same flames that devoured Mystic?"

Daniel did not answer, but looked down at the floor.

She placed a hand on Taregan's shoulder. "And you, my son,
must understand that Daniel mourns as we do, but he is in a different place of sorrow. Be patient with him. Time alone will heal
the guilt and anger in his soul—"

"I am not guilty! I was not wrong to go with the English!"

"Yes," Gilda chided, holding Daniel with a warning glance.
"You were. Your father would not have allowed you to go. He
did not want to become involved in the English war, and now it
has stolen his life. You must not encourage the English to take
other innocent lives, Daniel. You must stay home and let God do
as he will with the English. He is in control through all of this,
and we must watch and wait to see what he plans."

"Watch and wait!" Daniel's mouth was tight with mutiny.
"Mother, you talk like a foolish woman! The English need me;
they have promised to take care of us if we join them. And we *are*
English, have you forgotten? My eyes are blue, my skin fair, I
speak their tongue and read their books—"

"A man is what he is on the inside," Gilda answered softly,
pressing her hand to the angry curve of his cheek. "Your father
considered himself one with all men, regardless of their tongue
or beliefs. He wanted you to feel the same way."

"One with all!" Daniel spat the words in a mocking tone, then
pushed her hand away. Anger hung in the air between them like
an invisible dagger. "On the morrow I will leave with the
English," he said, thrusting his slim shoulders back. "There is
nothing for me here now that Father is gone. Taregan will stay
with you, but I will avenge my father's death and do whatever
the English require of me. They walk in God's way, too, and I am
convinced the hand of the Almighty intends to clear this land for
them and their descendants. And I will be one of them!"

"You will not talk to Mother that way!" Taregan roared, his
nose pinched and white with rage. He stepped forward, his fists
clenched, but Gilda put her hand on Taregan's chest, holding

him back. After a heated moment during which the brothers' eyes remained locked in malevolence, Daniel turned and stalked out into the night.

Gilda said nothing as her firstborn son walked away. For many years she had dreaded this moment; she had known it was inevitable. Boys grow into men, Fallon had often told her, and they will choose their own paths. But Gilda had never dreamed that Daniel would choose his path as a result of Fallon's death, nor that he would set out upon it so soon.

"Let me go get him, Mother," Taregan said, straining against her hand. "How can you let him speak to you that way? He's upset. Once these cursed English leave, he'll settle down and begin to think clearly again. I can get him in a headlock for you and drag him back here like a whipped pup—"

"Let him go," Gilda whispered, drawing the words from the bottom of her soul. She closed her eyes against the tears stinging the back of her lids. Today she had grappled with the loss of the one love of her life; on the morrow life would, of necessity, be different than anything she had known before.

She would deal with Daniel later, when her heart had mended. Now other matters demanded her attention. "We must warn Nixkamich's people," she whispered, opening her eyes and turning to Taregan. "The sachem's wife and children—there are many souls yet in the village."

"Dena!" Taregan whispered, his eyes widening.

Gilda moved to the leather pouches hanging on the wall. "We will prepare what we can and slip out when the English are soundly asleep. We'll take your canoe, so we should arrive at the village before daybreak. If all goes well, we can reach them before the English and scatter the women and children into the forest—"

Taregan nodded. "And then?"

"Then . . ." Gilda paused and looked around at the cabin she had called home for so many years. Fallon's chair sat in the corner, the books he had brought from the trading post, his traps and musket and the reeds he had planned to use for arrows. The heavy bearskin with which he had cradled her when she nearly died of smallpox. . . .

"Only God knows what will happen next," she said, closing the window on her memories. She moved toward the small table where her cooking utensils lay. "But if there is war, I do not think we will be able to come back to this defenseless place. Perhaps we can move into a Narragansett camp or even live with the Mohegans."

Taregan's face sobered as he realized her full intention, but he stood and reached for his buckskin leggings hanging over a stool. "I will make ready," he said, his voice deeper than she had ever heard it.

The night was black and icy with a wash of brilliant stars when Gilda and Taregan slipped from the house and paused before the circle of sleeping Englishmen. Taregan unconsciously stepped into his father's role, his eyes flitting over the invaders' muskets, swords, and knives. He mentally debated whether or not he should take one of the weapons, but decided that the risk of waking one of the soldiers was too great. He had his father's musket and his own bow and arrows, and he was adept with both weapons. Let Daniel keep company with the English; Taregan had no need of them.

Daniel slept stiff and still on the ground near Garvin Black, his thin arms crossed defiantly across his chest. Lines of bitterness and anger furrowed his forehead and mouth even in sleep. For the first time in his memory, Taregan thought that a stranger would have no trouble telling the twins apart.

He lifted his eyes to the treeline, listening to the breaths of the wind and the night noises. The soft and steady sounds of snoring punctuated the darkness, and Taregan took his mother's hand and led her past the sleeping soldiers. Three days from its fullness, the moon lit the jagged treeline with a cold white radiance and threw black shadows on the ground below. Taregan walked easily along the trail to the river, hearing the soft pad of his mother's footsteps in sync with the rhythmic pounding of his own heart. His father had trained him for this moment. He had to slip away successfully, for the lives of his mother and Dena depended on his efforts this night. With any luck, Taregan thought, when the sun rose the English would think that he and his mother still mourned inside the house.

His canoe lay hidden under boughs and branches at the river-bank, and Taregan slid the concealing limbs from the boat, then used a leafy branch to wipe their footprints from the landing. Gilda placed their few supplies in the curve of the bow, then stepped inside, tucking her legs beneath her buckskin skirt.

Gilda picked up an oar, and Taregan eased the vessel into the water and leapt in behind his mother, causing barely a ripple in the silver water. Paddling with long, clean strokes, they moved quickly upstream amid the night shadows on the river.

▼▲▼▲▼ *The damp fog of the swamps near Mystic closed around Garvin's ankles like a python, ready to squeeze and pull him under the earth. Fear of the unknown knotted and writhed in his stomach as he stepped hesitantly forward, but then a woman with golden skin and piercing cobalt eyes moved through his dream, a delicious invitation in her smile. Hair like black gold spilled over her shoulders as she swayed before him in a primitive rhythm, and Garvin forgot his fears. With a shuddering sigh he reached for her. His hand caught her arm, but she twisted from his grasp and vanished into the mist as his fingers raked the thickened air.*

Awareness hit Black like a punch in the stomach and he sat up, uncomfortably aware of where he was. His comrades in arms snored around him in varying degrees of slumber; next to him, the boy Daniel lay as stiff as a mean dog's tail. Garvin shook his head, momentarily jealous of the boy's adolescent energy, then glanced toward the house. The blue-eyed woman slept inside with the other boy, both of them mourning the man they thought dead—the man Garvin knew was under guard at Fort Saybrook.

Garvin pulled his dagger from the sheath at his belt. The blade curved like a snake in the moonlight—certainly it would win cooperation from the woman. He regarded the house with a lurking smile. If he reminded Bailie's woman that he held Daniel in his power, he might even convince her not to report this nocturnal activity to Captain Mason.

He grinned, confident of his plan and his prowess, and crept toward the house. The small lamp no longer gleamed in the window, and all was quiet within. The door swung open easily, and Garvin blinked, waiting for his eyes to adjust to the darker black inside. Through the slanting moonlight in the open door he saw two blanket-covered figures, one at the west side of the house, one at the east.

Garvin ignored the mat closest to him. That would be the boy, sleeping near the door to guard his mother. He moved silently, then paused as his boots encountered something soft. Stooping to pick it up, he held it to his face. Ah! It was the shawl she had worn, and still it carried the soft scent of a woman. He had been in the wilderness for far too long.

Readying his blade, he knelt beside the second mat and gingerly lifted the blanket, prepared to rest the knife upon the woman's slender throat. But under the covering he felt the matted fur of a bearskin. A ruse! Frowning, he stood and kicked the motionless form, confirming his suspicions. Crossing to the other mat, he furiously stomped the bulky form, scattering a collection of fox and beaver skins that had been hidden under the blanket.

Cursing under his breath, he rested his hands on his belt and considered his options. The woman and her son had slipped away, either to flee for their lives or to warn the Pequots in the village upriver. As a good soldier, he knew he ought to wake Captain Mason and tell him of this latest development, but then he'd have to explain why he had felt compelled to enter the house in the middle of the night.

Garvin sheathed his knife and squatted on the floor. It would be easy to invent an excuse. He could claim thirst or illness and explain that he had hoped the woman could give him aid. Though Captain Mason might privately doubt his story, Daniel was so hungry for approval that he would believe anything Garvin told him.

The English army could go hang itself, for all he cared. His concerns were not military but material; he'd come on this venture to spy out the land and scavenge what loot he could. Bending, he ran his hand over one of the furs on the floor, a thick bear-skin that had been expertly dried and softened. It would bring a fine price at the trading post, probably more than enough to buy the services of a trollop in one of the harbor towns or a fine jug of whiskey.

He would keep quiet about the missing woman and boy and come back later to clean out the cabin. From the look of things, Fallon Bailie had been a fine trapper, and the furs in this house would enrich Garvin's business for a number of months.

Leaning against the doorframe, he looked toward the sleeping men to make sure none of them stirred. None did. With a chuckle of satisfaction, Garvin stepped out of the house, closed the door, and moved back to the place where he had been sleeping. He hadn't found what he'd been searching for, but Garvin Black never let an opportunity go begging.

▼▲▼▲ He woke again amid a blizzard of curt orders and immediate responses. Captain Mason bawled commands while the soldiers folded their blankets and put away their supplies, steeling themselves for another day of battle. Captain Underhill scratched a rough map in the dirt, trying to figure the best way to approach the village without being seen. Daniel sat by Underhill's side, a curiously blank expression on his face.

Garvin tied his kerchief around his neck and pinned his mantle over his shoulders. The boy wore the look of a bewildered sleepwalker, his eyes wide but unseeing, his hands limp upon his knees. Garvin hurried toward him, afraid a sudden attack of misdirected guilt had left the lad incapacitated.

"Daniel, I'm glad you're going with us," he said, resting his hand upon the boy's shoulder as he knelt, "and it pains me to tell you this—"

"I'm not sure I should go with you," Daniel said, interrupting him. Then a flicker of curiosity stirred in his eyes. "What do you need to tell me?"

Garvin jerked his thumb toward the house, and Daniel rose

and followed him until they were away from the others. "I think we'd best not say anything to the captain, but this morning, before you woke, I happened to spy in upon your brother. He's gone, Daniel, and he has taken your mother. I'm wondering if they have run away."

"Taregan is gone?" A flash of doubt crossed Daniel's face. "With my mother?"

"Aye, most surely. And rather than warn the others and set them in an uproar, I thought we might quietly set out to find them. I'm sure you don't want them wandering in the woods—but where could they have gone?"

Daniel frowned, lost in his own confusion, then his face cleared. "They've gone to Nixkamich's village," he said, the old light in his eyes. "Taregan is in love with the sachem's daughter. Indeed, Master Black, I'd swear upon my life that we'll find them there."

Garvin nodded. "Good. Is this village far?"

"About half a day."

"And is it . . . prosperous? Will we find food, furs? The army is hungry, lad; we've got to eat."

Daniel nodded. "Yes. Nixkamich and his warriors were good hunters."

"Ah, then." Garvin clapped his hands on Daniel's shoulders. "You and I shall slip away for the purpose of talking to your mother and brother privately. We will hold the savages together in the camp until Captain Mason and his men arrive, then your brother and mother will be safe. What do you think?"

Again the doubtful look. "Why should we go ahead of the others? We are only two, Master Black, and the Pequots are armed—"

When all else failed, Garvin told the truth. "The Pequot camp will have many goods to be plundered," he said, stooping to look into Daniel's eyes as he lowered his voice. "I know the Indians, and I know each wigwam boasts a store of furs and blankets and mayhap even a musket or two. Why should these riches be burned in the blaze Captain Mason will set? But if you and I go

early, we can find whatever goods there be of value and set them
aside. Your brother and mother have probably already set the
savages to flight, but we can save the hard goods if we leave
now." He lifted an eyebrow. "Of course, if you don't know a
more sure way through the woods than these bumbling Englishmen—"

"I know a way," Daniel said, his voice firm. "We could take a
canoe upriver and then cut through the woods off the main trail.
We should arrive at least an hour before the captain and his
men."

"Let's be off, then," Garvin said, slapping the boy's shoulder.
He glanced around to make certain no one noticed their depar-
ture. "Before the day's end, my young friend, we may even find
that we are heroes."

▼▲▼▲▼ Taregan and Gilda found the trail leading from
the river to Nixkamich's village at the time of half-light before
dawn. Taregan was panting from exertion by the time they
reached the fortress, and the sentry outside the palisade nodded
sleepily as they approached. "We bring important news," Gilda
told him in the Indian tongue, and the aged warrior recognized
the urgency in her voice and pulled the brush and branches out
of the entry so she and Taregan could pass.

"Your sachem, Nixkamich, is dead," she told the handful of
old men who squatted around the morning fire at the center of
the village. They blinked, their eyes wide and uncomprehend-
ing. "The English are on their way to destroy this place. You
must not tarry, you must gather the women and children and
send them into the woods. Send them to the Narragansetts or
have them hide along the river. But they must vanish, and there
is no time to waste."

Moving with unexpected vigor, the men rose from the fire and
left to spread the word. Parting from his mother, Taregan hurried
to Nixkamich's wigwam. Pausing at the threshold, he peered
into the dimly lit hut. "Wake, Dena!" he shouted, searching the

shadows for her face. "The English are coming! Your father is dead!"

The sachem's wife, Sooleawa, lifted her head instantly. Without pausing to question Taregan or to weep for her husband, she prodded the other sleeping bodies scattered on the floor and urged them to hurry. The family's dogs rose from a sleepy tangle and walked toward Taregan, their heads down and eyes alert.

"Hurry, we must go," Sooleawa told her children. A slender figure under a blanket at the back of the hut stirred, and Taregan recognized Dena. Her dark eyes were wide with fear, but she did not hesitate to rise and follow her mother's example. Hassun, her younger brother, woke slowly, and Dena pulled his hair, lifting his head from his sleeping mat. "Get up or die!" she whispered hoarsely, not caring if she frightened the younger ones. "Taregan says we must leave now!"

"When are they coming?" Sooleawa asked as Taregan stepped aside so the younger children could leave the wigwam.

He shook his head. "I don't know. They camped at our house. Mother and I slipped away, but the English will probably set out as soon as the sun rises. We do not have much time."

"The elders will need help," Sooleawa said. "And so will we. Hassun—" She looked toward Dena's younger brother, a slender, alert boy of about twelve winters. "Run to the camp of the Narragansetts and tell them that the English are upon us. Hurry, Son, run like the wind!"

Without hesitation Hassun flew from the wigwam, rushing in desperate flight toward the second opening in the palisade and the path that led deep into the forest. Sooleawa told Dena to send the remaining children into the woods with the dogs, then she left to help the others.

Pules, Dena's three-year-old sister, stood crying in the center of the hut, and Dena stopped to lift the child onto her hip. "Are you certain the English are coming?" Dena asked, reaching out to Taregan.

The touch of her hand ran up through his arm, and for a moment he could not speak. Her pale face was like glass, lovely and fragile in the morning light, and in a distant corner of his memory he heard again Garvin Black's words about the stench of the enemy frying in the fire. If anything should happen to Dena . . . the thought made his pulse pound.

"I am sure," he said, his voice tight. "You must go into the woods. I will help scatter the others. The English fired the village at Mystic, and only a few managed to escape. They showed no mercy to the elders or the women and children. All but a few died."

"My father? His warriors?"

"All who were inside the fort."

A ragged whimper escaped her lips, and he wrapped his arms around her and Pules, crushing them to him. He held her for a long moment, then pulled back to look into her eyes. "I am sorry, Dena. But I have found consolation in knowing that my father died with yours, and today they are together in Paradise."

Her eyes misted as she gave him a look that was troubled, compassionate, and still, then she knelt and set Pules on the ground. "Run to the hiding place in the woods," she told the child. "Follow the others. And do not come out until I come for you."

"You should go with her," Taregan said, pointing toward the trail.

"No." Dena shook her head. "I will wait until the elders are out. My mother will need help with them."

She moved toward the door, but was suddenly back in his arms, her hands clasped around his neck. "Oh, Taregan, what will become of us?" she whispered, her voice breathless and urgent in his ear. Her lips touched his, featherlike, and then she was gone, lost amid the flurry of activity outside the wigwam.

For a moment Taregan could not move. But when an aging warrior walked past, tall and stately in his dignified tread, Taregan stepped forward and pointed him toward Pules, who toddled aimlessly on the trail. The old man extended his hand toward the child, leading her away.

By the time the tangerine tints of the sun had fully warmed

the camp, Dena had paused again by Taregan's side. "Last night the Spirit of God spoke to me in the wind," she said simply, slipping her hand into his, "and warned me of the sorrow to come. I was not surprised when you entered my hut. I think my heart already knew that my father had gone to heaven."

"Could God be in this?" Taregan asked, wondering aloud.

"He must be," Dena answered, tears flowing down her cheeks as she watched the slow parade of humanity leave her village. "And he is merciful, for he sent you to warn us. Perhaps Hassun will bring help from the Narragansetts in time."

"Mayhap," Taregan answered, though he did not believe it.

▼▲▼▲▼ Taregan strained against the reins of his own impatience as the Pequots of Nixkamich's village gathered their belongings and moved out of the family wigwams. The elders would not leave until the children had been prepared and sent down the trail, but once the young ones had gone, the elders began to sing the slow, eerie songs of mourning for the dead. The clan had lost their sachem and at least forty warriors. By Taregan's rough estimate, thirty men and women remained in the camp after the exodus of the children, along with Dena, Gilda, and Sooleawa. And the sachem's wife, he noticed, had no intention of leaving until the last man and woman had vacated the village.

"Hurry!" he called again, the word having lost its urgency in his overuse of it. "The sun is up. They will be coming."

The strained, nasal whine of an elder's death song cut short his admonition. Sooleawa, with Dena by her side, ignored Taregan and walked calmly from wigwam to wigwam to help the others gather pouches of food, tools, and wampum shells. Taregan stopped in amazement when he saw one white-haired elder move toward the riverside entry to the village, his bow and spear in hand.

"Honored friend," Taregan called, hastening to the old man's side, "these foes will not fight like the warrior you are. They carry the long guns of iron and will not hesitate to use them. Please, grandfather, come away with the others."

The old man stared at Taregan without speaking, then walked slowly toward the line of marchers moving toward the forest path. Taregan had hoped that the old warrior was among the last of the villagers, but then from the corner of his eye he saw the flash of Dena's embroidered dress. She walked toward the wigwams, away from the trail.

"Dena!" He ran and caught her arm. "Please! You must go. I will see to the others. You know I will keep my word."

"I cannot leave!" Her eyes filled with honest surprise. "I must help my mother. In my father's absence she must make sure the elders have escaped."

"Please, Dena, let me do this for you." The soft, satin skin beneath his hand would burn in the fire if she lingered. "Dena, I—I want you to live. You must go. Take the trail, take the children." The words came out in a rush, making little sense, but she smiled at the confusion in his eyes.

"God will watch over us. Let me go help my mother. I will find you later."

She pulled out of his grasp and flew along the path through the wigwams, her moccasined feet skimming the ground, and Taregan turned from the depressing sight of the mass exodus and moved to the entry from the river trail. Leaning against the logs of the palisade, he scanned the brush beyond the cleared field. A light fog hovered above the meadow, a slight breeze rustled amid the tops of the trees. His heart went into sudden shock as a flock of birds startled into flight. Surely the English had not yet reached the river trail!

Daniel stepped out of the brush, pale and unnaturally calm, and for a moment Taregan thought he stared at a ghostly vision of himself. But then Daniel came closer, waving, as if he had decided to take a morning stroll and had by chance found himself here.

"Well met, brother," Daniel called in English. "I see that you have been busy. Are there many left in the village?"

"Not many," Taregan lied, feeling his back stiffen. Something was wrong. Daniel was never this carefree in his actions or attitude. His studied indifference stood in marked contrast to his furious anger of the previous night.

"Hold those who remain inside," Daniel said, stopping. His smile of greeting flattened out as he folded his arms across his chest. "We will want to leave some as a present for the English. If you send them all out into the forest, the English will have no Pequots to conquer, and they will scour the woods until they find every last soul. Better to offer up those who remain and end it now."

"Offer them up?" Taregan gaped in astonishment. "Daniel, can you know what you are saying? Dena is inside, and our mother—"

"He knows," a deeper voice answered. Shouldering his way through the brush, Garvin Black came forward, his musket leveled squarely at Taregan's chest. "And your brother speaks the truth. Not another soul leaves this place, dear boy. Anyone who tries will be blown away by this musket." He stepped forward, pressing Taregan back. "Tell those who remain inside to fetch their bear skins, otter skins, any types of fur they have in the wigwams. Wampum beads, too. They must bring their goods to Daniel, who will place them outside the palisade. If the people obey, I will convince the English army to spare their lives." He gave Taregan a dry, one-sided smile. "I wouldn't let them kill Daniel's mother, so you needn't worry about that."

Taregan glanced from the Englishman to his brother. "You came here as a common thief?" he asked, shaking his head. "I am glad our father is not here. It would shame him to see this."

"Our father would be alive if not for the Pequot," Daniel retorted. "A few furs are nothing compared to what they stole from me. They will keep their lives."

"You will break our mother's heart. Would you hand her over to the English?"

The smile on Daniel's face twisted. "You must send Mother into the woods with the others who have escaped," he said, lowering his voice. "You and she can leave by the forest trail. You are not Pequot."

"I will not leave Dena and her people," Taregan said, lifting his chin. "You are wrong in this, Daniel. Once again you are wrong—"

"I will not leave either, my son."

Taregan turned in surprise as Gilda stepped from behind the palisade. He did not know how long she had been listening behind the wall, but one glance of her eyes told him she had heard enough. Her eyes brimmed with sorrow as she turned to her eldest son.

"Daniel, this is wrong," she said, holding her hands out to him. "Please, do not listen to the voices of hate that twist your heart. Your father would want you to stand with these people whose fires have warmed us so many nights."

"Mother, I do not want to hurt you," Daniel said, his voice breaking. He shifted uneasily. "Go, leave this place, and wait for me at home. The English are our friends, not the Pequot. Can you forget that the Pequot have killed so many—"

"I cannot forget that Nixkamich and his wife welcomed us when we came to this valley without a home. Sooleawa herself brought you forth from my womb, and without her help I might have perished in this place. And the people of this village have embraced the true God and his Son, so by faith they are our brothers and sisters. I cannot forget these things, Daniel. Though my heart grieves because your father is not by my side, I trust that God knows what has happened and why."

"My heart grieves, too," Daniel said, the muscles in his face tightening into a mask of rage. "And my heart knows that the Pequot are a cursed people. They drew my father to his death. That I cannot forget and I will not forgive!"

"Daniel!" Gilda's tone rang with rebuke, but Daniel was no longer a child she could command. Staring at his brother, Taregan felt the chasm between them open like a wound. For fifteen years they had walked together as brothers. How could Daniel choose a separate path?

"If you are not with me, Mother," Daniel said, venom in his voice, "you are against me and all the English. And the army is coming. I suggest you leave this place at once."

He stepped back, yielding to Garvin Black, who entered the palisade with the musket, pointing it at whomever crossed his path. "Talk to them," Black called over his shoulder to Daniel, "order them to bring their furs and hard goods. They must be quick, for Mason and his men are on the way."

Stepping past Taregan and their mother, Daniel shouted Garvin's orders in a loud, harsh tone. Taregan felt Gilda's eyes on his face. "Your brother is a fire-eater," she said, her voice trembling. "Iron-willed and hard as stone. We must be patient with him."

She moved as if to reenter the palisade, but Taregan caught her arm. "Go, Mother, with the children," he said, pulling her back. "I will stay with Dena and the elders. Daniel will not let them kill me, but you must not fall into their hands—"

"I lost a husband yesterday and a son today," she said, gently pulling free of his grip. She held his hand between her palms. "I will not lose another. I will remain here with you, Taregan."

Baffled by the strange turn of events, the remaining Pequots brought the furs, stores of grain, and wampum that Garvin Black demanded, then stood in front of their wigwams, their faces wiped clean of any emotion. Taregan knew they wondered why he and Gilda waited with them while Daniel stood with the stranger brandishing the musket, but they did not ask.

When the English arrived later as a militant, vengeful army, they found the remaining villagers assembled and calmly awaiting their fate.

Connecticut sent out forty men under the command of Captain John Mason, to supplant the Pequots by burning their wigwams and bringing away their corn, Uncas with about one hundred of his men in twenty canoes, going also to assist in the service.

We ran our vessels up into a small river, and by reason of flats were forced to land on the west side, their wigwams being on the east just opposite. But we meeting with a narrow place in the river between two rocks drew up our Indians' canoes, and got suddenly over sooner than we were expected or desired, marching immediately up to their wigwams, the Indians being all fled, except some old people who could not.

We were so suddenly upon them that they had not time to convey away their goods. We viewed their corn whereof there was plenty, it being their time of harvest. Coming down to the water side to our pinnace with half of Uncas' men, the rest being plundering the wigwams, we espied about sixty Indians running towards us. We supposed they were our absent men, the Mohegans that were with us, and did not speak one word nor move toward them until Uncas' men came within thirty or forty paces of them, then they ran and met them and fell on them pell mell, striking and cutting with bows, hatchets, and knives after their feeble manner: indeed it did hardly deserve the name of fighting. We made no shot at them, nor any hostile attempt upon them. Some of them grew very outrageous, whom we intended to have made shorter by the head, and were about to put it in execution, but one Otash, a sachem of the Narragansetts, stepped forth and told the captain that they were his brother's men and if we would spare their lives we should have as many murderers' heads in lieu of them which should be delivered to the English. We considering that there was no blood shed as yet, and that it tended to peace and mercy, granted his desire, and so delivered them to Uncas to secure until his engagement was performed, because our prison had been very much pestered with such creatures.

We then loaded our bark with corn, and our Indians their canoes. And thirty more canoes which we had taken with kettles, trays, mats, and other Indian luggage. That night we went all aboard, and set sail homeward. It pleased God in a short time to bring us all in safety to the place of our abode, although we struck and stuck upon a rock. The way and manner how God dealt with us in our delivery was very remarkable.

Thus we may see how the face of God is set against them that do evil, to cut off the remembrance of them from the earth. Our tongue shall talk of thy righteousness all the day long, for they are confounded, they are brought to shame that sought our hurt! Blessed be the Lord God of Israel, who only doth wondrous things, and blessed be his holy name for ever. Thus the Lord was pleased to smite our enemies in the hinder parts, and to give us their land for an inheritance: who remembered us in our low estate, and redeemed us out of our enemies' hands: Let us therefore praise the Lord for his goodness and his wonderful works to the children of men!

John Mason

▼▲▼▲▼ While Captain John Mason and the English sailed home in their pinnace, Uncas and his warriors secured the prisoners. With their hands bound behind their backs, the elders, women, and children who had not escaped climbed stiffly into the Mohegan canoes to be transported downriver.

Though the stout rope bit painfully into his wrists, Taregan rode in silence behind his mother. The rage inside him was a living thing, born of his brother's participation in their father's death and fanned by this latest betrayal. He kept his face blank and his hands calm lest the enemy Mohegans see his hatred, but violence bubbled beneath his impassive expression. He wanted to fight, to scream a war cry as he rushed the enemy, to have a fair opportunity to deal with these traitorous Mohegans. He and the others had faced the enemy without flinching as the army approached, but his blood boiled when a Mohegan warrior pulled Dena and her mother from a wigwam and delivered them to Uncas. As a warning to the other captives, the Mohegan chief had pulled a dagger from his belt and plunged it squarely into Sooleawa's heart as Dena screamed.

Still stunned, his own mother refused to talk except to murmur words of comfort to the others. She did not speak of Daniel or Fallon, and Taregan feared her fragile soul couldn't bear the burning memories that had scorched it in the last few hours. She spent her words upon the elderly villagers who traveled with them, and she demonstrated special concern for Dena. Whenever one of the elders began to sing one of the ancient chants of mourning, Gilda silenced the song by quoting words of Scripture in the Indian tongue. Though the Pequots of Nixkamich's village had no written language and could not read the Scriptures, they always fell quiet to hear the words of God from Gilda's lips.

"The prophet Habakkuk understood what we are feeling today," she called over the water as the Mohegans guided the canoes downstream. Her voice was a wall of energy; it had a force that commanded silence from all who heard it. "'How long, O Lord,' he cries to God, 'must we call for help, but you will not listen? How long shall we cry out to you, "Violence!" but you do not save? Why do you make us look at injustice? Why do you tolerate wrong? Destruction and violence surround us; there is strife, and conflict everywhere. Therefore justice never prevails. The wicked hem in the righteous, so that justice is perverted.'"

The other captives in the canoes murmured in assent.

"But," Gilda went on, "the Word of God reminds us of other truths. God is so great we cannot begin to know him. He draws up the vapor from the water and distills it into rain, which pours

down from the skies. Can anyone really understand the spreading of the clouds and the thunders within them? See how God
spreads the lightning around him, and blankets the tops of the
mountains. By his fantastic powers in nature he punishes or
blesses the people, giving them food in abundance. Lightning
bolts are in his hands. He hurls each at its target—"

"My heart wants God to hurl lightning at these Mohegans,"
one old woman yelled from a canoe across the water. The
woman snarled at the fiercely painted warrior paddling behind
her. "They talk of peace, but join with the English!" Without
missing a stroke, the Mohegan lifted his oar and smacked the
woman on the side of the head for her impertinence.

Gilda grimaced at the blow but continued with her words of
encouragement. "The world will not know peace until peace has
found a home in the heart of each man and woman," she called,
strengthening her voice. "And true peace is found only in Jesus
the Christ."

The clouds that had hovered overhead like ghostly shrouds
suddenly broke, drenching the captives in a strangling rain.

▼▲▼▲▼ The captives who were too old and infirm to
be of any use to the English were given to the Mohegan and Narragansett tribes. The surviving young and healthy Pequots were
quartered in the jail at Hartford.

Standing in line with his mother and Dena, Taregan tugged
helplessly on his bonds as the town magistrates began to pull the
women from the line of prisoners.

"Where are they taking us?" Dena cried, pinching her
trembling lower lip with her teeth in a vain effort to hide the fact
that she was about to cry.

"It matters not; we are in God's hands," Gilda answered. She
turned to Taregan. "As much as is possible, Son, live peaceably
with all men," she urged, her voice low and compelling. "Do not
make trouble for yourself. And do not worry about me."

A dusty soldier with a harsh grayish yellow face gestured for

Gilda to step out of the line, and she obeyed without comment. The man motioned then to Dena.

"Taregan!" she moaned, pressing her head to his shoulder as if he could hold her there. "Don't let them take me."

"Dena—" he struggled against the bonds that held him tight— "Do not worry. This cannot last forever. . . ."

The soldier reached forward and pulled her by the hair. Submitting, she followed, but her eyes remained locked upon Taregan's in a wordless plea.

"Do not fear," he called, his voice mingling with the cries of others who were being torn from their loved ones. "No matter where you go, my heart is with you."

Amid much wailing, the women were taken into a separate building. Though most of the Indians around him spoke no English and had no idea why the women had been separated, Taregan overheard the magistrates talking about the gold they would receive when the women were sold into household service.

He gritted his teeth, expecting the worst, when he and the other men were crowded into the jail. "How long will we be keeping the creatures, Captain?" one of the guards asked the tall man who seemed to be the jail keeper. "They're too quiet; they make me nervous as a wing bird in cat country."

"Don't worry yourself. We keep them only until the militia arrives with a pinnace large enough to transport them to the fort at Saybrook."

"And after Saybrook?" The guard spat a stream of dark juice toward a brass spittoon at the door. "I won't be sleeping nights if there's a chance these murdering savages might escape to haunt the woods again."

"There'll be no chance of that," the jailer answered. "They'll be bound and held under guard for the entire journey. They'll keep them in stocks at Saybrook until the slave traders dock, then it's to the West Indies with the lot of them."

The West Indies. Taregan had never heard the name, but the jailer's tone of voice made the place sound like hell itself.

▼▲▼▲▼ Every curve of the prisoner's body spoke defiance as Captain Osbart Ramsey glared down at him.

"I ask you again, sir, how you came to be at Mystic. Unless you were there to give aid and comfort to the enemy—"

"I have told you time and again," Bailie cut in, his icy blue eyes fastening upon the judge's. "I went to Mystic to find my son, who had left home to travel with Captain Mason."

"Why, then, did you not take your son and leave?" Ramsey said, consulting the parchment in front of him. "Garvin Black's recorded testimony states that he saw you attempt to enter the fort of the Pequots. He is certain that you intended to warn our enemy of the attack."

The prisoner shook his head. "I sought only my son."

"I have other reports here," Ramsey said, pulling a sheaf of papers toward him, "stating that you are known as a brother to the Pequot. Do you deny this charge?"

Bailie pressed his lips together.

"Ah, so you do not. Then why, Fallon Bailie, should I believe that you were not attempting to warn those you consider your brothers? Did you care more for their heathen souls than for the consecrated, God-fearing Englishmen who waited in the field below? Did you not realize that a warning, if successful, might have resulted in the death of the entire Connecticut company?"

A spark of some indefinable emotion lit the prisoner's eyes as he stared at his judge. "For many years both the Indians and the English have regarded my word as near gospel," he said, his smile tight. "And though God knows I was not at Mystic to warn my brothers, mayhap I should have been. Which do you think would be more precious to God, sir? Six hundred innocent souls, including women and children, or a company of bloodthirsty men bent on the cruelties of war?"

Ramsey slammed his hand down on the desk. "I have heard enough! I sentence you—"

"You have heard nothing!" Fallon raged in response. "You are so deaf and blind, you and the lot of your countrymen! You come here and rob the tribes, you kill and plunder—"

Ramsey bristled with indignation. "I sentence you to—"

"I am not finished! I *should* have warned the Pequots! If God had but given me an extra measure of strength I would have arrived in time to set an ambush for the English. I should have left my son in God's hands and sought the welfare of my native brothers, but I—"

Ramsey nodded to a guard, who forcibly clapped a hand over the prisoner's mouth.

"I sentence you," he repeated through gritted teeth, fighting the urge to scream at his unruly captive, "to ten years hard labor in His Majesty King Charles's navy. You are hereby assigned to *The Pollux,* under the command of Captain James Walker. The ship waits in the harbor. Now go from my sight, Fallon Bailie, and take care lest your treasonous, treacherous ideas go with you! May God have mercy on your wretched soul."

▾▲▾▲▾ Like autumn leaves from an oak tree, the days fell one after the other, indistinguishable in the crowded confines of the stuffy English jail. Twenty captives were crowded into cells intended for one man; food and water were strictly rationed. There was not room enough for even one man to lie down, so at night Taregan coiled into the shadows and pulled his knees to his chest. Pillowing his head on his knees, he fought against despair and tried to sleep as sag-bellied rats skittered across his feet in a vain search for crumbs.

The captive Narragansetts who had come to the aid of the Pequots were ransomed by their relatives, but no one dared to speak on behalf of the Pequots. After ten long days of waiting, the jailer announced to his guards that the pinnace had arrived. On the morrow the savages would be shipped downriver to Saybrook, and he, by God, was glad to be rid of such pesky, unnatural creatures.

Slumped into morose musings, Taregan nearly did not hear the jailer's approach. "Is one of you called Taregan?" the man asked, squinting as his eyes swept over the men jammed into the first cell. He turned away as if he did not expect an answer, but Taregan leapt to his feet.

"I am he. Taregan Bailie."

Slowly, the jailer turned. The man's lips pursed suspiciously as he looked at his prisoner, and Taregan's cheeks burned under his intense scrutiny. Stripped to his breechcloth and leggings like the others, he looked as sweaty and grimy as the most primitive Indian in the woods.

The jailer's upper lip curled in distaste as Taregan wrapped his hands around the bars of the iron door. "You," the jailer said, pointing with exaggerated firmness. "He told me you would speak English."

Taregan nodded slightly. "I do."

"Ah." The jailer lifted an eyebrow. "What a clever monkey you are. Well, there's a visitor for you." He indicated the door with a jerk of his head, then unlocked it with the key at his belt. As Taregan slipped through the opening, the jailer motioned for a guard. "Stay with him now, and keep your pistol on him. If he makes a sudden move, shoot him."

The guard pulled a pistol from his belt and smiled in secret amusement as the jailer opened the outer door and gestured for Taregan to lead the way. "This way, savage," he said, his voice faintly mocking. Taregan lifted his chin, conscious of the burning stares of the other prisoners and the pistol at his back.

The jailer led the way through an outer room, then came to another door and pushed it open. The small room beyond had no windows, but in the shadows Taregan could see a large wooden cross hanging on the wall and an English gentleman sitting on a bench. "We'll be outside. If you need help you have but to call out," the jailer told the man inside. "Don't get too close. The devils are crafty and cunning."

Taregan stepped inside, the door slammed behind him. He blinked slowly, allowing his eyes to adjust to the dim light, and stiffened when the seated figure rose and stood before him. "Have you finally come to your senses?" The voice was more familiar than his own—Daniel!

No one now would have surmised that the boys were twins. Daniel wore his hair neatly trimmed and pulled back with a ribbon at his neck. He was dressed in an embroidered doublet with paned sleeves and a double collar of fine lace. Instead of his customary breechcloth he wore fancy pleated breeches held at the knee with garters. Fine leather boots shod his feet.

Taregan took in the transformation in one searching glance, then lifted his eyes to his brother's mocking smile. For a moment, sheer amazement overshadowed the bitterness of his memories, and he reached forward and drew his brother into an embrace. "Daniel! I had hoped you were well!"

"By heaven above, you stink," Daniel said, stepping back slightly. He pulled a perfumed handkerchief from a pocket in his doublet and made a great show of holding it before his nose. "It is high time you had a bath. Master Garvin will insist upon it."

Taregan shook his head and grinned, still bewildered by the change in his brother. "If Father could see you now! What does mother think?"

Daniel's smile vanished. "That's one reason why I'm here, Taregan," he said, stuffing the handkerchief back into his pocket. "Mother is not with me. An English family in Hartford bought her to serve as their cook, but she flatly refused to work when she saw them whipping another Indian girl."

"Our mother? A slave?"

"In truth, she's not a slave now, but is here, in this jail, under the authority of Captain Jones, the man who brought you to me."

"Mother is *here?*" Taregan trembled, recalling the horror of the last ten days. "But this is no place for a woman!"

"Would you rather they hanged her?" Daniel hissed, leaning into Taregan's face. After a moment, he stepped back and took a deep breath to calm himself. "I wanted to leave you here for a good long time. I thought that if you took your fill of suffering with the Pequots you would come to your senses. I saw the pinnace arrive today; they will send all captives to Saybrook on the morrow. So I have come to ransom you. And when Captain Jones learns that you and I are English, he will realize his mistake and release our mother. I've thought it through, Taregan. We can build a house here in Hartford, and Mother can—"

"Is she all right?" Taregan interrupted, his mind still reeling from the news that his mother was confined in this terrible place. "Have you seen her?"

"I tried to visit her," Daniel answered, his voice brimming with bitterness. His brows came together in a brooding knot over his eyes. "I sent word to her through the captain. She replied that she had no son named Daniel."

A tear tangled in his eyelash and Daniel turned, dashing the wetness away. When he spoke again, his voice was quiet and stubborn. "Garvin Black has promised to hire both of us, Taregan. He is willing to forget that you defied him at Nixkamich's village. I work for him at the trading post on the river, and the good people of Hartford have no idea of our past history. Garvin says we are unique because we understand English and Indian ways and can speak either language." He stepped forward, eagerness burning in his eyes. "Garvin has promised to treat you and our mother with honor. I've considered everything carefully, and know exactly what we should do. The captain will release you if you declare yourself to be the son of an Englishman, for the English war is only with the Pequot. You can forget the past, forget our past associations, and become an Englishman from this day forward. It will work, you know. It is a good plan."

"But Mother will not abandon the Pequot. She stood with them at Nixkamich's village. She will stand with them now."

"Not if you send word to her and say that you need her. Make up an excuse, anything, and she will come to help you." Anger edged his voice as he added, "For you she would do anything."

Taregan sat down, hard, and lowered his head into his hands as his mind spun like a whirlwind. If he left with Daniel and sent a plea to his mother, she would of certain come out of the jail and claim her own English heritage. With her blue eyes and exemplary education, she would have little trouble adjusting to life in an English village. Mayhap her wisdom could go far in tempering English reaction to the Indians as the colonists pressed farther into the wilderness.

But leaving with Daniel now would mean denouncing that part of him that was Indian. It would mean denying the Pequots who had nurtured him through childhood and taught him to be a man. It would mean sanctioning the acts of the English invaders and mean-spirited, greedy men like Garvin Black. It would mean lying to his mother and walking on the streets of Hartford costumed in foppish clothes that served no purpose but to disguise the true manner of man underneath. It would mean passing Dena on the street as she slaved for some haughty English woman. . . .

A blur of tears clouded his vision. *Oh, God, tell me what to do. How am I to know what is right? My father is not here to guide me, my mother is as helpless as I. Daniel is my brother, flesh of my flesh, akin to my own soul, and though we have had our disagreements I cannot imagine living apart from him. It would be so easy to go with him and beg our mother to join us. It will be so hard to deny him and sentence my mother to jail and myself to uncertain exile. . . .*

English or Indian, which was he? The English possessed powerful guns and ironworks and mighty ships and books. They talked of God, mayhap many of them worshiped him in spirit and in truth. His father had been English, and his mother's mother. In fact, none of Taregan's ancestors were Pequot, for the Indian blood in his veins flowed from the tribe of the Powhatan, no friends of the Pequot.

But Daniel offered life in league with Garvin Black and those who would take advantage of the Indians. His own brother was asking Taregan to convince their mother to repudiate the goodness, gentleness, and virtue they had found in the Pequot nation. She would not; the very idea would offend her. She had chosen to stand with the Pequots at Nixkamich's village, and Taregan could not ask her now to renounce her decision.

In a surge of memory, he found his answer. *"The wrong thing is easy,"* his father once told him after he caught Taregan misbehaving. *"Certain ways seem right to a man, but the end thereof is the way of death. The right thing is difficult. Often we must suffer, often we must bring pain to the ones we love and endure it ourselves. And yet God commands us to do right."*

"I can't do it," Taregan said simply, lifting his head to look at his brother. "I won't go with you, I won't tell them you are my brother. They think I am Pequot, so a Pequot I shall remain. Mother has chosen to stand with the Pequots and trust in God. I will do the same."

A blue flame of defiance burned in Daniel's eyes. "You are a fool, brother. God fights for the English."

"No," Taregan said, standing to his feet. "God fights for truth. And he commands us to live in peace."

"Stop preaching at me! You sound like Father—"

"At least I didn't kill him!" Taregan roared, knowing his words had the power to wound. "You had no business going with the English; I told you not to go. Father went after you and he died trying to fetch you home. And now Nixkamich is dead, and Dena a slave, and our mother in jail because you did not listen. You've never listened to me, Daniel, never! Not even when I tried to teach you—"

Daniel closed his eyes against the tirade. "Guard!" he bellowed, interrupting the stream of accusation that poured from Taregan. "This savage is duller than a rock! I'll not trouble Master Black with the likes of him—"

Like an awakening giant, Taregan's temper rose and roared. Forgetting where and what he was, he ducked and drove his shoulder into Daniel's stomach, pressing the breath from his brother's slender body. As quick as a mad cat, Daniel turned and struck Taregan across the throat with the flat of his hand. Dazed from his sudden foray into violence and weak from partial starvation, Taregan stumbled forward while a scream clawed in his throat. Daniel's fists struck Taregan's face and ribs repeatedly, like the mouths of snakes, and Taregan clutched his stomach and bent forward, trying desperately to protect himself. A front snap-kick to the groin left him gasping on the floor as pain streaked up to his stomach and jolted every nerve. As he lay on the ground, his heart pounding heavily, a shiny English boot slammed into his stomach and cut off his breath.

They had often wrestled and tussled as children, but Daniel had never beaten Taregan in a contest. Until now.

"Be glad, brother, that I didn't kill you," Daniel said, his voice a thin whisper from across the room.

"I will kill you," Taregan gasped, feeling the warmth of blood on his face. "When I next see you, I will."

"Guard!" Daniel bellowed, moving toward the door. Footsteps echoed in the hall; the door swung open. "Go ahead, ship him down to Saybrook."

The guard flashed Daniel a wide smile. "He wouldn't do, heh?"

"No," Daniel answered. "He is not the man I thought he was. He is just like the others, a hopeless, helpless heathen."

▼▲▼▲▼ Back in the sweltering cell with his fellow prisoners, Taregan huddled against the iron bars, nursing his bruises. If only he had the strength of Samson, he would tear down these walls and free his mother and his Indian brothers! Let Daniel desert the family, he had done so of his own choosing! But Gilda should not have to suffer for the sins of others. She had done nothing but try to aid the neighbors and friends she loved.

Night swooped over the jail and darkened the single barred window that brought light and fresh air into the squalid cell. Taregan knew that when the sun rose again he would journey from this city for the last time. The image and story of Samson lingered in his consciousness—what had that mighty man prayed as he faced the morning in which he would give his life to avenge his people? In his mercy, could God work again in order for Taregan to free the Pequots and punish the English? He prayed again and again, begging God for a sign or a vestige of peace, but no answers came throughout the long and lonely night.

Around him the other prisoners sat mostly in silence, listening to ghostly memories of their own pasts. Few of them were from Nixkamich's tribe. Most were tattooed in some way with the tribal signs of the Pequot; many bore fresh scars from the recent fighting. But all of them wore expressions of aloof pride like a badge of honor. In nary an eye did Taregan see a hint of fear or submission, and in the manner of those sternly proud countenances he smoothed his face while he prayed for strength.

At length, he slept. A rooster crowed in the darkness, and through the embracing folds of sleep Taregan heard the creak of the door. Had the guards come so soon? His eyes sprang open and he beheld the jailer behind the iron bars. The man wore his full uniform and stood stiffly, his hands behind his back, a guard at his side. Behind them stood a woman in a dark skirt and plain linen blouse. *Mother.*

Taregan choked back a sob as her eyes moved into his. *Quiet,* her glance warned, *Wait.*

"They all seem well enough to travel," the captain remarked to the guard. The guard agreed, and they moved away from the cell. Gilda stepped into the space where they had stood, her broom moving steadily over the packed floor.

She swept quietly with her head bowed over her work, her knuckles whitening around the broom. Taregan crept toward the iron bars, then whispered a greeting in Algonquin.

"How are you, my mother?"

"Shhh," she warned, not lifting her eyes from the floor. "They will be back soon. But I had to see you, my son."

"Are you well? Daniel told me what happened."

"They have decided to put me to work rather than keep me in a cell. Even a prisoner must earn her keep." Her voice was low and surprisingly musical, almost pleasant. "I am glad, actually. The work keeps me strong."

In one swift, deft movement she drew near the prison bars and dropped to her knees so that she was eye to eye with Taregan. From a slit in her skirt she found a pocket and pulled forth a gold ring. Taregan recognized it immediately. It was the ring

with which she had married his father—the English ring her
grandmother had given her.

"It is yours now, Taregan," she said, reaching for his hand. She
pressed it into his palm. "But you must not wear it on your finger, or they will take it from you. I have lain awake nights wondering how to give this to you in safekeeping, and the Lord has
shown me what to do."

Smiling, she took the ring from his hand and reached for his
head. Fitting the golden circle snugly into the cup of his ear, she
gently pulled his long hair down to cover it. "You will wear it
there, and not lose it," she said, giving him a smile of purest
sweetness. "And one day you will give it to Dena, and then to
the son or daughter God will send you. And as you pass on the
ring, you must explain the charge engraved inside: *Fortiter, fideliter, feliciter.* Boldly, faithfully, successfully."

"Fortiter, fideliter, feliciter," Taregan whispered, trying to
memorize both the words and every detail of his mother's lovely
face. "But Mother, what if I don't—"

"Boldly we go into the world, faithfully we place our trust in
God, successfully we live according to his will," she went on,
ignoring his question. "This is your charge, my son. This is what
your father would have told you, were he here with you now."

Her words touched the secret pool of sorrow within him, and
he struggled to keep from weeping. "Mother," he whispered,
recalling in a rush of bitter remembrance how many times he
had taken that simple word for granted.

She did not answer, but ran the back of her hand along his
cheek. A weight of sadness lay upon her thin face, but streams of
intense, pure love poured through her blue eyes.

Taregan gripped the iron bars. "Mother, perhaps I can talk to
the jailer. I could ask to speak to Captain Mason. He knows
about our family, and he could ask Captain Jones to free us from
this place. We do not have to associate ourselves with Garvin
Black and the others like him—"

Gilda pressed a finger across his lips. "Captain Mason would
not give us an audience. We are witnesses to what truly hap-

pened at Nixkamich's village, and the truth bears little resemblance to the story Mason has told in the river towns. No, God has willed that we should part, my son, but I will hold you in my prayers until we meet again. For you will be able to come back, Taregan, I have every confidence. If your heart and purpose remain strong, you can marry Dena, and your children will walk along the river in this valley."

She covered his hands with hers and tilted her head to smile up at him. "The Indians believe that their souls cannot rest until they are buried in the land that holds the bones of their fathers. We do not believe that, of course, for to be absent from this body is to be present with the Lord, but I know that you will not be at peace until you return to your brother. You two slept together in my womb, you were formed on the same day, you have been together always."

"But Daniel is—"

Again her finger tapped his lips. "Daniel has been blinded by the lust of his eyes and the pride of life, but he will return to the ways his father taught him. And when he does, he will need you, Taregan. Promise me, swear to me, that you will come back to redeem your brother."

She paused, her heart on her face, and Taregan did not have the courage to remind her that he might not live long enough to keep his promise. With one misbegotten glance or one slip of the tongue, some English officer was likely to shoot him for insolence or insubordination before he even reached the West Indies, wherever that was.

But she was right. He would never be at peace until he confronted Daniel and made him pay for the sorrow he had inflicted upon their mother, their father, and an entire nation of people. The blood of seven hundred Pequots rested upon Daniel's head. Like the expert hunter he was, Taregan would return and follow the scent of that blood until God delivered Daniel into his hands.

He nodded before his mother's stubborn gaze. "I swear to you," he whispered, his voice cracking. "I will come back and find Daniel."

Her hand tightened around his. "Go with God, my son," she said, rising to her feet. "Know that while I live, I will pray for you."

Taregan pressed his lips together so she wouldn't see that he trembled with the need to call her back, to beg for comfort, to cry out his hopelessness and fear.

"Go with God," she repeated, then she picked up her broom and swept her way out the door.

The river lay heavily upon the valley, bright as a spill of molten metal from a furnace. The clumsy pinnace traveled slowly, her handlers fearing the shallows and the human cargo that lay in chains below deck. The English who guarded the prisoners were snappish and ill-at-ease, continually scanning the forests like wide-eyed owls. With every moan of the wind they seemed to shrink into their skins; at every rustling in the brush they pointed their muskets at the land and fired at shadows.

"They are afraid the Pequot nation yet lives to rescue us," one of the captives near Taregan remarked. "Uncas has them believing that Pequots still hide behind every tree."

"Are there many of us left?" Taregan asked, realizing the irony in his words. Though he was not of Pequot blood, the hand of God had thrust him squarely into the midst of that tribe's affairs.

The warrior shook his head. "Sassacus was not at Mystic. He still lives, as do a few of his warriors. But they are on the run toward Mohawk country."

"I heard about one group who elected to remain behind," another warrior said, keeping his voice low. "They were hiding in the Chomowauke swamp."

"The Owl's Nest?" Taregan asked. He knew the place, for his father had taken him hunting there. The swamp was a place of refuge, riddled with winding and serpentine paths that only expert hunters could navigate successfully. "Surely they are safe there."

The second warrior shook his head. "The people of the sachem Puttaquapouk took refuge in the swamp, but an English

captain called Stoughton was guided along the trail by Yotash, a
Narragansett sachem. Though the English could not see the
Pequots' hiding places, they cried out with loud voices and said
they would die sooner or later whether they surrendered or not."
The warrior's eyes misted as he paused. "The Pequots held out
until their women and children were nearly dead from starvation, then they surrendered and cried for mercy. More than one
hundred prisoners were taken: eighty women and children were
given to the English. Thirty men were bound and placed on a
boat and taken to the sea, where they were made to walk off a
plank and left to drown in the deep."

A heavy silence fell upon the prisoners who had been listening to the story. "And Puttaquapouk," the warrior went on,
"who had been spared on a promise to help the English find
other enemies, refused to help them further when he heard how
his men had died. The English captain Stoughton shot him in the
midst of the swamp, under a laurel tree laden with white and
gold blossoms. It is said that before he died, Puttaquapouk
cursed the swamp for starving his people and forcing their surrender, and since that day the gold of the blossoms has deepened
to the color of blood."

Taregan balled his hands into hard fists, fighting back the
tears that swelled hot and heavy in his chest.

For a full twenty hours they sailed southward without stopping to eat or sleep. Finally Taregan caught sight of torches burning through the black night. The square building at the juncture
of the Connecticut River and the great salt sea was Fort
Saybrook; the captives had arrived at their destination.

When the sun rose the next morning the prisoners aboard the
pinnace were herded into a huge holding pen that stirred with
dozens of men who had been transported earlier. Searching
through the crowd, Taregan was surprised to see a familiar face.
"Hassun!" he called joyously, recognizing Dena's twelve-year-
old brother. "Are you well?"

"As well as I can be in this stinking place," Hassun answered,
embracing Taregan. The boy's eyes snapped at the sight of an old

friend, and for the first time since his capture Taregan thought he could discern the barest outline of God's plan. Though Dena had been taken from his reach, he could demonstrate his love for her by protecting her brother.

"Are there others of your village here?" Taregan asked.

"Only one or two, much older than me," Hassun answered, settling onto the ground with an ease that bespoke familiarity with his surroundings. "They ignore me. They say I am unproven."

"You will be proven soon enough, I think," Taregan said, glancing around. Most of the captives in this group had lived less than thirty summers; none had obvious injuries. The men in this place, he realized suddenly, had been evaluated like prize cattle. Only the healthiest and strongest specimens had made it into this pen—what had happened to the others?

"What is this place? What happened to the others who came downriver with me?"

A shadow crossed Hassun's face. "Those who do not make it into this cage are used to pull plows in the fields, but none last more than a few days. How can a warrior allow himself to pull like a fat English cow? Those who refuse—" he looked down at his hands— "are shot. Or they run and are killed while trying to escape. The English do not understand that Pequot cannot be made into slaves."

And yet we are to be sold to slave traders, Taregan thought, not daring to speak his thoughts. *What good can possibly come of this?*

▼▲▼▲▼ In the sweltering days of August, when the holding pen at Saybrook was as hot and airless as a kiln, a new group of prisoners brought a stunning report. On the twenty-eighth of July, Sassacus and a group of twenty Pequot warriors had finally reached Mohawk lands. After their plea for alliance was considered and rejected by the Mohawk council, Sassacus and his warriors were executed. As evidence of their worthiness to be trading partners in river commerce, the Mohawks sent the Pequot scalps to Boston.

With this news to gird their strength of purpose, the English rang bells of celebration and looked forward to ridding themselves of the few Pequots remaining in captivity. When at last the sails of the largest wooden ship Taregan had ever seen moved across the bay, a trumpet blew from the lookout tower. The soldiers at the fort hastened to raise their signal flags in greeting.

"The ship is just in time," Taregan overheard one guard call to his companion. "Autumn approaches, and I'd hate to spend the winter sharing victuals with savages who'd as soon eat me as the scraps we toss 'em."

Like the others in the prison, Taregan stood at the hastily constructed fence and craned his neck for a better view of the ship. A flag identical to the red, blue, and white standard on the fort flew from a sail of the huge vessel; billowing white sheets of canvas curved out from tall poles like the bellies of pregnant women. The mighty ship lanced her way out of the bay and into the mouth of the river, then the Indians fell silent as huge iron chains spewed forth from openings in the side of the ship like a web from a spider. Once the mighty chains had rattled into the deep, the ship stood still. From their prison, Taregan could see men scampering like rats over her decks and a series of weblike ropes that stretched to the tops of the towering poles. Within a few moments of landing, the huge canvas sheets had been lowered and lashed to other beams that ran horizontally across the huge poles.

Hassun stood slack-jawed with amazement. "I have never seen such a thing," he murmured, his eyes fixed to the dock like a bird staring at a snake. "I have heard of the floating islands—"

"They are called merchant ships," Taregan interrupted, fully as fascinated as Hassun. He had seen smaller ships when he visited the English towns with his father, but he had certainly never expected to journey in one as large as this.

"The white cloths—," Hassun said, pointing toward the bundles atop the horizontal poles.

"The sails," Taregan explained. "When the English want the ship to move, they loose the sails and the wind blows them away."

"Where does the wind blow them?"

"Wherever they want to go," Taregan answered, his voice as cold as his heart.

▼▲▼▲▼ The raucous noise of drunken sailors filled the fort that evening, but by morning the hollow-eyed and hungover crew had unloaded its supplies from the islands of the Atlantic and stood ready to bring its cargo aboard.

Taregan jerked away from the fence when the wooden gate creaked and slammed open. The commander of the fort, a dark and vigilant guardian presence, stepped into the pen followed by a dozen soldiers carrying shackles, chains, and mallets.

"Each of you will be cuffed at the wrists and ankles," the commander shouted in an iron voice, not caring that few of the prisoners understood him. "You will board the ship today and leave these shores on the morrow. May God rest your souls, my savage friends."

While several of the soldiers stood guard with muskets, others approached and motioned for the prisoners to stretch forth their hands. A soldier near Taregan approached an awesomely muscled Pequot, who bristled at the sight of the chains. It was the warrior who had told the story of Puttaquapouk and the swamp's curse, and Taregan knew the Indian would rather die than be the first to submit to such a humiliating and confusing experience. These men had never seen iron chains and certainly did not look forward to vanishing into the bowels of the monstrous ship in the bay. The warrior had not understood a word of the commander's instructions and probably thought that death would now be an honorable way out of captivity.

Taregan stepped forward and thrust his upturned wrists toward the soldier, daring the Englishman to deny him. The soldier frowned, glaring back at the bold, black eyes of the warrior, then snapped a pair of iron cuffs around Taregan's wrists. Taregan did not move while he ran a length of chain through metal loops, effectively locking Taregan's hands together. The guard gestured toward Taregan's feet, and Taregan lifted his hands to shoulder level as the soldier knelt and fastened a pair of shackles around his ankles.

"You see, brothers," Taregan called over his shoulder in the Indian tongue, "they kneel before us as a tribute to our courage. The metal bracelets serve to link us together, for in unity we will find strength. Do not fear the shackles and chain, and do not defy them over so small an act. The Great Spirit of God watches over us; his strength shall be ours."

"What'd he say?" the commander demanded in English, but most of his men shrugged uselessly as they continued their work. But one blonde-bearded guard stared hard at Taregan, a grudging smile of admiration on his face. Had he understood? If so, Taregan mused, he might have spent time with one of the tribes . . . he might be an ally who'd be willing to get word to Gilda or Dena.

Shackled and bound, Taregan awkwardly inched his way over to the fence near the guard. He leaned against it with pretended indifference. *"Win-gap-po,"* he murmured in the Algonquin language. "Greetings to you."

The guard kept his musket trained on the group but looked at Taregan, his blue eyes bright and bemused. *"Win-gap-po,"* he replied in the same tongue, his voice barely above a whisper.

A bubbling furious excitement rose in Taregan's chest; he closed his eyes lest the others see his exhilaration. "Are you a friend?" he murmured, praying that the man would not prove to be a disappointment.

"A Christian brother," the Englishman replied, returning his gaze to the prisoners. He lowered his voice until it was the merest shadow of breath. "Later we will talk. After dark."

Taregan covered his mouth with his hand and coughed as a sign that he had heard and agreed, then he moved slowly back toward the others. For the first time in days he felt a spark of hope with which he could aggressively face the future. Perhaps his mother had not been speaking from a heart of vain dreams when she had bade him promise to return! If God had sent this man to encourage Taregan in this forsaken place, God could of certain enable him to keep his vow. This captivity was a test, a time of trial, and if Taregan could withstand the sufferings of the present time, his loved ones would be restored and justice done in the end.

As the afternoon wore on and his fellow prisoners were fitted with chains and shackles, Taregan withdrew to a corner and prayed that God would comfort his mother. *Protect her, almighty God. Tell her all I want to say, and work a miracle so that she may be rescued from bondage and slavery. Keep suffering far from her, sovereign God, for I know she would rather go to heaven and be with my father than endure the sorrows of earth.*

The sun had nearly set by the time the last prisoner was shackled. The guards were called to attention, and the long, single chain that ran through every prisoner's cuffs was tightened and attached to a stone wall. Bawling orders, the commander ordered the guards to throw open the doors of the fort, then the single line of prisoners stumbled out of the holding pen toward the dock where the slave ship waited to receive its cargo.

Taregan glanced around. There was no sign of the muscular blonde guard, no assurance that he would keep his word and speak to Taregan before the prisoners were taken aboard the ship. Taregan's pulse fluttered with anxiety as he placed his feet in the footprints of the man in front of him and followed the snaking line onto the dock. Two dozen sailors, their faces a curious mixture of ruddy skin and dark beards, lined the rail of the ship and jeered in a variety of languages. Not a single Pequot answered in words, but the renowned pride and fierceness of the Pequot nation shone through their glittering eyes. Their example stiffened Taregan's spine and lifted his head.

He stepped back, startled, when the English guard appeared at his side just before he was to step on the dock. "I can't set you free," the man said, not looking at Taregan but pretending to study the rear of the line.

"I wouldn't ask you to," Taregan managed to whisper. "But in Hartford, my mother is confined at the jail. Her name is Gilda Bailie, and she has been unjustly imprisoned. My brother, Daniel Bailie, works for the trader Garvin Black. He might be able to help her."

The man lifted an eyebrow, then turned his head and pretended to cough. "Bailie is an English name."

"We are part English, part Indian. I have chosen to stand with my Pequot brothers."

A flash of grudging admiration shone in the man's eye as he glanced at Taregan. "I will try to find this woman."

"There is someone else." The chain pulled Taregan inexorably toward the ship, and he resisted its tug, suddenly unwilling to go forward. "I was to marry a Pequot girl called Dena. I believe she is now a slave in Hartford. If you find her, tell her I am coming back. Though I die in the attempt, I will return and keep my promise to her."

For the first time the guard looked full into Taregan's face. His eyes clouded with hazy sadness and a trace of pity. "My name is Colton Bramwell, and I will pray for you. I will relay these messages when I am next in Hartford."

"Hey, you! Keep those animals moving!"

Colton made a halfhearted gesture with his musket, and Taregan obliged by taking a giant step forward.

"How do you intend to come back?" Colton whispered, stepping toward the ship. "The captain of this vessel plans to sell all of you on Barbados."

The chain tugged again, and Taregan followed it, then smiled in the calm strength of knowledge. "I am coming back because I swore that I would." He tossed the words over his shoulder as the chain drew him forward. "Pray for me, brother, and for these who go with me. And may God grant us mercy until we meet again!"

The next pull yanked him onto the plank leading to the ship, and Colton could not follow. But as Taregan moved across the narrow board toward the *Styx*, he felt Colton Bramwell's silent sympathy and smile of encouragement.

▼▲▼▲▼ The *Styx*, as best Taregan could tell in the gathering darkness, had four levels, and he and his fellow prisoners were stored aboard the third level with as much consideration as if they had been sacks of corn. Indeed, Taregan thought, feeling the slimy, filthy floor beneath his hands, the previous cargo had apparently been foodstuffs, and the prisoners would undoubtedly have to deal with the rodents and vermin left behind. The uppermost deck was the territory of the sailors; the crew's food, supplies, and hammocks filled the second deck. Below the Indians' deck, the orlop contained rocks, sand, and barrels of fresh water for ballast.

The Indians settled into their places without much noise, behaving in the typically silent and reserved manner of defeated warriors. Straining for the sounds of voices, Taregan heard the ship's captain commend the commander of the fort for such an easy handling of "345 red devils."

Red devils? Taregan glanced around, confused by the appellation. The Pequot certainly did not have red skin, nor red hair like his father, nor did they wear the bright red uniforms of the English. But then he caught sight of a recently arrived prisoner and the light of understanding dawned. Red paint. The Indians wore red paint on their faces and bodies when they went to war; an ancient practice designed both to encourage the painted warrior and frighten the enemy. It was such a common sight and understanding that Taregan had completely overlooked the connection.

Night drew down like a black cowl over the ship, and Taregan sat on the wooden floor with his fellows, his mind miles away with Dena and his mother. The ship rose and fell rhythmically, straining against the anchor cables as the river currents gently pushed it seaward. Listening to the soft lap of wavelets sloshing against the sides of the ship, Taregan could almost imagine that he

was reclining in his own canoe, the Connecticut valley to his right
and left, the mouth of the river at his feet, and home at his head. . . .

A glaring burst of light entered the cabin, and Taregan instinctively threw up his hand, forgetting about the heavy chain that
bound him to his neighbor. A young boy with a torch entered the
cabin, followed by an obese, balding man in middle age. The fat
man stared at the chained Indians, then grunted and thrust his
hands into the waistband of his breeches.

"If any of ye can hear and understand, I'm Bran Daman, the
captain of the *Styx*," he roared, glaring at the prisoners as if they
had personally committed crimes against him. "If any one of ye
does anything to cause me harm, I'll toss him overboard to the
sharks!"

He paused, seeming to expect some form of cowardice or
trembling before his threat, but the Indians merely watched him,
their faces as impassive as stone.

"I don't think they understand you, cap'n," the boy said,
ducking slightly. "I hear they speak Indian."

"Do any of ye speak English?" the captain shouted, waving
his hands in frustration.

Taregan quelled the urge to speak out. If he admitted the
truth, he'd have to talk with this man, an idea he found distasteful. No. Better to let his identity remain a secret.

No one else responded, either. Growling in frustration, the
captain turned and mounted the narrow stairway. "Feed 'em
when the sun rises, and take 'em one bucket of water, you hear?"
he yelled at the boy. "And then leave 'em alone! I'll have nobody
on my crew associating with savage cannibals, you understand?"

"Yes, cap'n," the boy answered, scurrying after his master.
The torchlight left with him, and a trapdoor overhead slammed
shut. Taregan had never known such complete darkness.

▼▲▼▲▼ He had thought their hold completely closed
in, but when the sun rose the next morning Taregan saw two
small openings, each no larger than a man's hand, high upon the

wall. In the light these openings afforded, he had a better look at the belly of the ship in which they had been confined. There were no walls to subdivide the crowded space, only three vast poles, which intersected the ship at the front, center, and rear. Giant beams, like bones in a man's rib cage, lined the walls, and wooden planks no wider than two hand-widths surrounded these beams like skin and kept the water out.

Shortly after sunrise a vast metallic clanking cut through the seamen's voices, and a stout pole at the rear of the ship began to rotate. Taregan realized that this pole was lifting the anchor cables out of the water, and after a moment the ship shivered as it flowed free of its mooring in the muddy bottom of the Connecticut River.

From across the hold he caught Hassun's wide eyes. "We are on our way," Taregan called, with more courage than he felt.

Hassun nodded, too frightened to speak, and several of the others stirred uncomfortably. A few stood and would have paced, but their chains prevented it. The best a man could do was stand and move from side to side for a step or two, then he had to sink back onto the floor and try to make himself comfortable.

Once or twice a whiff of pungent sea air filled the stagnant cabin, and Taregan breathed it in and closed his eyes, trying to imagine what the open sea might look like. Fear gripped him more than he wanted to admit, for though he had grown up on the water, he had never in his life been so far out to sea that he had lost sight of the shore. Even in the racing rapids of the Connecticut River, he had always known that he could swim to safety, but how could one swim through the vast salt sea? And how could one escape when he was buried three levels deep and chained to more than three hundred other men?

After an hour or two of daylight, the young boy came down into the hold, a basket of hard loaves in his arms. Breaking the loaves, he tossed a piece of bread to each man with the quick, cautious motion with which he might have fed a rabid dog, then turned and scooted like a rodent up the stairs. Taregan grinned and gnawed on his stale bit of bread. If they befriended the boy, perhaps they could convince him to remain long enough to deliver the promised bucket of water.

The day wore on, interminable in its length and filled with the muffled thunder of bare feet on the hollow decks above. In his imagination Taregan painted a picture of the ship upon the waters, for he could feel the vessel climb the slopes of waves, then slip down their tops and travel smoothly into the hollow beneath.

The hours melted into days, the days into weeks. In time the sounds of creaking blocks, straining sailcloth, and the rumble of the sailors' feet became usual and customary. The fear that had kept even the most stoic of the captive warriors silent eased somewhat; the men began to talk among themselves and share stories of battles past and the women and children they had left behind. They spoke of their loved ones as if they waited just upstream, only a day or two away. Taregan realized that this was how they had spoken on long nights around the campfire when they left their villages to hunt or make war, but most had never left the Connecticut River valley. They were farther from home than they had ever been before.

Taregan could not share in hunting tales without thinking of Daniel and his father, so he escaped the pain of confinement by revisiting his memories of Dena. During the night he dreamed of her, during the day he sat with his eyes closed and imagined himself the captain of a majestic and gleaming ship that spread her wings over the sea and moved with speed and grace through the living water. The brusque and familiar commands of the captain passed his own lips: "All hands ahoy! Out or down! Rouse and bitt! Show a leg there! Sheet home! All hands to the braces!"

"Almost I could wish for a sailor's life," he murmured one night as he struggled to find a comfortable position in which to sleep, "if I could command a ship to take me home."

Colton Bramwell

One of you will say to me: "Then why does God still blame us? For who resists his will?" But who are you, O man, to talk back to God? "Shall what is formed say to him who formed it, 'Why did you make me like this?'" Does not the potter have the right to make out of the same lump of clay some pottery for noble purposes and some for common use?

Romans 9:19-21

Of the three towns established along the emerald banks of the
Connecticut River, Hartford was the most central, flanked by
Windsor five miles north and Wethersfield four miles south. Garvin had chosen to establish his trading post in Hartford, and
Daniel now resided within the trading post. He loved the liveliness of the town. A thrill shivered through his senses every time
he stepped from the small building by the river docks and wandered into the bustling village.

A single road, which muddied when it rained and swirled
with dust during the heat of summer, ran through town. The
heart of Hartford lay at its midpoint, where a cleared field surrounded both the meetinghouse and an adjacent cemetery. This
field, which the Puritans called "the green," was anything but.
During the week, cattle grazed there on quick-sprouting weeds
and grass, and in the hour just before sunset the local militia
trained in the place, doggedly marching through piles of cattle
dung. Under continual trampling by man and beast, the village
green became a field of moist black earth as slippery as wet
paper beneath a man's feet. Daniel thought "the village muck"
would be a far more apt name.

Narrow lots flanked Hartford's main street, each large enough
for a house, a garden, a fruit tree or two, and enough pasture for
the family cow when the village herdsman brought the animals
home for the night. Families of low estate lived at the far ends of
the street; homes near the central village green rose taller and
grander than the others.

The hurry and hustle of the village were a far cry from the
quiet regularity of his home in the forest, and Daniel thoroughly

enjoyed the excitement of the fledgling town. The English and
Dutch argued loudly, lived dangerously, and drank fermented
beverages that burned the throat and left a man feeling a bit soft
in the head. Daily, almost hourly it seemed, canoes and small
ships arrived at the docks carrying traders with goods from the
far corners of the earth. From Narragansett, Mohegan, and occasionally even Mohawk Indians, Garvin Black took skins, furs,
corn, and fish; from the English and Dutch traders he obtained
candles, iron kettles, axes, and bolts of colorful cloth. Occasionally a prosperous merchant would pay in silver coins, which
Daniel carried straightaway to the silversmith. The smith melted
the coins down, then hammered the metal into spoons, plates,
and cups. "There being no safe place for coins," Garvin
explained, locking the silverware into a trunk, "dinnerware is as
good a bank as any. And the ladies of Connecticut will pay
dearly for such items, you wait and see."

Garvin's personal goods were kept in a small room built onto
the back of the trading post, and for many weeks Daniel felt a tri-
fle guilty whenever he entered the chamber. Garvin's big bed
filled half the space; Daniel's small cot hugged the far wall.
Beside Garvin's bed, a wardrobe bulged with furs, hides, kettles,
and other spoils from the ravaged Pequot camps, as well as the
booty Garvin had collected from Nixkamich's village. Once as he
sorted through the goods, Daniel thought he recognized a bearskin that his mother had tanned and softened, her favorite covering. But surely Garvin would not be so callous as to hoard
Gilda's possessions. He had been nothing but a friend in the past
difficult weeks, and often Daniel thought of him as a father. At
least at Garvin's supper table there was never a mention of Taregan or a suggestion that Daniel work harder. Garvin praised
and petted him, complimenting him on his quick tongue and
sharp trading skills.

But still a flood of memories swirled behind the wardrobe
door, and each time Daniel opened it he wondered if he would
drown in guilt. Once after he had brought a beaver skin from the
closet, Garvin caught sight of Daniel's stricken face. "Daniel, you

must not let things of the past bother you," he said, taking the pelt and tossing it onto the counter. "Today is all that matters; you can forget the troubles of yesterday."

"I can't help remembering," Daniel mumbled, feeling ashamed. "My father often said that only God can truly forget our sins. Often I dream of Nixkamich's village. I can still see the look on Dena's face when Uncas killed her mother."

"Forget those things; war is brutal," Garvin answered. "You must consider the goods in the wardrobe a ransom for your father's life. A small pittance, really, when you think about it. How much more the savages owe you, Daniel! Rejoice when you open that door, for your enemies are dead or gone, and the land is free for trade and expansion. And if the thought of God troubles you—" He looked around to be certain they were alone— "well, God is fine for the Sabbath and such, but let's leave him out of our weekdays, heh?"

"Leave God out?" Daniel wasn't sure he had heard correctly.

"Aye," Garvin whispered. "You'll be happier if you can learn to give him a proper, useful place. I know the law demands that we give him the Sabbath and our presence in the meetinghouse, but that's all I'll allow. If you're smart, you'll learn when to invoke his name and when it is more politic to refrain from references to the Almighty. Be strong, Daniel, but have faith in yourself. A man must make his own way in the world, as I have done. Follow me, boy, and learn to take care of yourself."

Daniel listened and believed. Believing Garvin Black was far easier than dealing with his memories and the nagging voice of his conscience.

From Monday through Saturday they haggled and traded; on Sunday Daniel joined Garvin and the other citizens of Hartford in the meetinghouse. The minister preached for two hours on Sunday morning, then again for another two hours on Sunday afternoon. The strict, still atmosphere of the tiny church was nothing like the happy, effusive attitude with which Fallon Bailie had led his family in worship, but Daniel liked the formal, proper atmosphere.

If, perchance, one happened to fall asleep during the long prayers, Bible reading, hymns, or sermons, the tithing-man's long pole would rap the sleeper's head and rouse him to attention. Even smiling and whispering, Daniel soon learned, were forbidden in church. Those found guilty of these sins had to pay a fine.

On the Sabbath, Garvin told Daniel, they must conduct their affairs in secret. "The Puritans do not work, laugh, shave, or play on the Sabbath," he told Daniel one afternoon as they lingered outside the meetinghouse. "That does not mean, of course, that you cannot laugh or share a joke with me in private. But no one can see you, lest you be reported."

"Why?" Daniel asked, perplexed. "My father and mother always set aside the seventh day to worship God, but we lived no differently on that day."

"Ah, my boy, it is one of the mysteries of divinity," Garvin answered, strengthening his voice as a pair of passing women eyed them suspiciously from under the brims of their hats. "And we are probably not allowed to discuss it on the Sabbath day."

When the women had gone, Garvin lowered his voice. "There are some things we do at the trading post that you must never tell any man. It is forbidden, for instance, to give strong drink to the savages, but the Indians will not meet my terms unless their wits have been addled a bit. Since they will do anything for a taste of the brandy, you may give them a sample from the jug under the counter, but never when an English man or woman is present."

Daniel nodded. "I understand."

"Give a savage strong brandy first," Garvin went on, thrusting his hands behind his back as he began to walk. "And as the haggling wears on, cut the drinks with water. You'll save me a pretty penny, and by the time the fire has taken ahold of their guts, the Indians won't know the difference."

They had reached the green beside the meetinghouse. The warm afternoon air, bathed in sunlight, carried faint hints of coming autumn days. A number of women had spread baskets and blankets on the ground for Sunday dinner. The colonists who lived in the woods outside the settlement preferred to carry their dinner to church and eat on the grounds rather than walk home and back again. Garvin Black and Daniel chose to eat with the church people for an entirely different reason.

For the last two weeks, Garvin had been paying particular attention to a dark-eyed newcomer known as the Widow Butler. She had arrived in Hartford only a month before, and Garvin had helped supply her meager house with the necessities of life. Sabrina Butler and her husband, Garvin informed Daniel, had been living upriver outside Windsor, but when a barrel of gunpowder accidentally ignited, her house as well as her husband were destroyed. Without home, husband, or hope of happiness, the Widow Butler had come to Hartford expecting to make a new life for herself.

She was a petite woman, clean, tidy, and approachable, with smooth, sweet-smelling skin. Under her kerchief Daniel caught sight of wispy brown hair, and her velvet brown eyes glowed with the sensitivity of a scholar. She was not exactly beautiful, he thought, but her hands were gentle and competent, her manner both refined and warm.

Today, as she knelt upon a rough blanket and opened her basket, her brown eyes flickered with genuine interest as she smiled up at Garvin. Like a gallant warrior he knelt at her side and helped her spread out the corn bread, corn cakes, and a huge bowl of sweetened squash. Daniel hung by the edge of the blanket, feeling like an intruder, but the Widow Butler smiled up at him, too, a sincere welcome in her eyes.

"The minister gave a good sermon today," Garvin said, his hand lingering over hers as he reached for a pumpkin pie.

A blush colored the widow's cheek as she lowered her eyes. "Aye, a very good one," she murmured, pulling her hand away. Almost reluctantly, she turned from Garvin and looked up at Daniel. "Why do you hesitate, Daniel? You are of certain a growing boy and need your victuals. Have a seat and help yourself. I baked all day yesterday in order to repay you and Master Black for your kindness—"

"It was not a kindness to help you," Garvin answered, sinking onto the ground. He stretched out his legs and leaned back upon his hands, still gazing at her. "It was an honor, Widow Butler. Our town does not receive as lovely a resident as you every day."

She squinted in embarrassment, but still she smiled as she withdrew a jug from the basket. "Apple cider?" she asked, crinkling her nose. "I'm afraid it is not very good. I haven't had time to make a decent batch."

"I trow whatever you make will taste as sweet as honey," Garvin answered, tossing her a wink. The anxiety in her face vanished as she pinked before his praise. She lowered her head, and Daniel saw that her hands trembled as she picked up a stoneware mug and began to pour.

"I fished two of the minister's sons out of the river yesterday," Daniel offered, hoping to turn the conversation to more mundane matters. "I expect they should have been at lessons with their father."

"How fortunate for them that you were there," Garvin drawled, leaning toward the widow. He gave her a wide white smile. "Our Daniel swims like a fish. One of his many gifts."

"Oh." The widow shivered delicately. "How on earth did you ever learn? I can't imagine being totally covered in water. I trow I would faint if I ever fell out of a boat—I have nightmares about being buried in water. I hear that the savages swim in the river, but surely no civilized person would attempt such a thing."

Daniel felt his ears burning. In a moment she might guess his heritage, or had he already given himself away?

"I'm sure the cool water seems inviting on a hot day, and children don't know any better," Garvin answered smoothly. He leaned down and sniffed the pumpkin pie. "Delicious, Mistress Butler, I'm sure. Must we talk all day, or may we eat?"

"We'll eat, of course," the lady answered, blushing furiously. "I'm so sorry, I didn't mean to prattle on."

"Such sweet prattle is easily forgiven," Garvin answered, pulling a plate from the bottom of her basket.

They passed the afternoon in pleasant conversation until the church bell tolled for the beginning of the afternoon service. Garvin and Daniel helped the widow pack the dishes into her basket, then Garvin offered to deliver the basket to her house while the widow went on to church.

"That would be most kind," she said, dimpling as she curtseyed. Garvin grinned until she turned for the church, then he suddenly unsmiled and hurried toward her house, the basket under his arm.

"So will you be marrying the widow?" Daniel puffed, hurrying to keep up.

Garvin's somber expression twisted into a grimace. "Ha! Not on your life, boy, and not in my lifetime, either."

"Why not? You like her, and of certain she likes you. She needs a husband, and you have no wife—"

"Her dead husband owed money to every merchant in Windsor," Garvin said, the corner of his mouth dipping in derision. "As soon as he promises to have and hold, whoever marries that wench will be poorer than a sailor on his second day of shore leave. No, Daniel, I'll not be giving up my treasure just to have a wench in my bed and kidney pie on the board at the end of the day. There are other ways to get what a man needs."

Daniel would have asked more, but an inner voice warned him that he shouldn't discuss such things on the Lord's Day.

▼▲▼▲▼ On a sharp summer afternoon a few days later, Daniel leaned against the doorframe of the trading post and studied two broken shadows cast upon the road by the bright sunlight. He played this game when trade was slow; he liked to compare visitors to their approaching shadows and see how accurately he had been able to judge one by first analyzing the other.

The shadows of a stout English woman and her servant were

now moving toward him from the center of town. The woman's broad silhouette all but engulfed the slender shade of the servant's. The serving girl walked with her head down and her bonnet tied tightly around her chin. She carried something in her arms, but whether bags or a basket Daniel could not tell, but the burden was heavy, for the girl swayed slightly as she walked, her shadow wavering back and forth on the road.

"I cry you mercy, young man, move out of the way. I need to see Master Black."

Too engrossed in his game to realize that they were upon him, Daniel jerked his head up and stared into the woman's broad face. "Master Black is inside," he said, stepping aside so the woman could pass. As the lady swept past him, he glanced at the servant. A strange, cold numbness filled his entire being when he recognized the girl before him.

Dena.

The supple leather garments she had worn in the Pequot camp had been replaced by a thin kirtle of cheap English cloth and a long-sleeved blouse that completely covered her slender arms. Her hair, which had once hung in a gorgeous raven plume down to her waist, was either gone or hidden under the severe English cap, pulled tight and knotted under her chin. The lovely face was the same, dominated by high, strong bones and large eyes. But a livid purple bruise outlined her cheek, and the lips that had been rosy and plump were bloodied and cracked.

"Dena!" Daniel burst out, shocked. His heart thudded like a drum when she lifted her eyes to meet his, and he fell into the Indian tongue without realizing it. "My dear girl, what has happened to you?"

Her eyes widened, the lovely face grew pale. She took a hasty half-step back, as if she had seen a ghost. "Taregan!" she whispered, nearly dropping the heavy basket in her arms.

"No," he answered, his heart sinking with swift disappointment. "Daniel." A weight of sadness overwhelmed the wonder in her eyes, and her thin face fell into lines of sorrow as she lowered her gaze to the ground.

The English woman abruptly turned around. "Welladay, what is this?" she asked, eying him carefully. "To whose house do you belong, young sir? And how have you come to speak that heathen tongue?"

"I work for Master Black," Daniel answered, ignoring the woman's scrutiny as he gazed at Dena's disfigured face. "And I talk to Indians every day as part of my job here. But how, mistress, came this girl by this bruise?"

The woman's face emptied of expression as her jaw dropped, her heavy cheeks falling in worried folds over her collar. "She's a clumsy girl . . . she fell and hurt herself. And why would a good English boy like you care what happens to one of the savages? You ought to mind your ways and avoid them, lest you pick up their ill-bred, lazy habits—"

"You say she fell?" Daniel interrupted. He put out a hand and brushed his fingers across the purpled skin, aware that Dena trembled beneath his touch. Why?

The woman frowned. "Do you dispute my word? Be off before I call your master or report you to the magistrate for slander. I've no time for dealing with the likes of you."

Dena did not speak again, nor did she lift her eyes, but shuffled after her mistress, her proud, confident stride stripped away. Daniel's spine stiffened as he watched her pass. If she had but given him one smile, one glance of entreaty, he might have been willing to redeem her from this fate, mayhap even to give her a home as his wife. But she was broken and weak, just like the rest of her people.

From out of nowhere, the realization that his mother might be bloodied and bruised like Dena crashed into his consciousness, and he let out a soft cry of despair. It wasn't right. He had wanted to protect his mother, he had tried to reach her in the jail. But she would have nothing to do with him, would not even acknowledge that he existed. And traitorous Taregan had refused to help him and followed their mother into slavery. . . .

The sight of Dena had opened the door on a host of memories he'd tried to bury. Resolutely putting her from his mind, he stalked out to the docks to help an arriving trapper unload his canoe.

▾▲▾▲▾ The late afternoon sun streaked the river crimson as Colton Bramwell stepped out of the shallop and surveyed the village lying beyond the dock. Hartford seemed a busy enough place, a welcome respite from the wilderness solitude of the fort at Saybrook, and Bramwell looked forward to spending his three days of liberty in the area. But a troubling responsibility lingered at the back of his mind, and Colton knew he would have no rest until he had fulfilled his promise to the young man who had boarded the slave ship. But how could he find two captive women in a territory that had expanded hundreds of miles in every direction? If the women had been sold as slaves, they could have been transported anywhere.

A knot of Narragansetts lingered near the door of the trading post at the dock, and Colton thought about going in to ask for information. But traders were notoriously tight-fisted and probably would tell him nothing unless he offered up a pouch of tobacco or a copper penny for their trouble. No, it would be easier to nose about on his own. After all, his father had always said that the Almighty promised to direct a man's paths, and paths were made for walking.

Turning from the trading post, he walked down the main road leading into town. A late summer rain had turned the road to mud that tugged on his boots with every step, but Colton ignored the mess and tried to study his surroundings. A number of lumber and mud houses lined the central road; merchants' signboards hung from the sloping eaves and swung gently in the late summer breeze. The cobbler's, hatter's, and pewterer's houses lined one side of the street; the tanner's, silversmith's, and cabinetmaker's the other. The smithy stood at the edge of the field outside the church, and adjacent to the smithy stood a small house with a sign proclaiming "Will Wilson, Wheelwright, liveth here."

Colton found the sign he sought on the far side of the muddy field. The village inn was a slanted, ramshackle building, probably thrown up in haste when it became apparent that visitors to Hartford would need a place to stay and might be willing to pay for a decent bed and a hot meal. Colton ambled toward the hostelry, nodding pleasantly at several men walking by. One young girl, a freckle-faced lass of not more than fifteen or sixteen, passed him on the road, and Colton impulsively put out a hand to stop her.

"Pray excuse me, miss," he said, tipping his hat in respect, "but I am searching for an Indian woman and girl who were recently sold into slavery from the Pequot villages. Would you be knowing of any family who might have taken them in?"

The girl took a half-step back and blushed furiously. "N-no sir," she stammered, her cheeks darkening to the crimson color of the cloak she wore around her shoulders. "And I shouldn't be talking to you, a stranger."

"But, miss—" Before he could finish, the girl darted toward the safety of another house, and Colton shook his head, amazed at his own stupidity. No decent young woman would speak to a strange man on the street, particularly one as dusty as he.

He settled his hat squarely on his head and quickened his pace until he reached the inn. Opening the door, he squinted for a moment through the dim light inside. A musty, heavy odor of boiling corn and meat filled the outer chamber, where a group of men sat around a table, intent upon a stack of parchments in the center. One gentleman, however, stood apart. Colton noted the man's white shirt and patched breeches and directed his attention to him.

"Good day," he said, removing his hat. "I am looking for a meal and a place to stay the night."

"Be you a soldier?" the man asked, narrowing his eyes as if he did not trust Colton's uniform.

"Yea, from Saybrook," Colton answered. "I have three days' liberty and had hoped to pass it here while I look for a place to settle. My term of service is up in a few months."

The man nodded, apparently reassured. "There's a room upstairs that'll hold you. There's two other men in it, trappers from the north country, but they won't mind bedding down with you as long as you don't mind their lice."

Colton grinned. "I won't mind. I'm sure their lice are cousins to the varmints that plague us at the fort."

"I'm sure you're right." The man jerked his head toward the fireplace where an iron kettle hung on a hook. "Have a seat at the board there, and my wife will spoon you out a bowl of porridge. The fee is three shillings a day for room and board, lodging, and wine at dinner. We don't serve intoxicating liquors and don't allow games, dancing, or singing. It is the law of the town, you understand."

"You need not concern yourself with me, I have none of those vices," Colton answered, moving toward the large board that had been propped on two sawhorses next to the wall. He was aware of the careful scrutiny of the other men as he moved through the room, but after he had seated himself and tossed his hat onto the board, they seemed to lose interest in him.

Colton rested his chin on his hands and stared at the flickering fire, listening to the men even as he pretended not to notice them. They were a party of five, spaced equally around the circular table, and all but one dressed in homespun green breeches and shirts, their long hair tied at their necks and their faces bronzed from the sun. They were trappers, Colton mused, from the lean, wolfish look of them, and skilled hunters, for a dauntless, intrepid air clung to each of them.

The youngest man, who still retained the slender waist and shoulders of adolescence, wore a gentleman's doublet and breeches, a flowering of lace upon his collar and sleeves. Sitting with his back toward Colton, he patiently refereed the discussion between the others. The trappers were offering furs in exchange for silver and other goods, and Colton realized he had interrupted a bidding war, which the young man skillfully resumed.

"And you, Jacques Bettencourt," the lad said, pointing to a man who spoke with the nasal accent of a Frenchman, "have you

beaver furs in the north country to equal those of Master New-
man? He has promised six beaver pelts for a single silver ingot;
can you match or better that offer?"

The Frenchman cursed and slammed his fist on the table.
"No, *mon dieu*, I will not do it! What you suggest is larceny, my
young friend, and your master will not allow this to go on!
Where is Monsieur Black, and why does he make us deal with a
stubborn youth?"

"My master," the boy said smoothly, leaning forward as he
folded his arms upon the table, "trusts me implicitly. I know, gentlemen, what a thing is worth, and I know how much the Indians
will pay to obtain the kettles and goods you bring from the harbor towns. You will not trick me. Do not think that because I am
young, I am stupid."

"The boy speaks the truth," an older man said, a grin breaking
across his weathered face. He propped a heavy boot upon a
nearby stool and rested his wrist upon his knee. "All right, Daniel, we will allow that the price of six beaver pelts is one silver
ingot. We will guarantee that our beaver pelts are as large and
thick as those of the north country, and you swear that Master
Black's silver is not tainted or shaved on the edges."

"You have my word on it," the young man answered, a smile
in his voice. The men broke up, some disgruntled, some relieved,
but there was much slapping of backs and barking for beer as
the innkeeper hurried to meet their needs.

The youth bent over the table, writing upon a parchment, and
something in his posture piqued Colton's interest. The trapper
had called him Daniel—could this be the brother he had been
sent to find? Colton slowly submerged himself into memory,
recalling the Indian boy's manner and physical characteristics.
This Daniel was very much like the Indian in form and stature—
yet he was very English. Indeed, there was nothing whatsoever
about him to bespeak an Indian heritage. Colton looked away,
convinced he had nearly made a mistake.

"Monsieur Bettencourt!" the boy said, turning so that Colton glimpsed the clean purity of his profile. "When might we expect to see you again?"

Merciful heavens! The lad's face was a mirror image of the one who had proudly stepped into the slaver's ship. The Indian boy had sent Colton to find a brother in Hartford, but this Daniel was a twin! Colton's eyes narrowed as he observed the youth. Of certain he was no Indian. The young eyes shone with the confident, almost arrogant light of an aristocrat; his manners would have been acceptable in the finest Boston homes; the lace ruffles at his wrist spoke of elegant sophistication. He spoke proper English without the slightest hesitation or trace of an accent, and obviously knew how to read and write. How could one twin be a Pequot and the other as English as King Charles?

Colton stared, fascinated, barely noting when the innkeeper's wife hurried up with a steaming bowl of porridge. "There, now, I'm sorry I've kept you waiting," she said. She clucked in solicitous sympathy as she set the bowl before him. "But that porridge will stick to your ribs, you'll see. Just take a spoonful, sir, and you'll be glad you came our way."

"Thank you," Colton murmured absently, trying to peer past the woman's formidable girth to watch the boy. From the corner of his eye he saw the woman's bosom heave in silent indignation, then he remembered his manners and lifted his gaze to meet his hostess. "Thank you kindly, mistress," he said again, picking up the spoon she had set on the board. "I am hungry, and I am certain you are a wonderful cook."

"Well now, I wouldn't say that," the woman said, swaying slightly in pleasure. Colton realized she would not leave until he sampled her fare, so he took a huge mouthful and smiled with the lumpy mush heavy upon his tongue.

"Delicious," he said, forcing himself to swallow as he spooned up another heaping mouthful. "But I would not have you neglect your other guests. They have been in a long discussion, and I am certain they could use sustenance now."

"Glory be, how right you are!" The woman turned to look at

the other men. "I'm sorry, gentlemen, for keeping you waiting! How may I serve you? Beer? Cider?"

Colton sat back, eating slowly and thoughtfully as he watched Daniel Bailie. The young man made a few more notations on his parchments, then rose to lift a mug of beer with the others. It was not easy to tell what sort of man this Daniel was, but one question hung heavy in Colton's mind: If Daniel's heart possessed the same measure of honor as his twin's, why hadn't *he* rescued his mother from jail and the girl from slavery?

Colton lifted his mug, determined to discover an answer.

Daniel leaned against the wall and pretended to guzzle with the others. His drinking, the friendly banter, it was all an act, part of the routine he and Garvin had developed. Soon these trappers would drink themselves into a near stupor, then they would stumble out onto the street. Daniel would point them toward the trading post, where Garvin would convince the drunken fools to give him a dozen pelts per silver ingot. If they were totally senseless, Garvin would take their pelts and send them on their way with a few useless trinkets.

The system worked beautifully, and Garvin assured Daniel that they were actually performing a service for the hapless trappers. "After all," Garvin explained, "they ought not drink so much. And if any one of them has the gall to appear and complain when they've found their lost wits, we've only to remind them that the sentence for public drunkenness is a morning spent in the stocks."

No one ever complained. Daniel was certain that when the trappers awoke the next morning, adrift in their canoes with nothing but memorable headaches, most of them would have no idea what had happened. They would shrug off their misfortune and head into the wilds again. There were, after all, plenty of furs in the forest.

These four, who had arrived together with a bundle of furs and hides, were now staggering toward the trading post. Daniel felt his smile stiffen and then melt as he watched them disappear into the gathering darkness; his face fairly ached from grinning at them. Now that he had done his part, he could relax.

He emptied his mug with a sharp jerk of his wrist, dully con-

scious of the soldier who had come in during the heat of the
negotiations and remained throughout the celebration. His piercing eyes seemed intent upon Daniel's face, and his continued
presence did nothing to calm the anxiety that spurred Daniel's
heart to beat unevenly. Had Garvin done something wrong? Had
the captain of the militia sent this soldier to interrogate Daniel?
After standing silent through several minutes of scrutiny, Daniel
turned to face the stranger.

"Do I know you, sir?" he snapped, pretending an anger he
did not feel. "I do not think we have met."

"No," the man said, shaking his massive head. The line of his
mouth curved, a mere twitch in the blonde-bearded face. "We
have not, but I have met one who looks exactly like you. The boy
I met, though, called himself an Indian. He wore leathers like the
savages and painted his face and chest in the manner of the
Pequot."

Daniel's gaze flew down to the empty mug in his hand as his
heart raced. Did this man mean to brand him a Pequot? It would
be a sentence worse than death.

"I am sure many people in the world resemble one another,"
he said, taking pains to remain calm. "I assure you, sir, that I am
not a Pequot. My father was Fallon Bailie, one of the first English
in this area. You can ask anyone in Hartford—they know I have
lived in this valley many years—"

"The Indians have been here longer than any Englishman,"
the soldier replied. He waved his hand. "But that is no matter. I
would not have thought you an Indian, in any case." The man
lifted his mug and took a long, slow drink, then returned the cup
to the board and resumed staring at Daniel. "One thing I have
learned in war, my young friend, is that a man may be one thing
on the inside and another on the outside." His eyes darkened as
they focused on Daniel. "The young man who lives behind the
same face you wear told me that he had a brother in Hartford
called Daniel Bailie. I assume you are that brother."

"I am Daniel Bailie, but I have no brother." The innkeeper's
wife stopped stirring her kettle and cocked her head, listening.

The soldier shrugged. "It is of no import. I came to seek a mother. The boy I met bade me find a woman called Gilda and a girl called Dena. I am to tell them that he has sworn to come back. Since you live here, would you know where I might find them?"

Sudden bands of tightness closed around Daniel's lungs, and he took a deep breath, resisting them. To admit the truth would confirm that he and Taregan were brothers and might cast him as a Pequot before this soldier and the innkeeper's wife. Though Captain Mason and Garvin Black knew Daniel's history, Mason had returned to Boston and Garvin didn't care. Most of the townspeople had no idea of Daniel's past, and he did not want to be anything other than English in their eyes.

He forced a laugh. "Hartford is a busy village, sir, and by no means could I know everyone. However, you might speak to Mistress Broughton, the pastor's wife. She may be able to tell you where to find these people you seek." He shifted his weight, leaning upon his other shoulder so he might see the man better. "This boy you met swore he would come back? Where did he go?"

"He boarded a slaver's ship at Saybrook. The captain said his ship was bound for the West Indies, of that I am certain. And yes, judging from the gleam in the boy's eye, if God allows it he will return. I do not think he is the sort of man who would break a vow."

A thin, cold blade of foreboding sliced into Daniel's heart, but he straightened himself and stepped away from the wall. "Excuse me, then, sir," he said, rolling up the parchments waiting on the table. "The stranger who looks like me can go or stay as he pleases, but I have nothing to do with him, his mother, or any Pequots. They are a cursed people, have you not heard? They will be fully exterminated. That tribe's name is not to be spoken in this valley, nor their manners to be adopted."

The man leaned forward and lowered his voice to an urgent whisper. "You have a quick tongue."

"So do you." Daniel spoke without thinking; his heart went into sudden shock when he realized what he had done. The sol-

dier had spoken this last phrase in Algonquin, and Daniel had
answered without hesitation.

The soldier leaned back, a lazy smile sweeping over his face.
"So you are not an Indian," he answered, picking up his hat.
"Indeed, you probably learned the language from your work at
the trading post, though there are veteran traders throughout the
colonies who do not speak as well as you."

"I am young," Daniel stammered, feeling his cheeks burn. "I
learn quickly."

"Aye, that you do," the soldier said, standing. He bowed
slightly. "Thank you for the recommendation of Mistress
Broughton. I will visit her on the morrow and hope that I will be
able to fulfill my promise."

Daniel stared at his hands as the man moved away, and not
until the soldier had disappeared could he lift his head again.

▼▲▼▲▼ The village seemed to sleep under a clouded
molasses-colored sky as Daniel walked slowly back to the trading post. His encounter with the soldier had unnerved him, and
for a moment he felt as though Taregan's spirit had risen with
the wind to haunt him. His mother was still alive somewhere
near this town, perhaps even in it, but since she had refused to
acknowledge him he had made no effort to inquire after her. She
had always preferred Taregan, and Daniel would not allow her
to wound him again.

A smudge of moonlight dappled through the cloud cover as a
warm wind blew, and Daniel knew that soon winter would
descend from the north. Life would slow as man and beast alike
drew near to their fires and settled down to survive the harsh
months ahead. How would his mother live in the jail or as a
slave? Did she have warm clothing? What had become of the
rich furs that had lined her bed at their house? He remembered
the bearskin in Garvin's wardrobe, and for a moment he wondered if he might be able to slip it away and deliver it to his

mother. But no. She had willingly walked away from her life to stand with the Pequot. It was her choice, not his.

A group of Narragansetts moved away from the porch outside the trading post; a pair of Englishmen stood near the docks and bickered loudly over the advisability of giving muskets to the Indians. Daniel ignored the lot of them and went inside.

He stopped just inside the door, suddenly uneasy. The Widow Butler stood near the table where Garvin kept the crocks of molasses and syrup, and from the way their heads inclined toward one another Daniel knew he had stumbled upon an intimate moment. He lingered in the doorway, hiding in the shadows, afraid to move in or out lest he be seen and embarrass the lady or his master.

"So you'll come to supper on the morrow?" the widow asked, looking up quickly. Her smile crinkled the corners of her eyes, and the sight made Daniel's heart constrict in pain. His mother had smiled like that.

"Aye, I'll come," Garvin answered, leaning with both elbows upon the tall counter where he kept his ledger book. "And what about the boy?"

"Oh, he's welcome, too," the lady answered, her cap bobbing in her enthusiasm. "I would never leave him out. My heart breaks for him, poor orphan child." She looked up at Garvin, her eyes glinting with interest. "How on earth did you come to find him, Master Black?"

"Ah, the will of God led me to him, I'm certain," Garvin answered, meeting her inquisitive gaze head-on. "It was during the battle at Mystic. The boy's father had turned traitor, and I had to break the news. The lad's been with me ever since that day."

"You are kind to consider him. There are many men who would not undertake to provide for an orphan."

"Daniel is useful. He knows the woods, he knows the Indian language, he knows—" his dark gaze focused on the woman's lips— "many things."

"Still," she said, lowering her eyes, "you are certainly a saint,

Garvin Black. And you've been so kind to me, charging me so little for the syrup and cloth—"

"I would charge you nothing at all," Garvin answered, his hand inching toward her arm. "Except that others would hear of it, and the minister would be asking my intentions before I was ready to proclaim them—"

"And what—," she asked, her slight body trembling as she leaned toward him, "if I may be so bold as to ask, are your intentions?"

Daniel slammed the door behind him and kept his eyes down as the two adults started in surprise and pulled apart. A lingering crimson shade upon the lady's cheek proved the effect of the conversation he had just overheard.

The Widow Butler paid for her maple syrup, covered her crock with its lid, and smiled at Daniel as she carried her purchase out the door. Garvin leaned on the counter as she left, letting his eyes roam over her figure in a way Daniel felt was indecent. When the lady had disappeared, he cast Daniel a knowing look.

"Ah, women," Garvin said, the grooves beside his mouth deepening into a lazy, complacent smile. "There are no better creatures on God's green earth, Daniel. You can be sure of that."

"So will you now be marrying the Widow Butler?" Daniel asked, pretending not to care. But he did care, tremendously. Eating dinner with the two of them was uncomfortable enough, with every other sentence flying past him carrying some sort of hidden, private meaning. Living with the two of them would be impossible. "I'm sorry, but I heard what she said about your intentions—"

"Well, I've no intention of marrying her." Garvin slapped the counter as he laughed. "Mercy no, son, why would you think I've changed my mind? A man does not get married until he is ready to settle down, and then he wants a young girl who's never been touched by another man."

"But you spend so much time with her—"

"The Widow Butler is lonely and capable, and a man needs a woman to feed him, mend his clothes, and keep him warm on winter nights." He paused and gave Daniel a lecherous wink. "You'll be knowing about these things soon enough. You won't find any girls in Hartford to warm your feet in the night, but I've heard the Indian chiefs will let you sleep with their daughters as a gesture of goodwill." Lifting the heavy crock of syrup to a shelf behind the counter, Garvin put it away and paused to wipe his hands on a damp cloth. "But who am I to tell you of this, forest boy? You grew up in the woods, surely you know these things."

"No," Daniel said, feeling his neck burn. He turned away and pretended to study the parchments he had brought from the inn. "The Indian village near us was—well, it was not like that."

"Welladay, there are other tribes that are plenty free with their women. I promise you—" Garvin slapped his heavy hand on Daniel's shoulder—"if things aren't going as well with the Widow Butler as I think they will be come the first snow, we'll pay a visit to Uncas at the Mohegan camp. We'll take a few iron kettles and some beads, and Uncas will be so grateful he'll give us his daughters for the night. Then, my boy, you'll understand why I'm courting the Widow Butler so patiently. Women make life so much more interesting."

Garvin slapped Daniel's back once more for emphasis, then walked away, humming a bawdy tune he'd heard the drunken trappers singing. Daniel stared at the parchments, his remarks blurring on the page. Memory transported him to a Mohegan village he had once visited with his father. He saw the wigwams, heard the chanting of the warriors and the singing drums, smelled the roasting venison. But every Indian woman wore his mother's face, and every pretty girl smiled at him with Dena's troubled eyes and cracked, bleeding lips.

His gorge rose suddenly, and Daniel gripped his stomach, overcome with nausea.

▼▲▼▲▼ Mistress Broughton, the minister's wife, was an unstylish, soft little woman with many chins; many children clustered about her skirts. Her face was ruddy and her eyes red-rimmed as Colton greeted her at the door of her house, but kindness shone in her gaze as she listened to his question and paused to think. "Indian slaves," she said thoughtfully, pressing a finger to her lips. "Most of the Pequots have not done well as servants, Master—"

"Bramwell, ma'am," Colton interjected, removing his hat. He bowed deeply. "Colton Bramwell."

"Master Bramwell." She gave him a smile that was more a mechanical civility than a spontaneous expression of pleasure. "The Indians do not wear the yoke of slavery with grace. Many have been returned to serve the Mohegans or the Narragansetts, and I've heard that a number have perished with pining for freedom."

"I am interested in only two: A girl called Dena and a woman who had been confined at the jail."

"The woman I know well," the minister's wife answered, nodding. "My husband visited her there. At first he thought her a Christian, but her views were so far removed from orthodoxy that my husband was forced to deliver her up to Satan."

Colton lifted his chin. "What became of her?"

"After she was injured, Captain Jones released her," Mistress Broughton answered. "I believe she now serves Master Morton, the cooper. There may be other slaves in his house as well. He is a busy man."

"Thank you, ma'am," Colton said, doffing his hat. He stepped away from the prying eyes of the grimy children. "I pray God will bless you for your kindness."

"He already has," Mistress Broughton answered, placing a protective hand on two tow-headed toddlers at her side.

A collection of newly made barrels in the yard advertised the cooper's house, and his workshop lay not more than fifty yards from the minister's home. Colton hurried toward the place, eager to dispatch the messages he had promised to bring. The sound of hammering greeted him as he stepped through the gate in the yard and approached the open door. "Master Morton?"

A big, florid man looked up from the barrel he had been

assembling. He frowned at the sight of Colton's uniform. "Yes, sir? Is there trouble?"

"No, no trouble," Colton said, touching his fingers to the brim of his hat. "I just have a message to deliver, that's all. I am searching for two Indian women, of late of the Pequot tribe. One is a girl called Dena, and the other is a woman known as Gilda. The woman, I believe, was imprisoned at the jail for a time."

The cooper spat upon the ground as if he found the inquiry distasteful. "I know both of them. My wife keeps them to work in the house."

Colton nodded in relief. "Are they in the house now?"

"No. The woman is sick, probably dying, and the girl has refused to work for several days. They are lazy and ignorant, sir. I keep them in the barn out back."

He jerked his head toward the rear of the property, and Colton could only guess that a barn of some sort lay in back of the building.

"With your permission, then, I should like to deliver the message I was given for them," Colton said. With luck, the sight of his uniform would sufficiently impress the man and prevent him from refusing.

But the cooper seemed not to care one way or the other. "Be my guest," he said, picking up his hammer. "And while you're at it, see if you can convince the young one to earn her keep. We hoped she'd be good for a few years when we bought her, but she's apt to die with the older one if she doesn't eat."

"She isn't eating?" Colton lifted an eyebrow.

"If she won't work, she won't eat," the cooper drawled, spitting again. "That's what the Bible says, isn't it?"

Colton bade the man good day and hurried from the building.

▼▲▼▲▼ The wooden structure at the back of the workshop was more like a doghouse than a barn. Scarcely tall enough for a man to stand in, the building had been thrown together to shelter hay and feed from rain and winter snow. Wide and squat, the structure had no walls, only a roof of substandard planking. Four timbers stood at each corner to support the roof.

But bales of freshly cut hay made walls of a sort, and some industrious person had carved a passageway out of the baled hay. Colton sank to his hands and knees and crept through the tunnel, mindful that the damp straw beneath him crawled with insects and other living things.

"Hello?" he called, moving forward cautiously. He did not know these women and was uncertain exactly how to address them. Would they believe his story? Would his news bring more heartache than joy? Mayhap he was wrong to persevere in this path; perhaps he should have dropped his quest after meeting the boy's rebellious brother. If these women needed help, it was Daniel Bailie's rightful duty to provide it. But he had come this far. It was too late to turn back.

In the distance he heard scurrying sounds, as if someone tried frantically to escape. The tunnel widened and the shadows deepened as he crawled. The air in this place was thick with dust, pollen, and the heat of the day, but at least the roof provided a sheltering shade. Colton came upon a small space, probably no more than five feet square, amidst the hay bales. There a woman lay upon a bed of straw, her eyes closed, her frame gaunt and pale beneath a homespun blanket far too heavy in this heat.

"Mistress Bailie?" Colton asked, sinking back upon his folded legs. Sweat dripped from his forehead and beaded under his arms. "Excuse me, ma'am, but I am searching for Gilda Bailie."

The eyes flickered and opened, and the woman's face softened as she looked at him. Strands of gray filtered through hair that had surely been as black as night once, but her eyes were the blue of the sea, the same bright blue he had seen in the eyes of the young man on the ship and the youth at the inn.

"I am Gilda Bailie," she said, her voice a hoarse whisper in the heavy stillness.

Colton removed his hat from force of long habit, then realized how foolish the gesture was. This woman was very ill, mayhap even dying, and would not care if he kept his hat on.

"Mistress Bailie," he said, tossing the hat aside in the hay. "I come with a word from your son."

"Daniel?" she said. Her eyes flickered with a deeply felt emotion he could not interpret. Her chest rose and fell in a sigh, the lines along her mouth stiffened. "Daniel no longer thinks of himself as my son."

"The message I bring is from another son. I met him aboard a ship at Saybrook."

Her breathing quickened, the blue eyes blazed with an inner fire brighter than the shafts of sunlight that broke through the wooden planking overhead. "Taregan! He is alive?"

She pressed on the ground, struggling to sit up, and Colton put out a hand, warning her back. "He is alive, and he bade me tell you—don't push yourself, ma'am—he told me to find you and tell you that he will come back."

She surrendered and reclined in the hay, smiling at his words. "Of course he will," she murmured. "As a bird that wandereth from her nest, so is a man that wandereth from his place. He will come home."

"He asked me to give the same message to someone else. Is there a girl called Dena in this place?"

Gilda's eyes darted suddenly upward, and Colton followed her gaze toward the roof. A crackling, rustling sound broke the stillness, and within a moment a pair of dark eyes peered toward him over the tallest bale of hay. "That is Dena," Gilda said, a small smile lighting her face. "She has been a daughter to me in these last few months. She was promised to Taregan."

"Promised to him?"

"They were to marry. Dena would have been my daughter if God had not worked in an . . . unexpected way."

"Dena," Colton called, looking up to where the girl lay atop the hay bales. "I pray you come down. I won't hurt you."

Like a frightened mouse, the girl slithered over the straw, sinking down into the clearing, her dark, tangled hair hiding her face. Her movements were quick and furtive, like a frightened dog who has been kicked one too many times, and she slid into a corner and crouched there, her arms folded across her chest.

"Dena," Gilda murmured, lifting a hand toward the girl. "He brings word from Taregan."

Dena looked at him then, her dark eyes wide and questioning through the tangle of her hair. Colton shifted uneasily beneath the power of those eyes, then a slow, hopeful smile rose to her face as her eyes filled with grateful tears.

"He said he will return for you," Colton said, unable to turn his gaze from the girl. Through the tattered clothing he could tell that she was painfully thin. "But you must live to wait for him." Wrenching his eyes away, he looked again at Gilda. "Have you eaten? Is the cooper giving you enough food?"

"I cannot work," Gilda answered, waving her hand helplessly. "I have tried, but since the accident—"

"What accident?"

"At the jail." Her voice was calm and matter-of-fact, totally empty of bitterness or regret. "One morning I tarried too long at the well, and the jailer kicked my back with his boot. Ever since that day I have been unable to use my legs. Dena asked Master Morton to take me, but when I could not do what he asked, he put me out here. And Dena will not work as long as I have no one to care for me, so the master gives us neither food nor water."

Colton winced as if his flesh had been nipped. "But how do you live?"

"We are Indians." This answer came from the girl, and the voice was surprisingly mature and self-assured. With one slow and regal gesture she lifted her hair, fully revealing her face, and Colton realized for the first time how exquisitely beautiful a woman could be. Though a smudge of dirt lay across one perfectly formed cheek, those wide, luminous eyes sat above a finely shaped soft mouth and a slender throat.

Colton caught his breath, utterly entranced. No wonder the young man had been desperate to return to this creature.

"We are Pequot," the girl spoke again, lifting her chin slightly as if a royal pedigree were contained within that simple statement. "We lived off the land before the English came to this place. I forage for berries, for nuts, I hunt for squirrels, I fish in the river. At night, when the English hide in their houses and bar their doors, I slip into the woods where God's bounty provides for us. He has not forsaken us, sir, no matter how many times you or your English minister surrender us to Satan."

"I would never—," Colton stammered, bewildered. "I mean to say, all English are not like . . . whomever has hurt you."

"The minister did not hurt us," Gilda answered, her voice soft and reasonable in the gathering gloom. "I know what I believe, and am persuaded that Jesus the Christ is able to hold me fast in his arms. Even before the English came, my husband and I tried to spread the gospel among the Indians. We were only partly successful. Now the English speak of God in their way, but I am not interested in any man's religion if his knowledge of God does not bring him joy and peace. I have no understanding of these long-faced Christians. If God is anything, he is joy. He is peace."

The blue eyes that were focused upon him softened. "With their hard goods and muskets the English are turning more Indians toward gods of pleasure and profit than to our Father in heaven. But I will not condemn all men for the sins of a few, my friend. You have brought joy to my heart this day. You have assured me that my son Taregan lives."

"He lives," Colton said, struggling to speak past the lump that had risen in his throat. "And he is coming back. As sure as God lives, I believe that he will."

"So do I," Gilda whispered, closing her eyes. "Taregan and Fallon will return to me. Thank you for endeavoring to find us."

"Fallon?" Colton asked, lifting an eyebrow. "Another son?"

"Her husband," Dena said, slipping to Gilda's side. "She will not believe he is dead."

"Is he?"

Dena glanced quickly at Colton. "Gilda is tired. She should rest. But you did not tell us your name."

"Colton. Colton Bramwell."

She nodded, then turned back to the woman lying in the hay.

"Well met, Colton Bramwell. I, too, give you thanks." She paused to wipe a sheen of perspiration from the sick woman's forehead with the edge of her skirt. "May God bless you."

His heart overflowing, Colton backed out of the hovel.

"May God bless you."

The woman's parting words rang in Colton's ears, and his heart constricted. He prepared to leave, but his feet would not obey. He stood transfixed, as though listening to some inner debate. Then he turned on his heel and went to find the cooper.

He found the man outside by the well, his neckerchief undone in the heat, his forehead dotted with drops of sweat. "Master Morton, I have a proposition for you," Colton said, pulling his leather purse from his belt. "Ten shillings, my monthly wages. The amount should be enough to purchase the freedom of those women."

"Ten shillings for those two?" the cooper muttered, his eyes gleaming at the sight of the purse in Colton's hand. He wiped his forehead and neck with the kerchief, then bit his lip. "I couldn't do it, sir, not for ten shillings."

"Surely you didn't spend that much to purchase them. And the older woman is sick; the younger one nothing but trouble to you."

The cooper tilted his head and squinted up at Colton. "Can you go twelve shillings? I've had to keep a roof over their heads, haven't I?"

"Ten shillings is more than enough for their freedom and their keep," Colton said, counting the coins from his purse. As he expected, the cooper was quick to extend his hand, and Colton dropped the coins onto the man's grimy palm. "This sale is predicated on one condition. I cannot take the women away now—I am still stationed at the fort. But in three months I will have finished my term, and I will come back to fetch them away." He deliberately exaggerated his frown. "I want both women strong and healthy when I return."

"I can't work miracles," the cooper answered, his voice flat. He held the money out toward Colton. "The older woman's nearly dead, sir, and what can I do if she dies? I'll not be having you haul me before the court and saying that I killed your servant—"

"Do your best before God," Colton answered, pushing the man's hand away. "Keep the money and swear that you will be honest and fair with me. I want the women fed daily, and warmed, and given a decent shelter so they do not have to sleep with rats. And a new kirtle and blouse for each. This money will buy all they need and still leave you a handsome profit. And when I return in October, I will reclaim my property."

He pulled his hand away, leaving the gold with the cooper.

"You would do so much—for two Indians?" the man whispered, staring at the gleaming coins in his hand.

"For those two, yes," Colton answered, resting his hand on the sword at his belt. "Don't be substituting others for them. I want the woman called Gilda and the girl Dena, do you understand?"

The cooper looked up. His stone face cracked into humanity for a moment. "Why, sir, would you do this?"

Colton caught his breath, surprised by the question. *Why am I doing this, Father? Clearly it is your will, but why?* Though no divine response was forthcoming, he nonetheless felt he was doing right. True, he had planned to explore the wilderness after his term of military service—the last thing he wanted was womenfolk to care for. But he had promised to find these two, and, having found them, he could not ignore the tugging at his spirit, could not leave them in their miserable condition.

"I don't know," he muttered as he walked away.

▼▲▼▲▼ "I'm going to have to turn you now," Dena said, kneeling beside Gilda.

"I know." Gilda straightened her arms, readying herself. Dena meant to remove the soiled straw beneath her and replace it with fresh hay. Weakened by her illness, Gilda summoned the effort to turn her head to the side so her face would not be buried in the dust, then held her breath as Dena's capable hands slid beneath her and flipped her body.

"God is good," Gilda murmured, pillowing her head on her arms as she breathed in the scent of the earth. "He was good to send the English soldier and gracious to keep Taregan alive. 'Twas a sign . . . I know this as I know that Fallon lives."

"How can you say that?" Dena asked, flinging the smelly straw from the spot where Gilda had been lying. "Look at us! God was good to my mother and father, he took them to heaven. But we are stuck here, in misery, in filth—"

She stopped suddenly, and Gilda knew the young woman would not go on for fear of hurting her feelings. Since the paralysis had struck, she had no control over her bodily functions and none but Dena to care for her. The girl had been more than a daughter in the past weeks, she had been a nurse, a mother, a guardian angel.

"God holds us even in this misery," Gilda answered softly, unable to deny the difficulty of their situation. "And today he sent the English soldier to remind us that we are not forgotten. Our Taregan lives, Dena, and as God lives, he and Fallon will return. And the soldier has a kind heart. I saw the goodness of God in his eyes."

"I saw only a soldier who pitied a pair of poor Indians," Dena said, scooping up an armful of fresh hay. "Though his pity was more than most people have given us, I would rather have had his respect. I am a sachem's daughter, and you were the wife of an Englishman who knew these woods better than any of these useless, silly creatures—"

"It matters not who we were," Gilda said gently, cutting off the tirade. She pushed her upper body off the ground to help Dena flip her legs. Dena's hands lifted Gilda's right hip, and suddenly she was on her back again, the rough planks of the roof overhead. "God has kept us alive for a reason. We should thank

him that we live, and that we are together. And now God has
sent someone to let us know that Taregan lives, too, and that he
will be coming home."

Gilda lifted her hands and clasped them across her breast, her
habitual posture for prayer. She paused, waiting for Dena to settle into her place. When the hay had stopped rustling, Gilda
closed her eyes as words of gratitude poured from her heart:
"Heavenly Father, how marvelous are your works! You set the
sun in the sky, you sent the moon to rule the darkness, you have
brought forth the blueberry and the walnut, you sent the pumpkin for us so that we might eat. Even in our solitude, you have
not forgotten these two of your daughters. You have set us
amidst an alien and strange people who do not know that we are
also your children, and yet you keep your hand of protection
upon us when they stumble and do not see the truth. For this we
praise your name, Father God, and for the deliverance of my son
Taregan, we thank you. Bring him home safely to Dena, whose
heart yearns to join with his, and while he is away, teach him all
he must know in order to be a man." Gilda paused, searching
her heart.

"Keep my Fallon in the palm of your hand as well. Help me to
be strong until we are reunited. I know that you, my Father God
who fills the earth with light, can do anything, so I ask in confidence and trust. All these things I ask in the name of my beloved
Savior, Jesus the Christ."

She closed her eyes, listening for the quiet noises of early evening, and heard instead the gentle sound of Dena's weeping.

▼▲▼▲ The setting sun seemed to quench itself in the
great ocean, leaving a coppery sheen on the water and a smoky
glow in the western sky, where Fallon's loved ones waited.

Keep your hand on them, Holy God, Fallon prayed as his eyes
skimmed the fiery horizon. His body bent in the subservient posture of a prisoner as he coiled the rope through his calloused
hands, but his free thoughts flitted to images and places far

away. *Strengthen them to fight the evil in the land. Guard Gilda, Taregan, and Daniel. Especially Daniel.*

"Ahoy there! You, Bailie!"

Fallon turned and straightened at the sound of Captain Walker's chilly voice. "Sir?"

"Gather the others below. We will have services. I know we're in need of them."

Fallon dipped his head, then looked away and sighed. Captain James Walker, proud commander of His Majesty's *Pollux*, was one of those confident people who, no matter what happened, always had known it would. He knew last week that Fallon's fellow prisoner John Bishop would steal an extra slice of bread from the galley; he knew Bishop would rather endure thirty lashes than confess to the crime. And so, without any formal charge, interrogation, or confession, Walker had Bishop whipped to within an inch of his life, then hung by his wrists from a yardarm for a full afternoon.

Fallon endured his shipmate's suffering without complaint, for he had suffered the same fate a month earlier. He traced his punishment not to any act of thievery, but to a quip he'd offhandedly made one morning about the captain's stony personality. Fallon forgot that any remark passed on the deck of a vessel sixty-three feet, six inches long was tantamount to a public statement, and before the sun reached its zenith that day, the captain had called all hands to the deck, accused Fallon of stealing food, and administered the punishment.

Now Fallon faced the port bow and called to his fellows. "Captain says we're to have services below." None of the men dared complain, but Fallon caught sight of more than one man rolling his eyes. Captain Walker's religious services, while dutifully attended and regularly performed, had less to do with the worship of God than with tormenting the prisoners. He led the service in a manner so dry and detached that the precious words of Scripture seemed to be coming from him after a prolonged journey through a parched desert.

But still the living water of God refreshed a thirsty soul.

Fallon used the enforced quiet and stillness to retreat to the wilderness, to Gilda. Somewhere she prayed for him; he was sure of it. He felt her prayers avail when his own spirit was too bruised to lift itself to thoughts of God's power and provision. Many, many times, Fallon was certain, he and Gilda had met before God's throne in prayer—and on those occasions he had returned to the bleakness of life on an endless sea with new eyes and bold hopes. God had not forsaken him and his family. Despite the injustice and treachery that had placed Fallon aboard a ship that did nothing but sail from England to the colonies and back again, ten years was not a lifetime.

He would return to Connecticut; he would find his family again.

"Land ho!"

Taregan sat up as the shout spiraled down from above. Staring into the dim light of the hold, he tried to pinpoint the voice that had slashed his sleep like a knife. He and the others had done little but sleep during the four weeks of the voyage, for in slumber they could escape the tedious monotony and deprivations of captivity.

His eyes squinted into the darkness, but he could see no one standing, no one who had called out. Had he been dreaming?

"They've spotted land?" Hassun asked, lifting his head. He was stretched out like an old dog on the floor, a collection of skin and bones held together by a youthful determination to live.

"You heard it, too?"

"Yes." Hassun propped himself up on one elbow. "Are we finally to get off this cursed ship?"

"I don't know," Taregan said, struggling to throw off the lingering wisps of sleep that clouded his mind. "Surely we are, if we have reached land."

But though the footsteps on the deck above thundered at a fiercer pace than usual and the sailors' sea chanties contained a joyous note that had been absent the week before, the ship sailed on through two more days. Bound by fierce pride, the other captives refused to ask anything of the boy who brought food and water, but Taregan's curiosity finally defeated his dignity.

"Tell me," he said, startling the boy as he prepared to break off a hunk of corn bread to toss to Taregan, "what land do you see when you are up above?"

The boy's jaw worked in silent amazement; his eyes bugged like a gigged frog's. "You speak English?" he finally squeaked.

"Yes," Taregan answered, ignoring the boy's stunned expression. "Tell me, what land lies outside? And why has the ship not stopped?"

"We are sailing past a string of islands," the boy said, too dazed to refuse to answer. "The sailors call them the West Indies." He lifted a hand to count on his fingers. "Saint Kitts and Nevis, Antigua and Garbuda, and Dominica. Today we will sail past St. Lucia, and then Barbados. We will land at Barbados, Captain Daman says."

"Barbados?" Taregan echoed, aware that every Indian in the hold listened. "What sort of place is it?"

The boy backed away. "I don't know. I've never been there. The captain says only a few people live there, mostly English. A few Dutchmen. The island grows sugarcane."

"Sugarcane?" Hassun whispered. He lowered his voice and spoke in Algonquin. "Ask him what this is."

"What is sugarcane?" Taregan asked, smiling to put the boy at ease.

The boy shrugged slightly. "I don't know. But I heard the captain tell one of his men that the first planter began planting cane ten years ago, and the plantations need more slaves to work in the fields. That's why the captain chose to take you there."

Taregan stared past the boy toward the line of captives on the other side of the ship as he translated the news. Their faces remained impassive, like stone, but he could almost feel their thoughts. Indian men did not plant crops. Farming was women's work, unthinkable for a Pequot warrior, beyond the realm of imagination. These men ought to have died in the forest or on the battlefield with their bows and tomahawks in their hands, singing their death songs in a blaze of courage and honor. How could they work in the fields like women?

Taregan turned again to the boy, whose hands had tightened around the handle of the breadbasket he carried. "Tell no one we have spoken," he said, smiling out of pity for the skinny, scared child. "And I will pray that God will bless you for your help."

The boy nodded a scared-rabbit kind of thank-you, then broke off a chunk of bread, handed it to Taregan, and moved on.

▼▲▼▲▼ The seamen broke into loud cries of jubilation before the sun set, and Taregan knew that the ship prepared to dock at Barbados. Lying flat on his back in the dark hold, he heard the flap of the canvas sails as they lowered, the creak and strain of cordage no longer needed, the metallic clank and rumble of the anchor as it spun off the capstan and settled to the bottom of the sea. The ship stopped its back-and-forth, up-and-down movements and seemed to rock gently upon the water, shivering slightly as the wind blew over the surface of the harbor. The noise above slowed and then ceased. A roar of absolute silence filled the ship.

From where he lay, Hassun raised himself up and looked at Taregan. "I cannot believe we are here," he whispered, his eyes dark and deadly serious. "I was certain God would punish these evil English slavers by sending the ship to the bottom of the sea. We ought to be in heaven with the others. How can we serve as slaves in a foreign place?"

"How can we know what God wills?" Taregan asked, his voice heavy with uncertainty. "When we lived in the woods, how could we know that a mad wolf did not wait outside the camp to take our life? Or that a snowstorm would not descend from the mountains and paralyze us with its freezing breath?"

"My father taught me well; I was prepared for those things," Hassun answered, lying back on the floor. The chains at his wrists clinked as he folded his arms behind his head. "I have never feared the wolf or the storm or the enemy. But I have never been a slave."

"If your tribe had gone to war with the Mohegan," Taregan went on, searching for words of wisdom, "you might have been captured and enslaved."

"I would have escaped or died trying," Hassun answered, flushing to the roots of his dark hair. "The trees, the wind, the river would have led me home. But I do not know this wide sea. How am I to find my way in this place?"

"God is God everywhere," Taregan answered, clinging to truths his parents had taught him. "The sea is his, for he made it, and his hands formed the dry land. This land is his, Hassun, just as the land of the Pequot was."

Hassun did not answer for a long moment, then he laughed softly. "Do you really believe that?" he asked, a faint bite to his words. "Or do you speak words you *want* to believe?"

Taregan could not answer.

▼▲▼▲▼ Night passed, and morning brought with it the slow, stumbling footsteps of seamen who had spent the night on shore. The sailors' feet drummed overhead for a long interval, during which Taregan sat silently, waiting. Finally the trapdoor lifted, screeching in protest. Captain Daman descended into the hold, a circle of keys in one hand and a whip in the other. A half-dozen seamen followed him, bleary-eyed and unsteady on their feet, but armed with muskets and pistols. The sight of the weapons lifted the hair on Taregan's arms.

The captain broke the silence in the hold with a crack of his whip, and the captives turned slowly to give him their attention. "Get up, you lazy devil dogs!" Daman roared, emphatically cracking the whip again. "Today I am rid of the lot of ye, and by nightfall I'll be a rich man! So up, ye insolent creatures, rise and walk!"

Not a man moved; Pequot pride would not allow it. Daman's face distorted with fury, and an artery throbbed in his neck. "Why you—," he snarled, his hand gripping the whip again.

In an effort to set an example of cooperation, Taregan stood. To his great relief, Hassun followed. One by one, the others chose to obey, but not before the captain's lashing whip had stung at least eight prisoners. When the last man stood on his feet, the captain stopped pacing and pointed toward the companionway. "Up, the lot of ye," he cried, snapping his whip with one hand and pointing with the other. "Men, don't be afraid to shove the muzzle of a gun to their noses if 'twill keep them moving. I want the stinking barbarians off my ship in this very hour!"

Their chains clinking, the captives moved toward the companionway, a line of stale bodies moving toward the thin stream of light that poured through the opening above. Taregan winced as he saw the backs and buttocks of some of his fellow captives. The men had lain in one position for so long that their flesh had festered and suppurated. In at least half a dozen wounds he could see that maggots had already begun their vile work. He and Hassun, being younger and more flexible, had been able to move about enough to keep the blood circulating throughout their limbs, but many of his fellow prisoners were little more than walking dead.

After climbing two sets of stairs, Taregan blinked in the bright light of morning, momentarily blinded by the dazzling path of the sun on the quiet sea. The great blue bowl of sky above was broken only by the piercing rays of the hot sun, and a whining, harsh wind lifted the matted hair from his neck and tossed it into the face of the man behind him. The air seemed suddenly sweet and pure—a delicious, rare fragrance—and like a man who has been rescued from drowning, Taregan drank in deep gulps of it.

Like spiders in their webs, the seamen coiled into the rigging along the masts and watched as the deck filled with the cargo of Indian slaves. From a platform high on the center mast, the captain examined the group, then conferred with a man by his side. "Should we wash 'em off?" His voice rang over the deck. "They're totally filthy. Might be worth an extra sixpence per man if we give 'em a dunking."

"Some of 'em might drown," his mate pointed out. "Most are mighty weak and thin. And what if they swim away?"

"Where are they going to go?" the captain answered, a wicked smile curling on his lips. "To the sharks?" He shook his head, then climbed down the yielding ladder of ropes around the mast. "They'll have to stay dirty. I can't risk one of 'em panicking and drowning the whole string. Herd 'em down the plank toward the docks. The auctioneer's waiting, and there's a crowd gathering already."

Taregan wasn't sure what lay ahead, but he gritted his teeth and lifted his chin, hoping that Hassun and the others would take courage from his example.

▼▲▼▲▼ Dirk Christoffels set his bundles in his push-cart and tucked his broad hands into the belt at his waist, momentarily distracted by the sight of the slave auction at the docks. He knew the *Styx*, one of the cruelest ships ever to anchor at Hole Town. Six months before, he had agreed to take two of Captain Daman's castoffs, sick, spiritless men who were a liability on the auction block. Though Dirk's wife, Alida, had nursed them, both of them died.

Dirk snorted in disgust as the latest group of captives lined the wharf. A crowd of English and Dutch planters milled about the dock, many with their purses already out. They were desperate for hands to work their sprawling fields and anxious to prove this island a success.

A familiar face caught his eye, and Dirk frowned. The figure was broad and solid like his own, and the shock of golden-red hair was unmistakable in any crowd. "Hans!" Dirk shouted, waving. The golden head turned, and his brother smiled and waved a greeting in return, but did not move from his place.

Dirk returned his hand to his belt as his own smile faded. How could two men raised by the same parents be so different? Their mother had died when both boys were young; their father had passed away three years ago. As the eldest brother, with the lion's share of the inheritance, Hans had suggested that they sell their father's modest house in Rotterdam and move to the island of Barbados. "A man can own acres of land there," Hans had promised. "We can forget about this bloody war with Spain and these low-lying bogs. Opportunity lies in the New World, Brother!"

The idea appealed to Dirk, and so he and Alida gave notice to their landlord, packed up their few belongings and their daughter, then set sail with Hans for the island of Barbados. Hans purchased a huge estate of nearly two hundred acres; Dirk had been content to settle for ten acres of an adjoining site.

"Twenty pounds! Twenty pounds for that one!" Hans yelled, bidding now on a muscular man with dark skin and darker hair, but even from this distance Dirk could see the flame of defiance in the slave's eyes. He had often tried to tell Hans that slavery was a shame and immoral, but his older brother refused to listen. "Go away, little man, and leave me alone," he'd say, thrusting Dirk's concerns aside as easily as he'd put away memories of the wife he had married and buried after only a short marriage. "You are only jealous of my success. You and Alida will do well to plant one acre this year, while I have one hundred fifty ready to cut."

"Your lands do not concern me," Dirk protested, quietly wondering if some secret jealousy did fuel his convictions. But one look at these proud men—stripped of their clothing and dignity and thrust into irons for the world to poke and prod—convinced him that his opinions were right. Better that he and his wife and daughter sow and cut and weed every single plant with their own hands than to subject other human beings to this kind of humiliating torment.

A flurry of movement in the line of captives caught his attention, and he moved his head slightly to establish a better perspective. One prisoner, a boy probably not more than twelve years old, had apparently tried to break from the line only to catch the captain's whip across the face. The boy stood silent now, his high cheekbone cut by the bite of the whip, his eyes somber and downcast: the body language of sorrow. The youth behind him, probably fifteen or sixteen, lowered his head slightly and murmured something to the younger boy. At the sight of the second lad, Dirk drew in his breath. The simple fact that he dared to speak at all was remarkable, for despite their aloof and defiant attitudes, most prisoners on the auction block were as scared as children. This second lad was either extremely compassionate, unnaturally courageous, completely mad—or perhaps all three.

Fascinated, Dirk left his pushcart and moved closer. Was the slave scolding the boy? No. Though the young man spoke intensely, there was no trace of anger or ridicule in his face.

The bids flew fast and furious, and the line of captives moved steadily forward. Once the biggest and strongest captives had been sold, the auctioneer separated the younger men into small groups. Dirk watched as the young rebel and his companion mounted the auction block. The second slave lifted his head for the first time, and Dirk felt shocked by a sudden elusive thought he could not quite fathom.

Despite the tanned skin and flowing brown hair, the young man's face bore a European stamp, complete with startlingly blue eyes. How had he come to join these enslaved prisoners of war? And what was his relationship with the younger boy?

Scarcely meaning to, Dirk insinuated himself through the crowd until he stood at Hans's side. "If you need other slaves," he said, pretending offhanded indifference, "buy this pair. I think they will make good workers."

"Those two?" Hans said, barely glancing up. He grinned at his brother. "See that cut on the boy's cheek? He's a trouble-maker, that one, and the last thing I need on my plantation is trouble. *Nee,* Brother, you are as wrong in this as you are in everything else."

"Please, Hans," Dirk pleaded, an unexpected passion overcoming his logic. "You must buy them. I will repay you if I am wrong."

"This from a man who abhors slavery?" Hans lifted his hands in feigned horror. "Forgive me, but have the oceans run dry? Or mayhap my ears deceive me."

"Please," Dirk said, placing his hand on his brother's arm. "The older youth has blue eyes. Don't you find that strange?"

"He's a freak or an illegitimate, which can only mean more trouble," Hans grumbled, but he did look toward the boys again.

The bidding had slowed since the strongest men had been purchased, and the auctioneer caught sight of Hans's upturned face. "Master Christoffels, surely you could use two strong young men?" he called, an edge of desperation in his voice. "They are small, they won't eat much."

"All right," Hans muttered, waving a hand. "Two shillings for the pair, but not a farthing more."

"Done!" the auctioneer called, slamming one hand down upon the other with a tremendous slap.

"I hope you realize the trouble these two will bring me," Hans muttered, turning to Dirk. "A rebellious boy and a freak. If they cause me any problems at all, I'm sending them to you. You'll take them and repay my two shillings whether or not slavery offends your delicate conscience."

"*Nee*, I'll not be working slaves," Dirk insisted, his eyes following the pair of prisoners as they were led off the platform. "I think you'll soon be thanking me, Hans."

▼▲▼▲ As Taregan followed Hassun off the wooden platform, the auctioneer faced the knot of waiting captives and rudely attempted to pantomime planting and cutting, apparently trying to describe what would be expected of them. Taregan bit back angry words, disgusted that these men assumed that Indians had the mental capacity of three-year-olds. Ignoring the auctioneer, he thrust his arms toward a sailor so the ship's chains could be removed. Once the filthy, dirt-encrusted shackles had been unthreaded and unlocked, another man slipped a noose over his head, then thrust Taregan's hands behind his back and his wrists through two loops. If he applied resistance to his bonds, the noose around his neck cut off his breath.

The Indians had used such a snare on their own prisoners and slaves. Taregan recognized the irony in the situation and threw Hassun a grim smile.

Their new master, a tall, broad man with hair the color of a summer sunset, approached to survey the twenty slaves he had just added to his estate. Apparently well satisfied, he paid the purchase price from a bulging money bag at his belt, then took the end of a rope looped around the neck of the first captive in line. Once again Taregan found himself part of a human chain and bound to a master he did not know.

This place was too bright, he thought, too bare and flat, too hot. Though of certain the Connecticut River valley had cooled with the breath of autumn, a hot dry wind blew across this island, sucking the moisture from his body as if it intended to dry his skin like one of the pelts Gilda had tanned in the warmth of the sun. Heat covered the island like a blanket, and the clear blue sky offered no hope of shade or comfort.

From the docks Taregan and the others followed the single street through a sizeable village, then walked along the beach for some time. The sand was white and sharp beneath Taregan's feet, a world away from the dark, moist earth of his valley home. Anger rose like a festering boil within his soul, prideful outrage that he should be in this place, in this condition. Against his will and through no fault or crime of his own he had been cast far from his home, his friends, the girl he loved, the people he called family. His father had been cut off from the living, his people dispossessed and murdered, his mother forced to labor for an enemy whose deeds shamed the God they claimed to serve. . . .

Holy God! His thoughts rose above the earth as his feet unwillingly followed the red-haired man who had just purchased his body but could never own his spirit. *Why have you allowed this to happen? Hassun thought you would sink the ship in the sea to avenge our loved ones and punish our enemies, and yet the wicked prosper and grow rich and mock the name of the Pequot, who are no more. How can you allow such men to prosper? Why does my brother walk free while I am trussed like an animal? He began the trouble, he ran away when our mother forbade him, he followed the evil English into war, he lured our father from the safety of our home to his death. My brother prospers with the English and ignores the mother who gave him life! He thinks nothing of you, so why do you not strike fear into his heart? I would give him something to fear! He is flesh of my flesh, bone of my bone, and yet I could strike him down with pleasure. I could watch him die and know that his death balances the evil he has brought upon us, even this sin of slavery.*

An eerie, whining sound rent the air as they walked, and from his place in line Taregan recognized a Pequot death song. Indian warriors only sang that song when death crooked its bony finger at them. Apparently one of the warriors behind him sang now to show that he was not afraid, that he would face death this day with honor and pride. Which one was it, Taregan wondered, not turning around. And how did he know that death approached?

The wail blended into the blustery afternoon like the chilly disquiet of a wolf howling before a full moon. From the innermost part of his soul, Taregan's heart lifted and joined in the defiant song.

Boldly, faithfully, successfully. Those were the words inscribed upon the ring that still nestled in the dimpled cup of his ear. Recalling his mother as she gave him the ring, Taregan straightened.

So be it. If this was his fate, he would boldly make his way toward whatever God had in store for him on Barbados. He would faithfully endeavor to leave the island, and he would, God willing, successfully confront and punish Daniel for the evil his actions had brought to their family—and to a nation of people.

For the better part of an hour they walked. Once Taregan's eyes had adjusted to the starkly bright sunlight of the tropics, he stared with amazement at the miles of white sand lining the shore while his mind curled lovingly around the thought of cool, shorter days at home. The steady wind shrilling across the island did little to dispel the sticky heat. Instead it blew sand into his eyes and hair and between his teeth. Strange-looking, nearly leaf-less trees bordered the ivory beach, and occasionally Taregan passed sunburnt, barefoot Europeans who stood at the water's edge with cane poles in their hands and baskets of fresh fish on their backs.

Of certain he had journeyed to the other side of the earth. Everything in this place gleamed with heat, even the eyes of passersby glimmered with bright ambition. For what? Within a matter of hours Taregan realized that the islanders' zeal focused on the offshore fields where gold grew in the form of sugarcane.

The group of newly purchased slaves straggled up the crest of a hill, and Taregan caught his breath as he reached the summit. Gone were the sparse vegetation and scrubby grasses that had fringed the beach; before him stretched fields of tall, dense cane. The stately plant looked to be more than twice the height of a man, and the uppermost portions of each bore a large, feathery plume, like the feathers warriors tied on their war clubs.

Hans Christoffels peeled himself away from the head of the line and stood in the center of the path, spreading his hand toward the green fields. "Take a good look there, my fine lads," he called in a deep, tobacco-roughened voice. "The cane. A sweeter, more valuable crop cannot be found. We grow it everywhere on Barbados, and I grow more than any man on the island."

"What is he saying?" Hassun murmured, unable to understand the man's heavily accented English.

"It is sugarcane," Taregan whispered, translating the unfamiliar word as best he could. "The sweet white sand the English brought to your village—it comes from those green stalks."

Hassun screwed up his face as though he would laugh, but Taregan cast him a warning glance. Their master paused and searched the line to discover who had spoken. Taregan lowered his head and hoped that Hassun would have sense enough to do the same thing.

They walked on in the sweltering heat, traversing acre after acre of the tall thick grasses, and soon came to a small rise crowned by a solidly built stone structure with a thatched roof. A longer, larger wooden building stood at the bottom of the hill like a poor relative. "That is my home," Christoffels said, pointing offhandedly to the stone house. "You will sleep over there."

He gestured toward the wooden shack, which seemed to squat upon the hot sands. A single low doorway led into the shelter, but Taregan was pleased to see that there was no door, no barred window, no evidence of chains. Apparently the remote location of the plantation and the isolation of the island itself were sufficient barriers to prevent a slave's escape. The others must have followed his thoughts, for they murmured among themselves in a flurry of Indian words.

Christoffels held up his hand for silence, then thrust his arms behind his back and began to pace before his new slaves. "I'm a fair master, but a hard one," he said, apparently not caring that the Indians understood very little of what he said. "You will work hard every day, for my fields are ready to be harvested. As long as you do not shirk your labors, you will eat and be satisfied. This house is yours," he pointed to the wooden shed, then jerked his thumb toward the taller stone building, "and that one is mine. Be sure that you understand the difference."

He paused, casting an eagle eye over the group as if he could discern with one glance whether rebellion resided in the soul of any man. "I have bought you with a great price, and you are mine. You will work for me; I will provide for you. If you have a problem, come to me. If I have a problem with your work, I will tell you. Anyone who disobeys my orders will be whipped. Anyone who disobeys twice will be returned to the auction block and sold to a master far less understanding than I."

His gaze rested for a moment on the face of each man. "If there are no questions, I will release you now. You are to go to the shore and wash yourselves, for you all stink. And tomorrow morning you will rise with the sun and work in the place I will show you." He gave them a slow, superior smile. "There is no way to run, nowhere to hide. This is a small island, only one hundred sixty-six square miles, and I know the people who own each and every bit of land. If you leave my land, it will not go well with you when you are returned."

A dim ripple moved across the back of Taregan's mind, and he cautiously lifted his head.

"What?" the master barked, his eyes expressing more challenge than curiosity.

"Have you no other slaves?" Taregan asked, looking toward the slave house. "Are we all—"

"You are all I have now," Hans answered, sniffing in arrogance. "And 'tis good you speak English—I was beginning to fear you were all as dumb as rocks. A fever claimed every slave I owned a few weeks ago, so tell your friends here to watch themselves, or God will strike them, too."

He nodded with satisfaction when no one else spoke or moved. "Good. As I cut your bonds, you are free to wash in the sea. Do not tarry there, but come back and make yourselves places in the slave house."

▼▲▼▲▼ "I hate him," Hassun said in Algonquin, staring at the gentle lap of waves kissing the shore. Barefoot, he stood in the shallows, his hands and ankles free for the first time in weeks, and yet he made no move to wade deeper into the water. None of the men did; the salt sea was a foreign entity to be feared. The pagan Pequot believed that the rivers, the land, and the wind possessed spirits that had to be placated before one could live in peace, and now their valiant hearts quivered before the spirit of the great salt sea.

Taregan inched a toe into the wavewash. Warm water tingled his skin, and he waded in to his ankles, hoping to show by example that the water was not an evil force. "See, brothers," he called, wading farther as the tide tugged at him. "This water is a cousin of the Connecticut. Both waters are creations of the Great Spirit and both are useful to us."

A few stone faces turned his way, but no one moved toward the water.

"Come, Hassun," Taregan taunted. "Is the sachem's son afraid of water with salt in it? I am not dissolved by its touch, and the dirt of the slave ship is wiped away." He gingerly moved into waist-deep water, inching forward lest the sandy bottom drop from beneath him. But the smooth and rippled floor under his feet was as steady as the surf roaring a few feet behind him.

Never one to be left behind, Hassun thrust out his lower lip and splashed forward. "I am not afraid," he said, grimacing as the salty water washed over his wrists and the abrasions left by the metal shackles. "Even though the water bites."

"It stings like an ant," Taregan admitted, speaking loudly enough for the others to hear, "but my mother said that seawater heals many ailments. It is God's gift to us, and it is good of our master to let us bathe in it."

One by one, the others moved with glacial slowness into the salty water. One or two of the older men, bewildered by the crashing waves, refused to go farther than waist deep, but most of the others followed Taregan's example and learned to submerge themselves as the waves crashed overhead. After a lifetime on the Connecticut River, all of the Indians were expert swimmers, but few had any experience with surf or the strong pull of the retreating ocean current.

As the sun slipped toward the western horizon, the men began to climb out of the water, stretching the stiffness from their shoulders and shaking their limbs dry. Taregan followed, then paused at the edge of the beach. The wave-washed sand before him was shining and smooth as an ice-covered pond. Every square of earth told a story, his father had taught him, and a tracker reading this bit of beach would have seen only advancing footprints, as if a tribe of men had walked out of the ocean to set foot on the island for the first time.

Could God wipe memories from his heart as cleanly? Could he begin life again in this strange place? He did not want to, but for the moment it seemed as though God demanded it.

"Come," Hassun said, climbing rapidly through the sand toward their new home. "The sun sinks, and I do not want to be out here after dark. I have heard that fearsome creatures live in the sea."

Nodding in agreement, Taregan followed.

▼▲▼▲▼ Weeks later, Taregan recalled that day as the first of his new life. Now he and his companions rose with the sun each morning and dressed in lightweight cotton breeches. They ate a quick breakfast of corn bread and beans, then ran to the beach for a fast swim. By the time Hans Christoffels came out of his house an hour after sunrise, they were expected to be waiting and ready in the clearing before the house. Anyone not in the clearing on time felt the lash of the master's whip.

They were a crew of nineteen (the warrior who sang his death song died in his sleep that first night), and they worked the cane in sections, rotating from one acre to another until the entire plantation had been planted, tended, or harvested. The rich, moist soil of Barbados grew cane as easily as summer grass, and the slaves gathered seedlings from the tassels of mature plants and planted them in tightly packed rows. Taregan was grateful to learn that the seedlings would not have to be replanted for several years; cane was a perennial grass that could be propagated from the fertile eyes of stalks growing above the soil line.

Along with the planting of new fields, Taregan and his fellows were expected to keep weeds from the already growing cane. Weeding was a loathsome job, for the cane was alive with rats, wasps, cockroaches, spiders, flies, and other biting insects he had never seen before. Taregan discovered that it was almost impossible to keep ants from stinging his legs while he struggled to weed and swat wasps at the same time. And if a rat chanced to scamper out and bite his foot, he had no room to maneuver in the narrow furrows where the cane grew.

Harvesting was accomplished year-round and required special vigilance on the master's part. After marking a field for harvest, Hans Christoffels would send for his brother, who unwillingly kept a musket leveled at the slaves as Hans handed each man a machete for cutting. When each slave was properly armed with his tool, Hans would pick up his musket and help his brother escort them to the chosen field. While the slaves hacked, slashed, cut, and stacked in an unending rhythm, the two men kept their eyes trained and their muskets ready in case any slave dared to consider insurrection.

The dense, junglelike growth of mature cane was cut by hand at ground level and stripped of leaves and the plumelike top while in the field. The exercise worked every muscle in the slaves' bodies: They bent to slash the cane, straightened to pull it from the earth, chopped the feathery plumes from the top, dropped the plumes to one side and the cane to the other, then moved on to the next plant, where the cycle began again.

While weeding was annoying work, cutting was a physical marathon that demanded every ounce of energy a man could give. After a day of cutting in the fields, Taregan's arms, legs, back, and ribs ached from exertion while his hands, feet, and face swelled from blisters, insect bites, and cuts. When the cutting was done, Dirk Christoffels again held the musket on the slaves while Hans collected the machetes. The harvest was hurried to the mill at Hole Town, where the cane passed through sets of large, heavy rollers that extracted the sugar. The raw sugar was then exported to European refineries on huge ships much like the one that had brought the Pequots to the island.

The work and their lives revolved around the cane. Hans Christoffels was apparently not a religious man, for he did not recognize the Sabbath for his slaves' sake or his own. According to the unwritten law of Master Christoffels, God made the first day of the week for planting, the second for weeding, the third for cutting, the fourth for hauling, the fifth for propagating, the sixth for trimming, and the seventh for plowing. His endless routine and rotation did not vary from week to week or season to season, and Taregan's memories of his other life grew faint as the days blurred into weeks, the weeks into months.

Taregan's muscles toughened into sinewy cords along his arms and legs; his back bronzed under the relentless rays of the tropical sun. In order to escape the heat, he and several other Pequots cut their hair, ignoring centuries of tradition. After a few months, his bare feet toughened so that he could not feel even the blistering hot sand beneath them. His eyes narrowed into a habitual squint due to the sun's brightness; lines of exhaustion creased his forehead and the corners of his eyes.

Under Hans Christoffels' unyielding hand Taregan became a man. The demands of the cane shaped and molded him; he moved with a restrained, slimly muscled grace he would not have known had he remained in Connecticut. As he matured, an idea slowly germinated within him. Mayhap this new strength and stamina would be required to free his mother from whatever bondage held her. Of certain he would need vigorous force to defeat Garvin Black—and Daniel.

With every day that passed, Taregan found comfort in the thought that he had endured a day he would not have to live again. God would soon bring him home to Connecticut and his loved ones, and the Almighty had a planned purpose for the pain of slavery and the resulting strength he had developed.

That possibility stood in front of each morning, giving him courage to face the day.

Thus did the Lord scatter his enemies with his strong arm! The
Pequots now became a prey to all Indians. Happy were they that
could bring in their heads to the English, of which there came
almost daily to Windsor or Hartford. But the Pequots growing
weary hereof, sent some of the chiefs that survived to mediate
with the English, offering that if they might but enjoy their lives,
they would become English vassals, to dispose of them as they
pleased. Which was granted them. The Pequots being
demanded, how many of them were then living? Answered,
about one hundred and eighty, or two hundred. There were then
given to Uncas, sachem of the Mohegans, eighty; to
Myantonimo, sachem of the Narragansetts, eighty, and to
Nynigrett, twenty, when he should satisfy for a mare of Edward
Pomroye's killed by his men.

The Pequots were then bound by covenant that none should
inhabit their native country, nor should any of them be called
Pequots any more, but Mohegans and Narragansetts for ever.

John Mason

▼▲▼▲▼ In September 1638, the Pequot War formally
ended when the remaining sachems signed the Treaty of Hartford, or the Tripartite Treaty, which declared the Pequot nation
officially dissolved. Thus did the Connecticut English conclude
their attempt at total genocide. With one aboriginal nation exterminated and the other two conquered and cooperative, the
English spread their houses and farmlands far beyond the confines of the three principal river villages. English families migrat-

ing south from Boston and the Massachusetts colony settled in
tents, dug caves into the hillsides, and took over abandoned
Pequot shelters.

Looking across the river from the dock at Hartford, Daniel
could see rows and rows of sod houses that seemed to have
sprung up overnight. Now that the Pequot were no longer a
threat, land-hungry colonists poured into the Connecticut colony.
A sense of the temporary seemed to hang around these small settlements of sod houses and wooden hovels; most had been hastily erected by men hoping to find furs or gold in the unexplored
forest along the river. The men came southward, deposited their
wives and children under some sort of shelter, then sauntered
forth into the woods, eager to earn a living with their traps and
muskets.

The influx of newcomers had been good for business. With a
steady and abundant income, Garvin built a proper wooden
house next to the trading post. Daniel slept in the cozy loft attic,
while Garvin made his bed near the huge stone fireplace that
dominated the northern wall. Garvin demanded that a fire burn
continually during the winter months. "I nearly froze as a child
in England," he often said, "for we had a pitiful fireplace and no
money for wood. As God is my witness, Daniel boy, I'll not willingly be cold again."

As time passed, the village on the river began to resemble
other prosperous colonies. The new arrivals moved into the surrounding countryside and fenced their gardens to keep livestock
and wild animals out. No longer could a man step outside his
gate and wander wherever he chose. The split-rail zigzag fences
protecting fields of parsnips, turnips, onions, peas, cabbage, and
carrots filled what had once been open forest. Often Daniel heard
visiting Indians complain about the sprawling barricades, but
there was no way the colonists could guard their crops without
them.

"A proper fence has to be pig-tight, horse-high, and bull-
strong," Daniel told a newcomer who had asked how to build a
barrier around his crops. "Let your animals roam in the woods.

No harm will come to 'em now that most of the savages have moved on."

The bear, deer, and beaver, which had abundantly populated the woods, moved deeper into the forest as the colonists' farm animals thrived in the area near Hartford. The colonists brought pigs, chickens, and goats from England, and hogs quickly became the staple meat of the colony. Wolves killed the domesticated pigs, but the tough boars could easily defend their sows.

Business at the trading post expanded beyond furs and staple goods to include livestock as well. Sheep, horses, and cattle arrived from England with the pigs and chickens, but not all animals fared well. Though valued for their milk and cheese, goats could destroy a garden in a matter of minutes. Sheep gave wool, but demanded grassy meadows and proved to be easy prey for wolves. Horses, Daniel tried to tell his new patrons, were not of much use, for few roads existed and the stout fences prevented convenient travel through the area. Most people either traveled by boat on the river or hiked along the narrow Indian trails.

Cattle and swine, though, were welcomed, and the tobacco ships that anchored downriver often ventured as far north as Hartford to set in supplies of meat and other goods. Using techniques Fallon had taught him, Daniel soon developed one of the most robust swine herds in the area. He once joked with the Widow Butler that he could use every part of a hog but the squeal. After butchering, the hog's intestines became sausage skins, the bladder held lard, the long hair from the tail was wrapped and used to sew buckskins. Salted-down meat from four good-sized hogs could fill a family's pork barrel and carry them through the winter.

As time passed, Daniel tried to put thoughts of his family and that other, more primitive life behind him. He wore the fine clothes of an English gentleman to church on Sunday, he spoke with the same lilting accent as the newcomers, he began to think like an Englishman. Involuntarily he began to speak of "our King Charles" and "our navy ships." An unconscious nationalism bloomed in his heart, blocking out thoughts of the past.

One Sunday the minister preached on belonging to the family of God, and Daniel thought deeply about the message as he walked home. Before, in the land of the savages, he had belonged only to his family. This feeling of loyalty to a far greater community frightened him somewhat—what would he be called to give for England if war came again? Could a country fairly demand and expect a man's life? A new thought whipped into his mind: Was it this sort of nationalism that had inspired his mother and brother to align themselves with the Pequot? If only their hearts had led them to the victorious side!

He shrugged, dismissing the thought, and thrust his hands behind his back as he walked home. Up ahead lay the small house where Dena lived with his mother, and, as was his habit, Daniel kept his head down and his thoughts directed elsewhere as he walked past the place. Dena never came to the trading post, and he wondered if she hated him so much that she could not bear to look upon his face. He had seen his mother only twice since she moved into the village house, and both times she had been carried in the hulking arms of Colton Bramwell.

He had been wholly taken aback when the Widow Butler told him that Dena lived with an invalid who was unable to walk. Why hadn't his mother listened to him? He had offered to take her away from the jail before she had been injured, but she had cast him off.

Stirred by an urgent need to be understood, he told the story to Sabrina Butler one evening at dinner after Garvin had fallen asleep by the fire. She listened with tears of compassion in her eyes, then ran her hand through his hair and murmured, "Poor Daniel."

His mother had abandoned him. He sternly told himself that he was right to abandon her as well.

In the wet season of 1642, Taregan realized that he had passed
his twentieth birthday and his fifth year of captivity. The hunger
to leave Barbados still gnawed in his heart, but his earnest
dreams had been defeated by common sense and the harsh, hot
light of reality. His loved ones were no more real than the wind—
they were memories, forever part of the sky and out of reach. But
thoughts of Dena were locked into his mind; fantasies of their
life together made his situation bearable.

In the dignified aloofness of warriors, each of Hans
Christoffels' slaves kept his private thoughts to himself. The captives lived and worked together, each man exorcising his personal demons through difficult toil and nighttime sweats. Life
was a disciplined routine, tedious but predictable.

Until Hans Christoffels ventured again to the slave market.
The twenty men he brought home this time were also Indians,
prisoners of war from an uprising against a different English settlement. Watching from the doorway of the slave house, Taregan
and his companions looked warily from one to the other as the
master paced before the newcomers and delivered his welcoming lecture. These men, still stiff and filthy from their voyage,
wore the tattoos of Mohegan.

Taregan felt his stomach knot at the sight of the Mohegan
markings and the stiff roaches of their hair. This tribe and their
sachem, Uncas, had betrayed the Pequot to the English! Without
their cooperation the English could never have waged war
against the fiercest tribe in the land.

Emotions Taregan had thought dead boiled in his soul. These
men deserved slavery, for they were traitors! And yet Hans

Christoffels would know nothing of this, could never understand the animosity between the two tribes. He had not watched
as Uncas murdered Sooleawa or heard Dena's agonized
screams. . . .

But these men were not Uncas, and the Mohegan were a large
nation with many sachems. It was possible that these men had
had nothing at all to do with the English war upon the Pequot.

Christoffels told the Mohegans to bathe in the sea, and they
turned with the same hesitancy Taregan and his company had
displayed. They had not looked into the longhouse that would
be their new home; they had no idea what awaited them on their
return. Indeed, Taregan thought, the men in the slave house with
him scarcely looked like Pequots anymore, for their leathers,
their hair, their war paint were gone. But they were still warriors,
and they would still hear the blood of their dead crying out for
vengeance.

Hassun was breathing heavily behind Taregan. "So the
English have finally turned on the Mohegan," he said, following
the movements of the captives on their way to the beach. "I wondered how long it would take. Soon they will rid the valley of
Mohegan, and then the Narragansetts. Uncas did not know that
he held a viper to his breast when he marched with Captain
Mason to invade Mystic and murder my father."

"These men are enemies of the English," Taregan answered,
turning from the window. He crossed his arms and leaned
against the wall. "They may not be enemies of ours."

"A tribe at war with the English is not always at peace with
our people," one of the older warriors spoke up. "But as for me, I
am at peace with the Mohegan. An Englishman and his iron rod
killed my father and brother. I will not cause strife in this place."

"Nor will I," echoed another man. Taregan looked around the
circle. The two warriors who had spoken wore the look of men
who have learned through suffering. Taregan knew in his heart
that their words were wise.

"But my heart," Hassun said, pounding his chest with his fist,
"cannot forget that my mother and sister were pulled from their

safe hiding place and presented to Uncas by a Mohegan warrior. That sachem murdered my mother. I cannot live in peace with Mohegan."

"Neither can I," another man answered, whirling in the center of the room. He lifted an arm hardened with layers of muscles, the triumphant salute of a warrior. "Uncas and his men killed my wife and children. I will not forget."

"Tell your heart to be silent," another man enjoined. "It may rage, but it must be still while you wear the bonds of the master. Will wrath bring back your wife and children? What good will anger do you in this place? What peace will revenge bring when you cannot find your way home?"

"These Mohegans may have lived far from Pequot lands," Taregan pointed out.

"And yet they may have been among those who raided our village," Hassun answered, a vicious gleam in his eye. "Perhaps one of these very men thrust me into his canoe and carried me away from my home."

Hassun paused and stared at the others, his eyes bold, black, and defiant. *What a sachem he would have been,* Taregan thought. *And yet the days of Pequot sachems are past, the tribe wiped from the face of the river valley as cleanly as our footprints were erased from the sand on the beach. Can our bitterness and anger be wiped away, too?*

"I would rather die tomorrow than work alongside the Mohegan," Hassun proclaimed, lifting his fist. "I would suffer a thousand blows from the master's whip rather than share my house, my food, or my strength. And any of you who are warriors, who follow the Pequot path and would carry forth our honor, must feel the same way."

"But God would have us submit to those who have the rule over us," Taregan reminded Hassun. "Sit, be quiet. Let your heart calm down."

"Would you submit to a man who entered your house and threatened to remove your head from your shoulders? No, Taregan, you would not. And yet you would allow the master to bring murderers into our lives. It is not to be borne!"

"If you must hate someone," Taregan answered, standing, "hate the man who brought the English to us! Hate Garvin Black or Captain Mason! Hate the court that declared war on our people!"

For the first time, Taregan sensed division in the group. Hassun's impassioned speech had roused the slumbering nationalism in the exhausted, beaten men, and a spark of pride burned brightly in their eyes.

Another man stood, a ragged battle scar upon his chest. "A Mohegan war club marked me here," he said, running his hand over the knobby scar. "And I will put one of these marks on the chest of any Mohegan who tries to walk in my shadow. He shall not come near me."

"I hear you!" another man shouted, springing to his feet with more energy than he had displayed in months. Suddenly a river of enthusiasm and wrath poured forth, and Taregan forgot for a moment that he sat in the slave quarters of a Barbados plantation. He could have been sitting in the wigwam of a war chief, surrounded by the tribe's bravest and fiercest warriors. One man grabbed a stalk of sugarcane and beat it against a beam in the building, the ancient gesture of striking the war pole, and others wrested the stalk from him and beat the beam, too, until the stalk was a withered, stringy mass of fibrous pulp.

Hassun led the war dance, singing and shouting with all his might, and Taregan knew that the younger man had been waiting, living, for this moment. His future as a mighty warrior had been cut short when the English intervened, but on this night, and mayhap one day soon, he would prove himself.

The traditions, the heritage, ran deep.

Vengeance would run its course.

And there was little Taregan could do about it.

Hans Christoffels

For thy violence against thy brother . . .
shame shall cover thee. . . . In the day that thou
stoodest on the other side, in the day that the
strangers carried away captive his forces. . . .
Thou shouldest not have looked on the day of thy
brother in the day that he became a stranger;
neither shouldest thou have rejoiced over . . .
the day of their destruction; neither shouldest
thou have spoken proudly in the day of distress.

Obadiah 1:10-12

Dena began each morning with a quiet prayer of thanksgiving for Colton Bramwell and his promise to Taregan. The small and sturdy English house Colton had built for her and Gilda was more comfortable than Dena could have imagined possible. The house was far away from the village green, but mud sealed the cracks between the wooden timbers and a bark roof kept the women dry and warm. The floor was simple planking, the interior walls cased with timber, the doorway low so that an intruder would be vulnerable as he stooped to enter. The modest one-room structure had no closets and was furnished only with two beds and a board, but Gilda told Dena that a small house could hold as much happiness as a big one.

At first Dena had felt guilty for accepting Colton's generous provision of freedom and a home. When she protested that he needed to save his money for his own future, he answered that he had no wife, no children, no parents. He yearned to learn hunting and trapping, he told her, and would appreciate having a home to come to when bad weather set in. He did not take to the woods naturally, Dena observed one day as she plucked porcupine quills from his hands, and he often made silly mistakes any Indian child could have avoided. But he was unselfish, kind, and gentle, and he spent most of his days and nights in the woods, eventually sharpening his skills enough to keep meat on the women's table and furs upon their beds.

As time passed, the threesome formed an interdependent circle. The women offered Colton a sense of family and the nurturing softness every man needs; Colton provided them with protection and a voice in village affairs. Dena fed and cared for

Gilda; the older woman schooled Dena in the English language and taught her how to behave in the structured society in which they found themselves. The villagers did not know exactly what to make of the odd arrangement. Although he visited every time he came to town, he never stayed the night. And since the three lived simple lives and kept to themselves, the citizens of Hartford were content to leave them alone.

Dena glanced outside her window. Snow blew across the road, moving snakelike in long, thin lines, piling up against the edge of the rail fencing bordering her house. The sight stirred shadowy memories of her family's wigwam where, on winter days, she and her parents and siblings would gather with the dogs around the fire. So much warmth had filled that home, so much life! The ache she felt over the people she had lost never really left her.

"Has Colton brought anything new?" Gilda's voice brought Dena back to the present.

Dena glanced toward the bed of furs where Gilda spent her days and nights. "A buck, last night. I have quartered the meat and will work on the hide later this morning. It was a fine animal."

"Taregan once brought me an enormous buck." Gilda's eyes misted as she visited the memory. "He bore it home on his shoulders, struggling under its weight. I can still see him, trying so hard to be a man like his father. . . ."

Dena said nothing, but turned to the stewpot over the fire. She had fond memories of Taregan, too, childhood remembrances of him in the woods, in the fields, climbing trees to impress her. Even now, as she wandered in the bare winter forest to gather wood, she often expected to see him peering at her from behind a tree or feel the sudden pressure of his hand upon her shoulder. The woods had once been full of his presence; now they mocked her with emptiness.

She dipped her wooden spoon into the pot and stirred. Such bright memories were sharp enough to pierce her heart, and she had learned to suppress them. Better to lock them away than be cut by their painful edges.

"I can see that you think of him, too," Gilda murmured from her bed.

Dena forced a smile. "Sometimes."

"When you see Daniel?" Gilda's fingers moved restlessly over the blanket that covered her. "I have longed to see Daniel, but I cannot bring myself to ask Colton to carry me to the trading post. I am afraid of the man he has become."

"I have seen him a few times," Dena said, her voice sharper than she'd intended. She took a deep breath to soften her tone. "Sunday I saw him walking to the church with Master Black. He is not much changed." In truth, he had become thoroughly English and probably as unscrupulous as Garvin Black. Dena had caught glimpses of him in the inn as he treated hunters to dinner so he could cheat them later. She had watched him at the river, smiling at the sachems he would make drunk with whiskey. She had seen him gaze hungrily at English girls who walked along the city streets and kept their eyes modestly downcast. She had tried to avoid looking for him. She wanted to think of him as just one of hundreds of men who lived and worked near Hartford, but every time his profile moved across a crowd she was drawn to it, fascinated by the impulsive thought that Taregan might have returned . . . but always, it was only Daniel.

"Fret not for him," Dena finished, forcing a smile. "I hear Daniel is a prosperous man."

"I cannot help but think of him," Gilda answered, her voice dropping to a whisper. "That is why I pray for Taregan to return. They are of the same flesh; only Taregan can reach Daniel. I know what he has become, Dena. I see it on your face when you mention his name." She paused, and when she continued her voice was husky and as golden and warm as a summer day. "And yet, Daniel is my son, and I love him no less than Taregan. But I cannot reach him. Taregan must come home."

Clenching her hand, Dena turned her head so Gilda could not see the storm of anger that broke on her face. She had seen the

fate of the Pequot slaves who remained in Connecticut, and few
survived the harsh treatment they received at the hands of the
victorious army. After five years of slavery, Taregan had to be
dead. He was not likely to find a compassionate Colton
Bramwell to redeem him from slavery.

A soft rattling sound cut through the silence of the house, and
Dena knew that Gilda had fallen asleep. Though the older
woman had not yet lived forty summers, the paralysis had aged
her ten years and weakened her hold on life. Dena straightened
and knotted her hair at the base of her neck. The war and its subsequent hardships had aged them all. Though only nineteen, she
felt as though she had lived two lifetimes.

A frigid wind blew in through a stubborn chink in the
wooden walls. She lifted another fur from the floor and tucked it
around Gilda's thin shoulders.

▼▲▼▲▼ An hour later, Colton's familiar rhythmic
knock sounded at the door.

"Come in."

He entered with a great deal of blustering and foot stomping,
but Dena lifted a warning hand and pointed silently toward
Gilda's sleeping form. Colton grimaced, frowning at his own
clumsiness, then tiptoed to the board and lay the bundle in his
arms on the table.

"I've been fishing this morning," he said, his voice a low whisper. "Caught enough for a decent stew for tonight and tomorrow. If you smoke the venison, it'll keep for later."

"Thank you, I'll do that," Dena said, reaching for a knife hanging from a peg above the stone fireplace. She unwrapped the
buckskin and admired the sleek silvery form of the large fish.
With one swift movement she brought the knife down, severing
the head, then paused to give Colton a smile. "Can I get you
something?"

"No," he said, sinking onto a stool by the board. "Just let me sit and rest. The winds are rising. We may be snowed in before long."

"I hope this winter isn't as hard as last year's," Dena answered, tossing the fish head into the fire. "So much snow! Gilda and I thought spring would never come."

"Neither did I," Colton remarked absently, studying his hands.

They sat in companionable silence for a long time as Dena filleted the fish, but she was aware of his eyes upon her. "Last week I worked outside, clearing the garden, when two ladies walked past," she said, giving him a sidelong glance. "They were newcomers to the village, and they asked how my brother was. I was surprised, never dreaming that they would know about Hassun, and then I realized they were asking about you."

Something flickered far back in his eyes, and Dena suddenly wished she hadn't spoken.

"They think we are brother and sister?"

"Yes," she said, feeling the burn of a blush upon her cheek. "It is an obvious assumption, since everyone knows you visit and care for us." She shook her head. "I don't even think they realized that I am Pequot." She whispered the last word as if it were obscene.

"You are a beautiful young woman," Colton said quickly. "I am sure that is all they see. And I suppose it is good they think we are family. In a way, we are."

"Mayhap," she answered, chopping the fillets into bite-sized chunks. She worked in silence for another moment, then swept the hunks of fish into the kettle over the fire.

"Are you well? Is there anything you need?" Colton asked, looking up. The power of his gaze made her uncomfortable, and she turned away, pretending to check on Gilda.

"I am fine," she said, her back to him. "We are warm, we are fed, and Gilda seems stronger. . . ."

They both knew this last statement was untrue, but Colton nodded as she turned again, a deep and personal interest radiating from the depths of his eyes. "I am glad that Gilda sleeps," he said, lowering his voice as if the mention of her name would wake her. "I have been wanting to speak privately with you for some time."

"Oh?" Dena settled onto a stool across from him.

"I have been thinking. . . ." He paused, seeming to gather his courage. His eyes gripped her. "There is no reason for us to pretend to be brother and sister—no one who looked twice at us would believe it. To keep the gossips from wagging their tongues, we should marry. If we help Gilda see that Taregan is not coming home—"

"Colton, speak not of this," she whispered. She wanted to clap her hands over her ears. They had been such good friends, and now, with one breath, he had ruined everything.

"Do you not see, Dena? I built this house for you. I want to live in it with you and fill it with our children—"

"No!" Dena leaned back, stunned. "You do not love me, Colton, you are confused. We are friends, we work together—"

"I loved you the moment I saw you in that barn." From across the board she could feel the surging power of his emotion. "Your hair was streaked with hay that day, your face dirty. And yet you were so devoted to Gilda, so loving—"

"What else could I be?" Pressing her hands against the table, she leaned toward him. "Gilda held me when a Mohegan murdered my mother. She has done everything for me. This thing you are asking would break her heart. Taregan is the first thing she speaks of in the morning, the last prayer on her lips at night. She prays for him and Fallon to come home, she waits for them, her hope keeps her alive—"

"Would you throw away your own happiness for Gilda's sake? Her days are numbered, Dena, but you are young and full of life. Think of yourself, think of me. I would do anything to release you from this useless loyalty you display toward a man long dead—"

Dead. The word caught her off guard, and she shuddered, facing for the first time the hollow loneliness that seemed to fill her. Taregan could not be dead! She would feel it in her heart if he had been taken from her forever. And yet . . . she shook her head.

He must be dead, for defeated prisoners of war did not live long in slavery.

"Dena." Reaching across the table, Colton placed his sheltering hand on her arm. She trembled at his touch, at the sight of desire in his eyes. "You feel it, don't you?" he whispered, sliding his palm over her skin until her hand nestled between both of his. "God has brought us together; you cannot deny it any longer."

"No," she whispered again, but he stood and leaned over the table, his face only inches from hers. A wave of heat rushed along her pulses. Her body itself betrayed her, she could feel the heat in her face.

Colton felt it, too. One of his hands pressed hers to the table, the other reached up and gently caressed her cheek. "I love you," he said simply, the warmth of his breath against her closed eyelids. "Let me speak to Gilda."

His touch courted her senses with gentle persuasiveness, and she almost surrendered to the warmth of his hand at her neck. She ducked her head, lost in the primitive yearnings his touch had triggered, then opened her eyes and felt a rock fall through her heart. Through some trick of fantasy, she had wanted, *expected*, to see Taregan's dark hair and dancing blue eyes before her, but the earnest face staring at her was Colton's. Her friend's.

She looked away, unsettled by the thought that she was in love with a ghost. But what was love, and how could she feel it for a man she hadn't seen in years? Love was emotion, but her emotions had died on the day the English emptied her village. Love was knowing someone, and since childhood Taregan had been a part of her life and she a part of his. But that part had been wrested away, cut off like an amputated limb. What then was left but memories of an old love, shadows of feeling linked to a best-forgotten past?

Those shadows would never leave her as long as she cared for Taregan's mother. Gilda kept his memory alive, his image before Dena, his name before the throne of God. Gilda talked as though Taregan waited just outside the door, and Dena's heart could never heal as long as Gilda lived with her. Colton should have realized this.

"You should not ask this of me, Colton," she murmured, finding her voice. "It is not honorable. It is a betrayal of the vow you gave Taregan."

For a brief moment, Dena caught a glimpse of a battle between desire and duty, then his eyes dulled and he pulled away, composing himself. "I apologize. You are right. After all, my promise to Taregan led me to you, and I should not be untrue to his memory."

"He said he would come back."

"And you still believe he will?"

The expression in his eyes brought the color rushing into her cheeks, but Dena clung to the edge of the table and nodded. "As long as Gilda lives, I must believe. She has faith, Colton."

He squinted slightly, his jaw moved sideways, and Dena saw both suffering and longing in his eyes. Oh, why hadn't Taregan come back? If he would, she could send Colton out to find a wife and children, to make a home of his own! Why had God led this man of honor and kindness to her while loyalty bound her to another? She ought to send Colton away, for she would never be able to forget his words or the touch of his hand. It was dangerous to linger near such burning desire.

And yet sending him away would mean that he would never again come to her door. She would not sew for him, his quick and ready smile would not warm her heart or make her laugh. . . .

She ran her hand over the table, searching for something to cling to. "Colton, as long as Gilda lives I cannot speak of this—"

"And if she dies?" His words whirled ominously in the quiet of the room, and Dena shivered with an eerie premonition of fear. Many in her tribe had believed that invoking the name of death brought bad luck.

"Speak not of it," she said, standing.

He bit his lip, then picked up his hat and stood across from her. "I guess I'll be going. I'll return in a few days." He turned toward the door, his broad back to her, and Dena struggled with her own self-control. It would be so easy to let those shoulders carry her throughout the rest of her life.

"Mayhap," she began, hating the harsh sound of her voice, "mayhap you should stay away awhile. We will need quite a store of meat in order to see the winter through."

"Wouldn't want to see the bottom of the pork barrel before spring, heh?" he said. He turned and gave her a weary smile. "Don't worry. I won't mention this day again. I would rather die than bring you sorrow, Dena."

Dena was so touched by his humble admission that she had to resist an urge to throw her arms around him. "Thank you. I just don't want to upset Gilda."

"I understand."

He moved toward the door slowly, and as Dena closed it behind him she heard Gilda call.

Colton stumbled through the courtyard, his feet as heavy as lead and his mind awash in regret. Five years of patient and careful nurture had been destroyed in a single moment of reckless abandon. He should have waited before speaking his feelings, but with the advent of winter he'd been thinking more and more about settling down with a wife. He was thirty years old and ready to begin a family. When he came through the door, Dena's eyes had brightened at the sight of him, and for a moment he had been caught up in the foolish notion that the house and the woman inside were truly his.

But the love of his life belonged to the young man who had asked him to deliver a message to her. Colton's fault lay in doing more than carrying a word of reassurance to Dena. He had cared for her, protected and sheltered her. In the process, he had learned to love her, and Taregan had become nothing more than a figment of his memory, a phantom in his imagination.

He clenched his hands into fists as he walked through the gate outside the house. How could a dead man exert such influence over two women? In his absence Taregan had grown to near saintly status, and a flesh-and-blood man could not fight against a heavenly saint. Would that Taregan were present in the flesh, so Colton could confront and challenge him. If he were here, Dena could see for herself what kind of man he had become and measure him against Colton. Unless the man had attained perfection, Colton was certain to rise the victor. He had become skilled in the woods, he was honest and faithful, he provided well for the women in his house.

Part of the problem lay in the fact that Taregan's image

haunted the streets of Hartford. Daniel Bailie was an ever-present looking glass reminding Dena of what Taregan would look and sound like if he were alive. Did her heart pound when she caught sight of her love's twin across the village green? Did the sight torment or please her? No wonder she could not rid her heart of Taregan's memory!

And Gilda, helpless in a fragile mortal coil, further compli-cated Dena's loyalty. Gilda lived only for her son's return, and Dena revered her so deeply that she would never do or say any-thing to bring the woman pain.

Yes, he had been foolish to open his heart and reveal the feel-ings hidden there. It would have been wiser to wait. And that was what he would do now. For unless God ordained otherwise, he could do naught else but wait for whatever God had planned for the two of them.

▼▲▼▲▼ Daniel groaned as the sun's first light broke through the crack in the shutters. The stale taste of last night's beer lay heavy and sour in his mouth, and he spat upon the floor as he sat up and struggled to open his eyes. He was in Garvin's bed on the first floor of the house, and he couldn't remember coming home. But if Garvin wasn't here—

Obeying a hunch, he leaned forward and cracked open the shutter. Through an early morning mist he caught sight of Gar-vin sneaking through the trees. The man had been spending occa-sional nights at the Widow Butler's house for well over three years now, and the magistrates had no idea that this bit of immo-rality occurred regularly within the bounds of their own town. The widow had been able to circumvent the town's law against single people living alone by hiring a live-in servant, but the woman who served Sabrina was deaf, partially blind, and slept like a stone. How much longer, Daniel wondered, would the widow plead for Garvin to marry her? Sooner or later her patience was bound to evaporate, for marriageable women were in short supply in the colonies. A single woman did not remain unmarried for long, not even a widow whose deceased husband had accumulated a mountain of debt.

"You should tell him he doesn't deserve you, Sabrina," Daniel murmured to the air as Garvin's heavy boots thumped outside the door. A hand pushed the door open, and Garvin stooped to enter, grinning wickedly at the sight of Daniel's bleary eyes.

"Did you drink too much last night?" Garvin asked, moving immediately to throw a fresh log on the fire. "You look a wee bit addled this morning. And I see you didn't make it up the ladder to your own bed."

"I drank what everyone else drank," Daniel answered, wiping his mouth on his sleeve. He turned toward the fireplace. "And I'm not the only one waking in a bed not my own. How is the Widow Butler this morning?"

"Round and saucy," Garvin answered, fanning the fire to encourage last night's coals. "Just the way I like her."

"Is she still hoping to be married?"

"Not now," Garvin answered, giving Daniel a sly wink. "I convinced her it would be more fitting if she continued working to pay off her husband's debts. I told her I wasn't going to marry into another man's indebtedness, and she swore she wouldn't be married in her underwear. So, for now, she's keeping quiet."

Hiding a grin, Daniel swung his feet to the floor. A man who married a widow was liable for the debts of the dead man if the widow brought any of his property with her. Since women could own nothing—not even the clothes they wore—a widow had to marry in the nude to avoid the liability. To prevent the immodesty of a naked bride, the law allowed a widow to marry in a large smock so she could dress beneath it following the ceremony, but Daniel knew the modest Sabrina Butler would never agree to such a humiliating arrangement.

"Does the late Master Butler still owe much money?" Daniel asked, calling over his shoulder.

"Not much," Garvin admitted, prodding the fire with a brass rod. "And he did leave her with more goods than liabilities. But she isn't willing to sell her things to pay his debts, nor am I willing that she should part with her things. And I'm in no hurry to be married. Why buy a field to plant corn when a perfectly good one is ready for harvest and begging for a man to tend it?" Satisfied with the fire, Garvin slapped his hands on his knees and stood up. "What goods came in yesternight? Anything of interest?"

Daniel shook his head. "Colton Bramwell brought in some beaver pelts. He had a deer carcass in his canoe, but I'm sure he took that to Dena."

Garvin cast him a questioning glance. "Is your mother still living with that girl?"

"Yes, I suppose so," Daniel said, yawning. "But I don't really care."

The corner of Garvin's mouth rose in a half smile. "Of course you don't. Well, shall we travel to the Mohegan camp today? I hear their sachem is intent on a copper kettle, and I've a new shipment in from Boston."

Daniel nodded, then forced his lethargic limbs to function. "I suppose so," he said, grimacing as he stood and braced himself against his pounding head. "There is no reason for us to remain here."

▼▲▼▲▼ Gilda jerked restlessly in her sleep. In her dream, she was walking along the river's edge, her legs blissfully graceful beneath her, wavelets splashing across her bare feet. An eastern breeze ruffled her hair and sent it flying behind her. She was young and beautiful again, and Fallon walked beside her, his voice warm in the silence like a comforting embrace. He was handsome, strong, and *alive,* just as she had always known he was.

A canoe waited on the misty shore of the wide river, and in the boat she saw her aunt Pocahontas, Sooleawa, Nixkamich, and many others who had already crossed from earth to heaven. The people in the boat smiled in welcome. Rather than frightening her, their peaceful expressions filled Gilda's heart with a desperate desire to join them.

"I am ready to go, my love," she said. Then, after squeezing Fallon's hand, she stepped ankle-deep in the sparkling water and left him onshore.

She put her hands on the edge of the canoe, ready to depart with the others, but Fallon's warm hand fell upon her shoulder.

"Must you go now?" he asked, his voice husky with tenderness. "Can you not wait . . . a little longer?"

"No." Her heart broke even as she whispered the word. "I haven't your strength, Fallon. I am so . . . tired."

His eyes radiated with gentleness and understanding. "Then look behind you. There is yet something you must do."

Turning, Gilda saw that two men walked hand-in-hand along the distant shore. There was something vaguely familiar about the way they moved, and as they drew closer Gilda drew in her breath. "Our sons!" she whispered, glancing up into Fallon's eyes.

"Taregan and Daniel will be together again," he murmured, coming closer until his hand tenderly brushed the back of her neck. He leaned forward and kissed her briefly, then pulled away. "Never fear and do not doubt. This dream is from the Great God and no other, and you must tell Dena of its message. Taregan promised to return, and God has promised that it will come to pass. Tell Dena so that she may share your gift of faith. Then you can join the others . . . and wait for me."

She turned again, studying the identical men on the shore through a blur of tears. They were still coming, walking together, smiling at each other. Then, slowly, one of them turned and began to wade into the water.

"What—," Gilda began, but Fallon interrupted her.

"This part is not for you to know," he said, lifting his hand to wave at his sons. He paused for a moment, smiling as if in anticipation of their reunion, then bent low to whisper again in her ear. "Wait for me, my love. I will not be long."

Wistfully, Gilda released the canoe and stepped back onto shore. When she turned again, she could see nothing but mist on the water.

▼▲▼▲▼ "Dena!"

Gilda's voice was more urgent and demanding than Dena had ever heard it, and she nearly dropped the bowl in her lap as she sprang up to answer Gilda's call. "What troubles you?" Dena asked, kneeling by the bed of furs.

Gilda's hand clasped hers in a tight grasp. "He is coming back," she whispered, her breathing labored. The ever-present rattle in her lungs seemed louder, and Dena felt a cold lump grow in her stomach as she looked down at the sick woman. Chilly tendrils of apprehension spread through her body as she clutched Gilda's cold hand.

"Who is coming back?" she asked, alarmed by the distant look in Gilda's eyes.

"Taregan. Fallon charged me to tell you. Taregan is coming back. But you must wait for him alone. It is my time to go with the others."

Dena feared that the woman had lost her mind, but a serene glow emanated from Gilda's pale face. Her smile was calm and peaceful, not frantic. "The love of your life is coming home, Dena," Gilda went on, liquid, loving laughter in her voice. "Like the bridegroom coming for his bride, he will come. Keep a lamp burning, and do not be overtaken by other things. Be ready, dear, for he is coming!"

"Of certain he is," Dena whispered, smoothing Gilda's hair from her brow as if she could soothe the woman's fevered mind.

"Will you remember?"

"Yes, I will."

"Will you believe?"

"Yes." Dena pulled Gilda's hand to her breast and studied the beloved face before her. If her promise would help this woman die a peaceful death, she would agree that bears could fly. "Yes, Mother Bailie, I will believe."

"Good." Gilda's eyes closed slowly, but the smile on her lips did not fade. Within a few moments, the rattling in her chest grew louder and her breaths further apart. Dena knew her death-watch had begun.

There was no one to call, no one to sit with her. The church at
Hartford had been less than enthusiastic in its reception of the
freethinking women, and Colton could be miles away on the
river by now. At one point near midday, Gilda called for Daniel,
and Dena stopped a young boy passing by and asked him to
fetch Daniel from the trading post. Within the hour the boy
returned and said that Master Black and Master Bailie had gone
to the Mohegan camp.

Exhausted, drained of will and thought, Dena settled back
into her place at Gilda's bedside. Though her heart wanted to
turn from the sight of her beloved friend dying, this woman had
come to her village at great personal risk to save Dena's people.
She was Taregan's beloved mother, and the only encouraging
soul Dena had known during the early days of her enslavement.
Waiting with her for death was the least Dena could do to honor
such bravery.

In the silence of the room, Dena began to sing the traditional
Pequot song of mourning. As Gilda struggled to draw her last
breaths, Dena picked up Gilda's *English Book of Common Prayer*
and recited a much-loved passage:

> *I am well pleased: that the Lord hath heard the voice of my
> prayer;*
>> *That he hath inclined his ear unto me; therefore will I call
> upon him as long as I live.*
>> *The snares of death compassed me round about: and the
> pains of hell got hold upon me.*
>> *I found trouble and heaviness, and I called upon the Name
> of the Lord:*
>> *O Lord, I beseech thee, deliver my soul.*
>> *Gracious is the Lord, and righteous: yea, our God is
> merciful.*
>> *The Lord preserveth the simple: I was in misery, and he
> helped me.*
>> *Turn again then unto thy rest, O my soul: for the Lord hath
> rewarded thee.*

And why? Thou hast delivered my soul from death: mine
eyes from tears, and my feet from falling.
I will walk before the Lord in the land of the living.

At sunset, Dena rose to find a bit of parchment and penned a
hasty note to Daniel: "Your mother is dead."

▼▲▼▲▼ In the midst of the great Western ocean, Fallon
lifted his head from his hammock and stared into the darkness.
His mind grasped for the dream of Gilda—held onto it with terrible longing—but it slipped away as smoothly as had the canoe
filled with the people he loved.

What does it mean, God? Am I to lose her before I find my way
home?

His heart resisted what his soul recognized as truth.

Her lovely, luminous eyes had brimmed with pain, her voice
had been tinged with exhaustion. 'Twould be selfish of him to
insist that she wait for him.

"Ah, Gilda, would that we could greet our boys together," he
whispered, his voice blending with the creaks and groans of the
sleeping ship. The darkness around him seemed deeper than
before. . . . Gilda's light had left the world.

Fallon clenched his fist and pressed it to his lips, silencing the
cry that threatened to break forth. The only things remaining to
him were the raw sores of an aching heart and his faith that God
would bring him home. Not to Gilda, at least not yet, but to the
sons for whom he would now live and pray with every energy
he possessed.

▼▲▼▲▼ Colton was at the docks, preparing to leave,
when Daniel Bailie arrived in a canoe and received the message.
The young man read the note, announced the news to Garvin
Black, then retreated into the house. Colton waited a moment,
almost certain he would reappear to help Dena prepare his

mother's body for burial. When he did not, Colton left his canoe tied to the dock and went to Dena's house himself.

Dena had dressed Gilda in her best clothes and the finest furs in the house. Colton asked whether Gilda should be buried in the cemetery at the church, but Dena shook her head. "Gilda patterned her beliefs after the Word of God, not the orthodoxy of the church," she said simply. "She could not accept the Puritans' level of conformity. And of certain they would never allow a woman identified as a Pequot to be buried in their hallowed ground. Let her be buried here, Colton, by this house, under the oak tree."

While Dena combed and braided Gilda's long hair, Colton went in search of the minister and discovered that Dena was right. The clergyman declined to perform the funeral ceremony, citing "religious differences" for his refusal. And so, early the next morning, Colton and Dena lowered Gilda's body into the gaping hole near the oak tree, then stood in stunned silence as Daniel walked through the gate, his arm linked with the Widow Butler's. The two newcomers said nothing as they paused by the graveside, and Colton broke the silence by reciting the Lord's Prayer and the Twenty-third Psalm. Then he folded his hands and gave Dena an apologetic glance.

"I'm sorry, but there is much I don't know about this woman," he said, suddenly regretting his ignorance. "She did not talk much of herself. I don't know who her parents were or where she came from, and I suspect Dena doesn't know, either."

Daniel glanced up sharply, and Colton knew his words had struck a nerve. "I know," Daniel interrupted, glancing up to face the group. Though his face was blotchy with suppressed emotion, his blue eyes strafed the gathering with icy rage. "Gilda Bailie was the granddaughter of the great Powhatan and the niece of Pocahontas. She was descended from the first Englishmen to ever set foot in this land and was as much an Indian as any warrior who roams this woodland. My mother embraced the best of both worlds and disdained the worst. She was English without being proud or pompous, an Indian who scorned ignorance and brutality. And now she is with my father and my brother. And now," his face twisted in a wry smile, "she is at peace."

"She has always been at peace," Dena whispered, lifting her chin as the cold wind ruffled her hair. "She told me once that if we do not have peace within ourselves, it is vain to seek it from outward sources. She had peace in the midst of the war, in her illness, and in her . . . loneliness."

Something in her words made Daniel flinch, Colton noticed, but Dena went on.

"She believed that her husband still lives and that Taregan will return," she whispered. Colton felt his heart twist in pain. "Gilda's last words were a prophecy of sorts. She told me not to give up hope, to keep faith in Taregan's promise to come home."

Colton stared at the ground, his hopes as dead as the woman within the frozen soil.

"Dena, you can't believe that," Daniel said stiffly, voicing Colton's opinion. The Widow Butler lifted a gloved hand to his shoulder.

"I don't know what I believe," Dena said, twisting her hands into her shawl. "I only know that Gilda is gone, and I shall miss her."

Her chin quivered as if she would cry, and Colton bowed his head and led the group in a prayer of thanks for Gilda's testimony and a plea to comfort those who would mourn her. Dena was sobbing as he ended the prayer, and he stepped forward and put his arm about her shoulders in a brotherly embrace. *Perchance,* he thought as he murmured words of consolation in her ear, *this is a sad, but necessary step toward our future together. Now that Gilda is gone, Dena will grow lonely and God will soften her heart toward me.*

He found a strange comfort in the thought.

▼▲▼▲▼ Colton left soon after the burial and did not return to Hartford until the harsh winds of January began to blow. The town crier had just begun to toll the curfew bell as Colton spied the light burning in Dena's window. Like a moth to a flame he drew near it, his pulse quickening at the thought of seeing her again. He knew she had dismissed the law against a woman living alone, saying she was a Pequot, not a Puritan. Surely the last six weeks had helped her sort out her feelings. The tiny house must have felt empty while he was away, and he would willingly give up his life as a trapper and hunter if only she would say the word.

He rapped on the door and heard her quick footsteps within. The door opened a crack, then her face lit in a genuine smile at the sight of him. "Colton!"

He stooped to enter and barely managed to stop his eager arms from enveloping her in a fierce embrace. "How lovely you look, Dena! I have prayed for you often and wondered how you are faring."

"I am fine." She stepped toward the table and gestured toward the bench by the board. "But you must be hungry. Sit, Colton, and let me ladle a bowl of porridge for you. There is meat in the stew, and vegetables left over from the summer garden—"

"Do not trouble yourself too much," he said, but he removed his hat and sat on the bench, watching her bustle about in a flurry of domestic preparation. Shadows wreathed the room as she reached toward the shelf holding bowls and spoons, but the flickering firelight only intensified her beauty and grace. She chattered endlessly about the townspeople, trying too hard, he thought, to fill the room with conversation when it brimmed already with the unspoken feelings between them.

When she finally set the swimming bowl before him, he reached up and caught her slender hand. "Sit with me."

"Of course." A smile played briefly upon her lips. "What kind of hostess would I be if I did not sit at meat with my guest? Even in the Indian camp, we knew the importance of manners—"

"You talk too much." He did not release her hand but pulled her onto the bench beside him, locking his fingers between hers. It was an unexpectedly intimate gesture that brought a quickened pulse to the slender column of her throat. "I have not come here to eat dinner or talk about your neighbors. I do not care what the minister said or what Widow Butler wears to church. I came here to talk to you, to open my heart and beg you to marry me."

"Colton, I—"

He pressed a finger across her lips. "I wasn't finished," he whispered, lowering his head so that he breathed into her ear. "I built this house for you, Dena, with the hope that one day you and I might be wed beneath its roof. Now you need not fear breaking Gilda's heart. Taregan has been away five long years, so he no longer has claim over you—"

"But I promised to marry him!"

"You were naught but a child."

"I was fifteen, not a child. My father could have given me in marriage at any time."

"Would you wait forever for a dead man?"

"Taregan is not dead! Hours before she died, Gilda dreamed that Taregan was alive. She said he would come back for me—"

Her eyes blazed with Gilda's fantasy, and Colton grimaced as if she'd delivered a hard blow to his stomach.

"You would risk your happiness on the deathbed ravings of a woman who never recovered from losing the husband and son she loved?" His words were suddenly raw and angry. She was either mad or cruel, but she could not love him, else she would not do this. After all he had done for her, this was a weak reason to refuse him.

"At first, I did not know whether to believe Gilda or not," Dena confessed, lowering her eyes to the table. "At the time I thought she was imagining things, seeing what she so desperately wanted. But Gilda was so serene when she died, Colton. Such peace could not have come from the devil's lie."

"This talk of dreams and visions is nothing but Indian superstition," Colton muttered darkly, refusing to meet her eyes. "Your primitive roots are showing."

From the corner of his eye, he saw her chin lift in defiance. "Our village was not primitive," she said, her voice as cold as the bitter wind blowing outside. "We made promises and kept them. Our word was our honor. Often it was all we had."

"It is all you have now," he said, standing. "The word of a dead man. Will that age-old promise keep you warm this winter? Will it put food on your table or babies within your womb? No! I have kept you alive these past years, I have put this roof over your head! And yet you spurn my love and care as if it were a worthless thing—"

"I do not spurn your kindness," Dena answered, pulling her shawl more tightly around her shoulders. "Nor do I deny all you have done for me. I have great affection for you, Colton. I could not love a brother more. I had hoped that you would consider me a sister in Christ and regard me with the same tender affection I hold toward you. But my heart has been promised to someone else, and even if I wanted to give it to you, I could not."

"Does tender *affection* make you feel like this?" In one swift movement his arms caught hers and lifted her to her feet. Brushing his lips lightly against the smooth, musky skin of her temple, he heard her gasp. When he bent his head to kiss her, her head turned so that his lips brushed her cheek as she struggled to move away.

"Why do you resist me?" he asked, his heart in his voice. She trembled in his arms, but whether from fear or passion he could not tell. "Can you tell me that you have not yearned for this? That you do not want a man next to you in the night and children at your breast? You are a lovely woman, Dena, and these things should be yours!"

"They *will* be," she said, pulling away from him. "When Taregan returns!"

He let her go, and she backed hastily away and leaned against the wall, her face pale, her eyes as gray and dark as a stormy sky.

Colton struggled to maintain control of his voice. "You speak bravely for a woman with no prospects."

Her chin lifted higher. "I speak as a woman who believes in a man's promise. I have given much thought to you, Colton, and to Taregan. I have wondered what love is, and whether I truly love Taregan or just the memory of him."

"And?" he whispered, trying to shake off a sense of foreboding.

"And I found my answer when Gilda died, but I was too blind to see it right away. She spoke of Fallon that day, and her love for him was as real in that moment as it had been while he lived. And yet she had lived without him for five years! Her *commitment* to him kept her love alive."

She stood upright and resolutely folded her arms. "I do not know what or where Taregan is, but I have his promise to return, and I have given my promise that I will wait. He is coming home soon, and he will find me waiting for him. That is what love is, Colton. As long as there is a chance that he lives, I will wait."

"If he lives," Colton said, clenching his teeth as pain raked his soul, "do you think he has waited as resolutely for love? If, wherever he is, his master has given him a bride, do you think he will refuse her? Do you think your beloved Taregan will restrain the passions of a man in order to be true to you, a girl he has not seen in years? He supposes that *you* are dead, Dena! If he hears any news of this colony, he will think that not a Pequot remains alive in this river valley."

"It matters not. Taregan told you that he would return for me. And I promised to wait—"

"Many years ago." Colton moved abruptly toward the door and settled his hat upon his head. "I withdraw my proposal of marriage, then. You have made your choice."

He turned to leave, but heard the rustle of her garments as she moved forward. "Colton." The word was barely a whisper, but his ears were so attuned to her that if she had but quickened her breath he would have turned.

"What?"

"God has someone for you, but it is not me, and it is not my place to say whom it might be. Before Gilda died I was loath to send you to another woman, for you were my comfort, my protector and foundation, but now I release you to find love on your own. Forget me, dear Colton, and forgive me for hurting you."

"That is far easier said than done," he muttered, then he opened the door and stepped out into the night.

Dirk Christoffels reined in his horse at the top of Sturges Bluff. At his left hand lay the western vista of Barbados: silver sea, shimmering skyline, and endless cobalt sky. To the north, before him, stretched his brother's acres: mile after mile of emerald cane gleaming in the sun. The stalks undulated gently as the dry trade winds blew across the island. Less than a mile to the east, Hans's slaves worked, their machetes catching the sun like the silver flickers of trout in a shallow stream. Dirk frowned, noticing how the slaves worked in two separate groups. The group of latest arrivals faced the east as they worked, the first group kept their backs to the newcomers and cut toward the west.

"*Vader,*" Arabella said, poking him irreverently in the ribs, "is Uncle Hans rich?"

"I don't know." The saddle creaked as he turned to study his teenage daughter. Despite the heat, her sunburnt face brought a smile to his lips. "*Ja,* I suppose he would say so. He owns more land than anyone else on the island."

"And slaves," Arabella answered. "And their cost is very dear, that's what *Moeder* told me. Is that why we don't have slaves, *Vader?* Are we so very poor?"

"We don't have slaves because I believe it is wrong to profit from the misfortunes of others," Dirk answered, turning back to study the men in the field. His horse nickered softly, impatient to be off. "I do not even own you, *mijn dochter.* God sent you to us. You are his child, lent to us for safekeeping."

Arabella didn't answer, but hugged him tightly, pressing her face to his broad back. As Dirk kicked his horse and moved slowly down the hill, he felt very rich indeed.

▼▲▼▲▼ Dirk reached the house just before sunset, and Hans seemed glad to see him. The slaves had surrendered their machetes to a hired hand in the field and were now straggling up the road, hot, sweaty, and tired. More than one of the men cast a scornful glance toward their master, not caring if Dirk noticed. Those glances, he thought, did not bode well.

"Have you noticed, my brother," he said as Hans led him and Arabella into the cool shade of the stone house, "that your men do not cooperate? I saw two distinct groups in the field today. And none of them looks kindly upon you."

Hans threw back his head and laughed. "*Ja*, and what master is regarded kindly by his slaves? They do not work together because they come from two separate tribes, as I discovered not long ago. I told them I didn't care about their ancient tribal warfare or the grudges that they might bear toward one another. As long as they cut the cane, they may stare and growl at each other all they like."

"One of the first group seemed particularly threatening," Dirk ventured. "The young one, the boy with feathers tied into his hair."

Hans nodded as he poured himself and his brother a drink. "That would be Hassun. He fancies himself an Indian prince or some such nonsense. The lad puts on so many airs it is a marvel the others haven't strung him up."

"One of them has interesting eyes," Arabella spoke up, smiling at her uncle. "He has blue eyes. How can an Indian have blue eyes, Uncle Hans?"

Hans lifted his burly shoulder in a shrug and passed Dirk a mug. "How can a cow be born with pink eyes? A freak act of nature, child, and little more. If you walked closer to that one, little girl, you would find that he stinks just like the others. He is no different. Though, of course, I wouldn't be letting you walk close to the men."

"I am no longer a child," Arabella answered, taking a deep breath. "I am a woman of sixteen."

Dirk smothered a smile. His daughter had not ceased to

remind him that she was mature now and nearly ready for marriage, but apparently she had not had an occasion to inform her uncle.

"Forgive me, my dear," Hans grinned, bending in a mocking bow. "I forgot that our lady has recently celebrated a birthday. Will you be leaving us soon to start your own life?"

"Let's not rush my Arabella," Dirk said, resting his hand on his daughter's curls. He cocked his head and gazed at her in pride. "Though she is of age, Arabella is too sheltered and idealistic to face the world. I will keep her by my side until she is ready."

"And I will keep my eyes open for decent suitors." Hans lifted his glass in a toast. "To the future, and the excellent young man whom our Arabella will marry. Do not take offense, Dirk, but I doubt you have the proper connections to find someone who would make a suitable suitor for our lovely Arabella. Why, any man from the continent would take one look at the dirt under your fingernails and run for cover—"

"I'll not deny that you've done well, Hans," Dirk answered, trying to keep his temper from flaring as it always did whenever Hans began his you're-not-ambitious-enough sermons. "But we have always done things differently. My farm may be small, but it is worked with my own hands, the sweat of my own brow—"

"To you, then." Refusing to be chided, Hans winked at Arabella, then drank. Smacking his lips with relish, he lowered the mug and grinned at Dirk. "I work, too, you know. And it is not wrong to work these men, for they are criminals. If they had done nothing wrong, they wouldn't have been sold into slavery."

Dirk rolled his eyes, amazed that his brother could not see the truth. "You can't believe that it's right to profit from the wrongs of others—"

"*Vader*, may I go outside?"

"Of course," Intent upon his brother's taunting face, Dirk sent her away with an absent wave. "If slavery is right, then why didn't our father own slaves?"

"Our father was a simpleminded gentleman," Hans offered,

lifting his mug for another swig. He sighed in satisfaction after swallowing. "And our mother was a fragile lily totally without ambition. She made no demands on him, and he did not earn any great sums."

"He earned enough for you to buy two hundred acres here," Dirk pointed out. "Your inheritance was no trifling sum."

"*Ja*, but he could have made his money into a fortune," Hans answered, thumping his mug onto the table. "So I will do it for him."

"I still think slavery is a shame," Dirk mumbled, turning to the single window in the house. The breeze blew the shutters against the stone, making a hollow, knocking sound. "And these slaves are at enmity with each other. Trouble is brewing, I can feel it. Look how the one group does not even go into the house with the others."

"Bah, you worry too much," Hans answered, moving toward the door. "Come, let me show you the new machetes I bought at Hole Town. They cut through the cane twice as easily."

Slumping in resignation, Dirk followed his brother out of the house.

▼▲▼▲ Aware that every dark eye outside followed her, Arabella walked down the hill with a sure and steady step. She wasn't in the least bit afraid of the Indians, no matter how brutal her uncle claimed they had been. They were as thin as starving puppies, and something in their velvet eyes reminded her of ill-used animals in need of care. More than two dozen of the men lounged outside the slave house, enjoying the cool of the evening, no doubt, and she gave them a timid smile.

They did not smile in return. She looked at each man in the circle, hoping that at least one would speak and tell her something about America and his life there, but the men grew silent and sat or stood or reclined where they were with an indolent, tomcat grace.

Finally she looked into the face of the young man who had

caught her attention earlier. He stood by the slave house, his arms crossed over the golden skin of his chest. High cheekbones accentuated the cobalt blue eyes that squinted toward her in some secret amusement.

She took courage from his expression. *"Goeden dag,"* she whispered in a low voice, gazing up into his bronzed face. *"Spreekt u hollands? Spreekt u engels?"*

Tilting his head, he gazed at her with a curious expression, as if she were either some unparalleled work of art or as crazy as a coot. Arabella wasn't sure, but she thought that his cheeks deepened in color. Had she embarrassed him?

"I speak English," he finally stammered.

"Good." She gave him a pert smile and folded her hands in front of her skirt. "My name is Arabella Christoffels. Your master is my uncle, and my father is the other man who comes here on occasion."

The young man nodded slowly, glancing over her shoulder as if her uncle and father walked there. Slightly unnerved, she glanced backward to be certain that they did not, then she smiled at the man again. "I saw that you have blue eyes and thought that perhaps you have a story to tell me."

His left eyebrow shot up, and for a moment she feared he would laugh at her, but he only smiled and shook his head. "I have no stories, Miss Christoffels, no more than any of the others here. And it is probably not right that we should be talking in this way. I have a feeling your uncle would cover my back with lashes if he knew I had spoken to you."

"Nee, I wouldn't allow him to hurt you—this conversation is my idea. Have you a name?"

"Taregan Bailie."

"Taregan Bailie." She repeated the name softly. "I thought Indians did not have surnames."

He uncrossed his arms and thrust his hands into the waistband of his breeches. "There is probably much you do not know, miss."

"I'd like to learn." She stared at him intently, fascinated, and an unusual gleam in his hair caught her eye. "What is that gold thing in your ear? Do the Indians of your tribe wear earrings? I have seen slaves with bones and wires in their ears, but have never known any with golden rings—"

She stepped forward, eager to see him more clearly, but he backed away, hastily retreating into the mass of other men who watched with undisguised curiosity.

"Arabella!" Her father's sharp voice cut through the astonished silence. Without looking, she knew that he jogged toward her. "What are you doing there? You have no place amongst the slaves!"

"I was talking to one of them," she said, extending a gloved hand in Taregan's direction. "One of these men speaks English very well, *Vader*."

Breathing heavily, her father caught her by the arm and yanked her toward the house. "Hans says they do not speak English. They are too dull to learn."

"But I talked to him!"

"He may have spoken one or two words, but that is all." Safely away from the slaves' quarters, her father whirled and planted his broad hands on her shoulders. "Arabella, *mijn dochter*, sometimes you allow your kind nature to lead you into foolish situations. You could have been hurt, or taken hostage, or violated in some way. You wandered like a lamb into a pack of wolves, and only God's mercy has kept you from harm—"

"I saw no harm," Arabella answered coolly, annoyed that her father did not think her capable of handling herself. "They were so pitiful-looking, and thin—"

"They are not your problem."

"But they belong to our family, and we should be doing something to help them—"

"They are not part of us. They should not even be on this island. And you are not to speak to them again, do you hear me?"

Arabella opened her mouth to protest, but decided against it when she saw the gleam of anger in her father's eye. He rarely scolded her, but this time he meant business. On this matter it would be best not to press him.

"*Ja, vader.*" She bowed her head meekly.

"Promise me."

"I promise. If you don't want me to speak about what I saw—"

"What? What did you see?"

Arabella struggled to contain her enthusiasm. "A gold ring. The blue-eyed one wears it in his ear. Do you think he stole it, *Vader*? Or maybe he found it in the dirt. I wanted to ask him about it when you interrupted me, but I'd be happy to ask him if you think I should—"

"You'll ask him nothing." Her father's face clouded. "You're to stay away from them, do you hear? Especially the blue-eyed one."

She frowned in an exact imitation of his expression. "*Ja, Vader.*"

"All right then." He released her, but did not take a step until she did, keeping himself between her and the slaves until they had returned to the house.

▼▲▼▲▼ "You, there! Bailie!"

Taregan paused, turning to answer the master's summons. Hans Christoffels rarely spoke to his slaves except to bawl orders, and nothing good ever came of being singled out.

"Come here and kneel before me."

The other men murmured in surprise behind him, and Taregan's mind raced as he slowly moved toward the master. This had to be some sort of punishment for his conversation with the girl yesterday. Her promise to protect him meant nothing, of course, as the master was surely about to demonstrate. The whip lay in his hand, and his bright eyes gleamed beneath his golden hair.

Taregan knelt, struggling to keep his anger under control. To lose his temper would surely cost him his life, and what good would he then be to those who waited for him at home?

He closed his eyes, fully expecting to feel the sting of the whip across his back, but instead a probing, obscene finger fumbled at his ear. Finding nothing, the master's hand moved to Taregan's other ear and groped through his hair. Then a long, low whistle of surprise cut through the silence.

"Where'd you get this, boy?" the master demanded, the ring upon the tip of his fat finger. He moved it before Taregan's eyes, taunting him. "Did you steal it? From whom? No, I don't guess you could have stolen it, so you must have found it in the earth. Well, this is my earth, and you're my property, so this is mine, too."

While Taregan swallowed a hysterical urge to punch the master in the face, Hans Christoffels rubbed the ring against the fabric of his shirt, then bit it. "'Sreal gold." His mouth lifted in a menacing, sarcastic smile. "I'd thank you, boy, for letting me have this, but why should I thank you for giving me something that's already mine? So I suppose I'll have to punish you instead, for not returning my property sooner."

Taregan's nails cut into his palm as he clenched his fists. If not for Gilda and Dena he would scream at this injustice and fight for the only precious object in his life . . . but the people at home mattered more than a circular bit of gold.

"Nothing to say, heh?" Hans asked, his face twisted in contempt. "Then lie on the ground, facedown, and remain silent while I teach you a lesson."

From the crowd, Hassun howled in frustrated anger, and Taregan shot him a warning glance as he prostrated himself in the dirt and braced for the blows to come.

▼▲▼▲▼ Once his Pequot companions had fallen asleep inside the slaves' quarters, Taregan rose from his mat and soundlessly slipped into the moonlight. Pain from the broken skin on his back kept him awake, but more troubling were the thoughts and feelings that stormed in his soul.

The moon had risen high in the sky, and bright, swiftly moving clouds scuttled before its surface. Taregan paused, reveling in the familiar sight of the moon, losing himself in memories of other nights when he had lain with his father and brother in its silver glow and listened to the haunting call of the owl and the whippoorwill.

The girl had opened the black veil that hung over painful memories at the back of his mind. He had not spoken with a woman in over five years, and her youthful beauty had brought the image and memory of Dena into painful flesh-and-blood reality.

He heard—no, *sensed*—movement behind him and turned to see one of the Mohegans an arm's distance away. The man was a scarred, aged warrior with a hard jaw, tendoned neck, and deep chest. Taregan nodded gravely. Out of respect for the uneasy truce between the two tribes, he and this man spoke not at all by day, but Taregan had often caught the man's eye and read an invitation in the smoldering dark depths. At last the time had come for them to meet.

"You are like the English," the man said finally in the Algonquin language, crossing his arms across his chest. "You have their eyes."

"My father was Wematin, Englishman and blood brother to Nixkamich of the Pequot," Taregan answered, staring again at the moon.

"I have heard of him," the warrior answered. His veiled, liquid eyes studied Taregan's face for a moment. "I was with Uncas when he traveled with Captain Mason to Mystic."

Taregan felt the wings of tragedy brush lightly past him. "Mystic?"

"I have wanted to speak with you of this. But I was not sure you would want to hear."

"I want to hear," Taregan answered, crossing his arms. He turned so that he faced the man directly and fastened his eyes to the warrior's. "Tell me what burns in your heart."

"I saw something in the woods that night," the Mohegan said, his face firmly set in deep thought. "I saw two Englishmen. One man with blood-colored hair hid behind the English army. He wore colored buckskin and carried a bow and quiver. The other man, with hair as black as night, waited behind a tree with an iron musket. This man wore the uniform of the English."

"I may know the dark-haired man," Taregan answered. "He is tall and thin, with a long, bony face and hawkish eyes."

"Yes. He has killed many times. For many moons before the attack at Mystic he visited the villages of the Mohegan, Niantic, and Narragansett and promised a musket to any warrior who would kill an Englishman on the river. Many died, and my people received muskets from this man called Black."

"Garvin Black." The confirmation left Taregan momentarily breathless. He closed his eyes, fearing the man's next words. "When you saw Black in the woods at Mystic . . . did he kill the red-haired man?"

The warrior shook his head. "The black one spoke roughly to the other, holding the iron musket on him. He demanded the first man's coat, then marched the blood-haired man through the woods, away from the English." The Mohegan shifted uneasily. "I followed. Then the black-haired one bound the other and sent him away with two warriors of my tribe."

"Sent him away?" Taregan's eyes widened in surprise. "He did not enter the fort?"

The Mohegan's eyes narrowed. "No. They went back the way the English had come, toward the river. I heard later that the man was called a traitor. An English officer sentenced him to serve upon one of the king's ships."

A bubbling, furious excitement rose in Taregan's chest; he stared wordlessly at the Mohegan warrior, his heart pounding. Garvin Black had lied! Fallon had not entered the fort at Mystic, he had not perished in the flames! He had survived the battle— he might still be alive now!

Mother was right. Bless God, thank you Holy Father, Mother was right!

"Why would Garvin Black do such a thing?" he asked, thinking aloud. "Why did he do any of these things?"

"Black said the Pequot had the best beaver rivers and land, but they had refused to open their lands to the English," the warrior answered, his eyes studying Taregan with a curious inten- sity. "He said the English were angry because some of their people had died upon the river. He promised that the Pequot would disappear if we did what he asked."

"And my father was a leader among the Pequot," Taregan whispered. "They respected his counsel. So Garvin Black had to send him away. He couldn't kill him—too many eyes about. But he had to silence my father's voice among the tribes."

He took a step backward, stunned by the realization that the Pequot War had been nothing but the result of greed. With lies, murder, and avarice as his tools, Garvin Black had persuaded the English to hate thousands whom they had never seen and to kill as many as they could. Hiding behind the names of justice and retribution, he had practically exterminated a nation.

Taking a deep breath, Taregan reached out and grasped the warrior's shoulder. "You have done me a great service, brother. You have restored to me the father I thought was dead. I will do what I can to keep peace between your tribe and mine while we are on this island."

"We are dying . . . here," the Mohegan answered, tapping the space over his heart. He turned slowly toward the spot where his fellow tribesmen slept on the ground. "But we can die in peace."

▼▲▼▲▼ Hassun was awake and sitting in a patch of moonlight when Taregan reentered the slave house. "Do you usually relieve yourself in the dark of night?" Hassun asked, all traces of friendship and humor wiped from his face. "And do you often stop to talk with our enemy when you do?"

"What do you mean?" Taregan answered, lying down on his mat.

"I saw you!" Hassun hissed, leaning over Taregan. "I saw you talking with the Mohegan! What are you thinking, Taregan? They are our blood-enemies, the ones who united with the English to kill our people—"

Taregan folded his arms across his chest and blinked up at the ceiling. "Tonight I have learned something," he said, keeping his voice low. "The Mohegan was present at Mystic. He saw Garvin Black abduct my father. And this same Garvin Black, the trader, bribed other tribes with the promise of muskets if they would kill Englishmen on the river."

He lifted his head and looked at Hassun. "The war was a mistake, little brother. Our people died as a result of one man's evil. The Mohegan are not to blame, for they were deceived."

"They cooperated! Their thirst for the white man's evil goods drove them to obey!"

"They were a branch on the vine of wickedness, but the root—" Taregan clenched his fists— "lies in Garvin Black. He knew full well what he was doing."

He set his jaw in determination. "I do not hate the Mohegans, Hassun. I will not lift a hand against them, for they have suffered as much as we. But Garvin Black must die. If God wills, he will die at my hand after he has admitted the truth about what happened to my father." Lifting his hand, he turned to the younger man. "As my father lives, I swear to you that Garvin Black will die."

▼▲▼▲▼ Though Taregan did not speak of it with the others, Hassun moved quickly to spread the news that at least one of the Mohegans on the plantation had taken part in the shameful assault at Mystic. Throughout the next several days, the Pequots' anger, kept alive by a deep-seated fire of resentment that had never gone out, rose and simmered beneath the surface as they worked.

Taregan sensed the change in the atmosphere and divined its source, but he could do nothing to dispel or diminish it. His own soul churned with outrage and hostility, but his desire for vengeance focused upon the shape and name of one white man alone. As he chopped cane in the field, Taregan imagined Black's narrow face on each slender stalk before his blade; he dreamed of finding Black in the forest and surrendering him to the bloodthirsty Mohawks for torture and death. Mayhap, he thought one night as he sat outside the slave house and chewed on a sliver of cane, he'd tie the greedy trader up and leave him to burn in his cursed trading post. And if, perchance, foolish, blind Daniel still followed this fiend, he'd tell him the truth about their father's alleged murder and then smile as Daniel lit the match.

Worn and weary after a day of cutting the cane, Taregan slipped into the slave house and stretched out on his mat. He scarcely had time to clear his thoughts before he withdrew into a deep and dreamless sleep.

He did not know how long he slept, for his body was too tired to register time or movement, but in the dark of night a blood-curdling war cry jerked him back to reality. He sat up, instantly awake. Glancing around in the darkness, he saw that only a pair of very old men still lay on their mats. Huddled like gray shadows on the floor, their eyes shone with bewilderment. Without stopping to think, Taregan sprinted for the doorway.

What he saw outside made his heart pound in a frenzy of horror. More than a dozen of the Pequot slaves had somehow managed to steal long machetes from Hans Christoffels' supply shed. The vicious blades worked with deadly efficiency in the defenseless circle of the Mohegans. The agonized cries of the startled victims shattered the night.

Dear God, what have they done?

"No!" Taregan screamed, waving his arms as he ran into the melee. "Not this! Do not slay one another! Hassun! Have mercy! Machk, Askook, stay your hands!"

A light blazed from the stone house on the hill as the circle of Mohegans boiled. The men sprang forth from their pallets as though they had been waiting, tensed and ready, for one final chance to prove themselves fierce and proud warriors. Taregan flew toward Hassun, who grappled with one of the Mohegans. Blood from a cut on his forehead transformed his visage into a glistening devil mask more fierce than anything he could have painted with the red clays of home.

"Hassun!" Taregan watched in hypnotized horror as the figures around him struggled against each other. In a dance of death they pirouetted in the moonlight, arms locked with arms, forehead against forehead, anger against fierce pride. Many of the machetes were now wielded by Mohegans, and warriors without weapons picked up firelogs to deflect the deadly blows. Three Mohegans already lay dead, their blood staining the sand. Taregan shivered when he recognized one of the dead as the warrior who had told him the truth about Garvin Black.

Pounding footsteps sounded from the hill, and Taregan whirled as the master ran down the path, his musket in hand and his nightdress flapping in the wind. "Be still, or I'll shoot!" he yelled, reaching the perimeter of the fight, but Hans Christoffels had not been born and bred to battle. As he struggled to lift the long rifle, Hassun ran forward with a machete and cut the master in half.

Waves of grayness passed over Taregan as Hans Christoffels tumbled to the ground, his mouth open, his face frozen in a paroxysm of fear. The musket flew from his hands as if thrown, slipping over the ground until it landed at Taregan's feet. He felt himself stare stupidly at it for a moment, then he picked the gun up, pointed it toward the sky, and pulled the trigger.

The blast ripped through the night like the thunder of war. Waves of silence began from the warriors nearest him and spread over the clearing. The Pequots froze, blood streaming from their bodies and their machetes. The clearing was a sight from hell. Bloodied bodies lay scattered over the sand like broken toys, and a dark pool of blood puddled on the sand next to the master's body.

"What evil have you done here?" Taregan shouted, the roar of the gun still echoing in the night. "You have shamed your forefathers this day! You have angered the Great Spirit! Murder is the work of the evil one, not of those who call themselves Pequot!"

"The English called us murderers. Tonight we have proved them right!" The cry came from Hassun, but the pitch and tone were so heightened that Taregan nearly did not recognize his voice. The young man's face glowed red in the moonlight, the wind lifted his hair like a dark cloud of death behind him.

"You have avenged yourselves upon the wrong people," Taregan said with a helpless wave of his hands. Suddenly limp with weariness, he stood the musket on the ground, then let it fall into the sand. "On the morrow there must be an accounting for these dead. Our lives are over, my brothers. You have killed your master, and the English lords in Hole Town will hang us—all of us—for this deed. There will be no escape."

He dropped his head in a silence that was the holding of breaths.

For a moment no one spoke, then Askook lifted his machete high. "We can do something! We can toss these bodies into the sea and tell the English that we slept through whatever happened here. We can say the Mohegans killed the master and fled away—"

"The sea will fling the bodies back to us," Hassun said, disdain dripping from his voice. "Lying is the coward's way. We have avenged our people upon these Mohegans, and I will stand and proudly proclaim that I have done so. If I die, I die. As a slave away from my people, I am already dead."

Fury lurked beneath the smile he gave Taregan. "I have avenged every stripe upon your back, my friend. The man who stole your birthright and whipped you like a dog is dead. My heart rejoices in this deed."

Taregan stood still and looked toward the dark horizon, the rhythmic crash of the ocean tide the only sound in the night. His mind skittered away from the unsolvable dilemma before them, and for a moment he idly wondered if Daniel had fathered a child. If so, Taregan would never see his niece or nephew. Hassun would proudly, gladly surrender them all to certain death. The young Indian did not dream of returning to Connecticut. He lived for nothing but vengeance.

Taregan lowered his eyes to the carnage around him. All twenty of the Mohegans lay dead, as did the master and two of his Pequot brothers. What a bloody night—and for what?

"I did not want to die," he murmured, turning toward the beach.

He had not gone more than twenty paces when he felt someone rush toward him. "Then you will not die with us!" Hassun's
voice rang in his ear. The youth leapt onto Taregan's back while
a silver blade bit through the darkness and slipped across Taregan's neck. Warm blood spilled over his fingers as he clutched
at Hassun's arm, then something struck him on the back of the
head and he fell forward into the sand.

    ▼▲▼▲▼ The glory of the sunrise was diluted by angry
gray clouds that swirled overhead like warring lions waiting to
breathe death. Hassun felt his panic rise as he gazed at the
bloody battlefield in the light of morning. Taregan was right, the
English magistrates of Hole Town would not hesitate to round
up and hang the entire group of slaves. The coming day would
be his last upon the earth.

Quietly, resolutely, he walked to each of the others and placed
a comforting hand upon each man's shoulder. When he had
saluted each warrior, he sat by the fire and began to sing his
death song. Each of them would face death in his own way, but
at least Taregan would be spared. The English would find him
on the beach, see the shallow cut on his neck, and surmise that
he had been trying to run for help when he had been cut down.
He would not be condemned as a conspirator, but proclaimed a
hero.

Moving as silently as a shadow, Hassun stood and walked
toward the beach. Gusts of wind blew through the cane and rippled the eddies in the tidal pools. Hassun passed Taregan's
unconscious form and walked steadily toward the sound of the
surf. Black arms of rain reached down from clouds over the sea.
There was no escape from the dark water that surrounded him.
No way home, no way off the island, no way to survive the system that had made him a slave. . . .

The cold water bit his ankles, but Hassun trudged on, singing
his death song with renewed vigor. He was not afraid to die, but

he would not let the English conquer him in death as they had in life. *The sea will spit my body back. They will know I am to blame.*

The water pressed around his knees, his thighs.

Was this a coward's way out? No. Yes. Perhaps.

His heart skipped a beat as the cold water sloshed against the warm flesh of his bare chest, but Hassun continued to move his heavy limbs through the water. Something stirred in the sea beyond, and he moved toward the splash, not caring if he met a shark. The water deepened, and he swam toward the west. Cutting the cane had made him strong. He might swim for hours, but he would not reach land.

A harrowing headache pounded Dirk Christoffels' temple, a remnant of the paralysis of horror that had earlier left him speechless. He had arrived at his brother's plantation as the sun climbed overhead, and for a moment he thought the grisly scene before him was but a trick of his overwrought imagination. The surviving slaves—savages, in truth, they were—had lined up the bodies in a neat row. Pensive and resigned, they sat like statues before the dead, each man lost in his thoughts. Later, after the shock and horror had passed, this fact had surprised Dirk. They had not run from their murderous crime, and each slave had willingly admitted his part in the heinous uprising. Each man, too, had sworn that the injured man found on the beach had tried to stop the destruction.

The governor's magistrate finished chaining the last captive's hands. "I'll take them away now, unless you want another word with them," he said, doffing his hat in respect for Dirk's grief. "I can assure you, they'll be hanging by sundown."

Dirk woodenly shook his head, grappling with the realization that his capable and ambitious older brother was gone. Hans's bloated body now collected flies as it lay in the sun. "I want to bury my brother and these other men," Dirk said, rising to his feet with an effort. "Do you know some gentlemen, sir, who would spare the time to help?"

The magistrate crinkled his nose. "Give your brother the Christian burial he deserves and burn the others," he said, jerking his head toward the line of dead slaves. "Why fill good land with their bones? I'd be happy to send someone to help you dig a burning pit."

Dirk looked toward the sea, keeping his eyes far above the line of dead men. "I'd appreciate the help."

The magistrate looked again at the bloodstained sand and the machetes lying about like abandoned toys, then squinted toward his captives. "On to Hole Town," he yelled, cracking the whip in his hand. "Justice will be done today. You devils will greet the sunset with a rope 'round your necks."

Away they went, as silent as death, without once looking back. When the entire company had disappeared behind the rise of the cane, Dirk turned toward the house and lifted his hands to the sky in an expression of surrender. "My wise brother, Hans," he said, feeling as if an entire section of his body had been torn away, "would it have pained you to listen just once to your younger brother? Now I must bury you in the acres of which you were so proud."

▼▲▼▲▼ "I must do what?"

"Tend to the injured man, Arabella. He has developed a fever." Her father's face reddened in exasperation. "I have to go to the governor's office and register my account of the massacre. Your mother has taken to her bed with grief. You are the only one left to nurse him."

Her father was an endless surprise. Days ago he had warned her that the slaves were dangerous, and now he wanted her to nurse one. "But—he was one of them! He was there when they killed Uncle Hans!"

"This man tried to stop the bloodshed. Do you think I would let him near you if I believed him a threat?"

Arabella looked at the ground and pressed her hands together. "*Nee, Vader.*"

"Take the horse and ride out this morning. I left him in the slaves' quarters."

Her father turned and walked away, and Arabella forced her unwilling feet to move toward the stable. In the space of forty-eight hours her family's world had crumbled like a sand castle before the surf. After the shock of hearing about the slaves' rebellion and her uncle's gruesome death, she had realized that her father now owned more land than anyone else on Barbados. That meant more profit, more money, more prestige—and more work.

Her expectations sank as rapidly as they had risen. As long as her father refused to own or work slaves, the land would suffer. Two hundred acres were too many for one family to cultivate, too much cane for three people to cut.

The bay mare waited patiently in the barn, saddled and ready to go, and Arabella stood on a low railing of the stall and flung herself across the animal's broad back. Nickering in pleasure, the mare turned toward the fresh scent of the sea and set out at a fast trot.

Arabella followed the shore, running the mare on the sand, until she reached the marker at the edge of her uncle's plantation. A trail cut through the sea grasses, and she squinted down it, half fearing that a bloody savage might yet leap forward and hurl a machete at her. But nothing moved but the wind in the reeds.

She turned the mare onto the trail and soon entered the clearing outside her uncle's house. If she had not known about the tragedy, she might have supposed it a typical day with the slaves working in the fields and her uncle watching over them. The house was quiet, like a cat sleeping in the sun; a shutter on the window banged against its frame, blown by the wind.

Arabella slid from the saddle and tethered the horse to a post in the sand, then gripped her basket of supplies. Lifting her long skirts in her free hand, she took a deep breath and marched resolutely toward the silent building that had formerly housed the treacherous slaves. If the man she sought was not inside, she ought to burn the hideous shack to the ground. . . .

But there he was, on a grass mat, and she grimaced at the sight of him. Pale and sweaty, he lay in the shadows, his body uncovered but for a pair of canvas breeches that ended at the knee. His chest heaved as though he struggled to breathe, and ribbons of red from the blackened wound across his throat crept over his tanned skin. His dark hair lay disheveled around his head and shoulders; his face glowed with the unnatural brightness of fever.

She came closer, peering at him, and gasped when she recognized the blue-eyed man with whom she had spoken before. His pale face was cut as clear and sharp as a cameo, and she felt a wave of gratitude that the knife had not marred his facial features. His thin body, though laced with tough-looking sinews, was more youthful than intimidating. She should have known he'd be the noble one.

Pressing her hand to his shoulder, she felt the burning heat of fever. "Oh," she murmured, more alarmed than frightened by the sight of her patient. She dropped the basket of cloths and bandages and picked up a bucket standing by the doorway. Running to the well, she filled the bucket and hurried back to her patient, sloshing water all over her dark skirt.

Kneeling in the shadows at his side, she dipped one of the cloths into the pail. "Here," she said, squeezing a few drops of water onto his cracked lips. Reflexively, he pressed his lips together. Encouraged, she wiped his face, feeling the heat of fever through the fabric. "Dear God," she murmured, "am I tending a dying man?"

His heavily fringed eyelids flew open at the sound of her words, and she found herself staring into troubled pools of blue, deeper and brighter than the waters of the sea. His wounded throat worked as he struggled to find his voice. "You should not be here," he croaked, his bloodstained hand reaching up to clasp her wrist.

"You are ill," Arabella answered, firmly pulling free from his grasp. She dipped the warm cloth into the bucket again to cool it. "You need someone, and I am available." She flashed him an impenitent grin. "I'd rather tend you than cut cane anyway."

"The others . . . ?"

"Are all gone," she answered, wringing the cloth over the earthen floor. "All dead, including my uncle." She could not keep an edge of bitterness from her voice. "I suppose you cannot tell me what happened here."

Closing his eyes, he shook his head so violently that the wound opened.

"See what you have done," she chided, gently pressing the cloth to the bleeding cut. "You must lie still. The men who remained here when my father came told him the entire story. They also confessed to the magistrate. Your name has been cleared, Taregan Bailie, and the others are hanged. Only one man is unaccounted for, and the magistrate has men searching for him—"

"Hassun?"

She tilted her head. "*Ja,* that is the one. How did you know?"

He grunted. "I know him."

At the touch of the cold cloth on his chest, he shivered, but Arabella continued cleaning and cooling him, then went into her uncle's house for a blanket. When she came back, he was sitting up, his legs bent as if he intended to walk.

"Where do you think you're going? Lie back down."

"Salt—I need the seawater. It will heal this cut."

"It would sting the sense out of you, not that you have any to begin with."

He lowered his head and glared at her, the first real display of energy she had seen from his weakened body. "You know nothing, girl. Stand out of my way."

Arabella moved to block the door, her hands on her hips. "My father sent me to tend you, and I'll not shirk my duty. You haven't the strength to walk to the sea and back!"

"I need the seawater!"

"Lie down, and I'll fetch it myself. I'd rather do that than have to tie you to the horse and drag your sorry carcass back to this place after you've collapsed!"

For a moment she thought he would try to push his way past her, then suddenly he smiled. "I do beg and pray you," he said as elegantly as any English lord on the island. "If you would fetch seawater to wash this wound, I would be most grateful."

Slightly mollified, she folded her arms and tipped her head back to look at him. There was something almost regal in his posture and way of expressing himself. What had he been, this Indian called Taregan, before he had become her uncle's slave?

"First you must drink of the fresh water in the bucket," she said, not moving from her place. "I'll not be toting that heavy pail back and forth to the pump just for your pleasure."

He nodded in quiet acquiescence and knelt before the bucket. Cupping his trembling hands, he lifted mouthful after mouthful, then dropped his hands into his lap. "Please, the salt water," he said, not looking at her. "Please."

Smiling in satisfaction, she took the bucket and walked toward the sea.

▼▲▼▲▼ Two days later, Taregan looked up to see Dirk Christoffels enter the cabin. For a moment his heart sank in disappointment, for he had come to enjoy the brown-haired daughter's visits. But this meeting was certain to be significant. As Hans Christoffels' heir, Dirk now held Taregan's life in his hands.

"You are better?" The man filled the doorway, but unlike Hans, Dirk carried his hat in his hand as he entered the room.

"Yes," Taregan said, rising from his mat. "Thanks to your daughter and her kindness."

"Don't stand up," Dirk said, holding out a hand. He squatted on the floor and regarded Taregan with a strong and steady gaze. "My daughter has told me that you are much stronger. Apparently the fever has left your body."

"It has," Taregan answered, crossing his legs. He leaned forward and rested his elbows on his knees. "Your daughter has been a very patient nurse."

A reluctant smile cracked the planter's sturdy face. "Patient? You give her too much credit, my friend. My Arabella is anything but patient. Sympathetic, talkative, idealistic, and loving, yes. But patient? *Nee.*"

Taregan lifted his head at the word *friend*. What sort of master addressed his slaves with such a term?

Dirk saw the question in his eyes. "You are probably wondering what is to become of you. Now that my brother is dead, I am owner of all his property, including you." He twisted the hat in his hands. "But I could never own another man, so this day I grant you manumission. If you wish, you are free to go."

A sudden exultation filled Taregan's chest to bursting. Home! He could take passage on a ship, go back to Connecticut, find his mother, Dena, and Daniel—

But he had no money, not even a decent suit of clothing. Mayhap he could purchase passage by selling himself into indentured service, but the indenture was worse than slavery. Men who figured to own servants for only seven years tended to work them without regard for their future well-being. No, he could not sell himself, for what good would he be to his loved ones if he were in chains?

"I cannot leave," Taregan said, looking at his hands. "I did want to go home, sir, but I have no money to hire passage on a ship."

"In that case—" Dirk cleared his throat— "I have a proposition for you, Taregan Bailie." He glanced up quickly. "That is your name? Arabella said it was."

"It is."

"All right." Dirk sank onto the floor facing Daniel. "We might be able to help each other, you and I. Arabella has spoken highly of your courage, while your actions here have defined your character." At this he raised his eyes to Taregan's face in an oddly keen, swift look. "I have land and no one to work it. You are free and strong, with no land to work. Together, Taregan, you and I might do our best to work these acres of cane. 'Two are better than one,' so the Bible says, 'because they have a good reward for their labor.'"

"Work the land for you? Two hundred acres? Alone?" Taregan asked, incredulous.

"Not *for* me, *with* me," Dirk answered. "I own ten acres,

enough for a single man to handle. But many of Hans's acres are already planted—they need only to be harvested. I believe God will bless our labor if we give him his due, so we will work six days out of seven, as the Bible has commanded. God's hand will double our efforts, Taregan, and we shall prosper in this venture."

"But I cannot stay here." His throat constricted around the words. "I must tell you, Master Christoffels, that upon leaving Connecticut, I made a vow to return. Now God has been good enough to free me, but if I am bound to your land—"

"Not *my* land, *our* land," Dirk interrupted. "Give me but five years, Taregan, to establish a pattern of planting and harvesting. At the end of five years, whatever acres are profitable we shall divide into two equal parcels, and you will be free to sell your acres or stay, whichever you please."

Listening through a vague sense of unreality, Taregan weighed the sincerity and the motives behind the man's words. In all the dealings he had observed between the two brothers, Dirk Christoffels had been kind and true, maintaining a Christian attitude. He had consistently refused to own slaves, he had never chosen to labor on the Lord's Day, and Taregan had never seen a whip in the man's hand.

But five years! Such a long time to tarry on this windswept island when he could be on his way home. In five years his mother might be dead, Dena married to someone else, Daniel thoroughly corrupted or even destroyed by the evil inside Garvin Black.

But if this was not God's provision, what was? God had freed him from slavery and now seemed to be providing a way home.

Taregan extended his hand. "We are agreed," Taregan said simply as Dirk took his hand. "We will work these lands together, and five years from today we will each own an equal part."

"*Ja*," Dirk said, relief apparent on his face. "I will draw up a written agreement." He flushed suddenly. "Pardon me—perhaps I am wrong to assume that you know how to read—"

"Do not fear, Master Christoffels," Taregan answered, grinning. "I read and write. My mother taught me everything I would need to know to live in the English man's world."

A slow smile spread across the planter's face. "*Ja*, God is good. All right then, we must first get you out of this filthy shack. My brother's house is yours, Master Bailie, my friend. I will keep my wife and daughter in our house; it is too much trouble to move them. Burn this accursed hovel whenever you are able. We will not speak again of the horrible thing that happened here."

He combed his hair back with the fingers of both hands and looked out the window toward the open sea. "My brother—may he finally find rest—chose to walk a different path. I know he was a difficult master and probably not close to your heart, but I mourn for the man he might have been." He suddenly lifted his brows. "I nearly forgot," he said, digging in a small pocket in his breeches. "I have something for you. I found this in Hans's pocket, and Arabella tells me it is yours."

From his pocket he pulled out Taregan's ring, lifting it on the palm of his hand like a peace offering. Taregan shot Dirk a questioning glance, but there was only friendliness in the man's smile. Wordlessly, Taregan took the ring and slipped it on his smallest finger. Never again would he hide it.

"There is one thing I need to know," he said, looking at the unfamiliar gleam of gold upon his hand. "The missing slave— has he been found?"

The light in Dirk's eye faded. "*Ja*. He washed up yesterday a few miles down the beach. The magistrate sent word to us a few hours ago."

Taregan nodded, blinking back unexpected tears.

▼▲▼▲ Months later, Dirk often thought that the one bright thread in the mantle of memory over Hans's death was the discovery of Taregan Bailie. Over and over Dirk thanked God that the young man had been spared from the massacre, and he wondered what set Taregan apart from the other savages who had killed and died for the sake of honor. Taregan was an honorable man, as God-fearing and respectful as any soul on Barbados, yet he possessed the confidence of a lion. Projecting a quiet air of authority, he confronted problems with the utter frankness of the firm and practiced hunter. "He is not a man who accepts second best in anything," Dirk told the magistrate when he came to check on Taregan's progress. "I do believe he is a gentleman."

Despite his ability to command respect, his was a warm soul. His gentleness showed itself in the respectful way he treated Arabella's animals. With an unusual love for beasts, she poured her life into her chickens and the few livestock on the property, and Taregan often stopped to help her feed and tend her flock.

One evening after a backbreaking day of cutting cane, Dirk happened to stumble upon Taregan and Arabella in the barn. A ewe had birthed a lamb the previous day, and the little creature struggled for life. It bleated constantly for attention, but its frail, spindly legs could not support its weight despite the ewe's efforts to prop it up.

"The bones are weak," Dirk heard Taregan say. "I do not think it will live."

"Oh, no," Arabella moaned. "Isn't there anything we can do? Can we give it more milk? I could hold it up so that it will be able to nurse from its mother—"

"Nothing," Taregan said, his hand running lightly over the lamb's downy coat. "If you support it today, it will never grow strong enough to drink on its own. Who will hold it tomorrow? And the day after that?"

"Taregan, I can't stand to sit here and watch it die! We've got to do something! That pitiful bleating tears at my heart—"

"It is saying good-bye," Taregan answered, stroking the lamb in a regular, soothing rhythm. "Suffering is a natural part of life, Mistress Christoffels. Soon the lamb will sleep, and its pain will end." A flicker of a smile rose at the edges of his mouth. "Have you never said good-bye to someone you loved?"

"No," Arabella whispered, visibly melting at the young man's smile.

From his hiding place in the shadows of the barn, Dirk watched Arabella lean toward Taregan. The woman inside of her had come alive in the past months, and Dirk could almost feel his daughter's thoughts. Confused by the ex-slave's easy charm, she stood in awe of the young man, fascinated by his gentle ways and his knowledge of wild things. Of certain she was caught up in the eager tremors of adolescence, but Dirk was not certain his daughter should be dreaming of Taregan Bailie. . . .

"Arabella!" he called, forcing a light tone into his voice as if he had just walked into the barn.

"What?" The face she turned toward him was taut with disappointment.

"Your mother sent me to fetch you. She needs help with dinner."

Arabella sighed, then extended a hand for Taregan to help her up. Dirk watched as those bronzed fingers closed around his daughter's creamy skin; her hand lingered on Taregan's for a moment longer than necessary. But she walked away without a backward glance. At least she had some pride.

Is it the savage in him that attracts her, or the civilized gentleman? Dirk wondered, turning to watch her go. And though Taregan shows her nothing but brotherly affection, he is a man in the prime of life and without a woman of his own. . . .

Dirk frowned. Perhaps he had done wrong to exact a full five years' commitment from the attractive young man. If Taregan felt nothing for Arabella, he might be tempted to use her and then cast her off. Of course, it was unlikely, given his noble nature, but passion burned hot in the young, and Arabella had practically cast herself at his feet today. What might she do in the years to come?

Lingering in the shadows of the barn, he studied the young man bent over the baby lamb. What if this striking youth fell in love with Arabella? He might assume that Dirk would not approve of an ex-slave for a son-in-law.

"But you would be wrong, my friend," Dirk murmured.

A few weeks later Dirk hitched the mare to the wagon, then helped Taregan load bundles of cane. When the bundles had been securely lashed to the tall poles standing upright along the sides of the wagon bed, both men climbed aboard. Dirk flicked the reins and pointed the mare toward the sugar mill.

The sun was hot and the trade winds sticky as they moved down the rutted road toward Hole Town, and Taregan stretched his lanky frame over the bench seat and pulled his hat low over his eyes. With his hands crossed behind his head and the brim of his straw hat hiding his eyes, he was the perfect picture of an islander: tanned, lean, and strong.

"What will you do when our time together is done?" Dirk asked, casting a quick glance toward his partner as he guided the horse over the scarred road. "You will be a rich man, Taregan Bailie. You might be forgiven if you forgot about Connecticut and spent the rest of your life on Barbados. More slaves enter the port every day, and the acres we are leaving fallow grow more valuable with each passing month. You could sell them at a great price—"

"I'm not interested in money," Taregan answered from beneath the brim of his hat. "Only in enough to get me home."

"Mayhap, then, something else might hold you on Barbados," Dirk answered. "Love, perhaps." He paused, but the only sounds were the creaking of the mare's harness and her plodding footsteps over the packed sand. "You could marry *mijn dochter*," he went on, his voice light. "I know she holds you in high esteem. You would then inherit my portion and be a far greater

man than my brother ever hoped to be. Master of Barbados, heh?
What do you think?"

The head under the hat moved slightly. "I think," Taregan
replied, his words precise, "that I should be honest with you. I
not only have a mother in Connecticut, but a brother . . . and a
woman. We were promised to each other in marriage before I
was captured."

"But that was seven years ago, Taregan!"

"I gave my word. Her father gave his. And I believe she waits
for me still."

"Was this girl an Indian?"

Taregan nodded. "Yes, a Pequot."

"How do you know she still waits for you?"

A tanned hand lifted the hat, and Taregan's blue eyes blazed
into Dirk's. "How do we know anything? We trust God, and
keep our word, and pray that others will do the same. I gave a
vow to my mother and a promise to the girl I loved. I will honor
both. For those reasons alone, I cannot remain on Barbados." He
tapped the gold ring on his finger. "This was my mother's wed-
ding ring, and her mother's before that. When my mother gave it
to me she reminded me of the charge inscribed inside: *fortiter,
fideliter, feliciter.* Boldly, faithfully, successfully."

Dirk rode in silence for a moment, digesting this bit of information. His business partner was an ex-slave who quoted Latin.
Each day he discovered new elements of Taregan Bailie's personality. His mind bulged with unasked questions, but he rode in
silence, waiting for Taregan to continue.

"Though I may never be the man my mother hoped I would
become," Taregan finally finished, "I can at least be faithful
and keep my promises. I must return to Connecticut. That
much I can do."

Dirk pressed his lips together and flicked the reins across the
mare's sweaty back. He had thought himself a resolute soul until
he met this man.

"So," he answered, drawling his words into the sun, "I can do nothing to change your mind? I fear *mijn dochter's* heart will be broken if you leave."

"Your daughter is a compassionate and nurturing soul who will make some man a wonderful wife. I would not hurt her for the world."

Dirk bit the inside of his cheek and kept his eyes on the road. "Do you feel nothing for her?"

"Kindly affection, as I might have felt for a sister."

"I see."

A cloud moved in front of the sun, casting unexpected shade, and both men sighed in relief as the mare sprinted forward, eager to reach water and rest.

▼▲▼▲▼ For four years Taregan and Dirk planted, weeded, cut, and harvested together. With the profits from the cultivated fields they hired free men to plow and plant more acres, and soon nearly all of the two hundred ten acres rippled with cane. Europe was starved for the sweet crop and its by-products, molasses and rum. While the average plantation yielded twenty tons of cane per acre, the Christoffels' fields yielded thirty.

Dirk believed that their greater output was due to God's blessing. Though he and Taregan hired free men to work the crop with them, other plantation owners invested in slaves, most of whom now were native Africans stolen or gathered as spoils of tribal warfare. Ten thousand Europeans had lived on the island in 1640. "But at this rate," Dirk grumbled one afternoon as he and Taregan walked past an auction of African slaves, "within thirty years this island will be home to fifty thousand people, two-thirds of them slaves."

God's hand not only blessed but also protected the Christoffels' plantation. From December through June, fierce dry trade winds blew relentlessly across the island, often damaging the crops, but the Christoffels' fields seemed always to emerge unscathed. "*Ja*, I knew that you were a good man, Taregan Bailie," Dirk said one afternoon as they swam in the sea to cool off after a hot day in the fields, "but I didn't know how good."

"I have done nothing to merit such a compliment," Taregan said, feeling himself blush. "You are a fine manager, Dirk. You have organized the work."

"*Nee*, I'm beginning to think we prosper because your prayers reach higher than mine," Dirk said, laughing. "Hans used to scold me for praying because my cane never grew as well as his."

"Brothers are a bother," Taregan said, frowning as he thought of Daniel.

"I forgot that you had a brother," Dirk answered, paddling lazily toward shore. "Is he much like you?"

"Exactly like me," Taregan answered, turning onto his back. "And yet nothing like me."

"*Ja*, I understand," Dirk called over his shoulder. "We love them even though they make us crazy. As difficult as my brother was, still I miss him. Listen to one who understands, Taregan. When your parents and your brother are gone, you feel as though you're beginning to disappear yourself."

Something in his words made Taregan hesitate. For some shapeless reason, his anger toward Daniel had cooled over the last few months. Like the Mohegans, Daniel had been deceived and blinded by the charming aspects of an evil man possessed with the spirit of the destroyer himself. But no matter how strong the evil influence, Taregan did not think Daniel could ever be as ruthless as Garvin Black. Their parents had taught them right from wrong; they had instilled the fear of God and the honor of righteousness into both of their sons.

In a strange and unexpected way, thoughts of Daniel dulled the cutting edge of Taregan's loneliness. Did they still look alike? Had Daniel taken a wife? Did he live with the English, or had he established a homestead in the woods? Would Taregan ever see him again? "Please God," he found himself murmuring, "keep Daniel safe—"

He stopped, pressing his lips together. Of certain his prayer

had not flown any higher than the mosquitoes buzzing above
the beach. His mother had always made the twins apologize to
each other before the family's evening prayers, because, she said,
God wouldn't hear the plea of an angry heart. Daniel was a
world away, so Taregan couldn't apologize for the anger he'd
expressed the last time they talked. He could confess to God his
anger toward Daniel, but that confession wouldn't wipe his
heart clean enough for God to respect his prayer. His soul and
mind still burned with anger toward Garvin Black.

He turned in the sea and began a slow, smooth stroke toward
the shore. With hatred and anger resident in his heart, he had of
certain not done anything to merit divine favor. Dirk's generous
nature had more likely earned the blessing of God.

"My friend," Dirk called, drying off with a towel as Taregan
climbed out of the surf. "You will not be so lonely if you marry
and have sons. I wish I'd had sons myself, for they make the
work easier, but it was not in God's plan. Alas, I have but one
dochter, a lovely girl who will not pay the slightest heed to the
young Englishmen who come to court her."

"Perhaps it is because they come to court her property and
not the lady herself," Taregan answered, hiding the smile that
threatened to creep across his face. "Arabella is a compassionate
soul, but she can recognize a shyster as well as anyone."

"Or," Dirk said, tilting his head as he dried his thinning hair,
"mayhap it is because her heart already belongs to a man who
might have sons to work this field. A man who will give me
grandsons so I will not have to cut this cursed cane when I am
three-and-sixty years old."

Taregan laughed, long-used to Dirk's blatant hints. "You
might find that you would enjoy granddaughters," he said, sinking onto the sand. "You obviously enjoy matchmaking. Do you
think you could find husbands for a passel of granddaughters?"

Dirk scowled, but after a moment a smile curved to his lips
and stayed there as he moved toward the road that led to his
house. Taregan remained on the beach, watching the blurred and
bloodred sun sink beneath the horizon.

▼▲▼▲▼ The hour after dinner was Taregan's favorite time of day, a rare interval of solitude and reflection. He knew Arabella and Alida would have liked him to linger at their house after the evening meal. They loved to unburden their hearts at the end of the day, but Taregan did not want to foster the impression that he planned to ask for Arabella's hand. Once or twice he had remained in their house to watch the sunset, but soon he realized that they had become two couples. Dirk and Alida sat in one corner of the room, whispering the day's confidences, and he and Arabella lingered in another.

Now he said his good-byes quickly and set out upon the path to his own house. Better to let some English youth come calling after supper to hear the secrets of Arabella's soft heart.

Taregan stood in the doorway of the stone building that had housed him for more than four years. Soon his time of partnership would be over, and for many months he had debated what he should do next. For a while he had actually considered forgetting the past. It would be easy, even pleasurable, to settle on the island and live the life of an English gentlemen with black slaves to do his work and rear his children.

But he had worn the chains of slavery and felt the sting of the victor's whip. His throat still bore the burgundy stain of a traitor's blade. Such things were not easily forgotten.

Mayhap, he thought, he should sell only a portion of his property on Barbados. He could make a temporary journey to Connecticut, for he might not find his father, his mother, or Dena. As long as he owned land on the island, he could always come back and resume his position in the casual, windswept society.

But an inner voice urged him to give all, to follow his instincts, to obey the homeward call.

He was not an islander, never would be.

His place was in the woods, his voice one with the wind and the bear.

From the doorway of his house he could see the western sea spreading before him. Hot, water-scented winds blew across the dark-surfaced waters, and through the thickened air a dull-gray light began to inch across the ocean. Taregan stood as though fastened to the floor, studying the light and the odd movement of the waves. Shivering with a cold that was not from the air, he sensed a storm approaching from the opposite direction of the winds.

He circled throughout the house, obeying an old instinct to gather his belongings in a single place. In the center of the room he piled his clothing, his musket, his machete, the unread Bible Dirk and Alida had given him at Christmastide. The island was frequently deluged with storms that blew over palm trees and shacks, and thus far the stone house had withstood every blast of nature.

But this storm prowled like a lion outside the door. From the barn Taregan heard the frightened whinny of his yearling colt, a hard-won and extravagant purchase he had made with his share of last season's profits. Taregan ran for the stable, then led the skittish horse up the hill. Despite the bawling winds and the dark clouds that boiled overhead, the colt wanted no part of the house. Taregan looped the animal's halter lead over a post, then slipped off his shirt and threw it over the animal's head. Once the colt could not see, it followed meekly. Taregan pulled it into the house and barred the door shut.

"There, my brave little one," he said, resting his hand upon the colt's muzzle. The animal's eyes were wide with fear, but the creature stopped trembling at the sound of Taregan's voice. "It is only a little wind." Taregan made a mental note to bar the shutters at the window as soon as the animal had calmed. "We have had storms before, haven't we?"

The horse whinnied softly in response, and Taregan affectionately slapped the animal's flank and moved to bar the shutters. Then, covering his pile of possessions with a thick blanket, he settled on the floor next to them and closed his eyes for sleep.

It would be a long night, and he wanted to be ready for whatever might happen.

▼▲▼▲▼ Taregan bolted upright as a gigantic ripping noise tore through the house. Water spattered upon his cheek and knifed his bare arms. How could he be wet? Then he looked up. The roof had disappeared, and a yawning black hole gaped where before there had been rafters and thatch. The claws of the wind tugged at him, pulling at the blanket on which he slept, sending papers and books flying throughout the room.

The colt tossed its head and bounced in agitation, and Taregan rose to comfort the animal. The wind snatched away the words he called to the horse, but Taregan managed to grab a shirt to cover the animal's head again. Though blinded and held within Taregan's sheltering arms, the colt continued to tremble, its sides heaving with every quick breath.

Beneath the howling scream of the wind Taregan could hear the crashing roar of the sea. How far would its rogue waves encroach upon the sands? How many acres would be destroyed by this temperamental fit of nature?

Clinging to the colt, he buried his face against its smooth neck, relishing the absolutely normal, living smell of it. The wind goaded him, pulled at his shoulders as if it dared him to leave the sheltering stones of the house and step into its full fury. The gale outside had increased from its first warning blasts to a great roaring current of air, a torrent so laden with gushing rain that Taregan had to hold his head down and cup his mouth sideways to breathe.

He wasn't sure how long he and the stone house withstood the pounding storm, but after a while the darkness seemed to thicken and congeal around him. Rain slapped the sand outside, falling straight as if shot directly from God's arrow, and Taregan lifted his head. Of certain the worst was over.

The colt, too, sensed the change in the air pressure and lunged forward, eager to be out of the confines of the stone walls. Taregan let it go through the doorway, then he followed it out into the open.

The waves continued to roar and pound upon the beach, but the whining, blustering wind had ceased. He looked up and thought he could almost see the shimmer of stars above, the same star formations he and Daniel had gazed upon while the Pequot elders spun stories about the meanings of the bright clusters. The air hung still and dark and warm, the remaining fronds on the palm trees shivered as if paralyzed after their fierce dance with the wind.

An unusual scent stirred in the air, and Taregan lifted his head. He could smell the salt of the sea, the wet smell of rain—and smoke.

Something was burning.

Running toward the road, he glanced over the fields in the direction of Dirk's house. Even against the dark of the night sky he could see the red glow of fire. How could a house burn in the middle of a rainstorm?

Forgetting everything else, Taregan raced toward the tongues of leaping flame.

▼▲▼▲▼ The flames danced in the dying wind with whoofs and puffs and streams of sparks whirling off into the terrible darkness. Arabella stood outside the burning house in her nightdress, a thin, soaked shawl clutched around her shoulders. Tears flew down her cheeks, mingling with the rain.

"Taregan!" she sobbed when she saw him. "Help them! *Moeder and Vader* are still inside!"

Without hesitation, Taregan ran toward the low doorway. Part of the roof had collapsed, but whether due to the storm or the fire, he could not tell. Alida lay just inside the door, her neck twisted under a heavy beam. She had probably died the instant the beam fell.

"Dirk!" Taregan shouted, crawling on his belly to breathe the thin air near the floor. "Where are you?"

"Here." The word was barely audible over the snap and crackle of the flames, but a few feet away Taregan found Dirk pinned beneath the same beam that had killed his wife. The heavy timber covered him from shoulder to ankle, and Dirk's face had purpled beneath the pressure of its weight.

"Arabella?" Dirk whispered huskily through his pain. "Alida?"

"Arabella is outside, she is well. Be still, and I will get you out."

"*Nee*, there is no time. My leg is crushed. You and Arabella must find Alida and get to shelter. The storm—"

"It has passed, Dirk, and this wood is wet, so the fire will not reach you. If you will lie still—"

"*Nee*, Taregan. The storm is half passed. This is the calm before the end. You must find Alida—"

"Alida is dead."

The amber flames in Dirk's eyes dimmed as his head fell back upon the ground. When he spoke again, his voice was calm and reasonable. "You must take Arabella to the stone house, and you must go now."

He stiffened suddenly in a spasm of pain, and Taregan jerked with all his might on the stout beam that held Dirk in a fatal grip. But a team of horses could not have moved it.

Taregan paused and rubbed his stinging eyes. The smoke was strong and thick; the harder he worked, the more it choked him. But he could not leave this man who had given him everything—

"You must go," Dirk said, an edge of desperation in his voice. His hand stretched to reach Taregan's. "She is my only *dochter*, Taregan, she is all that matters. Nothing else. I give you the land, the horses, everything. But promise me that you'll take care of my *dochter*."

Taregan bent low to look into Dirk's eyes. "I promise. You know I'll do what I can."

Dirk's eyes closed. "Good." His facial muscles twisted in a twinge of pain. "Now take her to your house and live. And may God go with you."

"I'll take her. And then I'll come back for you," Taregan promised in a despairing whisper. He slid out the same way he had entered the house.

As he made his way back to Arabella, the rain hit with a sudden dense slanting rush of thick drops. The wind came sliding down over the island, and the sound of the surf grew louder. "Hurry!" Taregan said, taking her elbow.

"No!" Hysterically she pulled out of his grasp, flailing her arms like a child. "I can't go, I won't go, you can't make me leave them!"

Without a word, Taregan picked her up and heaved her across his shoulder, running for home like a hunted deer.

▼▲▼▲▼ The next morning the sun rose on desolation as complete as a battlefield. Acre after planted acre lay as flat as a beaten coin. Taregan's few possessions were ruined and his high-spirited colt thoroughly spooked. But his losses were nothing compared to Arabella's.

Dirk had been right. The storm had taken a rest and returned with increased fury, and the nightmare began again. Arabella clung to him and cried like a baby during the tempest, but the stout stone walls of Hans Christoffels' house remained strong, reinforced by Taregan's frantic prayers.

When at last the storm abated, he left Arabella asleep on a wet blanket and returned to Dirk's house. Those stone walls had collapsed completely, burying the man and his wife in a pile of blackened rubble and charred wood. Taregan tried for the better part of an hour to uncover the bodies, then decided that he should leave them as they lay until he could get help. Dirk and Alida were not suffering now.

With a heavy heart he turned again for home, wondering how he would explain the harsh reality to Arabella.

▼▲▼▲▼ With quiet dignity she accepted the news that both her parents were dead. She had wept and screamed most of the night, and Taregan suspected that her emotions had almost completely drained away. "How did the fire begin?" he asked, approaching the subject as gently as he could.

"The roof fell in, and an oil lantern spilled," Arabella answered, thumbing tears from her eyes. "*Moeder* had just filled it."

She kept to herself most of the day, walking out once to visit the ruined house and survey the desolate fields. When she returned, her tired twenty-year-old face looked middle-aged; there were hollows beneath her eyes, dark, bruised-looking circles. She spent the afternoon curled into a corner of the stone house with Taregan's ruined Bible in her hands, a last link to her parents.

The remains of the slave house had been washed out to sea; nothing remained of the hovel but a spot of smooth sand. The barn that had housed Taregan's horse was a pile of rubble. Taregan gathered a few planks of broken wood and piled them together for a fire. If they couldn't be dry, at least they could be warm.

"Your partnership with Papa is finished," Arabella announced when she joined him beside the fire. "My mother and father are dead, and I suppose I am now your business partner."

"Come, we'll talk." Taregan motioned for her to be seated on a mat of fallen palm fronds. When she had settled next to him, he turned to her. "Your father would never want you to go into business."

"My father," she said, her uplifted finger trembling with repressed emotion, "wanted you to marry me. And since you will not have me as a wife, you shall have me as co-owner of these acres."

"Arabella," Taregan said, running his hand through his hair in an exasperated motion, "I am not a planter. This is not my home. I have wondered what I should do, and now my way is clear. As soon as the island has recovered from this storm, I will sell my property and see that you are established under the care of a suitable guardian."

She lifted her chin in the stubborn gesture he knew well. "Why will you not be my guardian?"

"Because I am leaving. As soon as my share of the plantation sells, I am going home, back to Connecticut." He looked back to the fire and hesitated, not wanting to say anything that would bring further hurt to her soft brown eyes. "I have family there."

"And who do you think will buy these ruined acres?" she snapped, her eyes large and fierce with pain. "The entire crop is destroyed; it will take months for the remaining roots to sprout again—"

"There is enough money in the land itself to make me more than rich," Taregan said, picking up a scrap of wood. "You, too, are far wealthier than any other young lady on the island. If you want to return to the Netherlands—"

"There is nothing for me there."

Taregan shrugged and broke the damp wood. "Then any number of young men on this island would be happy to become your husband." He tossed the broken branch into the flames. "You are a lovely girl, Arabella, and bright. Any man—"

"Would be happy to have me," she finished, frowning at the fire. She sat still for a moment, then leaned forward and ran her dainty finger through the sand. "Some would say you are a scoundrel for leaving me unprotected, Taregan Bailie. My father would cringe to think—"

"I will not leave you alone. For nine years I have waited to go home, and I don't suppose it will hurt me to wait until I fulfill my vow to your father."

"Then take me with you." His startled gaze met hers, and she rushed on. "There is nothing for me on Barbados, nothing but money-hungry planters who would sell their very souls for a bag of gold to buy a dozen slaves. If you won't take me as a wife, take me as your ward. *You* be my guardian, Taregan, as my father asked. Don't leave me behind."

Words escaped him as he gazed at the determination in her face. Never had he seen such fire, such strength in any woman's eyes, save those of his mother. Like Gilda Bailie, Arabella Christoffells would not give up, Taregan knew that too well.

He reached for her hands. Mayhap this was God's will, after all. Men said that God worked in mysterious ways. . . .

"All right," he said, holding her at arm's length. "As soon as a buyer offers a fair price for part or for several parcels of land, we will go."

She gasped and sat back, clearly stunned.

"Did you think I would refuse you?" he asked, looking over at her.

"Indeed," she murmured, a blush rising on her cheeks. "I had no idea you could be won so easily.

Dena

Leave there thy gift before the altar,
and go thy way; first be reconciled to
thy brother,
and then come and offer thy gift.

Matthew 5:24

The wielded shovels left deep wounds in the earth beside the rubble of Dirk Christoffels' house. Taregan and Arabella stood silently in the crowd of mourners who had come to pay their respects. Since the hurricane, the entire population of Barbados had been engaged in mourning the dead and rebuilding that which had been destroyed.

Despite the morose and sorrowful atmosphere at the graveside, Taregan knew that the planters gossiped about him and Arabella. Without a doubt, they were now the two wealthiest people on the island.

"'Tisn't fitting," one of the men's voices drifted toward Taregan. "A mere girl and an Indian slave. 'Tisn't right that they should own so much."

Taregan threw a warning glance toward the planter; suitably ashamed, the man lowered his eyes. Arabella seemed not to have heard the comment. Kneeling at the graves of her parents, she kept her hands clasped at her breast, her eyes closed. After a long moment in which her lips moved in a soundless prayer, she opened her eyes and reached for Taregan's hand.

"I've heard from a Dutchman on the other side of the island," she said, lifting her skirts as she stood. She kept her voice low so the eavesdroppers would not hear. "He and a consortium of others are ready to buy if we still wish to sell."

"I still do," Taregan answered, turning his back to the other planters. "But you must think carefully, Arabella. Once you sell your property, all that your father worked to give you will be gone."

"Not entirely. I will have a purse full of gold," she said, facing him. The last traces of girlishness and uncertainty had evaporated from her features. She had always been lovely, but now she seemed a capable and mature woman. "And I will have you to guide me. Please, Taregan, let us not argue again. I have nothing here, nor anything in Europe. Take me with you to this Connecticut of yours, and God will lead me afterward."

He had already offered her a hundred reasons why she should not go to America, but she had swatted them away as easily as mosquitoes in the evening air. Reading the determination in her eyes, he pressed her hand to his arm and turned to regard the graves one last time.

▼▲▼▲▼ The sky was clear from rim to rim as Arabella followed Taregan aboard the ship that would take them to Boston. Schools of fish ruffled the shallows near the docks, as skittish and quick as the beating of her heart. She could barely remember her family's journey from Rotterdam to Barbados, and she counted this as the first real journey of her life. Certainly it was the most adventurous, for never had she faced the future without the protective shadows of her mother and father. Indeed, she would not have found the courage to face it now if not for Taregan, her reluctant guardian.

Their 210 acres had sold within a month of the hurricane, and she had watched with delight as Taregan's natural caution and reserve evolved into a state of controlled excitement. With a skill and intensity that surprised her, he concluded their affairs on Barbados and booked passage on a ship to Boston. They shared a single trunk, for they had not many possessions to transport, and on the day they were to set sail Taregan escorted Arabella to the port at Hole Town and bade her wait for him on a bench near the docks.

The reason why became apparent before long. With a secretive smile, he left her in the sparse shade of a palm tree and disappeared into a tailor's shop. When he emerged a few moments later, Arabella had difficulty recognizing him. Gone were his usual canvas knickers and sandals, in their place he had substituted a pair of dark green broadcloth breeches, stout leather boots that reached nearly to the knee, and a doublet in a matching green with an elegant lace collar. A large ostrich-plumed hat with a tilted brim completed the outfit.

Though his attire could not compete with the extravagant outfits the other planters wore when trying to impress each other, the effect of a gilded and plumed Taregan was so astonishing that she could only gape when he walked toward her.

"What?" he asked, lifting a brow. "Am I so like a monkey that you must mock me with that dropped jaw? The tailor has been working many days to outfit me—"

"*Nee*, you look nothing like a monkey!" she stammered, feeling the burn of a blush upon her traitorous cheek. When would she learn to hide her feelings? "It's just that you look so very— different. There is nothing of the Indian about you now, Taregan."

"I thought it best that I alter my rough appearance," he answered, suddenly serious. He sat next to her on the bench. "I do not know the fate of the Pequots who remain in Connecticut. Indeed, I don't know what has become of any of the Indian nations. And for your sake, Arabella, it would be best if you did not travel with a man who appears savage. And though I hate this finery—" he held up a hand where lace dripped in a profuse bloom from the sleeve of his doublet—"still, I am assured it is the costume of Boston."

"Whatever you think of it," she said, leaning back with pretended nonchalance, "it suits the English part of you, Taregan Bailie. You are quite a handsome picture."

He stood and swept the ridiculous hat before her. "After you, my lady. We've a boat to catch and a journey to begin."

Arabella stood and adjusted the bodice of her traveling gown. "You must admit, my Taregan," she said, taking his arm as he led her toward the docks. "You look quite the landed gentleman."

He had not answered, but led her toward the docks and the

gangplank, greeting the captain with monumental self-confidence and grace.

Now Arabella stood at the ship's railing, the wind on her cheek and the sun on her face. She closed her eyes and sighed in bittersweet anticipation. America! Her father had dreamed of going there, but her uncle had dismissed the idea as preposterous. "The land is too wild and savage," Hans had always protested. "A man could starve to death in that wilderness while waiting for supplies to reach him."

But she and Taregan would not starve. Locked safely away in their trunk, hidden under her bodices and sleeves, chemises and petticoats, were four bags of gold coins and several finely wrought silver pieces—more than enough to purchase whatever they might need once they reached Boston. Between the treasure in her trunk and the watchful protectiveness of the gentleman pacing behind her, Arabella felt confident that her new life in America would be a good one.

And yet, she mused, staring out over the wind-whipped waters of the bay, life was nothing without love. In Connecticut she would begin a new life, and she prayed every day that Taregan would be able to finally silence the ghosts of his past and find life's meaning in a new love—hers.

▼▲▼▲▼ After four weeks at sea, Boston rose one morning before the voyagers' eyes, its chimneys and gables rimmed with the first gray-pink tatters of dawn. Despite his effort to appear calm and self-possessed before Arabella, Taregan felt his pulse quicken at the sight of the city. He was almost home! After nine long years, he would finally keep his vow.

A sleepy line of gulls squabbled languidly over a spill of fish along the docks, and the ship came around fast, heeling over so that the silk-black water lipped at her port sills as she faded into her berth at the docks. Despite the early hour, a thrill of expectation had spread among the passengers, and most of them joined Taregan and Arabella at the windows in the lower hold. The foot-

steps of the crew thundered overhead amid the happy cries of
the passengers. Overcome with curiosity, Arabella leaned out of
the window at a dangerous angle. "Careful," Taregan said, reaching to pull her back into the ship. "I'll not be ruining these fine
clothes just to pull you out of the bay."

She laughed, a delicious three-noted giggle, and her eyes
shone mirror-brilliant with excitement. "You've nothing to fear,"
she said, refusing to retreat. "I know how to swim, you know. I
grew up on an island."

Taregan grinned at her, caught up in the feeling of exuber-
ance, and pressed his hands to the windowsill. He leaned out
with her, filling his mind and heart with the sights and scents of
home.

At sixteen years of age, Boston still wore the awkward unfin-
ished look of a frontier town. Even at this early hour, crowds of
pedestrians clogged the muddy streets and wooden sidewalks
where lanterns pushed at the lingering gloom. Many-fingered
swirls of dark smoke puffed from chimneys that seemed to leap
from the bay, dragging up clusters of timbered houses that stood
aloof and proud in coats of blinding white paint.

"It's beautiful!" Arabella breathed, her eyes fixed on the city
beyond. "So many houses in one place! How many people live
here, Taregan?"

"I don't know," he answered, trying to conceal his own
astonishment. Arabella counted on him to lead her through this
new world, but after living on an isolated plantation and in the
cathedral solitude of the woods, the bustle of the harbor and
town overwhelmed even Taregan.

When at last the gangplank lowered, Taregan paid a cabin boy
to deliver their trunk to the nearest inn, then he escorted
Arabella from the ship. As he stepped from the wooden dock
onto the dark soil of his birthplace, an eerie feeling swept over
him. His mother and father had been born in this land, had
worked it, breathed life into it. If God was willing, both of them
lived upon it still.

"Taregan?" Arabella was staring at him, a concerned expression on her face. "Your thoughts are a thousand miles away."

He smiled slowly as his eyes drank in the wide horizon. "I was just thinking. To Adam in the Garden, paradise was home. To the rest of us, home is paradise."

Her hand slipped into his, and he squeezed it. "Come, we'll find the inn and clean up," he said, shaking himself out of his reverie. "The trunk will arrive soon, and you can change your dress if you like."

He turned onto what looked like a main street as Arabella's wooden-soled shoes clattered beside him. "Wait, tell me what you will do," she said, pulling on his arm to slow his stride, "while I'm changing."

"I will write a letter to my brother," Taregan said. He pressed his lips together as he thought of facing Daniel after so many years and so much misunderstanding. "He must know that I have come home and that I intend to find him. There is something I must make him understand."

▼▲▼▲▼ The inn at Boston was a large, spacious building with a common room downstairs and four rooms upstairs. Taregan deposited Arabella in a room she would share with a dour-faced spinster from England. Chuckling at her expression of discomfiture, he went to his room, a narrow, dark chamber filled with two narrow beds. A basin and pitcher sat on a small table near the window, and Taregan slipped out of his doublet and splashed water on his face, neck, and arms, bathing as best he could without soap or a proper washcloth.

He and Arabella had received red-carpet treatment from the innkeeper as soon as Taregan explained that he planned to pay in gold. Immediately obsequious and reverent, the innkeeper had scurried to make proper preparations, and for the first time in his life, Taregan felt the rush of wealth's power. Frowning, he shrugged the feeling off and went upstairs, reckoning that though he was now better dressed than he had been when he left

America, the shipboard journey had left him no less in need of a bath.

Never in his life had he been rich, and he found it strange to think that any luxury he could need or want was within reach. Before the English came he had never thought of himself as poor, for he and his brother had all they could ever have imagined needing. Like the Indians, they counted a man rich if he had a full belly and a fur upon which to sleep.

But in Boston, money spoke with a voice as loud as thunder. Quite unused to the kowtowing and bowing the innkeeper had displayed when Taregan promised to pay in gold, he made a mental note not to speak of his wealth unless absolutely necessary. But, he had to admit, rich was better than poor. The sea voyage had been incredibly luxurious compared to his journey to Barbados in the slave ship, for he and Arabella had enjoyed twice-a-day meals, freedom to move about the ship, a basin of water to wash their hands and faces, and sleeping hammocks pitched from the rafters overhead. And though most of their fellow seafarers would tonight wrap themselves in their traveling cloaks and bed down in assorted barns or by the side of the road, he and Arabella would sleep in proper beds with a strong roof over their heads.

A rap on the wooden door interrupted his thoughts, and Taregan opened it to find the innkeeper standing there, a stack of fresh linens in his hands. The man bowed in a stiff, formal gesture. "Your trunk has arrived, sir."

"I'll fetch it up," Taregan said, shaking water from his hands.

"No bother, sir," the innkeeper said, bowing again as he offered Taregan a towel. "I'll send my boy up with it directly. And I thought you might like to know that Boston has one of the finest cook's shops in New England. I can direct you there, if you and your ward would like a bit of supper—"

"A cook's shop?" Taregan asked, taking the towel.

"A shop that sells food," the innkeeper said, his birdlike eyes gleaming. "Delicious food. Though they are not licensed to sell spirits, they will give a thirsty man a draught of beer if you ask for it."

"Thank you, it would be nice to eat something other than sea biscuits," Taregan answered, smiling. "I'll tell Miss Christoffels. If you'll just have our trunk placed in her room—"

"Under lock and key," the innkeeper promised. With another formal nod, he turned to leave.

"One more thing," Taregan said.

The innkeeper whirled around, ever ready to serve. "Yes?"

"I need parchment and a pen. And someone to deliver a letter to Hartford on the Connecticut River."

The innkeeper scratched his head for a moment, then snapped his fingers. "Ah, I have it, 'twill be no trouble. I have the supplies downstairs, and there's a trader nearby who'll be leaving for Hartford on the morrow. For a shilling, he'll gladly carry your letter for you."

"Is he trustworthy? My letter is very important."

"If your gold is good, so is he," the innkeeper said, winking. "Is that all, Master Bailie?"

"Yes," Taregan answered, still uncomfortable hearing himself called *Master.* "It is."

Within the space of five minutes the innkeeper reappeared with parchment, pen, ink, and sealing wax. Taregan sat down upon the bed and penned a brief message, signed the letter, and sealed it. Going downstairs, he left the letter and the promised shilling on the innkeeper's desk, then stepped out into the streets of Boston.

He did not know where he wanted to go, but something drew him away from the inn and the docks, away from the bustle of merchants and seamen and trappers. Walking toward the heart of town, within a few moments his ears heard what his heart had been seeking: songs of praise, lifted high to God. Hans Christoffels had not allowed his slaves either the time or the opportunity to worship. By the time his freedom had been mirac-ulously restored, Taregan supposed his heart too black with anger and hate to be of any use to God, and so he avoided the church on Barbados. In over nine years, he had not once heard a hymn or a verse of Scripture save those he had pulled from memory. . . .

And now, music poured from the windows of a small church:

He that within the secret place of the most high doth dwell,
He under the Almighty's shade shall lodge himself full well.
My hope, he is, and my fortress, I to the Lord will say:
He is my God; and I in him my confidence will stay.
Surely out of the fowler's snare he shall deliver thee,
Also thee from the Pestilence infectious shall free,
He with his feathers hide thee shall, under his wings shall be
Thy trust: His truth shall be a shield and buckler unto thee.
Thou shalt not be dismayed with fear, for terror by the night:
Nor for the arrow that with speed flieth in the day light:
Nor for the Pestilence that doth walk in the darkness fast:
Nor for the sore destruction that doth at noon day wast.

Taregan paused, marveling in the glorious sound of the song. The tune he recognized as the melody of a bawdy chantey the sailors had sung at least a hundred times every day as they worked the ropes and furled the sails. But the words struck the chords of memory, reminding him of a psalm his mother had taught him years before.

"The ninety-first," he whispered, recalling the passage his mother had read from her Bible.

The song came from a building of squared logs that sat atop a hill in the center of town. It was a plain structure with a thatched roof and unplastered exterior walls. Peering through the open door, Taregan guessed immediately that it was a Puritan church, for long benches filled the interior. A handful of men sat on one side of the room; a group of women on the other. *It is not the Sabbath,* Taregan mused, *and yet their devotion still urges them to meet for praise and morning prayers.*

Drawn by a powerful sense of the familiar, he slipped through the door and sat with the men while a tall, stern-faced man in

the front of the room held up a book and led the group in
another song. Taregan sneaked a peek at the book in the hands of
the man next to him. Titled *The Whole Book of Psalms, Faithfully
Translated into English Meter*, its pages listed musical texts and
referred the singer to a contemporary tune that would fit the
rhythm of the words.

After another quarter hour of singing and half an hour of
prayer, the gathering dismissed. The men and women around
him stood and left, anxious to be about their daily work, and the
tall man who had led the singing left the building without even a
backward glance at Taregan.

Within a few moments, he was alone. He sat in the hush of the
room, the words of prayer and praise still ringing in his head. An
odd nostalgia swept through his soul, a yearning for the innocence and clear conscience of his youth. In the early months of
his captivity, he had regularly lifted desperate pleas for help,
health, and safety to God. Yet, since learning about Garvin Black,
his conscience had risen to block the windows of heaven. No
man had the right to petition God when he fully intended to
murder another. No man had the right to thank God for forgiv-
ing love when his own heart burned with hatred.

And yet what he had just witnessed left him feeling shaken
and contrite, almost confident enough to address God again after
so long a silence. Something in the concentrated power of so
many unified voices moved him beyond words.

Rising to his feet, he walked to the front of the building. A
Bible lay upon a small table at the front of the room, and Taregan
sank to his knees before the book and clasped his hands in
prayer. Perhaps his heart was still too dark to address the
Almighty, but if the thief on the cross had found mercy and compassion, surely there was hope.

"Father God," he prayed, using the form of address his
mother had taught him. Unconsciously, he slipped into the
Algonquian tongue of his youth. "I give you thanks for bringing
me again to the birthplace of my mother and father . . . for lifting
me out of the chains of slavery, for restoring me to freedom and

blessing me with more riches and power than I ever dreamed of possessing. I pray that my mother is well, that Dena is strong, and that I will find my father." He paused as a still small voice reminded him of Daniel and Garvin Black. "As for my brother," he whispered, trying to still the whirlwind that had begun to spin in his soul, "I pray that he would be strong and able to bear the rebuke I will bring down upon him. May he be ashamed, and yet may his eyes be opened; may your rod and staff of correction be gentle, yet strong enough to drive the evil influence of Garvin Black far from him. I would teach him a lesson, Holy God—"

"Is it not God who teaches us?" a voice behind him interrupted. Surprised that someone had crept up without his hearing, Taregan jerked around.

A tall and straight man stood behind him. His dark hair curled neatly around his ears, and his eyes seemed impossibly gentle. He wore neither the robes of a clergyman nor the elaborate doublet and lace collars of an English gentlemen, but a simple leather coat and breeches. In his clasped hands, however, he carried a Bible, and for an instant Taregan assumed that he had been interrupted by yet another Bostonian who had come to seek private worship in the church.

Then he paused. Did all Bostonians speak the Indian tongue well enough to understand Taregan's fluent and fervent prayer?

"I intended my discourse for the ears of God alone," Taregan answered in English, a slow blush burning his cheek. He rose to his feet and regarded the interloper with a level gaze.

"I apologize, I meant no insult," the man answered, extending his hand. "My name is John Eliot. I am pastor of the Roxbury church about two miles from here. I like to visit this place whenever I come to Boston, and I was so taken by your proficiency with the savage tongue that I could not help interrupting." He bowed slightly. "Far be it from me to prevent a gentleman's prayer."

"You say you mean no insult, but again you have given one," Taregan answered, his words clipped. "For I am no gentleman, despite the foppish clothes you see me wearing. I speak the

Indian tongue because I am one of the people you call savage."
He felt his mouth twist in an awkward smile. "And if there are
so few of my people left in these parts, mayhap the English are
far more savage than the Pequot, Mohegan, and Narragansetts."

Eliot inclined his head slightly and studied Taregan more
closely. "*If* there be few left? Have you been away?"

"I have been in Barbados for nine years, sold as a slave by
those who overran the Pequot fort at Mystic."

"And yet you do not look like an Indian."

"My father was an Englishman, my mother half-English and
half-Powhatan. My brother and I were raised among the Pequots
when my parents moved to Connecticut from Virginia."

The man's eyes narrowed in disbelief, then he nodded slowly.
"Ah, I begin to see the goodness of God in this. He answers
prayer in the way we least expect."

"What?" Taregan was not in the mood for riddles.

"Will you be so good, sir, as to come to my house for dinner?
My wife, Hannah, would be delighted to talk to you. And if you
have but recently arrived, you cannot have made plans."

"You do not even know me."

"As sure as the gospel, my friend, I know God has sent you. I
need you. And I apologize for having offended you." The smile
he offered seemed to come from his heart. "Please, sir, will you
come?"

He waited, his expression open and trusting, and Taregan
wanted to laugh at the man's audacity. But he had no plans for
dinner, and this man was unlike any minister he had ever met.

"I am traveling with a companion, a young lady. She is my
ward."

"Bring her, by all means. I have six children, so the more we
have gathered around my table, the merrier we will be. The
house is in Roxbury, and I will send a carriage for you and your
ward. I suppose you are staying at the inn near the docks?"

Amazed at the man's persistence and insight, Taregan nodded.

"And whom shall my groom ask for when he calls at the inn?"
Taregan let out a short laugh touched with embarrassment.

How easily he'd submitted! This man was either a genuine saint or a crafty purveyor of the black arts.

Gathering his dignity, he gave the man a formal nod. "Tell him to ask for Master Taregan Bailie."

John Eliot walked with a light step as he left the Boston church. How good God was! Ever since his arrival in Boston fifteen years before he had been telling his congregation that their principal end should be the propagation of the glorious gospel among the Indians. The people at Roxbury were good folk, but they worked so hard to keep food on their tables and shelter over their heads that they preferred to remain at home and pray for the savages rather than actually *do* anything with them. The language was an insurmountable barrier, they insisted, and the heathens too barbarous, lazy, and idolatrous to ever be converted. Some even went so far as to say that Indians were complete savages incapable of reason. The only hope of converting them, or so the argument went, lay in conquering and enslaving them. Then perhaps their proud souls would be humbled enough to receive the glorious gospel.

But John had dreamed of converting Indians since his days at seminary. While at school in England he had thrilled to read Daniel Price's 1609 sermon encouraging Prince Henry in the colonization effort: "You will make . . . a savage country to become a sanctified country; you will obtain the saving of their souls; you will enlarge the bounds of this kingdom, nay, the bounds of Heaven. And all the angels that behold this, if they rejoice so much at the conversion of one sinner, oh what will be their joy at the conversion of so many!"

Emboldened and encouraged by those words, Eliot came to America with high hopes, but thus far his work had been entirely among his own people. "We must not sit still and look for miracles," Eliot urged his congregation. When they would not listen, he turned to his council of elders. "We must be up and doing the work of God, and the Lord will be with us. Prayer and pains, through faith in Christ Jesus, will do anything."

But thus far his prayers remained unanswered and his pains ineffective. He could not speak the Indian language effectively; he could not understand the workings of the Indian mind. He employed an Indian boy as a house servant and spent endless hours questioning the young man, but still his efforts fell short of his marvelous goal.

Now, gloriously, God had at last revealed his plan! He had sent an answer to John's fervent prayers: a finely dressed Englishman with the heart and tongue of an Indian. Surely the young man had been formed by God's hand with this eternal purpose in mind.

His heart quickening with hope, John Eliot hurried toward home to warn Hannah that they would have supper guests.

▼▲▼▲▼ "Taregan, do we have to leave Boston right away?"

Arabella popped her question without giving him a chance to greet her. He had just rapped on her door to fetch her for dinner, but apparently she had been thinking all afternoon about how to best ambush him. She had certainly dressed for a surprise attack: she wore a new gown from her trunk, a delicate blue silk creation that, with its full skirt and large puffed sleeves edged in fine lace, accentuated the young woman's slim figure. The bodice neckline dipped lower than any he could ever recall her wearing, and she had tied her hair up into a bun with dainty ribbons dangling among the ringlets that framed her face. A feather fan hung from her wrist, an elegant touch provided by the dressmaker's shop in Hole Town. Such fineries had never existed on the Barbados plantation.

Taregan took a step back, stunned by the unexpected transformation. This pretty woman was a stranger, completely grown-up

and poised beyond belief. How could the island child have
become a polished woman so quickly?

The answer rose from the center of the brass bed: the sober-
faced gentlewoman with whom Arabella shared the hotel room.
"Now, don't forget to thank your hostess, and remember to lift
your skirts when climbing from the carriage," the dowager murmured, smiling in approval as Arabella swept past Taregan into
the hall. "And have a lovely evening. I know the Reverend Eliot
and his wife; they are fine people. He's quite the scholar, you
know."

Taregan waited until the door closed before following Arabella
down the stairs. "Did you have to tell her all our plans?" he
hissed, hoping his voice wouldn't reach through the hall.

"Are we on a secret mission?" Arabella answered, her chin rising as if to balance the luxuriant weight of hair at the back of her
head. "Taregan, I've been thinking. Mistress Redfield says there
are no decent dressmakers or silversmiths in Hartford, and we
really ought to remain in Boston to prepare ourselves for Connecticut. Can't we linger here until you hear from your brother?
He will reply to your letter, don't you think?"

"I wrote that I was coming," Taregan answered gruffly. "And
winter is approaching, Arabella. Travel on the river is not easy in
winter. You're used to the warmth of the tropics; you won't like
our bitter wind."

"I can handle a little cold," Arabella answered, her eyes
flashing fire. "Let us wait a month, Taregan, please. I'll follow
you into the wilderness like I promised, but I want to enjoy the
city first. Please? I've never in my life seen anything like this.
There's so much to see and do; Hole Town could offer nothing
like Boston. . . ."

Despite his eagerness to continue home, the honest emotion in
her eyes touched him. True, he had not wanted to take her to
America, but once he had agreed to bring Arabella he had been
grateful for her company. She was a good companion, more like
a sister than a responsibility, and the liking he had always felt for
her had gradually deepened to affection. For all that his heart

clamored to return to Hartford as quickly as possible, he could not in good conscience deny Arabella this request.

Surely a month would not make that great a difference.

"All right," he conceded, opening the door to the street. The minister's horse and buggy waited outside. "One month. Shop all you like, spend all you want. But keep an eye to the forest, because we should reach Hartford before the leaves fall."

"Done," Arabella agreed, smiling at him. She gasped in appreciation of the fine carriage waiting for them, then lifted her skirts and climbed in. Taregan followed, conscious of curious and frankly envious glances from a dozen passersby.

▼▲▼▲ "Welcome, my friends, welcome to our home."

John Eliot's words rang with genuine warmth, and Arabella was stunned and more than a little puzzled at the enthusiastic friendliness in his smile. Planters on Barbados were relaxed, refined, and friendly, but this man seemed about to burst with anticipatory adrenaline.

Hannah Eliot's greeting was no less effusive, and Arabella made polite replies and casual conversation as she and Taregan joined the minister, his wife, and their six children around a lovely table set with linen tablecloths, china dinnerware, and silver knives and forks. Arabella found it difficult to keep from gaping at her hostess's lovely possessions. The six children, dressed exactly like their adult counterparts, ate around the lower end of the table with the family servant and spoke not a word to interrupt the adult conversation. Oh, that she might have such a home someday!

While Reverend Eliot and Taregan spoke in low voices at the corner of the table, Hannah endeavored to involve Arabella in conversation. Eager to talk about her talented husband, Hannah quietly remarked that John was not only pastor of the Roxbury church, but also an author of several books and pamphlets. "He is also one of the translators of the Bay Psalm Book, without which we wouldn't sing a word in this country," she remarked, wagging her finger for emphasis.

Totally unfamiliar with the work, Arabella could only nod in agreement. But when dinner was finished and the dishes cleared, Eliot poured out the passion that burned in his eyes. "I knew God sent you to me when I heard you praying," he told Taregan, his voice rising in tone and urgency. "Last month I addressed some Massachusetts Indians living near Dorchester under the sachem called Cutchamekin. I gave them a sermon and waited for their questions about the gospel, but they asked instead about the cause of thunder, the course of the winds, and how the tides operate with regularity. I had prepared my sermon in their tongue, but not answers to these questions."

Disappointment shone from his eyes even now, and his voice dropped as he conceded his defeat. "I don't know how to approach the Indians, Taregan Bailie. I need the advice and wisdom of someone who does. Someone like you."

"He could also use a bit of encouragement," Hannah remarked lightly, coming back to the table and sitting next to her husband. "No one seems at all interested in helping him. His cause is about as popular as pork in a synagogue."

Eliot smiled at his wife's joke, then spread his hands as he explained. "My work is resented by the sachems, who fear they will lose their people's loyalty. The white traders discourage my work because they fear I will turn the Indians from trapping furs and trading for whiskey. My own church people are jealous of the time I invest in this work, and the town officials are afraid I will encourage the Indians to move closer to the English settlements." He shook his head as if overwhelmed by the opposition. "I cannot speak the language fluently; I do not know how to turn the natives from idolatry. We know all men are depraved without Christ, yet they stubbornly cling to their belief that every man is good at one time or another—"

"If you truly want my advice, I will give it," Taregan interrupted. "Whether or not you take it is up to you."

"If God's truth is in your words, I will heed your advice," Eliot answered. "Please, speak. I am listening."

Taregan leaned back in his chair. "First," he said, drawing a deep breath, "you make too much of our differences. There is much we have in common. Both the Indians and the English believe in one great God above. Both know that the world is not of our own making. Both acknowledge that supernatural forces influence our daily lives. Both invoke the aid of higher beings. Both engage in private prayers and communal ceremonies—"

"But the Indians are so—" Eliot spread his hands helplessly— "*misguided*. They do not understand that they cannot live in harmony with God apart from salvation."

"The Indian lives in harmony with his world," Taregan answered, his eyes darkening. "He lives in peace with the forest, the wind, the winter. You must teach him of the other world that he does not understand. You must give the *Manitou* a name, Jehovah God. You must tell him that the spirits that bend his paths are in truth God's holy angels or Satan's demons."

"I just can't understand why they won't listen to me," Eliot said, shaking his head. "We have so much to offer them—"

"You think as a typical Englishman," Taregan answered. "You are amazed and frustrated when the Indians do not want to live in your stuffy cabins, attend your English schools, give up their own religion, copy English government, or adopt your medicines. You think they have nothing, but the Indians have a culture, a government, and a history. You would be wise not to ignore what the Indians already have, but learn to work within their society."

Arabella felt her heart swell with pride as she listened. This man, her friend, was instructing Boston's foremost theological scholar.

Eliot sat silently, tapping his fingers on the table as he digested this news. "And you say your parents were able to lead an entire village to salvation in Christ?"

Taregan nodded. "A Pequot village. The other sachems were not as quick to believe as Nixkamich, so the entire nation was not much influenced. But Nixkamich told his people the proper name for God, and they understood."

"And yet still they lived as Indians? Hunting, and painting themselves, and warring like savages?"

Taregan's nostrils flared in a flash of temper. "Why shouldn't they live as Indians? That is what they were."

"But how can they be Christians unless they be civilized? I have hoped that our converts will put aside heathen ways and learn to plant, to move to proper villages and dress modestly, to forgo their heathen chanting and dancing around the flames of war—"

"Do not the English war with their neighbors?"

The minister lifted a finger. "Only when there is good cause."

"Just so, the Pequot fought only when necessary to defend their homes or their way of life. And as for the chanting— Nixkamich's village continued to dance as their forefathers did, but they danced in praise to God for making the corn grow and for filling the woods with game."

The minister shook his head. "Words of godly praise will not change a heathen practice. Their chanting is still uncivilized. The roots go deep into the devil's work."

"And yet this morning I listened to a song in the Boston church. The hymn praised God for his deliverance, yet we heard that same tune aboard our ship with vastly different lyrics—"

The minister abruptly leaned forward, glancing to see if his wife paid close attention. "I assure you, Master Bailie, we do not sing those vile words."

"Will words of godly praise change a heathen tune?"

"The words of God sanctify the melody."

"Then words of God can sanctify the dancing. Did not David dance before the Lord in jubilation? Does not the psalmist command us to lift our voices, our hands, to make noise and shouts of praise?"

John Eliot did not answer, but pressed his fingers to his lips and leaned upon the table, thinking. At length he lowered his hand and gave Taregan an honest smile. "You have given me

much to consider," he said, pushing back from the table. "Next
week I am planning to preach again in an Indian village. Will
you come with me?"

Arabella held her breath, half afraid that Taregan would
refuse. But he stood and bowed to the minister. "Apart from my
father, you are the only Englishman I have met who seems to
honestly care for the souls of the Indians," he said simply. "I
would be honored to join you. And to help you prepare, if you
should need me."

"I need you," John Eliot answered, standing. "God has only
begun to show me how much."

"Be you Daniel Bailie?" The trapper slid a sealed parchment along the table in the trading post. Though the ink had smeared, Daniel could read the address: *Daniel Bailie, Hartford, Connecticut.*

"I am," Daniel said, picking up the letter. He turned it over. A simple, nondescript seal marked the back. No initial, no clue as to the sender's identity.

The trapper grinned, revealing a gaping hole where his two front teeth should have been. "Then I've earned my gold," he said, a beery breath blowing across the table.

For a moment Daniel forgot the letter. "Gold? Someone paid you in gold?"

"Aye, to deliver your letter. Said I must bring it straight to Daniel Bailie and no other."

The trapper paused for a moment, studying Daniel's face, then shook his head in a drunken daze and lumbered out of the trading post. Curious, Daniel took the letter to the lantern and broke the seal.

> To my brother, Daniel Bailie, greetings.
>
> I have today landed in Boston and will soon follow this letter to Hartford. I intend to find you and whatever may remain of the life and home I knew before I was most foully and unjustly sold into slavery. It has been nine years since I left the land our mother and father prepared for us, and my heart still burns to avenge the attack upon our father's character.
>
> I have news for you, brother Daniel, about the Pequot War and our father. My heart is so filled with bitter

venom it cannot be borne. I will be in Hartford, God willing, before the first snow.

Taregan.

Daniel felt the room spin slowly around him. Taregan, alive!
And, from the trapper's description, wealthy! How could such a
thing have happened?

Wrecked, he sat down and ignored the creaking of the door as
someone entered the trading post. Taregan was coming home.
He had not forgotten. He had sworn to kill Daniel before he left.
When he learned how their mother had died, he would not be
happy with just killing Daniel, he'd insist upon torture, too.

A thunderbolt jagged through him as he crumpled the parchment. The news was horrible and terrifying, but Garvin would
know what to do. Since Taregan had never borne any great love
for Garvin Black, this news would concern him, too.

Ignoring the woman at the counter, he pushed his way
through the door and went to find Garvin.

▼▲▼▲▼ Three days later, in the Widow Butler's house,
Garvin pushed away from the board and rested his hand on his
bulging belly. "I can't imagine a better supper," he said, swatting
the rear of Sabrina's skirt as she brushed past him. "If you've got
any stew left in that pot, why don't I take it to Daniel? I think
he's a wee bit put out that he doesn't get to enjoy your company
as much as I do, Sabrina Butler." His eyes narrowed as they
trailed over her figure, and though her back was to him he knew
she was blushing. "Of course, I wouldn't want him to share all
the benefits of your company."

"Garvin, I need to talk to you," she said, her voice as thin as a
reed. He winced. Usually that tone meant she would bring up
the subject of marriage or whine about something else he had
neglected to do, and he wasn't in the mood for such talk. Daniel
had been in a foul mood for three days, fretting about his brother's arrival.

"Can't we talk later?" he asked, reaching for her arm.

"No," she retorted, turning and making an abrupt gesture, almost as if she would slap his hand away. Garvin tilted his head, dark thoughts racing through his mind. Had his filly suddenly become skittish? Had some other man or a nosy woman approached her?

"What is wrong with you?" he asked, wiping all traces of playfulness from his voice. "Why do you take that tone with me, woman?"

"Garvin, I—"

"Sit down." His hand caught her arm and pulled her, hard, onto the bench next to him. She sank in an ungraceful heap, then made an effort to compose her pale face while he stared at her. She reminded him of a rabbit when she twitched that way, her eyes red-rimmed and runny, her nose pointed and sharp.

"I am with child."

He blinked, certain he'd misunderstood. "You're what?"

"You heard me." She lowered her voice and leaned over the table as if the walls themselves might report her to the church authorities. In a trembling whimper she repeated, "I am with child."

"Of certain you're too old. You're no virgin bride—"

Her expression twisted as though his words had stung. "I am not too old. I am five-and-thirty, young enough to bear children for a husband."

Garvin sighed and rested his forehead in his hand. Women were such a trial. If not for the small pleasures they provided, he'd ship them all back to England or wherever else they came from. But she spoke the truth; he had told too many lies to be easily deceived. Mayhap he had finally been caught in a web of his own weaving.

"How did you manage it?" he finally asked, lowering his hand.

"How—how did I—why, you *know* what happened, Garvin! And it won't be borne in this village nor in any other in New England! The magistrate will have me jailed, or exiled, or turned out into the woods!" She bit her lip as tears filled her eyes. "And so I'm asking you now, Garvin Black, what are you going to do?"

"Have you talked to an Indian woman?" he asked. "What about the girl Daniel knows—what's her name, Dena? I hear the Indians know how to rid a woman of a baby while it is still unborn."

She had been pale before, but now her face blazed whiter than a winter snow. "Kill the baby within my womb?" she asked, her hands flying to protect the secret place where the baby grew. "Why, I could never do such a thing! It is bad enough that I allowed you to compromise my position in the village, but I would not commit murder for you. Though I love you more than life itself, I won't be killing your child—"

"Are you sure it is mine?"

He regretted the words as soon as they left his lips. She'd been indignant at his suggestion that she abort the baby, but the implied accusation in his last comment brought fire into her eyes. She stood, a whimper escaping her lips, and her hand drew back to slap him.

He was faster, moving to pin her arm behind her back.

"Get away," she screamed, struggling in his grasp. "Go away! I'll call the magistrate. I'll tell them all that you've done, Garvin Black, and I'll—"

"Hush," he answered, pulling her close. He had won her with tenderness, so he'd use the same strategy to keep her quiet. An idea formed in his mind, and he acted upon it, lowering his head until his breath warmed her ear. "I'm sorry, darling Sabrina, I'm sorry. Forgive me. Only a knave would say such a thing, but you know I've always been a knave at heart."

Her struggling eased somewhat, and he relaxed, confident in his power over her. "You *are* a knave," she mumbled, her lips against the fabric of his shirt.

"Aye," he answered, lifting her chin. He ran his free hand over her tousled hair. "There's only one thing to do. We'll be married before God and the church, in a proper way. And when the babe comes, people will just think it was born ahead of its time."

She pulled her head back as her eyes probed his. "Truly, Garvin? But you said you couldn't marry me as long as I owed my husband's debts—"

"Hush, woman, and do you think me a pauper? I will pay the debts and make an honest woman out of you."

"And you're truly happy about the baby? I want to give you a son, Garvin, someone you can love and provide for—"

"I'm as happy as a hog in new slop," he answered. "Now kiss me, love, before I change my mind."

She kissed him, throwing her arms about his neck, alive and happy in his embrace. "When shall we be married?" she asked when they pulled apart. "On the morrow? Or the day after?"

"Soon," he said, settling back on the bench and pulling her upon his knee. "But first I shall send you to Boston with a bagful of gold to buy whatever you will need for our home and for the baby."

"To Boston?" Her face lit in amazement. "You'd send me to Boston?"

"Yea." He met her expression of pleasure with a careful smile. "I'd go with you, but I can't get away just now, and I need Daniel to remain with me. But I want you to go, to stay in a decent inn, eat whatever you want, buy whatever you think we will need. Leave your maid to care for your house, and have a merry time on your own."

"Garvin!" Sunshine broke across her face; she drew his head toward her and planted little smacky kisses over his forehead and cheeks.

"And while you're in Boston," he said, bearing up under her affection as best he could, "I want you to take care of a little business for me. Look for a certain man and write me with any news you may gather about him."

"A man?" Resting her cheek against his head, she sighed in contentment. "Is he one of your traders? Or a merchant?"

"No, it is business of a happy and secret nature, my love," he said, settling his hand about her waist. "You may inquire about the man, even speak to him if you like. But you must not let him

know that I have sent you, nor should you say anything about
Daniel. The man we seek is Daniel's brother, Taregan Bailie."

▼▲▼▲▼ On the morning of October twenty-eighth, as
the last of autumn's faded leaves clung to the trees, Taregan
joined John Eliot, Thomas Shepard, Daniel Gookin, and John Wilson of Roxbury. They rode five miles on horseback to Nonantum,
a small village on the south side of the Charles River, where the
sachem Waban waited to hear from the English man of God.

"Have you never been afraid to enter these villages?" Taregan
asked while they were riding. "You have said that the sachems
resent you."

Eliot shrugged. "Once one of the petty chieftains met me at
his village gate with a knife. I told him that I was about the work
of the great God and that he was with me, so I feared not any
sachem in the country. 'Touch me if you dare,' I told him." Eliot
grinned good-naturedly. "I thanked God that he did not."

Taregan was pleased to see that Waban did not wait for them
with a knife this time. The sachem welcomed the English minister into his wigwam with curiosity and friendliness in his smile.
Most of the village and all of Waban's family had squeezed into
the wigwam. Smoke from the pipes of the elders hovered along
the saplings supporting the bark roof; nearly naked children
scampered underfoot and moved easily among the crowd.

Taregan stood back against the wall and folded his arms,
struggling to keep his mind above the flood of memories that
washed over him at the sights, smells, and sounds in the village.
Eliot began to speak the Algonquian tongue, and the sound of
his flat accent made the children giggle. Not despairing, Eliot
continued, attempting to lead the children in prayer and a
simple catechism. After a while, the young ones grew quiet,
gazing at the minister with wide eyes.

Eliot chose Ezekiel 37:9 for his text, and not an Indian dared
speak while he read: "'Then said he unto me, Prophesy unto the
wind, prophesy, son of man, and say to the wind, Thus saith the

Lord God; Come from the four winds, O breath, and breathe upon these slain, that they may live.'"

Taregan found himself approving of the minister's words. The Indians related immediately to the image of the wind—much of their folklore and worship centered around the spirits of the wind, sun, and moon. Eliot spoke in a graceful and warm delivery. In vigorous crescendos, his voice rose and fell to rebuke sin. A penetrating liveliness made his words like thunderbolts that struck the heart of each listener.

Truly, Taregan thought, *what I am seeing is beside and beyond the mere power of man. God is in this. Even though my heart is imperfect, God has chosen to use me. He brought me to Boston for this reason.*

"'God that made the world and all things therein, seeing that he is Lord of heaven and earth, dwelleth not in temples made with hands,'" the minister quoted, lifting his gaze from his Bible. His eyes seemed to probe the souls of every individual in the wigwam. "'And hath made of one blood all nations of men for to dwell on all the face of the earth, and hath determined the times before appointed, and the bounds of their habitation; that they should seek the Lord, if haply they might feel after him, and find him, though he be not far from every one of us: For in him we live, and move, and have our being.'"

In him we live and move . . . As John Eliot's voice continued, guilt avalanched over Taregan, breaking his heart with its weight. His parents had led him to salvation as a small child, had taught him the truths of God's Word and the precepts of holy principles. But though God had never left him, Taregan had wandered from the awareness of the Almighty and allowed bitterness to supplant the close fellowship he had once known and enjoyed with the Creator God of the earth.

Of certain his desire for revenge had wounded the Spirit of God, but Taregan had assumed God would cast him aside for continuing in his anger and hate for Garvin Black. How many times had he thought that God didn't or wouldn't care about him because his heart was dark and vengeful?

But now the Spirit of God touched a burning finger to Taregan's soul. *You can't walk away from me, my child. No matter where you go or what you do, still my hand will guide you, protect you, mold you. For you are mine, in me you live and move and have your being.*

With crystal clarity, Taregan saw that God had saved his life on Barbados more than once. In his timing, God had provided Taregan's freedom and the fortune with which he could return home. God had directed him to the little church in Boston, then to the house of John Eliot. He'd been a fool to think that he could ignore God as easily as he had disregarded the Bible Dirk had given him for Christmas. He could no more live without God than he could live without . . . Daniel.

Caught up in the pain of realization, Taregan crumpled forward with his hands upon his knees. No one in the wigwam noticed his anguish, so engrossed were they in the exchange between the minister and one of the village elders.

"Does the English man's god hear Indian prayers?" the elder asked.

"Certainly," Eliot answered. He pointed to a basket lying near the door. "See that basket? The earth is like that basket, made of straws of differing colors. The God who made English men and Indians knows and understands each of them, for he made them both."

I made you both, Taregan, you and Daniel, just as I made both Jacob and Esau. Esau was separated from a brother who wounded him, but after many years he met Jacob with forgiveness and an embrace. Can you not do the same? Forgive Daniel his association with the evil man; trust me to provide justice and mercy.

Taregan stared past the wigwam's fire as the voice of God echoed in his spirit. He thought he had forgiven Daniel for the sorrows of the past, but now he saw with pulse-pounding certainty that he had looked forward to watching Daniel cringe when Taregan told him what really happened at Mystic. Even after nine years of suffering and separation, Taregan had planned to confront Daniel in yet another contest, to prove himself right and Daniel wrong. . . .

But God knew his thoughts. As John Eliot described the blackness of a heart beset by sin, Taregan applied the words to his own life. The Indians in Waban's wigwam needed salvation; Taregan needed reconciliation with the God he had set aside in order to dwell upon the sins of others.

His eyes caught sight of the gold band upon his right hand. *Boldly, faithfully, successfully.* For the last nine years he had lived *bitterly, foolishly, selfishly.* But God, in his unmerited grace and mercy, would draw him close and restore him to loving fellowship.

"Father God, forgive me," he whispered, bowing his head in contrition.

▼▲▼▲▼ An ebullient John Eliot returned Taregan to the inn, and Arabella noticed a thoughtful change in her guardian from the moment he alighted from his horse. "Did all go well at the Indian village?" she asked as a groom led the horse away.

Taregan looked up and gave her a rare smile, beautiful with brightness. "Very well," he answered. "Waban and his people desire to be baptized and follow Christ. They have asked the Reverend Eliot to petition the Court to grant them land for a special village in which they may live as Christians."

"That's wonderful," Arabella answered, clapping her hands together. Her smile faded at the serious look in Taregan's eye, and she followed him from the yard into the inn's keeping room. Taking a seat beside him on a bench there, she pressed her hand to his arm. "What are you not telling me, Taregan? I know your moods, and your thoughts have wandered away again."

He combed his thick black hair with his fingers, then shrugged. "A light shone among my people today," he said simply, his thoughts still far from her. "And that same light shone upon my heart." His eyes focused upon her as if he had just realized she sat beside him. "And we are going to Hartford to meet my brother. We will leave on the morrow."

"Not tomorrow!" Arabella cried, lifting her hand to her throat.

"My dresses won't be ready until next week! You said I might order anything I wished—"

"All right." Taregan lifted a hand, conceding. "We will leave when your dresses are done. But try to hurry the sempstress along, will you? Grease her palm with an extra shilling so we can be on our way." His eyes drifted toward the front window as his thoughts left her again. "The winter winds grow cold."

"I'll try to hurry her," Arabella answered, wondering what had happened to him.

> To Garvin Black
> The Trading Post at the dock
> Hartford, on the Connecticut River

My dearest Master Black:

I have been in Boston for two days and had no trouble finding the young man Taregan Bailie. I took a room at the inn nearest the harbor dock, as you suggested, and found the young man and his traveling companion here. He is very handsome and so very much like our Daniel! Indeed, even a mother would be hard pressed to tell them apart.

He is apparently wealthy, as you suspected, and travels with a lovely young lady he calls his ward, though I am of the opinion they could be kindly affectionate toward one another given the time and proper circumstances. They have told me that they intend to remain in Boston for two more days, but I did as you suggested and begged that I be allowed to travel home with them. Though Taregan is most anxious to return to Hartford, Arabella (his young companion) prevailed upon him to wait for me, and so we shall journey together when my purchases here are made. I hope you will be pleased with what I have provided for our new home.

As you enjoined me, I have not told Taregan that I am acquainted with our Daniel, nor did I mention this fact to Arabella. I think Daniel is very kind and thoughtful to want to surprise his brother. But we will leave soon because Taregan wants to reach Hartford before the winter makes travel too difficult.

I am eager to return home, too, my love, so we can be immediately wed. I trust that you have spoken to the minister.

Until I see you again, I remain, Your most devoted servant,

Sabrina Butler

Garvin lowered the letter to the counter and turned to Daniel. "He is there?" Daniel's face was grim.

"Yes. And he is still intent upon coming here before the winter hits. The man who delivered the letter to me did not say when he had received it, so they may be traveling even now."

Garvin's eyes moved toward the shuttered window at the front of the trading post. It was bolted tight. "Are you still willing to be rid of your brother?" He turned his gaze upon Daniel. "I must have your resolution in this. There can be no backtracking once we undertake this action."

"I am willing. I have no choice—Taregan vowed to kill me. He holds me responsible for our father's death, and when he finds out how our mother died, his anger will know no bounds."

"I have made a plan to rid each of us of our troubles." His eyes moved into Daniel's, measuring the younger man's resolve. "Are you certain you have the courage to undertake this path? This is your chance to prove yourself, but your courage must not fail."

"As long as I do not have to face him directly," Daniel answered, bitterness dripping from his voice like venom. "He always bested me. There is something about him, some special gift—he always wins no matter what I do. But if there is a way to trap him—"

"Man is an animal and can be trapped more easily than most," Garvin said, smiling darkly. "And you will not have to face this favored brother of yours, nor will anyone suspect that you have had a hand in this. Do not shirk from what I tell you. Follow my instructions to the letter, then hide yourself in the woods for a fortnight. And tell no one, ever, about this, or we will both face the gallows."

Daniel nodded slowly.

"Good." Garvin glanced around to make certain they were alone, then he picked up a lump of charcoal from the fireplace and traced a wavy line upon the counter. "This is the Connecticut. Do you know the place where the brook from Feeding Hills flows into the river? The river forks in twain, then comes together again a few miles downstream."

"The rapids?" Daniel asked, his features twisting into a horrified expression. "Of course I know the place. My father once tried to teach me how to row through the eastern fork." He shuddered visibly. "I hate the place."

Garvin nodded. "That is good. No one will suspect you if you have always avoided the spot. But on the morrow you must go to a point upriver of that place and wait until your brother and his party come. And when you see them, you must lay the most cunning trap your imagination can devise. . . ."

Taregan, Arabella, and their new companion, Sabrina Butler, left
Boston with a family moving west until they reached Chicopee
on the Connecticut River. There Taregan traded the horse and
wagon for a large and stable flat-bottomed canoe. He would
have preferred something lighter and faster, but he would be
rowing with two unsteady women, each of whom traveled with
a heavy trunk.

He carried little for himself, only a knife in his belt and a musket, which he kept at his side. He did not want to meet his
mother and Dena dressed like an English dandy, so he left the
trappings of the English behind in Boston, donning instead the
simple leather breeches favored by the Indians and a soft shirt of
tanned deerhide. Loosening his hair to blow in the wind, he tied
a bearskin mantle about his shoulders and a kerchief around his
neck to hide the thin red scar that would forever remind him of
the uprising on Barbados. Nothing in his appearance must alarm
either his mother or Dena.

As the bitter winds of November ruffled the still waters of the
river, Taregan held an oar in his hands for the first time in years
and pressed the canoe out onto the water. Every nerve in his
body leaped with exhilaration as they set out, and for a moment
he was a boy again, paddling his father's canoe as his mother
sedately rode up front.

Taregan shook the memory from his mind and concentrated
upon the work at hand. The river lay heavy upon the land,
bright as crushed diamonds against the bleak brown of
approaching winter. Gleaming water rippled gently toward the
shoreline as his boat cut through the river, and occasionally he

spied a fisherman or hunter who would raise a hand and wave in salute. The passage would be easy, for they traveled with the river's flow, and his job consisted mainly of steering the canoe away from the shallows and keeping the two women and their goods safely balanced.

Their new acquaintance, Sabrina Butler, had agreed to the river journey, but she balked when it came time to venture into the canoe. "I hate the water," she said, her birdlike hands nipping at her arms as she hugged herself. "I traveled by sea to Boston from a ship at Saybrook Fort that was much larger. I've never journeyed in anything as small as this canoe, I've never seen the water—" she held out her hand—"right in front of me."

"I promise you that Taregan is an able rower," Arabella said, settling in at the rear of the craft. "You have nothing to fear, Sabrina." At length the lady was seated in the bow, her trunk behind her back for support, but her back remained as straight as a spear and she gripped the sides of the boat so tightly that her knuckles whitened.

Taregan relaxed as the wind caressed his face. The soft lap of the oars pulling against calm water, combined with the sight of the wide river, calmed and reassured him. This much of Connecticut had not changed. Perhaps his mother and Dena would not have changed much, either.

The miles streamed out behind them, the canoe's white path stretching straight and true as the river carried him southward toward his home.

"Taregan," Arabella called from behind him, interrupting his thoughts, "did you hear what the settlers were saying about you back at Chicopee?"

"No," he answered over his shoulder, not breaking his rhythm.

She laughed softly, a warm sound in the chill of the afternoon. "While you were seeing about the canoe, one of the Indians whispered that you were a great sachem returning to your people. Another said you were a departed spirit come back to life."

"How did they explain the two English women with me?" Taregan answered, laughing.

Sabrina Butler, pale and uncomfortable in the bow, held tight to the sides of the canoe as she turned her head. "Perhaps they think you have taken two wives," she said, making an effort to smile. Despite her fear, humor glinted in her dark eyes, and both Taregan and Arabella laughed.

Arabella had met the woman in the inn and instinctively liked her, for she was warm, friendly, and eager to talk. Taregan had been interested in her once he learned that she lived in Hartford. Yes, she told him, she knew an Indian woman called Dena, and though she had never heard of one named Gilda, it was possible that she lived outside the village. When Taregan asked about Daniel and Garvin Black, she smiled and said, yes, she knew them, too, but her conscience would bother her if she gossiped about her fellow townspeople. If Taregan wanted to know more he would have to learn it for himself once they reached Hartford.

Though Sabrina Butler was a good conversationalist, she was not a good traveler. More than once, Taregan regretted allowing her to join them on their journey downriver. She seemed to suffer from some sort of sickness during the bumpy overland journey, and quite frequently she vomited her dinner. She tired easily, shivered like a homeless puppy in the chill winds, and fared little better on the water. Taregan placed her in the front of the canoe so she could hang her head over the side of the boat if she felt sick. But Sabrina Butler was eager to be home and did not complain.

Arabella, a true island child, traveled with ease, never fussing despite the fact that her skirts were frequently wet and the weather colder than anything she had experienced in years. Taregan suspected that she was trying to prove herself capable of becoming a woodsman's wife, but he said nothing. If she did choose to remain in Connecticut, this testing might prove useful.

▼▲▼▲▼ In the dark place in the woods where she had gone to relieve herself, Arabella adjusted her kirtle, smoothed her bodice, and tucked a few stray hairs back into her fur-lined cap. They had spent the night sleeping under the stars, wrapped only in bearskins Taregan had bought in Chicopee. The experience had left her feet cold and her confidence shaken. Though Taregan snored soundly and Sabrina Butler slept like one dead, Arabella had tossed and turned for hours, tuning her ears to the frightful night noises surrounding them. Odd wind-borne sounds came to her, keening wails that seemed to rise from nowhere, quiet whispers of night shadows, the sound of her heart battering against her ears. When she finally slid into a thin sleep, Taregan shook her gently and told her it was time to rise.

Some adventurer she was, she thought with disdain. Though life on Barbados had accustomed her to blazing heat and hard work, the abundant fields of green cane had done nothing to prepare her for the vast canopy of forest that loomed over both sides of the river and threatened to engulf her as she slept. Taregan told her he felt safe and hidden in the trees; she felt terrified and trapped.

But she dare not complain. She helped Sabrina and Taregan bundle the furs and stow them in the boat, then she kicked dirt over the embers of the fire Taregan had built to warm them through the cold night. Wrapping a bearskin over her shoulders, she settled in the back of the canoe, ready to face another day. Two sleepless nights bore down on her with an irresistible warm, delicious weight, and she nearly nodded off until Taregan whispered her name.

"Arabella, look."

Her heavy eyes flew open. Taregan had taken his oar from the water and was pointing to a structure on the west side of the river. "What is it?" she asked.

"A sawmill," Sabrina answered, her head turned toward the building.

"*Ja,* of course," Arabella answered, looking back at the shore. The forest did not tower here. The trees had been cut and cleared as thoroughly as if an army of beavers had struck, and the water along the shoreline was thick and brown with the detritus of the mill. Apparently the mill had been abandoned; the place was as silent as the grave.

"My father and I used to fish here," Taregan said, his eyes glinting with disbelief and frustration. He jerked his thumb over his shoulder. "Back there, about a mile inland, is the place where Nixkamich had his village. My brother and I visited there often."

"So your home was near here?" Arabella asked softly.

"Farther downstream," Taregan said, putting his oar back into the water. He turned resolutely from the sight of the sullied shore and pushed the canoe downriver. "Nothing is as it was. The fish are gone, the bears will move away. God was merciful to take Nixkamich to heaven. His heart would break to see the land like this."

Arabella shivered and gripped the edges of the bearskin on her shoulders. She had never heard such a mournful, defeated note in Taregan's voice, and the sound of it lifted the hairs on the back of her neck.

Colton had awakened with frost on his beard and hair, but as the wind herded dull gray clouds over the trees, the winter sun wiped all traces of white from the earth. Now the sun bathed the bare forest with dazzling light, and he paused to revel in the beauty of it. Under his feet the fallen leaves were brown and black and stained with death, but above him the sun promised to warm the earth with its breath and awaken life once again.

The sound of human voices touched his ear. Cocking his head, he turned toward the river. He could be hearing the militia on maneuvers, or a party of Indians, or perhaps a group of fur trappers like himself. But it was the Sabbath, so no decent Puritan would be traveling, not even this close to sunset.

Curious, he sprinted southward at an angle so he could catch sight of the boat when it came into view. He wanted nothing to do with the militia or other trappers, but if a party of Indians passed he might approach to ask them about the disappearance of the beaver. There was a rumor circulating among the traders that the sachems had devised bad medicine to make the beaver go away, and while Colton didn't believe that tale, still, he wondered if the creatures had migrated to one of the Connecticut's tributaries.

Reaching the river, he dropped down behind a fallen log and waited until the voices came to him again. He blinked when he recognized the treble voice of a woman—no, two. Two women and one man on the river. English women! Who were these folk and why weren't they minding the Sabbath like all God-fearing Puritans?

He reared up his head and blinked again at the canoe that

came into view. He immediately recognized the pale woman in the bow of the boat as the Widow Butler from Hartford. And behind her rode Daniel Bailie—at least, it looked like Daniel. But he was dressed in Indian garb. . . . Colton frowned slightly, then shrugged. It had to be Bailie, for both he and the widow spent a great deal of time with Garvin Black. A stranger rode behind Daniel, a young woman with the face of an angel.

Colton couldn't help gaping as he watched. The woman held a bearskin to her shoulders as if she were cold, and tendrils of soft brown hair escaped the cap that framed her doelike brown eyes. Her face and hands were as tanned as an Indian's; her long neck curved beneath her cap like a bird taking wing. The girl possessed a windblown, glowing, happy look, unusual for a newcomer to these parts, and her voice lilted with a melodic accent that Colton couldn't place.

"Where the devil did Daniel Bailie find her?" he grumbled, the serpent of jealousy hissing in his heart. It was bad enough that Dena had decided to wait for the brother that would never come home, now it appeared Daniel had claim on the only other girl who had ever piqued Colton's interest.

Intrigued, he sprinted along the riverbank, hiding behind the brush, struggling to keep pace with the swiftly moving boat. The girl rode confidently, now resting her arms on the side of the canoe, and Daniel seemed to pay her no undue attention. Mayhap she was not intended to be his bride. Mayhap this was some scheme of Garvin's, some young woman he'd arranged to auction off to the highest bidder—

It was a rude thought, but Garvin Black had been known to suggest cruder things. In that moment Colton forgot about his quest for beaver. If he could ride with them to Hartford, he'd be on hand to defend this girl's honor if and when an unsavory situation arose.

"Whoa there!" he shouted, splashing into the water while he waved his hands. Daniel instantly withdrew his oar and held it up like a club; the young woman's face froze in panic. The widow screamed.

"Who are you?" Daniel called, still brandishing the oar.

Colton understood their concern. The sun hovered near the horizon, and fiendish sorts had been known to follow a boat and murder its inhabitants when they made camp. There were two trunks in the canoe; people had been waylaid for less. "I'm Colton Bramwell, you fool," he yelled, stopping when the cold water reached his waist. "Halt, Daniel! I am no threat! I'd like a word with you."

The current carried the canoe past him, but the widow stopped screaming and leaned back to say something to Daniel. He listened intently, then dragged his oar in the water until the canoe slowed. "Come back, Daniel!" Colton pleaded, his legs feeling the cold. "Before I freeze to death out here!"

The canoe turned, slowly, and crawled upriver. When the boat was even with Colton, the man in leather called out. "Be you Colton Bramwell who was once a soldier at Saybrook Fort?"

"You know I am," Colton called, exasperated. "Come, Daniel, take me with you to Hartford. You will save me a day of walking."

"He is Master Bramwell, of certain," the widow answered, nodding confidently at her companions. "I'd know him anywhere."

The canoe came closer, but still Daniel kept the boat out of Colton's reach. "Do you recall, soldier, meeting one at Saybrook who was sold with the slaves?"

"Who?" Colton asked, perplexed.

"A young man, who asked you to bring word to two women in Hartford."

Colton nodded soberly, wondering if Dena had told Daniel the story. "I do."

"And did you fulfill your duty?"

"I spoke to the woman and the girl as I promised." He frowned. "But I never spoke to you of it. How have you come to know this?"

In an abrupt movement, the man jumped out of the canoe, rocking the women and setting them both to squealing. Splashing through the frigid water with the unconcern of an Indian, he came forward and extended a dripping hand. "My name is Taregan Bailie," he said, his dark eyebrows rising in pleasure. "And I must thank you for keeping your word. I swore to them that I would come home, and so I have."

Colton took a quick breath of utter astonishment, then he began to laugh.

▾▴▾▴▾ They shared a campfire that night, and as Colton and Taregan dried out and warmed themselves around the fire, Arabella wrapped herself in a thick fur and lay down in such a position that she could watch the newcomer without being observed.

When he had first charged out of the woods toward them she had thought him some sort of wild animal. But at close range, she mused, he was one of the most exquisite men she had ever seen. Tall and straight, strong and supple, he moved with the hard grace of one who has total control of himself. Muscles bulged and slid under the leather shirt he wore like a second skin, and his blond hair curled onto his shoulders in such a way that her fingers ached to subdue it. Intelligence and hard-bitten strength were etched into every feature of his face, from his sparkling green eyes to his stubborn chin. He was, she decided, as handsome as Taregan, but in a totally different way.

The two men laughed and talked with easy familiarity, and she found it difficult to believe they had only just renewed an acquaintance scarcely begun nine years before. Taregan asked almost immediately about Dena, and Arabella could not deny the joy that snapped in Taregan's eyes when Colton gravely remarked that she was well and yet unmarried. "She waits for you," he said simply, a tinge of sadness in his voice.

"And my mother?" Taregan pressed.

Colton stirred the fire with a green stalk and did not speak for a moment. "When I found her and Dena in slavery, your mother had been gravely injured. I redeemed them with a few wages I had saved, and your mother lived for several years with Dena. But she never regained her strength. Though her spirit rose victorious above every challenge she faced, her body weakened. She died four years ago."

He seemed preoccupied for a moment, as if a memory had suddenly surfaced and overshadowed his awareness of their conversation. "Your mother had a dream before she died," he said, watching the fire. "She told Dena that you would come back. I don't think Dena quite believed it until that day, but something in Gilda's words convinced her. Even now she is waiting for you."

As tears of joy and sorrow mingled in Taregan's eyes, dashed dreams and disillusionment raked at Arabella's heart. She would never marry Taregan. He had never offered or promised more than protection and affectionate friendship, and she had been wrong to hope and pray for more. As certain as night succeeded the day, he belonged to this woman Dena. If she had waited so faithfully in the face of impossible odds, Dena and Taregan deserved every happiness.

Arabella sat up, and the movement caught Taregan's eye. He lifted his head, looking at her, and she knew that he understood everything that was in her heart. "I wish you and your woman every happiness God can bestow," she whispered, smiling in sweet surrender. "You were right. She has waited."

Taregan thanked her with his eyes, then abruptly stood and walked into the woods. Colton seemed to understand his need to be alone, for he did not question or rise to follow. When the yawning blackness of the woods had swallowed Taregan completely, Arabella drew the bearskin closer to her shoulders. "Will he be safe in the dark?" she whispered, trying not to wake Sabrina.

Colton shifted his position to see her better. "If he is anything like his brother, dark and light are much the same to him. They were born in this river valley. Nothing here can threaten them."

"Nothing—but the English," Arabella said, moving her eyes into his.

His eyes were a stream of gold in the dark. "So he has told you his history?"

"Yes."

"And yet you followed him to this land?"

"I had nothing and no one in Barbados. Taregan and my father were partners and friends. He is like . . . a *brother* to me."

Was that a sigh of relief? She couldn't tell, but Colton tented his strong, capable-looking hands and gazed at her across the dancing flames. "You should sleep," he said, a genuine note of concern in his voice. "The roughest part of the river lies ahead."

"I'm not afraid," she answered, though she shivered at the husky tone of his voice.

"I didn't think you would be." He lay down across from her, pillowing his head on his arm. She tried to follow his example and lay back upon the ground, but a thousand questions raced through her mind.

"Master Bramwell?" she whispered.

"What?"

"Are you coming with us on the morrow?"

He lifted his head, and his smile was unlike anything she'd ever felt before.

"The entire English army couldn't keep me away."

Relying upon his knowledge of the river and his understanding of his brother, Daniel found their encampment. Taregan had chosen a place at least one hundred paces from the river, a spot dense with trees and evergreens and blue shadows. The crackling fire offered a dancing halo of light and caressing fingers of smoke and heat as it played over four figures sleeping beneath bearskins.

For the better part of ten minutes Daniel lay flat on his belly against moist dead leaves on the damp earth, his head lifted to study the face of his sleeping brother. It was an eerie sensation, like looking at a ghost of the past. Taregan's face had not much changed, but it had widened and grown strong, and Daniel saw that they were still identical shadows of one another. He knew what trials had brought furrows to his brow—what had etched those same furrows into Taregan's forehead? If his mission were less important or less urgent he would have enjoyed a conversation with this alter ego, but time and circumstances would not allow it.

For a moment he had been dismayed to see Colton Bramwell in Taregan's company, but the ambush would still be simple, far easier than he had dared hope. Taregan wore the typical uniform of an Indian woodsman, leather breeches and a shirt of tanned deerskin. Still, Daniel's broadcloth shirt was similar in color . . . he would just have to hope events passed too quickly for anyone to notice the differences.

Daniel grinned when he saw that Taregan wore moccasins. He had known his brother would chose the soft shoes, for though most trappers wore stout boots, the Indians still preferred their moccasins. Regardless of all that had happened, Taregan was still a savage at heart.

He took in the kerchief around his brother's throat and wondered fleetingly why Taregan wore it. Then he shrugged. No matter. He would tear a strip of material from the hem of his shirt. It would have to suffice.

There remained the matter of Taregan's shorter hair, but Daniel could easily trim his hair with his hunting knife. Their voices had always been similar, and as long as he avoided the eyes of the two women, mayhap they would not notice when he stepped in to take Taregan's place.

But he would have to draw Taregan away, and something must be done with Colton if the plan were to work. Daniel slipped from the sleepers, as silent as a ghost, and slipped again into the shadows. Everything would have to be prepared by sunup.

▼▲▼▲▼ The rising sun swallowed up the chill wind that had whistled over the river, and silence, thick as wool, wrapped itself around Daniel as he waited for the canoe. Watching the water as it flowed by, he shuddered—then chastised himself for his weakness. For all that he feared the river, Taregan was a far greater threat. He smiled, thinking of the trap he'd laid. Unless Taregan had undergone a total personality shift, the lure would not fail to draw its bait.

Daniel's whole being concentrated in his right ear for the sound of voices, and, in time, they came. On his knees, he crept to a maple tree standing between him and the river's edge and flattened himself against it to peer out. The heavily laden canoe and its four occupants slowed in the water.

"Look there," Taregan said, lifting his oar as he pointed to the place where Daniel had trampled the low-lying shrubbery. "Is that a pool of blood?"

Dragging his oar, Colton turned toward the sight. "I think so. Should we stop?"

Listening from shore, Daniel held his breath as Taregan looked downriver and searched the horizon. "We're about half a mile from the rapids, right?"

"Rapids?" The Widow Butler gripped the sides of the canoe; her eyes like a frightened bird's. "Are they dangerous? You promised me that this trip would be smooth."

"Nothing to worry about," Colton explained in a soothing tone. "There's a fork in the river about a quarter-mile south of this place. The east fork is rough water, but the western fork is quite calm."

"So we'll take the western fork?" The young woman in the boat behind Taregan turned bright eyes upon Colton. "Will we still arrive at Hartford before sunset?"

"Mayhap," Colton answered, grinning at her. "If you women will be quiet long enough for us to do our work."

"We will be there well before dark," Taregan said, his eyes intent upon the trampled shore. He threw Colton a challenging smile. "Are you up to a hunt, my friend? We could bag our dinner and still reach Hartford before dark."

Colton stroked the waters; the canoe edged toward the shore. "It could be a wounded deer," he said, studying the bloodied grass. "Perhaps she slept here in the night and has left to forage for food."

Taregan brought the canoe closer. "If she lost that much blood, she won't last the day," he called, his voice carrying easily over the water. He threw Colton an impudent grin. "I was once the best hunter in these parts."

"In truth?" Colton asked, throwing Taregan a glance of jaunty superiority. "But now your time has passed, my friend. I am the greatest trapper. In fact, I'd wager a beaver skin that I could find that doe and bring her down before you."

As Daniel knew he would, Taregan rose to the challenge. "There are some skills a man does not lose," he said, placing his oar into the canoe and picking up his musket. "Remain here, ladies," he cried, leaping easily from the boat into the shallows.

"You're leaving us here?" the young woman cried, a note of panic in her voice.

"Naught will harm you," Colton answered, splashing behind Taregan. He bent and pulled the canoe onto the shore, seating it firmly in the muddy bank. "We're just going to do a bit of tracking. You'll be thanking us once you have a bite of my venison stew."

"Don't take long," Sabrina Butler called out, her face paler than usual. "We're all alone here!"

Daniel smothered a smile as he watched the two men follow the trail of blood he'd planted in the woods. It was a deer's blood, but they would not find a carcass. Daniel had laid a bizarre, serpentine route that wound for half a mile into the woods and then forked, as if the dazed deer had doubled back upon its own trail. The fork would separate Colton and Taregan, and the possibility that the doe had doubled back would keep them on the chase, confident in the knowledge that they were close to their prize. . . .

Taregan had always been the superior woodsman, but even now Daniel possessed far more cunning.

He waited until the two men disappeared in the undergrowth, then began a leisurely count to one hundred. When he reached ninety, he shook his newly shorn hair loose like Taregan's and took a deep breath. Then he raced from his hiding place toward the women in the canoe.

"Quickly," he yelled, ignoring their dazed faces. "Sabrina, grab an oar! You—" he pointed to the other woman, who stood in the back of the canoe peering into the woods— "sit down and be still!"

"Taregan, what is it?" the younger woman asked, sinking into a frightened heap. "Where's Master Bramwell? What happened?"

"We were ambushed by a pair of renegade trappers," Daniel snapped, taking the place in the canoe where Taregan had been. He grabbed the oar and pushed against the muddy bottom, sending the canoe away from shore.

"Where's Master Bramwell?" Sabrina asked, flailing uselessly at the water with the extra oar.

"He is dead," Daniel said. The woman behind him gasped, but he did not pause. Three strong strokes cut the canoe into the current—Taregan would have been proud of him!—and when the boat picked up speed, he leaned forward and yanked the other oar from the widow. He paddled forcefully, propelling the canoe forward, and soon saw the fork in front of them. He carefully steered the canoe toward the eastern side of the river where the water ran faster. Though his movements were less sure than Taregan's, the women, distracted by his news, paid no attention.

"Dead?" the young woman whimpered. "How could he be dead? We heard no shots—"

"An arrow," Daniel replied, amazed at how easily the lie sprang to his lips. "I used my shirt to bind his wound and then saw that he was already dead."

He glanced over his shoulder at the girl to see if she had caught anything unusual in his speech or inflection, but she stared mindlessly at the shoreline, her thoughts still centered on Colton Bramwell.

Taregan followed the bright spots of blood for nearly a quarter of an hour before he stopped, bemused and puzzled. Despite the delicate deer tracks in the mud, these marks had not been made by an injured animal. The drops of blood were too evenly spaced, too predictable, and the hoofprints too close together to have been made by an animal mad with pain. The crimson droplets appeared only when he might have lost the trail.

He crouched upon the earth and listened, but nothing but the wind broke the quiet of the woods. Had he bragged foolishly? Surely he had missed some clue, some obvious thing that any hunter should know. Animals went to water when they had been hurt, and the deer would have sought deeper woods when the sun rose. . . .

He searched his memory for a clue but found only his father's voice, Fallon's patient instruction about the ways of animals in the wild. Despite his confusion, Taregan smiled. The pattern of blood drops and tracks reminded him of puzzles his father invented to test his sons in the forest. Taregan had solved them all without difficulty, but Daniel—

Daniel. His heart thumped against his rib cage. Could this possibly be Daniel's handiwork? Surely not. For though Daniel knew Taregan was en route to Hartford, he would have no idea when he might arrive.

If not Daniel, then who would want to distract him from his journey? An angry Indian? Riverfront thieves? Army deserters?

Taregan turned toward the shore, resolutely leaving the trail behind. Unless his instincts had completely atrophied in the years he had been away, trouble had descended upon the riverfront.

Someone with evil intentions had been enticed by two English women and a canoe laden with treasures from Boston. . . .

He broke into a run, sobered instantly by the frightening possibility that he had discovered the truth too late.

▼▲▼▲▼ Holding the canoe on its course, Daniel steeled himself for what lay ahead. Already he could hear the low murmur of the rapids that would draw the canoe like a magnet. Even in a small, fast vessel he'd had difficulty on this part of the river. No one in the world could get a heavy, poorly balanced canoe through the water ahead without capsizing.

"Taregan," Sabrina said, turning slightly toward him. Her knuckles were white against the dark brown bark of the canoe. "Isn't this the east side of the river? You said the eastern side was dangerous—"

He had prepared for this. "The murderers who killed Master Bramwell will expect us to take the western side," he said, keeping the canoe steadily on course for the rapids. "We can lose them if we take the eastern fork." He forced a smile. "You must trust me, Widow Butler."

▼▲▼▲▼ Staring straight ahead, Sabrina trembled at the shock of recognition. During her time in Boston she had often mentioned her impending marriage, but never had she told this young couple that she was a widow. She'd thought it best not to invite speculation about her first husband, and never, not once, had Taregan called her anything but Miss Butler or Sabrina. Never would he call her Widow Butler.

Daniel called her nothing else.

Terror stole her breath, which came in short, painful gasps as she gathered the courage to turn and look over her shoulder. Daniel was behind her; she should have recognized the shrewd gleam in his eye. Seeing him thus, straight and determined, he was so like Garvin, and nothing at all like his brother.

"Daniel!" she whispered, mesmerized by the difference in the two men.

His mouth twisted into a mirthless smile, but he did not deny the name.

"What are you doing?"

"Taking you to your husband, Widow Butler."

The conversation was cut short by a shrill scream. Behind Daniel, Arabella's eyes were wide, and her finger trembled as she pointed forward. When Sabrina turned again she saw why.

The living river roared just ahead.

▼▲▼▲▼ An angry gray boulder loomed just off the bow, and at the last minute Daniel cut into the water with his oar, turning the canoe. In front and behind him the women screamed, and the sound ripped at Daniel's nerves even as he struggled to keep the boat upright in the water. He should have let the craft break up on that first rock, but the horror in the widow's eyes had unnerved him.

Why was he doing this? For Garvin. Because Garvin had promised to make certain that Taregan would not bother Daniel.

The water ahead spat up in white plumes; another set of rocks towered ahead of them. Daniel paddled quickly on the right side of the canoe, then switched to the left, digging in with all his might in order to turn the unwieldy boat. The widow was not screaming now, she had turned to yell at him. "Don't you know he came back for your sake?" Her voice was ragged and sharp above the noise of the river.

"You don't have to tell me why he came back! I know why!"

The white water rose and snarled at them; massive black rocks roared up from the water's depths. The bow of the canoe dipped and rose again and again, sending sprays of frigid water into the air and over all three passengers.

The widow would not look at the water; still she stared at him, her eyes wounded and dark, like his mother's. Daniel tore his gaze from her face and worked the canoe, struggling to fight

the darkly nagging voice in his head as his body worked to keep
the boat afloat.

"Just shake her up a bit on the rapids by dumping the canoe," Garvin had said, *"just enough to make her lose the child in her womb. She
hates the water; she'll faint or grow ill, and she won't have to bear the
shame of an illegitimate child. You will be doing a merciful thing, Daniel, and if you do this for me, I'll personally take care of your brother.
Trust me, lad, and do exactly as I tell you."*

Garvin's plan had seemed so simple, and tricking Taregan
had been but a bit of challenging fun. But the full reality of what
Garvin intended suddenly struck Daniel with the force of a physical blow. He may have already taken things too far, for the
widow trembled like a leaf and her face contorted in an emotion
that looked like fear, but might well have been pain. He could
not stand before the hurt in her dark eyes knowing he had had a
part in destroying the child she already loved.

If he could only get the canoe to shore, mayhap the widow
could still be helped. He and the women could carry the canoe to
the point where the forks reunited. He'd slip into the woods and
leave the women for Colton and Taregan to find, and he'd go far
away, perhaps wander south toward Virginia where a man could
earn a fortune growing tobacco. . . .

But the river would not show mercy. Like an old and vengeful
enemy from his past, the most massive boulder in the stream
rose from its lofty position, water eddying around its base like a
tidal pool, relentlessly pulling the canoe. Daniel stroked until his
shoulders burned and his stomach cramped, but the water
sucked them forward until the boulder bludgeoned the canoe.
He heard the sharp and brittle crack of weathered wood, then
the impact pitched everything into the churning water.

For a moment the world went black and a rushing sound
filled Daniel's ears. Fighting the current and a wave of numbing
terror, he swam away from the treacherous underwater tides and
forced himself to follow the bubbles rising to the surface. His
lungs burned as he gasped for air, and he swam to a calm pool
and treaded water, searching frantically for the others.

The young woman was lying in shallow water on the opposite bank, her hair plastered to her face and shoulders, her heavy skirts engulfed in the crystal stream. But she leaned upon her elbows, thank God, and held her head above the water.

"Are you safe?" Daniel called.

"Yes," she yelled, raking wet hair from her eyes. "But I don't see Sabrina!"

Frantic with guilt, Daniel swam into the current and dove, opening his eyes wide for any sign of the Widow Butler. Bits and pieces of the battered canoe brushed past him in the water; once an oar knocked him on the side of the head with bruising force.

Finally, when he was numb from the cold and thought he could bear no more, he saw her. She stood erect under the water, moving slightly in the current, her eyes still wide and wounded, her hands outstretched, her mouth open. The hem of her dress had caught on one of the trunks from the canoe, weighing her down so that she had never had a chance.

Gulping back a frantic sob, Daniel dove one final, desperate time, propelling himself downward until he grasped the widow's skirt and ripped it free of the sunken trunk. A soundless cry escaped him as he gathered her lifeless body in his arms and lifted her to the surface. By the time he could stand, grief had blossomed like a tumor in his lungs, taking up the space he needed to breathe. He threw his head back and gasped to fill his seared lungs with air.

"Widow Butler!" he cried, stumbling out of the water. "Sabrina!" Her skin was icy under his touch, and he whimpered as he carried her to the grassy shore. The sun lit a spot there, mayhap its warmth would revive her. Mayhap God would work a miracle; his father had often spoken of God's mercy. . . .

"Sabrina, you must wake up!"

He laid her on the grass, then lifted her cold hand and chafed it. "Wake, please! I didn't mean for this to happen. Please, Garvin is waiting for you. . . ."

But the silence of death mocked him. She was as quiet and unresponsive as the charred body from Mystic that Garvin once dropped at Daniel's feet. This was another senseless death caused by Daniel's foolish behavior.

Terrified by the burden before him and trembling from the cold, he turned and saw the other woman watching from across the shore. The look on her face was horror distilled to its essence, and when his eyes met hers, she began to scream.

Stunned by the force of the sound, Daniel staggered into the woods, disappearing as utterly as a shadow at noonday.

▼▲▼▲▼ Colton paused, his attention drawn from his frustration over not finding the wounded deer. An odd, faint sound came from the southeast, far away from the point where he and Taregan had left the canoe. He concentrated, then stiffened in alarm. It was a woman's scream! Could it be Arabella in need of help—?

With the sure speed of a forest creature, he sprinted toward the sound. Within a few moments he had reached the point where the two forks of the river joined together, and on the far shore he could see Arabella, her hair and clothes wet and her face covered by her hands. Without hesitation, Colton stripped the heavy bearskin mantle from his shoulders, lifted his musket over his head, and plunged into the icy waters.

▼▲▼▲▼ Arabella's story was unbelievable. "The man came out of the woods, told us you were dead, then took us through the rapids," she told Colton, choking back tears. "It was as if he wanted to kill both of us."

"What man?" Colton asked, his mind reeling. "Who would want to hurt you?"

"I don't know," Arabella answered, shivering. "But he looked exactly like Taregan. I thought it *was* Taregan until Sabrina began to scream at him. But Taregan would never . . . *could* never do anything like this."

She lifted a trembling hand and pointed to the west. Squinting, Colton could make out an indistinct shape on the grass. "Is that—"

"Sabrina Butler," Arabella finished. "She is dead. I've been watching ever since he pulled her out, and she hasn't moved."

"'Tis settled, then," Colton said, slipping his arm around her and pulling her close. "I'm taking you to Hartford myself. I know an Indian trail that leads to Windsor. We'll stop there to get you dry clothes, then we can find a boat to carry us to Hartford. The magistrates will want to hear this tale."

"I think Sabrina realized what his intentions were," Arabella said, still sobbing as he lifted her to her feet. She wiped her eyes with the back of her hand and looked at him with eyes like black holes in her pale face. "But why, Colton, would anyone do this thing? I haven't hurt anyone, and poor Sabrina—"

"I think I know," Colton answered, settling his face into grim lines. "And we will let the magistrates decide the truth."

▼▲▼▲▼ A mile upstream, Taregan returned to the site where he had beached the canoe. As he feared, the boat was gone, but a host of footprints on the bank told him what had happened. His and Colton's prints led off into the brush near the pool of blood; the women had never stepped out of the canoe. But someone, a solitary person wearing soft-soled moccasins, had come from the brush and taken the canoe with the women. From the depth of the footprint and its relative size, he guessed the interloper to be a man. When he inserted his foot into the stranger's print and saw that one matched the other, he knew he would be searching for Daniel.

He paused, studying the flow of the river and the movement of the wind. Of certain Daniel would not want to take the women north, but why would he take them at all? The question hounded him as he shouldered his musket and began to walk south along the riverbank. Daniel had surely received Taregan's letter, but the letter contained no threat, nothing to make Daniel wish to harm Taregan's companions. So why would he kidnap

Sabrina and Arabella? Did he hope to hide behind their skirts as Jacob hid behind his wives and children when he returned to face Esau?

Taregan pressed his lips into a determined line and concentrated on the southern horizon. No matter what Daniel's reasoning, the problem could be worked out when they met. The past was forgiven. Their mother watched from heaven, and Dena still waited for Taregan. None of Daniel's actions would spoil those truths.

▼▲▼▲▼ "Magistrate," Garvin drawled, removing his pipe as he scanned the northern river a day later, "I believe the man you seek comes in yonder canoe."

Thomas Norton, the chief magistrate of Hartford, stood and craned his look for a better view. "That's a canoe of Indians, sir!"

"Not all of them are Indians. The man in the bow, the young one, is the man you seek. Ask his name. I think he will confess that he is Taregan Bailie."

The magistrate stepped closer to the dock, shaking his mighty head in sorrow. "It is a pity, Garvin, that such a shameful thing should happen among our people. But I thank God that the young girl could swim. He would have killed them both."

"I am certain he did not intend to kill the Widow Butler," Garvin answered, remembering to cast the magistrate a mournful look. "He intended to murder the heiress. I myself have pieced the story together after talking to Master Bramwell and the poor girl. It appears that this Taregan Bailie couldn't abide the thought that she might have developed a fondness for our Colton. Mayhap this prodigal brother didn't want to see her give her share of the money to another man."

"A lot of good the gold will do him now," the magistrate said, lowering his voice as the canoe neared. "It is still at the bottom of the river."

"We know where it is, and Colton has assured me that a good

diver can bring it up," Garvin said, shrugging. "The little lady shall have her half of the gold."

"And the other half?" the magistrate slanted the question with a lifted eyebrow.

Garvin puffed on his pipe. "Why, it will go to the murderer's closest kin, I would imagine," he said, his eyes following the progress of the canoe near the dock. "And the man has a brother here in Hartford."

The Indians allowed their passenger to leap out onto the deck; the young man thanked them in their own tongue and waited for a moment as they began to row away. When he finally turned to face the knot of men waiting on shore, Garvin drew in his breath, marvelling. The man was indeed a mirror image of Daniel. As young boys he had thought them as alike as two halves of the same apple, and time had maintained the resemblance.

"Excuse me, sir," the magistrate called, stepping into the young man's path. "I would have your name."

Garvin felt himself flinch when the twin's blue eyes rose and lighted on him. For a moment the young man frowned as though puzzled, then his eyes stirred to anger. "My name," he answered, still focused upon Garvin, "is Taregan Bailie."

"Taregan Bailie," the magistrate said, carefully pulling a pistol from his belt, "you are to come with me to the Hartford jail. You are under arrest for the murder of Sabrina Butler and the attempted murder of Arabella Christoffels."

Clearly he wasn't expecting that bit of news. The indomitable pride chiseled into his handsome face broke for an instant; he stared at the magistrate in a paralysis of astonishment. "Murder?" he asked, his voice hoarse with surprise. "Sabrina Butler? Arabella?"

"We have heard the entire story," the magistrate said, jerking his thumb toward the road. "I will ask you once again, sir, to come with me. On the morrow we will convene a court to hear your case."

"My brother," Taregan said, crossing his arms as if he refused to move from the spot where he stood. "I must see my brother, Daniel Bailie."

"Daniel is not here," Garvin said, standing slowly to his feet. Their eyes met again, locked. Garvin gave Taregan a smile as hard as a river boulder. "Your brother has gone inland to hunt. He said he would be gone at least a fortnight, so I do not expect him for many days." He looked to the magistrate. "You have my word that Daniel is not to be found in these parts."

With a calm assurance that Daniel would never possess or understand, Taregan Bailie turned from Garvin and nodded toward Master Norton. "Then I am in your hands for tonight," he said, lifting his arms above his head in the manner of a captured prisoner. "And in God's hands on the morrow."

▼▲▼▲▼ The supper tables of Hartford buzzed for two nights in a row. The first night the men of Hartford told their wives the shocking story of the murder on the river, and the second evening they disclosed the story of Taregan Bailie's brazen entry into town and subsequent arrest by the magistrate. The story expanded with each telling. Taregan had arrived in full Indian battle dress, painted like a savage, and in the company of warriors eager to defend him, their long-lost sachem. Only after Garvin Black and Master Norton fired a pistol at the murderer did he relent and surrender.

The village children, wide-eyed with numb terror, scooted from their supper tables and repeated the story to each other as the sun lingered in the west. By the time darkness drew down over the horizon, the good people of the town barred themselves in their houses and thanked God that peace had been preserved in Hartford, Connecticut.

But the dinner table in one house was unusually silent. Unwilling to leave Arabella in the town's public inn, Colton brought her to Dena's house, knowing that she would not hesitate to extend compassion to a weary and distraught stranger. After one look at Arabella, weak and still shivering from the cold, Dena put the girl to bed with hot bricks and heavy blankets. When she finally slept soundly, Dena drew Colton away from Arabella's side and sat with him in the semidarkness.

"Tell me the truth," she said, sensing a dark secret behind the few words of explanation he had given. "Who is this woman, and why have you and the magistrate huddled together for the last two hours?"

The wood of the high-backed settle creaked as Colton shifted his weight. "I don't know if you will still want her here after I tell you the story."

"Tell me, let me judge my own feelings."

Colton locked his fingers and stared into the fire. "Her name is Arabella Christoffels."

"All right. But who is she?"

"A planter's daughter from Barbados. She arrived at Boston a few weeks ago—with Taregan."

Dena felt everything go silent within her. Taregan had come home, but with this young woman! Why did he return to Connecticut with another woman when she, Dena, had waited a lifetime for him?

Her emotions bobbed and spun like fallen leaves on the river, and she closed her eyes, forcing herself to calm down.

"Is she his—*wife?*" Her voice broke on the word.

"No, they are not lovers." Relief coursed through her soul, and Colton lifted a warning hand. "She is his ward and under his protection. That is why these are such grievous and serious charges."

"What charges? Where *is* Taregan?"

"He is in the jail. There are those who believe he tried to murder this young woman, and in the attempt caused the death of Sabrina Butler."

Dena pressed her hands to her face, confused. Colton might well have said Taregan had flown to the moon and stolen the sun and made more sense.

"Taregan could never murder anyone."

"I want to believe that, Dena, as much as you do. But Taregan is not the man we knew. We knew a young and innocent boy, but he was sold into slavery, remember? Last night he learned that his mother is dead. And though he inherited half of a wealthy estate in Barbados, Arabella inherited the other half. There are those who say he is hard, bitterly angry, and greedy. They wonder if he desired her share of the gold for himself."

"I cannot believe this. A man cannot change so much."

"I find it hard to believe myself. 'Twould be easier to believe such treachery of Daniel than of Taregan, but Garvin Black swears Daniel has been a fortnight in the woods, hunting." He bowed his head and murmured, "I do not trust Garvin, but truth be told, I could not imagine Daniel capable of murder."

She let her head fall back against the wood of the settle, and her eyes glazed over as she stared at the fire. The charges against Taregan were insane, a mistake, but why would Colton lie? He no longer fancied himself in love with her. From his tender care of the young woman on yonder bed, Dena felt certain Arabella had captured his heart.

Desperate, Dena tried another approach. "If he wanted this woman's gold, he could have married her."

Colton leaned forward, his hands upon his knees. "So I thought until Arabella told me that she once loved Taregan and asked him to marry her," he said, staring into the fire. "She wanted him to remain in Barbados, but he would not. The woman he wants is you."

Dena squeezed her eyes shut, resisting the words. Under happier circumstances she would have wept with joy, but the tears brimming behind her closed lids were heavy with bitter sorrow. The Great God had obviously worked a succession of miracles to free Taregan and bring him home, so why had he allowed Taregan to be welcomed by terrible calamity instead of her own loving embrace?

Colton's hand, familiar and comforting, fell upon her shoulder. "I should leave you now," he said, standing. The fire threw his long shadow over the wall where Arabella slept. "Taregan will be tried on the morrow. Arabella must testify." He looked down at his hands as if he did not know what to do with them. "You may come or not, as you please."

She did not answer, but curled into a tight ball upon the wooden settle as if it were the only reality in a shifting, uncertain world. After a moment the front door opened and closed, sending a breath of bitterly cold air into the room, but Dena did not move from her place.

▼▲▼▲▼ With his hands bound behind him, Taregan followed the magistrate into the tightly packed meetinghouse. He had not been given a chance to clean up or make himself presentable, and in the midst of the stiffly starched and perfectly dressed Englishmen, he knew he looked like a savage from the brush, one step removed from the Indians they had pretended to master, but still feared.

A panel of judges, three clergymen, sat in straight-back chairs at the front of the room. Taregan was led to a chair before the judges; the magistrate sat at his right hand. Behind him, the church had filled with townspeople, including Garvin Black. Taregan did not want to look through the crowd. He did not want to see Dena for the first time in nine years in this way, in this place.

One of the clergymen stood and led the meeting in prayer; another opened a book and read the charges. Taregan Bailie, born and reared in a Pequot village—the room seemed to shudder at the word *Pequot*—formerly sold as a prisoner of war into slavery, now a free man without a country, stood accused of the murder of Sabrina Butler, a widow of Hartford, and the attempted murder of Arabella Christoffels, an unmarried maiden of Barbados, now of Hartford village.

"What say you to these charges?" the sternest minister asked, peering down his long nose at Taregan. "Guilty or not guilty?"

"I am guilty of much, but not guilty of these things," Taregan answered, standing. "I believe Miss Christoffels herself will testify that I am incapable of hurting her or any other woman."

The clergyman rolled his eyes in amused disbelief and nodded to the magistrate, who motioned to Colton Bramwell. After casting a troubled glance at Taregan, the burly trapper led a fragile-looking Arabella through the crowd to stand before the council of judges.

"Do you, Miss Christoffels," the first judge said, holding up the Holy Scriptures, "swear upon this holy book to tell the entire truth, so help you God?"

Arabella placed her small hand on the Bible. "*Ja,* I do," she whispered.

The crowd murmured in collective approval, and one of the clergymen held up his hand for silence. "Tell us, Miss Christoffels," the second judge intoned, "what happened two days ago upon the river."

"Taregan slowed the canoe and pointed out something in the woods," Arabella said, looking very vulnerable and frightened.

"Did you see this thing he pointed out?"

"*Nee,* sir, I did not. But he told Colton—that is, Master Bramwell—that it might be a sign of an injured animal in the woods. Then he wagered that he could find the animal before Master Bramwell."

The third judge drummed his fingers on the desk before him. "So Master Bailie enticed Master Bramwell from the canoe. What happened next?"

"A man, a *different* man, reappeared after a few moments and said that Master Bramwell had been killed by an enemy and that we had to get away quickly. He got in the canoe and turned it toward the eastern fork in the river, even though Colton had warned us that the rapids were not safe."

"A *different* man, Miss Christoffels? Why would you allow a stranger to get into the canoe?"

Arabella's worried eyes flitted toward Taregan for a moment, and her hands tightened upon the chair. "I did not know it was a different man."

"Speak up, Miss Christoffels, we can't hear you if you whisper. Why didn't you know it was a different man? Was the sun in your eyes? Had you suddenly gone blind?"

"No."

"Then tell us, what did this man look like?"

"He looked like . . . Taregan Bailie. But only at first. It wasn't Taregan."

"Did the man have dark hair?"

"Yes."

"The same build, height, the same features?"

"Yes."

"But surely he wore different clothing. Did you notice his clothing, Miss Christoffels?"

"I didn't notice—it all happened so quickly. . . ."

The third judge paused and drummed his fingers again. "If this man looked exactly like your guardian, Taregan Bailie, how can you be sure it was a *different* man?"

"Because Taregan Bailie would never hurt me!" she cried, nearly rising from the chair.

"Calm yourself, I pray you!" the first judge said, frowning in disapproval.

"Let me remind you, young woman, that the court will decide intent, as well as guilt or innocence," the third judge said, tenting his fingers. He paused a moment as Arabella composed herself, then he continued. "How well do you know the accused, Miss Christoffels?"

"Very well. He worked for my father for four years, and my uncle for five years before that."

"As a servant?"

"As . . . a slave. But my father granted Taregan his freedom."

"Have you always known him to be kind and gentle?"

"Yes," she answered. But the defiant flame in her eyes dimmed before the judge's steady gaze.

"*Always*, Miss Christoffels? Was there never a time when he disappointed you?"

"Only once." Her voice lowered. "I once asked him for a serious favor, and he refused. But he had good reasons for his refusal."

The first judge cleared his throat loudly. "All right. So this man who looked exactly like Taregan Bailie got in the canoe and turned it toward the rapids. Why would he do such a thing?"

"He said someone was chasing us," Arabella answered, looking at him. "He said they'd never expect us to head into the rapids. So suddenly we were in rough water, and the boat was having . . . trouble. I thought we all were going to drown."

"But this man in the canoe with you—he was quite confident?"

"No. I saw his face. . . . He was truly afraid."

"Was it the same face you see in this room now?" the first judge asked, pointing to Taregan.

A wave of loving anxiety swept through Taregan as Arabella turned to meet his gaze. "It was not the same face," she announced, her voice bold and confident. "The man on the river had eyes full of fear, but, as you can see, sirs, Taregan Bailie is not afraid of the truth. Though the faces were similar, I am confident Taregan Bailie was not the man in the boat."

"Then who was?"

Arabella lifted her chin as she turned to face the judges. "Have you forgotten that Taregan Bailie has a twin brother? Find him, sirs, and ask his whereabouts during the attack!"

A murmur of dissenting voices, a palpable unease, washed through the room. Taregan felt it and knew that the people of Hartford did not believe Daniel capable of abducting two women. *He* was the stranger, his the unknown personality.

"Daniel Bailie is not on trial here!" the third judge said, slamming his hand upon the desk. "We have a sworn statement from his master. Daniel Bailie has been absent from Hartford for over a week. And your thinking, young woman, defies logic. How would Daniel have known about the gold in your trunk? Whereas Taregan Bailie knew of it, as he knew you had developed a fondness for Colton Bramwell, as he knew he would lose your fortune if you decided to marry another man."

"Money had nothing to do with it! Taregan cares nothing for money! He could have had it all! He could have married me, but he would not!"

There was no movement, not even the whisper of sound as the questioner leaned back in his chair. Finally he spoke again: "He would not have you, Miss Christoffels? You are kind and civil, well-bred and prosperous, every inch a gentlewoman. What kind of devil would refuse a gentle lady in need?"

"He had his reasons," she whispered, staring miserably at the floor. Though she shrugged casually, Taregan saw that her fingers nervously shredded the lace handkerchief in her lap. This activity did not go unnoticed by either the judges or the crowd.

"If you were to die, Miss Christoffels," the second judge began again, his voice more gentle than before, "to whom would your fortune go?"

She looked down at her lap. "To Taregan, I suppose."

"To a man who had nothing, a former slave whose reason and God-given conscience have been seriously seared by dreams of newfound wealth?"

"That's not true!"

"Miss Christoffels, do you love Taregan Bailie?" the second judge persisted, smiling blandly. "Isn't it true that you would say anything to defend him?"

"Yes! I mean no," she answered, tears brimming in her eyes. "No, I would not lie to this court, and yes, I love him, as dearly as a brother, and would defend him with my dying breath. I know Taregan, I know his heart, and I know that he would never hurt anyone. He had nothing to do with Sabrina Butler's death! I swear to you that he did not!"

The crowd murmured in excitement as Arabella's agonized voice rose and fell. The judges rapped for silence, then the third judge faced his companions. "But the man who drove Sabrina Butler into the rapids had the same face, the same hair, the same body as Taregan Bailie," he said, his stentorian voice rumbling through the meeting hall. "And his brother, who might have been considered a suspect in this offense, had no motive and was safely out of the area."

The judge's hard, gray eyes fixed on Taregan. "Have you anything to say in your defense, Master Bailie?"

"Yes, I do," Taregan said, standing. He knew that he looked like a condemned criminal already—his hands bound, his clothing soiled, his black hair unkempt and dirty. He represented everything the villagers feared, the nightmares that woke them from deep sleep and left them gasping for breath in the darkness.

He closed his eyes and prayed for wisdom. It would be easy to insist that they find Daniel, to throw suspicion on the other brother, but he had come to Hartford to make peace with Daniel, not to destroy him. And these people would never believe that one of their own was capable of such a crime. Daniel had lived among them for years as a quiet trader and Garvin Black's obedient shadow. Taregan had been the angry one, the defiant rebel who left with the dreaded Pequots and had the gall to return a rich man.

No, the way to freedom did not lie in accusing Daniel.

He paused, gave Arabella an understanding smile, then met the eyes of his judges. "I did not commit this crime," he said simply, folding his hands as best he could. "God is my judge. He knows my heart, and he knows I am innocent."

The judges nodded, then, as Arabella whimpered and dabbed at her eyes, the three men huddled around the desk.

"Taregan Bailie," the first judge said when they had separated, "in the face of irrefragable eyewitness testimony we find you guilty of murder and attempted murder and sentence you to hang at sunrise on the morrow. May God have mercy on your immortal soul."

Dena ran from the meetinghouse, her shawl about her head, her
hand to her mouth. Guilty! Why would Taregan come home only
to hang? Nothing made sense, not his words, his manner, or his
halfhearted defense of himself at the conclusion of the trial.

Grabbing up her kirtle, she flew along the street, dodging the
small knots of people who huddled to discuss the events of the
morning. The gate of her small courtyard beckoned like a
mother's embrace, and she slipped inside and hurried to the side
of Gilda's grave. "Mama Bailie," she cried, falling to her knees
on the winter-hard earth. "God did speak through your vision,
but what can he expect of me now? I'm glad you're not here to
witness this, I'm glad Daniel is away. It would break his heart to
know that his brother had been found guilty of such a crime—"

A sudden thought whipped in among her words and stole her
breath away. She had spoken in a flood of unthinking emotion,
and now she knew her words were lies. Daniel would not be
brokenhearted to hear what had happened to Taregan. He had
expressed no love and little interest in his brother's fate since
those early days when Taregan and the Pequots were captured
and taken downriver. Daniel considered himself an Englishman;
he would be embarrassed to see his brother dressed like an
Indian before the village clergy while he proclaimed his innocence. And yet Daniel knew the woods and the river as well as
Taregan—better, in fact, for he had not been away for these many
years.

She swayed on her knees as the truth hit her. Taregan hadn't
taken those women in the canoe, Daniel had! He had told Garvin
he planned to go hunting, but in reality he had lain in wait for

Taregan and his passengers to return to Hartford. But how had Daniel known that Taregan would return?

She clenched her hands and knocked her fist against her forehead. Somehow, he had known! Sabrina Butler had journeyed to Boston on a mysterious errand and reappeared in Taregan's canoe. If she had written Garvin about meeting Taregan, Garvin might have told Daniel that his brother had finally made his way home. . . .

Her heart turned to stone within her chest. Even if she could prove Taregan's innocence, there was no time. Unless Daniel miraculously appeared before sunup and confessed his crime, the sentence would be carried out. And if Daniel hated his brother enough to commit a cowardly murder in Taregan's name, he certainly would not appear before tomorrow morning's execution.

Clutching her shawl tightly about her shoulders, she stood and hurried for the jail.

▼▲▼▲▼ "Taregan Bailie?" The jailer leaned in the doorway, smiling in a controlled, unmirthful way. "You have a visitor."

Taregan pulled himself off the wall and stood, wiping dirt from his breeches. After the shame of this morning, who would come to see him?

A woman moved past the guard, a slim figure in an unfashionably narrow skirt. She held a shawl around her shoulders, but her face remained obscured by shadows. "I knew you would come home to me," she whispered.

"Dena?" Struggling to mask his sorrow, Taregan painted on a warm smile and moved closer to the iron bars. "I wondered if you would come."

"I came." She stepped closer, moving from shadows to sunlight, and the beauty of her countenance left Taregan momentarily breathless. A genuine smile lit her face, and it was as though candles brightened the dark room. Long dark hair framed her oval face and fell in a plume of black gold to her waist. The young girl had grown into an incredibly beautiful woman, and the expression in her eyes made his heart shudder with regret.

"I came, Taregan, because I have been waiting for you."

Her words lacerated him. If he had realized this morning that not implicating Daniel would mean breaking Dena's devoted heart . . . he clenched his fists, unable to pursue the thought. "I am glad you came," he said, forcing the words. "I wanted to personally release you from your vow of faithfulness to me, and I must apologize for the years that vow has cost you—"

"Taregan, don't be a fool!" Rushing forward, she thrust her arms through the iron bars, her hands reaching for him. Like a drowning man he clutched at her, not caring what the jailers or the minister outside might think. He had waited many, many nights to feel this woman's arms about him, and threats of death or censure had no power over him now.

"I have come full circle," he said, his hands cradling her head. "The last time I saw you was in this jail, do you remember? It seems strange now for me to have the entire cell to myself. There were twenty other Pequots here with me the last time—"

"Do not speak of the past," she whispered in an aching, husky voice he scarcely recognized. "Since the war, I have lived for the day of your return. If you die on the morrow, I fear my heart will die with you."

"Dena." He drew a ragged breath as his hand found her slender waist, stroked the black silk that tumbled down her back. Drawing her close, he looked through the bars and drank in the enchanting eyes that had haunted his dreams and filled his waking hours with hope. Her face was like gold in the flickering sunlight cast by the small window. His groping fingers touched her full lips, traced the high ridge of her cheekbone. He forced a smile to his face. "This is not the reunion I dreamed of."

"It is not over, Taregan." Her hand went to the back of his neck and pressed him to the bars, holding him tight. Her gleaming eyes, like stars in a black sky, searched the depths of his soul. She spoke slowly, her voice a warm embrace in the chill air. "I know you are innocent. I know Daniel sank the canoe. Sabrina

Butler was in love with Garvin Black, and she must have alerted Daniel that you were coming. He and Garvin are up to evil, I know they are—"

"Hush, my love." His finger fell across her parted lips, and he lowered his forehead to the bars. "I have learned that God works in ways far removed from our thinking. What I am about to say is for your ears alone. Do I have your promise that you will not repeat it?"

His eyes met hers; she nodded slowly.

"When I last saw Daniel, during the Pequot War, I swore to return and kill him. I hated him until I learned that Garvin Black was the true author of the war and its resulting evil. My anger removed itself from Daniel, but my heart still yearned to kill Garvin Black. I suffered and sweated and labored in Barbados only so I could come back to take his miserable life. But when we reached Boston, something happened to me."

"What?"

"A miracle." He smiled, wishing that she could look inside his heart and read all that had been written there in the last month. "I heard a minister, John Eliot, speak to the Indians outside Boston. He is not the typical Englishman, Dena, but a sincere, loving soul who truly desires God's best for our people. When he spoke of God's love and man's black and sinful heart, I realized that my fault was greater than the most ignorant Indian in the group, for I had thought that I could turn my back on God and all that my mother and father had taught me. I was totally consumed with avenging my sorrows upon Garvin Black. I had no peace because I put the shadow of willful sin between myself and God."

He held up his hand and pointed to the ring on his finger. "Do you see this? It is inscribed inside with the charge my parents gave us. Daniel and I were to boldly, faithfully, successfully go into the world as children of God, but only in the last month have I begun to fulfill that pledge. Tomorrow I will walk out of here boldly, faithfully, successfully. I know that whatever happens will be God's will."

Dena shook her head, confused. "You are willing to die because you feel guilty for the past?" Her voice, without rising at all, had taken on a frantic urgency. "Taregan, the sun will rise in less than twenty hours! What will you do to save yourself? We could send a party of men to find Daniel. He could be questioned—"

"We will do nothing," he said, taking a step away from her. His hands fell from the bars to his side. "My mother told me that I must come back to redeem Daniel. I had no idea then what she meant, but now I understand why she chose that particular word. Daniel is lost; he has been deceived by evil. But if I give my life for his crime, he will see the error of his ways. He is my brother—I know he will return to the path in which he should walk." He tilted his head and gave her a wry smile. "I can see the workings of God in this."

"No, you cannot do this! Daniel will not know what you have done, he will not care! He will fancy that he has escaped judgment and profited from your death! It is rumored that Garvin Black is already planning how he and Daniel will spend your half of the inheritance—"

"Daniel will know," Taregan said. He placed his hand over his heart. "We are closer than mere brothers. Daniel will know what I have done; I think he knows it already. In here." He tapped the flesh over his heart, then bowed his head so he would not see her tears.

"Then I am a widow before I am even a wife," Dena said, speaking in the low voice reserved for dreaded things.

Taregan could find no words to answer her.

▼▲▼▲▼ Miles away, at a table at the Windsor inn, a sudden pain struck Daniel's heart. He pressed his hand over the spot, catching his breath.

"You all right?" the innkeeper asked, his eyes narrowing in concern.

"Fine," Daniel answered, gasping for a quick breath. "It is

nothing." He waited for a moment until the pain had passed,
then picked up his mantle and saluted the innkeeper as he left.

Walking toward the docks, he studied the position of the sun
in the sky. Of certain by now Taregan had been tried and found
guilty for the murder of Sabrina Butler. The magistrate would
not know that an unborn baby also died that day, nor would he
know that Garvin Black had engineered the entire plot. "Both of
our problems will disappear at once," Garvin had promised, and
Daniel had been foolish enough to believe that Garvin only
intended to purge the unborn child from the poor widow's body.

Now he knew better. Garvin had known that Sabrina was terrified of water, and he wanted her dead. Whenever Daniel closed
his eyes to sleep he saw Sabrina's wide eyes gazing at him in
wordless rebuke, her hand floating up to him for assistance he
had been too late to give.

A similar fit of regret and grief had seized him on the day of
his mother's funeral, but again, he had been too late. How many
lives had he ruined? He had cheated countless hundreds of Indians, colonists, and trappers, and the people he should have
helped most he had wounded most grievously. He should have
swallowed his pride and helped Taregan escape from Saybrook,
but petty sibling rivalry had stood in the way of his noble intentions. He should have brought his mother out of the jail, but his
injured pride had not allowed him to beg for her release. He
should have refused Garvin Black's plan to ambush the women
on the river, he should have honored Sabrina Butler's request for
protection, he should have done so many things. . . .

Regrets and sorrows filled his past and present. His father had
often said that God had one overriding purpose for each man's
life, and true joy was found when he fulfilled that purpose. Daniel knew that his present path was far removed from the one
God had intended for him. Time after time he had been invited
to set foot upon that original path, but he had been too filled
with fear or jealousy to obey.

But not this time. Turning abruptly, he hurried back into the
inn and caught the innkeeper's eye. "Two sheets of parchment,

please, and pen and ink," he called, walking to a table. The innkeeper hurried to the desk where his supplies were kept and pro-
duced them. Daniel laid a shilling on the table.

"So much?" the man asked, eying the gold piece with suspicion.

"Yes," Daniel said, smiling. "This letter will be of great value."

> To the magistrate and clergymen of Hartford Village,
> Connecticut River:
>   I, Daniel Bailie, do swear to you that Garvin Black did
> conceive a child in the Widow Butler's womb and mis-
> lead the lady to believe he would marry her. Proof of
> this truth exists in the lady's house. In a small trunk
> within the keeping room you will find a collection of
> infant clothing she had begun to gather for the baby that
> would arrive.
>   Master Black, also in my presence, has denied that the
> Holy Scriptures are the Word of God and has instructed
> me not to attend to these same Scriptures. I know this is
> a severe violation of the heresy law that promises death
> to anyone who persists in such words and deeds. If you
> confront Master Black on these matters, I will swear to
> this truth in open court and before the entire assembly.
>   I am yours respectfully,
>   Daniel Bailie

After spreading sand on the parchment to absorb the excess
ink, Daniel dusted the letter, reread it, then copied out an exact
duplicate on the second sheet. After sealing both letters, he put
them in his doublet pocket and bade the innkeeper a good day.
The sun was beginning to sink toward the west, and he had at
least a two-hour walk before he would reach Hartford.

▼▲▼▲▼ "Taregan Bailie, you have another visitor."
With a screech of protest the iron door opened, and a pair of
booted feet stepped into the cell.

Taregan lifted his head from his knees, surprised by the announcement and the fact that the jailer had actually allowed someone into the cell. His visitor must be a minister, for there was no one else who would wish to speak to him. Dena had left in tears, vowing that she could not look on him again, and Colton had appeared for one bittersweet, reluctant interview in which he informed Taregan that he planned to marry Arabella himself so she would not be without protection in the world. Two clergymen had already come into his cell to pray for his soul, the minister at Hartford church and one from Windsor, for Taregan's notoriety had traveled quickly. He could not imagine who else would come to see him in his final hours.

"I have already made my peace with God," he murmured, not looking up at his guest.

"Then make your peace with me."

His throat constricted when he looked up and saw himself as he had been a month earlier: a young man dressed in doublet and breeches, with an English hat, English boots, an English air of superiority. *Daniel.*

"I wonder," Taregan said, emotion clotting his throat as a latent surge of anger rose within him, "that you have the courage to show yourself before I am dead."

"You give me too little credit," Daniel answered, the corner of his mouth twitching in what might be called a smile. "You always have."

Taregan stood slowly, tilting his head as he regarded his brother with an appraising eye. "If we are truly so much alike that Arabella could not tell us apart," he said, his eyes traveling from Daniel's finely crafted boots to the cocky ostrich plume in his wide-brimmed hat, "then I am a handsome fellow indeed."

Daniel did smile at this. "Of course you are. And I make a rather striking Indian."

They stood in silence for a moment, each knowing the truth of what happened on the river and the certainty of the morrow. And yet Taregan could not guess why Daniel had come.

"I received your letter," Daniel finally volunteered. "You

wrote that you were coming with a 'heart so filled with bitter venom it cannot be borne,' do you remember? Knowing that you had sworn to kill me when we last met, I asked Garvin what I should do. I knew that even if your heart had softened, you would be enraged when you learned how our mother died." A wistful note rang in his voice. "You always were her favorite."

"She loved us both equally," Taregan answered, crossing his arms, "but we received her love differently. In fact," he smiled, "her last words to me were of you. She begged me to come home and help you." He shrugged. "So here I am, waiting to die. I have done all I can and must leave your fate to God."

Daniel laughed, though his eyes glittered with some secret pain Taregan could not understand. "My fate! You speak as if I have done something wrong! One would almost think that I was the condemned criminal instead of you."

Taregan frowned as a sense of foreboding descended over him. Had Daniel's heart been so hardened that it could not change?

"Ah, don't pout at me, brother! We have things to share on this night, our last together! I must tell you that I have been a trader with Garvin Black, that I have cheated a few men and loved a few women. But, all in all, I am known as a loyal and quiet Englishman with a talent for staying out of trouble. Now it is your turn. Tell me what you have done in our time apart."

Taregan stared at his brother, disturbed by the mocking light in Daniel's eyes. "There are things I must tell you, too," he said slowly. "I worked as a slave on a plantation in Barbados. I spent five years cutting sugarcane. A group of Mohegans joined our plantation, and from one of them I learned that our father did not die at Mystic. He was there, not to warn the Pequots, but to fetch you home."

Daniel drew in a sudden wincing breath, but his expression did not change. Taregan waited a moment, then he continued. "Garvin Black surrendered our father to the English, who condemned him to serve at sea. I had planned to look for him after finding Dena again, but," he shrugged, "I suppose now that responsibility will fall to you."

Daniel's face darkened, but his eyes remained impassive.

"After I learned that our father still lives," Taregan went on, marveling that his words seemed to have no effect, "many of my Pequot brothers plotted an uprising against the Mohegans. I tried to stop it—"

"Of course you did, my brave brother," Daniel impatiently interrupted, pulling a small flask from his pocket. "And obviously you were successful enough to win the master's approval and his daughter's trust." He lifted the flask to his lips for a moment, tilted his head back, then lowered it and looked pointedly at the band of gold on Taregan's hand. "Do you remember, brother, the charge our father and mother gave us when we were young? Boldly, faithfully, successfully, and all that? We each had the same responsibility, but mother gave *you* the ring. Apparently our parents knew I could not be trusted with it."

"I will give you the ring now," Taregan said, struggling to slip it from his finger. "It is rightfully yours."

"No, let the gravediggers fight for it," Daniel said, waving Taregan's hand away. He offered the flask to Taregan, who stared at it for a moment, then took it and drank a long, deep swallow. A vaguely familiar scent assaulted his nostrils, a nostalgic memory his mind was too tired to identify or replace.

"This morning I remembered something else our father told us," Daniel continued, sinking to the floor as he watched Taregan drink. "Something about finding one task and doing it well. One purpose for life."

"I remember," Taregan said, wiping his mouth on his sleeve. The liquid burned as it traveled down his throat and brought warmth to his belly.

He handed the bottle to Daniel, who shook his head. "You need it more than I."

"I found my task," Taregan said, uncorking the flask again, "last month, so I suppose I can face death knowing I have fulfilled my purpose."

"And what was this monumental thing?"

"I met John Eliot, a minister from Boston. He is determined that the Indians understand the gospel." Taregan lifted his shoulder in a shrug. "I helped him understand the Indians. I do not know what the eternal consequences will be, but Eliot says that God brought me to him in his divine timing. After our discourse, for the first time, the Indians responded to Eliot's explanation of the gospel."

Daniel listened intently. After a moment of silence, he waved his hand. "Well, if you have found your life's mission and fulfilled it, we shall have no worries about the morrow, shall we?" he asked, leaning back against the stone wall of the cell. "I will wait for the dawn with you, brother."

The announcement caught Taregan unprepared. "You will?"

"We are brothers," Daniel answered, all traces of flippancy erased from his voice and expression. "We came into the world together, we will face death together. I will not leave your side until . . . you no longer need me."

Too moved for words, Taregan sank down against the opposite wall, then lifted the flask to his lips again.

▼▲▼▲▼ Daniel kept up a steady stream of small talk for over an hour, noticing with approval that Taregan had nearly drained the flask he'd purchased from the Indian woman.

"He will sleep heavily," the old woman had promised, her eyes as hard as dried peas and her mouth drawn up into a disapproving knot. "For the space of a day and night he will not move."

The potion seemed to be having the desired effect. Taregan's speech gradually slurred, his eyelids grew heavy, and his conversation silly as the exhaustion of the past few days bore down upon him. His head slid sideways against the wall, his mouth opened slightly.

With the grace of a cat Daniel leaned forward, listening. When he was certain that Taregan drew the deep, heavy breaths of

sleep, he glanced toward the outer room where the jailer kept a
deathwatch. No shadows moved, no sounds disturbed the stillness. The jailer was old and his eyes dim; he had not even
remarked upon Daniel's resemblance to the prisoner in his jail.

Daniel slipped out of his doublet and breeches, then pulled
his shirt over his head. When he had stripped to the skin, he
struggled to remove Taregan's clothes, then dressed his sleeping
brother in his own English finery. He patted the doublet pocket
to be certain the copy of the parchment letter remained inside.
The original letter had already been delivered to the magistrate's
house.

Calmly and deliberately, he dressed in Taregan's breeches,
leather shirt, and moccasins, then untied his hair so that it
flowed over his shoulders. He used the ribbon from his own hair
to bind Taregan's, then tied Taregan's grimy kerchief around his
own neck. For a final touch, he picked up a handful of dirt from
the earthen floor and smeared it over his face, then wiped Taregan's face clean with a handkerchief from the doublet pocket.

When he had finished, he stepped back and stared at his other
self, the brother he had spent a lifetime loving and despising.
Tomorrow no one would know that an exchange had been made.
The guilty soul would pay for its crime; the innocent man would
go free.

"Jailer!" Daniel roared, rattling the bars of the cell.

The old man moaned, the shadow in the outer room grumbled to its feet and moved across the floor. Finally the man
appeared in the doorway, bleary-eyed and frowning.

"My brother has drunk himself unconscious," Daniel said,
pointing with an air of disdain to the mound that was Taregan.
"Pray send someone to remove him."

"And where but the jail should I send a drunken man?" the
jailer retorted, his frown deepening as he glared at Daniel.

"Pray have mercy on him," Daniel answered. "He was over-
come by the news of my execution. Take him to the house of the
Indian woman called Dena. Beg her to take him in for my sake.
She will, for this man is my brother."

The jailer waved his hand and nodded sleepily. "I'll get help," he said, rocking across the room on hips stiff with rheumatism. "I'll have him out of here directly."

When the jailer had gone, Daniel dropped to his brother's side and rested his hand on Taregan's face. "You always were the better man," he whispered, his voice breaking. "And yet, on the morrow, I shall finally prove myself the braver. This I do, Taregan, to find my own peace, and because peace is never won but by victory over shame and sin." He leaned closer to whisper in Taregan's ear. "Take care of Dena for me."

Muffled voices drifted from outside the jail, a door creaked, then two men walked in with the jailer. "Stand back," the jailer ordered, brandishing a pistol. "We'll risk no foolhardiness while we're carrying this man out."

Daniel lifted his hands and placed them atop his head. "I assure you, there is no trickery here," he said, watching them carry Taregan away.

Dena spent the night tossing and turning upon her straw mattress, watering the fabric with tears while she prayed for deliverance, for peace, for some measure of comfort. At one point in the night men's voices moved past her door and she froze as a whisper of terror ran through her. Had the clergymen learned of her association with the convicted murderer? Had Garvin Black heard that she visited Taregan, and would he guess that she had discerned the truth? Would he implicate her in the crime in order to silence her as well?

Evening finally faded to light, and her small house filled with dusky gray shadows. Outside, footsteps tramped along the frozen street toward the village green, and voices cut through the stillness of morning to reach her ear.

She heard a drumroll, a sudden silence, then a continual murmur, as though the wind had picked up Taregan's soul and carried it heavenward in a flurry of sound.

Dena lowered her head into her hands and tasted the bitterness of tears. She knew what she would see if she could find the courage to open her shuttered window and look outside. A body was hanging from the gallows on the hill, and a somber crowd in black cloaks was slowly dispersing as the minister offered a prayer and a warning to his assembled congregation.

Someone rapped on her door, and she wiped the tears from her cheeks.

The magistrate stood outside, an anxious smile on his face. "Excuse me, Miss Dena, but the deceased man had one last request."

"He is dead, then?" She could not bear to look toward the hanging hill.

"Yes." The magistrate turned his hat in his head and fell silent for a moment. "But his brother visited him in the night and drank himself into an unconscious condition. The condemned man said you'd take care of Daniel until he awoke. We didn't want to bring him into your house last night, so we left him in your garden—"

Slipping her cloak from its peg near the door, Dena wrapped it around her shoulders and stepped outside. Among the withered cornstalks of her garden, a man lay curled on the ground, his hands clutched to his stomach as though it pained him.

"He is drunk?" she asked, confused.

"Yes. Ordinarily I'd have kept him locked up, too, but considering the situation, I thought it best to show a mite of mercy."

Dena wrapped her cloak more closely about her arms and nodded. The last person she wanted inside her house was Daniel Bailie, but if Taregan had wished it she could not turn him away.

"If you'll bring him inside, magistrate, I'll see to him." Her voice was calm, but inside she railed in anger.

I curse you, Taregan Bailie, for asking me to do this thing! Has your charity no limits? You know this man committed the crime for which you have paid, and yet you ask me to care for him!

She wanted to scream, but she could not give way to emotion in front of the magistrate. Instead she held the door open as Master Norton dragged Daniel's long and lanky form into the house.

"Whew, but he stinks," the magistrate complained, huffing as he tried to avert his head from Daniel's face. "I don't know what kind of whiskey he's been getting down there at the trading post, but this stench is stronger than most."

"Lay him here, before the fire," Dena commanded, pointing to the floor. "If he didn't mind spending the night among the withered corn, I don't imagine he'll miss the warmth of a bed."

"No, I suppose not," the magistrate chuckled, dropping the man by the fire. He sobered instantly. "Is there anything I can do for you, Miss Dena? I understand that your people were once on real friendly terms with these boys—"

"Many years ago, I was Taregan's friend," she said absently, studying the man at her feet.

"Well, I'd appreciate it if you'd give Daniel a message for me when he wakes. I read his letter and am prepared to take action against Master Black. I might need Daniel's testimony in court, but a signed statement is probably evidence enough."

Dena looked at the man sharply. "Action against Master Black? *Garvin* Black?"

"That's right," the magistrate said, nodding soberly. "Blasphemy is a capital crime. We won't tolerate it."

"I'll tell him," she murmured, her eyes drawn again to the man on the floor.

The magistrate hemmed for a moment more, then excused himself and slipped from the house. Dena sat back on her settle, watching Daniel sleep. How alike the two brothers were! Yesterday she had pressed her lips to Taregan's in a bittersweet farewell kiss, and it was difficult to believe that she hadn't kissed the lips of the man in front of her. But Daniel's handsome face had always taunted her, a visible reminder that Taregan was out of her reach. She bit her lip as pain swayed through her mind. Now even the hope of Taregan was gone forever.

The man stirred, lifted his hand to his chest, and groaned. A gleam of gold caught Dena's eye, and she saw the ring upon his hand. Of course Taregan would have given the family ring to Daniel. What was a ring, when he was preparing to give his life?

Daniel stirred again, turning his head toward the warmth of the fire. As he did, Dena noticed a fine, hairlike scar across his neck, a vivid red line she hadn't seen before. Where had Daniel received such a scar? To her knowledge he had never fought in a battle or been wounded while hunting. . . .

Hope suddenly rose in her heart like a startled bird, and she flew from her place to his side. A strong and pungent odor assaulted her like a slap in the face, and she pulled away and covered her mouth with her hand.

The magistrate hadn't smelled whiskey! The scent was hop blossoms! And every Pequot knew that the cones of hop flowers, when cooked and drunk in a potion, put the drinker into a deep, dopelike sleep. Daniel would know how to procure hops, how to use them, and he could have had only one purpose in mind. . . .

"Taregan?" she whispered, bending low. She placed her hands on his cheeks and patted them lightly. "Taregan? You must wake now! Hear my voice and come back from wherever you are."

The blue eyes opened and blinked slowly, as if they would not focus.

"Dena?" Her name rasped upon his tongue.

"Taregan? My love, it is you! Can you wake? You've drunk hops, darling, Daniel brought them to you so that you would sleep."

"Daniel?" His forehead wrinkled in confusion and he sat up, throwing her off with his arm. Glancing down, he absently patted the English clothes, then his features twisted into a horrified expression. "No! What is he thinking?"

He struggled to rise, but Dena caught his hand and pulled him down. "Don't, Taregan, it is finished. There is nothing you can do."

"There must be something!" He resisted her and pulled away, stumbling to the window. She waited silently, her heart swimming through a haze of feelings and desires, while he threw open the shutters and stared for a long moment at the body twisting in the wind. His head lowered, and his shoulders shook as he sobbed.

"Taregan," she whispered, the misery of the night still haunting her, "I didn't know what Daniel was going to do. And I'm not sure why he did it."

"I was supposed to come back and redeem him," Taregan said, his voice in tatters. "I promised our mother."

"You were right to return," Dena interrupted, not sure what else to say. She rose to her knees. "Taregan, you are right to weep for him. But do not sorrow for him. Daniel did what he wanted to do."

He turned and looked at her, and at the sight of his anguish she closed her eyes, her heart aching. "Daniel always did exactly what he wanted to do. He was headstrong, you cannot deny that!"

He did not answer, and when she opened her eyes he had returned his gaze to the gallows, his knuckles white around the windowsill. "I should have saved him," he said, his voice thick. "I should have guessed that he would try something. I should have known."

Rising to her feet, she moved to his side. "How could you know? You couldn't read his mind. You hadn't even seen him in years, how could you have known what he would do?"

"We were brothers," he answered, his gaze fixed beyond the window. "We were twins. I always knew what he was thinking . . . and I should have known last night."

He turned and ran his hand through his hair in a distracted motion. "I must tell the magistrates," he said, agitated, confusion on his face. "They have hung the wrong man."

"No!" She stared at him with deadly concentration. "What good would your death do now?"

"Oh, Dena." His trembling arms circled her waist and held her close. "I just wish I could have spoken with him again. We didn't talk last night . . . of this."

She lifted her hands to his shoulders, pulling his head down to gently touch her lips to his cheek. As she pressed against his chest she heard the rattle of parchment from within his doublet. "Taregan," she whispered, pulling away, "mayhap he does have something else to say to you."

With unwilling fingers, Taregan fumbled at the edge of the doublet and reached into the pocket in the inner lining. He withdrew an unsealed letter and unfolded it. "This is a letter to Magistrate Norton," he said after scanning the page. "Daniel says he will swear that Garvin Black fathered a child by the Widow Butler and that he is guilty of blasphemy."

"Magistrate Norton mentioned it this morning," Dena said,

nodding. "This must be a copy of the letter. Daniel must have wanted you to know of it if the magistrate approached you."

She ran her hand across the back of the page. "There is more, Taregan, written here."

He turned the page over. In an unsteady hand, Daniel had written two stanzas of a poem.

"It is a poem by John Donne," Taregan said, his eyes swiveling to meet hers. "Arabella had a book of his poetry."

"Read it to me," Dena said, resting her hand on his arm.

Taregan spoke slowly, feeling his way through the verse:

> *Our two souls therefore which are one,*
> *Though I must go, endure not yet*
> *A breach, but an expansion,*
> *Like gold to airy thinness beat.*
>
> *If they be two, they are two so*
> *As stiff twin compasses are two,*
> *Thy soul the fixt foot, makes no show*
> *To move, but doth, if the other do.*

"Do you still think you can make things right by taking his place on the gallows?" she asked, leading him to the settle. He sat down, weak and wretched, and she sat beside him and drew his head onto her shoulder. "You can't, Taregan, for each man must find God's path for his own life. But today Daniel has made his peace with God, and with you."

They sat in silence for a long moment. When he spoke again, Taregan's eyes were wet with regret. "I didn't want it to end this way. Daniel was deceived, but I was the one whose heart soured with bitterness."

"Speak not of the past," Dena whispered, framing his precious face with her hands. She softened her tone as his eyes moved to meet hers. "Taregan, you said you came to redeem Daniel, but not a single one of us can redeem another. Daniel had to surrender himself, don't you see? His life was all he could give you. This was his way of making things right."

"His purpose," Taregan replied in a choked voice as his eyes narrowed in pain. "He kept talking about his purpose."

"Yes," Dena whispered. She struggled to sort out her thoughts, arrange them, impose order upon anguish. Suddenly, like a light shining into a dark place, understanding dawned. "Taregan," she said, taking both his hands in hers, "your death won't help Daniel now. But if you truly want to redeem him, be the man he wanted to be, live the rest of your life as Daniel Bailie. Don't you see, my love," she whispered, pleading frankly, "Daniel was always jealous; he wanted to be you. If you wish to honor his name, do as our people have always done. Take a new name, the name of your brother, Daniel Bailie. If you do not, he has died in vain."

His face seemed to open so that Dena could look inside and watch her words take hold. She saw bewilderment there, a flicker of despair, and finally, acceptance. A soft and loving curve touched his lips as he drew her into his arms. "Then today my life begins anew," he said, his voice simmering with barely checked emotion. "Colton will care for Arabella and her fortune in gold. The magistrate will prosecute Garvin Black for blasphemy upon Daniel's testimony. And we will finally be together, my love, for now and always."

Dena exhaled a long sigh of contentment and moved her lips closer to his ear. "You did not fail Daniel. God changed his heart. Your brother did not toss his life away; he surrendered it for the brother he loved."

With a half-sob, Taregan pulled her closer, then rested his forehead on hers for a long, long moment as she twined her arms about his neck. "I suppose," he began, his voice a bit unsteady, "that Daniel has finally found the victory he always sought."

"Yes," she answered, combing her fingers through his hair. "You two really are very much alike. Nobleness, faith, and self-sacrifice were your weapons in war. Those same qualities have enabled Daniel . . . to make peace."

Magistrate Norton closed his prayer book as the joyful couple kissed by their garden gate. Though the stubborn minister had not allowed Daniel Bailie to take an Indian bride in the church, his refusal had neither held up the ceremony nor soured the mood of the celebrants. As they accepted the good wishes of Arabella Christoffels, Colton Bramwell, and a few other friends, the groom glowed with quiet contentment and Dena basked in a warm bunting of happiness.

Though his choice of a bride was unexpected, Magistrate Norton had to admit that Daniel Bailie had dramatically changed since his unfortunate brother's execution and the trial of Garvin Black. That evil man had been dispatched with all proper haste, especially when it became apparent that blasphemy was but one of his capital crimes. He went to the gallows screaming out his anger at God and at Daniel Bailie in particular, and the magistrate was surprised when Daniel and Dena did not show up for the hanging. He'd have thought Daniel eager to see his former master hung. The magistrate's usual dour expression twisted into a wry smile.

Apparently love occupied the young man's mind more than justice.

Arabella Christoffels and Colton Bramwell married, too, and journeyed westward for broader lands and more plenteous furs. Norton had counted himself fortunate to be present when the treasure-filled trunk was brought from the river and opened in full view of the village. Half of the goods were doled out and given to Colton and Arabella Bramwell; the other half ceremoniously presented to Dena and Daniel Bailie, as Taregan's next of kin. Norton noticed that Arabella smiled at Daniel Bailie with marked affection, but she clung to Colton Bramwell's broad arm as though he were the only man in the world.

▾▴▾▴▾ Four months after the furor caused by Taregan Bailie's return and subsequent trial, a grizzled veteran of the sea stepped onto the Hartford docks and announced that he sought anyone with the surname Bailie. News of the stranger traveled quickly through the town, and Magistrate Norton saw Daniel Bailie weep as he clasped the old man in his arms and cried out his gratitude to God.

Fallon Bailie joined Daniel and Dena in the small house and spent his afternoons in the garden Dena had planted around the graves beside the house. Often as Magistrate Norton passed the spot, he heard the old man talking to himself. The gossips of Hartford claimed that he spoke to the woman and the young man buried there, but Norton could not believe that a man so sound in mind and spirit could be thoroughly unsound in matters of the heart.

A year after Fallon Bailie's return, a letter addressed to Taregan Bailie arrived from Boston. The magistrate promptly delivered it to the Bailie house, expecting that Daniel would know what to make of it, and within two weeks Daniel and Dena had packed their possessions into a canoe. When Norton asked why they were leaving Hartford, Daniel would only say that he had business with John Eliot in Boston.

Fallon Bailie, Daniel explained, would remain in Hartford. He had waited ten years to reunite with his beloved Gilda and his sons, and the old man claimed that his days of wandering to and fro on the earth were done.

Fallon Bailie lived out his days in the small house Colton Bramwell had built for Dena. Since the garden plot already held the graves of Gilda Bailie and her son, other Indian dead were laid in the small fenced area, and soon the plot was officially known as the cemetery for Christian Indians. Fallon became the caretaker and a beloved figure, albeit an eccentric one. To anyone who would listen he told tales of Ocanahonan, a city far away, and a time when Indians and Englishmen lived together in peace and the love of God. Magistrate Norton could not bring himself to tell the peculiar old man that he had mislabeled the head-stones in the cemetery: the young man buried beside Gilda was Taregan, not Daniel.

But the people of Hartford accepted Bailie's bizarre tales and his quirks, and they often remarked upon a laurel tree that grew from the center of Gilda Bailie's grave. Its flower was not yellow and white, as other laurels were, but bore a crimson stain in the center of each blossom, bright and bloodred like the laurels of the swamp where the last Pequots died.

REFERENCE LIST

All the passages from John Mason's journal are actually from *A Brief and True Report of the Pequot War*, which he wrote after the fact. The entries have been lightly edited. Historical information for this book came from the following sources.

Bourne, Russell. *The Red King's Rebellion*. New York: Oxford University Press, 1990.

Bowden, Henry W., and James P. Ronda, eds. *John Eliot's Indian Dialogues*. Westport, Conn.: Greenwood Press, 1980.

Chartier, Roger, ed. *A History of Private Life, Volume III: Passions of the Renaissance*. Cambridge, Mass.: Belknap Press, 1989.

Grant, Bruce. *Concise Encyclopedia of the American Indian*. New York: Whip Books, 1989.

Hauptman, Laurence M., and James D. Wherry, eds. *The Pequots in Southern New England*. Norman, Okla.: University of Oklahoma Press, 1990.

Hawke, David Freeman. *Everyday Life in Early America*. New York: Harper and Row, 1989.

Jacobs, Wilbur R. *Dispossessing the American Indian*. New York: Charles Scribner's Sons, 1972.

Marcus, Robert D., and David Burner, eds. *America Firsthand, Volume I: Settlement to Reconstruction*. New York: St. Martin's Press, 1989.

Mason, John. *A Brief and True Report of the Pequot War*. Ann Arbor, Mich.: University Microfilm, 1736.

Noll, Mark A. *A History of Christianity in the United States and Canada*. Grand Rapids, Mich.: William B. Eerdmans Publishing Company, 1992.

White, Jon Manchip. *Everyday Life of the American Indian*. New York: Indian Head Books, 1979.

Winslow, Ola Elizabeth. *John Eliot, Apostle to the Indians*. Boston: Houghton Mifflin Company, 1968.